Scribner
A Division of Simon & Schuster, Inc.
1230 Avenue of the Americas
New York, NY 10020

First Scribner trade paperback edition July 2015

SCRIBNER and design are registered trademarks of The Gale Group, Inc., used under license by Simon & Schuster, Inc., the publisher of this work.

For information about special discounts for bulk purchases, please contact Simon & Schuster Special Sales at 1-866-506-1949 or business@simonandschuster.com.

The Simon & Schuster Speakers Bureau can bring authors to your live event. For more information or to book an event contact the Simon & Schuster Speakers Bureau at 1-866-248-3049 or visit our website at www.simonspeakers.com.

Interior design by Jill Putorti

Manufactured in the United States of America

10   9   8   7   6   5   4   3   2   1

Library of Congress Control Number: 2014000288

ISBN 978-1-4767-2732-5
ISBN 978-1-4767-2733-2 (pbk)
ISBN 978-1-4767-2734-9 (ebook)

THE
REMARKABLE
COURTSHIP
OF
GENERAL
TOM THUMB

~ A NOVEL ~

NICHOLAS RINALDI

SCRIBNER

NEW YORK   LONDON   TORONTO   SYDNEY   NEW DELHI

For Laura, Andrew, Elle, Leonardo,
Francis, Timothy, Hasan, and Nicholas—
and for Jackie, who swept the clouds away
and made the chrysanthemums grow.

THE
REMARKABLE
COURTSHIP
OF
GENERAL
TOM THUMB

NICHOLAS RINALDI

LIFE IS A ROAD

Not I, not any one else can travel that road for you.
You must travel it for yourself. . . .
Perhaps you have been on it since you were born, and
did not know. . . .

—Walt Whitman, *Leaves of Grass*

Long before the war started, it was already there, breathing, rumbling, hidden. It was in the clouds, in the rush of the rivers and in the rain, in the way people talked, the things they said and didn't say. The worry, the awareness that things were wrong and getting worse.

I remember my father saying there was no easy answer, there would be a war and a lot of killing. He looked me in the eye. "And aren't you glad, Charlie, that you're a tiny runt of a dwarf and won't have to carry a gun and fight." It wasn't a question, it was a casual observation that he left hanging in the air. And it made me miserable because even then, young as I was, I didn't like the idea of being left out of anything, especially this wild, strange thing my father was talking about, filled with smoke and thunder and charging horses.

But the war hung back, biding its time. It whispered, it murmured. And maybe, I thought—maybe it would change its mind and go home to wherever it came from. But that was a big maybe, so big you could walk around inside it, and there was no place to hide.

I had been a large baby, nine pounds two ounces. My mother never tired of telling me that. After half a year, I measured twenty-five inches, head to feet—but afterward, nothing. I was twenty-five inches tall, and was stuck at that height until I was fifteen years old. Then I was growing again, but slowly, an inch a year, sometimes less.

It used to bother me, the way my mother was always saying I'd been a big, healthy baby. In part, I think, she was letting me know I had given her a hard time when I was born. But there was something else, too, which I eventually understood. She wanted me to know there was nothing wrong with me at birth. She had delivered me in perfect condition—normal, not a dwarf—and if, after six months, I suddenly stopped growing, it wasn't her fault, it was mine.

That may, in fact, have been the way it was: a secret willfulness deep inside me, invisible even to myself. A decision to be different. Not a conscious choice made on a certain day, but something written in my bones. And the irony is that my smallness was not the curse my parents first thought it was, but a blessing, for them and for me. Though I have, of late, come to understand that blessings, like gift horses, may come with a bad set of teeth.

I spent my first years in a small house on a narrow street, and have vivid memories of my two sisters, both older than I. They used to run around the house in their flimsy cotton shifts, or in nothing at all, throwing pillows at me. They would grab my arms and swing me back and forth, then toss me in the air and bounce me on the bed. I liked that.

They taught me my ABCs, and I watched as they wove their hair into long braids that they piled high on their heads. In their best Sunday clothes, their dark red satins, they were the prettiest girls in the neighborhood. I have pictures of them, pasted in a large book of photographs that I keep. Pictures of my parents, pictures of Barnum, pictures of Queen Victoria, Louis Philippe, Lincoln, Queen Isabella, and too many others. Pictures of pictures. Memory is a barbed hook. No matter how you struggle, you never get free.

I was four years old when Barnum discovered me, and soon to turn five when I first appeared on the big stage at his American Museum. Barnum told the world I was eleven, lest anyone imagine I was just an undernourished slow grower and not an authentic dwarf. And, on the theory that an English dwarf would be of more interest to Americans than a homegrown dwarf from Connecticut, he announced that I was English-born and had just arrived from London.

My mother was furious. Bad enough that he lied about my age and changed my name to Tom Thumb, but it was nothing less than outrageous to declare that I was English-born, and to print it on a poster. Since my mother had never set foot in England, it was tantamount to saying she wasn't my mother!

She fumed and fussed so much that Barnum offered to tear up the contract and let her take me home to Connecticut—a quick end to my career before it even started. But no, not for the world was she going to let such a thing happen, and Barnum must have known that all along.

My first performance was in the Christmas pageant, which ran for three weeks. Mary Darling, the house magician, played the Holy Mother, and the Bearded Lady was Joseph. I was the Infant in the manger. A few janitors with strong singing voices were the shepherds. Sheep were the sheep, and a camel was the camel. After "Silent Night" and a few other carols, I leaped out of the manger and performed my whirling, churning, acrobatic breakdown dance. Then I hopped back into the manger and listened to the bone-rocking, spine-tingling, ego-building applause. It was exciting to be the newborn Savior. I was looking forward to the time when I would cure lepers, raise the dead, and change water into wine. But I would skip the part about being nailed to a cross.

The Museum was on Broadway, across from St. Paul's and the Astor House, and what a place it was. Big, brash, and splashy. I still remember the first time I saw it. The building stood five stories high, and it spread wide, filling the corner at Broadway and Ann Street. Sunlight blazed on the white marble, and there were massive painted plaques between the windows, images of the live animals that could be seen inside. A tiger, a bear, a buffalo, an orangutan, a pair of zebras. And, daily, huge, gaudy banners were hung from the balconies, listing the day's special attractions—

LIVING MONSTER SNAKES

MYSTERIOUS GYPSY GIRL

FAMILY OF ALBINOS

BOHEMIAN GLASS BLOWERS

WILD INDIANS IN SAVAGE WAR DRESS

And, on days when I was performing, an enormous banner for me—

GENERAL TOM THUMB
SMALLEST MAN IN THE KNOWN WORLD

On the second-floor balcony, a brass band played one tune after another, welcoming the crowds that came pouring into the Museum—some heading for the theater, others browsing through the many halls and galleries that were filled with paintings, statues, ancient coins, medieval suits of armor, muskets and three-cornered hats from the time of the Revolution. A poster by the ticket office boasted that the Museum contained over 100,000 CURIOSITIES.

In the wide halls, there were large glass display windows, floor to ceiling, showing bearskins and leopard skins, the skeleton of an ape, the jaw of a dinosaur, stuffed birds, a stuffed moose. Plenty of living animals too, in cages on each floor, and an entire menagerie in the basement.

In an alcove on the third floor, there were three Egyptian mummies in various stages of unwrap. I liked those mummies, and often wondered how they felt, lying there, with strangers like me going close and staring.

At the Museum, there was a tutor who worked with me several hours a week. Kwink was his name. "Just Kwink, without the mister," he said. He had large brown eyes and a bushy head of white hair. His method was to bring me around to four or five exhibits, and we studied the accompanying information cards. He explained the words I didn't know, and I wrote them down in a book of blank pages that he gave me. We looked at stuffed birds and animals, many that I'd never heard of, and a large collection of rocks and crystals, all new to me. I learned what a kimono was, and how to spell it. I touched a cannonball, and learned a bit about that, too. A canoe from the West Indies. A toga, a sari, a walrus tusk. A machine that tested your strength and a machine that talked with a human voice.

It was fun. I was learning new words, and after each session, I had to write ten sentences, each with one of the new words in it. I enjoyed that. New words and new facts, and how to write and remember.

On the fourth floor there was a scale model of Paris with an enormous number of tiny buildings carved from wood. Kwink had spent an entire year in Paris, and he pointed out some of the famous buildings and streets. Paris, yes. I was hungry for it, and worked harder than ever on the French words and phrases that Kwink taught me.

*   *   *

Barnum's office was on the second floor, next to the Hall of Mirrors, which held trick mirrors that made you look like anything but yourself. In one I was a giant, in another I was shorter than a puppy. In yet another, my head was larger than my body, and I was upside down—amusing, yes, but to see myself like that made me dizzy.

On the same floor, there was a whole gallery of wax figures, including George Washington and all of the Presidents, along with Queen Victoria, Napoléon, Jesus, Moses, and the Siamese Twins. And, toward the end of my first year at the Museum, a wax replica of me in my blue Napoléon uniform—General Tom Thumb.

Best of all, though, in that five-story house of wonders, it was the people—the acrobats, jugglers, trapeze artists, ropedancers. The Tattooed Man, and the Albino Lady. The sword-swallower and the fire-eater, the fortune-teller, and the Bearded Lady. There was a dancer, Josephine West, with a beauty mark on her right cheek. Whenever our paths crossed, anywhere in the Museum, she would pick me up and waltz me around, swinging me in the air as if I were a poodle.

And Nellis, the Man Without Arms, who could write with his toes, pencil on paper. With those remarkable toes, he could load a pistol and pull the trigger. When he was in a shooting mood, he displayed his talent in the basement shooting gallery, hitting the bull's-eye with every shot. He wanted me to be part of his act, shooting an apple off my head—and, with youthful enthusiasm, I considered it an exciting idea. But Barnum forbade it, and threatened to fire Nellis if he ever came near me with a gun.

The Snake-Charmer let me handle her snake, and the African Earth Woman let me pound on her tom-toms. The Albino Lady followed me on all fours and blew her hot breath on the back of my neck.

Zobeide Luti, one of the Circassian Ladies, let me watch while she washed her hair with beer so it would frizz up and make her look Circassian. She was beautiful, as Circassian women are said to be. But, as I later learned, she wasn't from Circassia—if, in fact, there even was such a place. She was from Beekman Street, within walking distance of the Museum. The other Circassians were also local—one from Brooklyn, one from the Bronx. Two were Hungarian, from Long Island. Years later, they were still around and still beautiful, still washing their hair with beer.

As the days and weeks wore on, the person who interested me more and more was the house magician, Mary Darling. She had slender arms, long fingers, hazel eyes, and an exotic head of red hair. She was an ingenious conjuror. She could make feathers fall from the ceiling like flakes of snow, then make them disappear. One day she pulled a white mouse out of my ear and put it in my pocket—but when I reached in, there was nothing there.

Hers was a sad story. She had stolen a bunch of money from her father, and ran off with a lover, who took the money and abandoned her. She went crazy for a while and spent some time in an asylum. But she recovered, and there she was, at the Museum, and thriving.

As I watched her rehearse her tricks, my feelings for her grew. But I came to understand, painfully, that she had no real interest in me. I was a toy, a child, a dwarf—much loved by the crowds, but still, to her, merely a dwarf, an amusing distraction. She wanted to incorporate me into her act, pulling me out of a big straw hat, then making me vanish in an empty whisky keg. But Barnum killed it. He thought it would demean me and tarnish my image.

Still, Mary Darling, with that gleam in her eyes, and so daring. For every performance, she dressed as a man, in black evening wear, jacket and pants and a red cravat. I was four when I first met her, then quickly five. And she was—what? Nineteen? Twenty-two? She was a magician, she could have been a hundred and who would have known the difference? Those eyes, that sly, ironic smile. I sometimes imagined that she would wave a wand, or snap her fingers, and I would suddenly be six feet tall and exactly her age, and off we would go to some hidden isle in the Pacific. But a dream, that's all it was.

The third floor held its share of exhibits, and it also held the entrance to the theater. When I first arrived, the theater was of modest size—but Barnum was always expanding, and, before long, the theater was large enough to seat three thousand. It was there that his actors presented plays, and there, too, on the enormous stage, that the acrobats, fire-eaters, and aerialists appeared, and the Kiowa and Cheyenne chiefs from the Far West, when they visited New York.

And on that stage, I offered my song-and-dance routines, wearing a kilt when I danced my Highland fling, and a three-cornered hat when I sang my Yankee Doodle song. Barnum taught me. He gave me the words, the timing, the fancy foot movements, and that special way of leaping out, front and center, as the curtain rose—

> *Yankee Doodle ride your horse,*
> *Yankee Doodle randy—*
> *Be quick to kiss the pretty girls*
> *Sweet as sugar candy.*

I was a fast learner, good at picking up the moves. Quick, too, with the songs, the jokes, the puns, the wicked smiles.

At five I often drank a few sips of wine with my dinner. On my sixth birthday I lit a cigar onstage, and the audience out there, the mothers and kids, the laborers, shopkeepers, immigrants just off the boat—they loved it. Even the clergymen, who considered me a gift from God. I could read and write, add and subtract, and even had a few words of French, the bad ones, which I'd learned not from Kwink but from a janitor who'd grown up in Marseille.

"Precocious" is the word our family doctor had for me. My parents used that word often, whenever they couldn't think what to make of me. But the truth of the matter is that in some ways I was, at times, just plain bad, with a will of my own and a mind full of mischief.

I already knew something about sex, the general idea of it. At home, in Bridgeport, I'd seen my mother and father performing with great zest under the sheets, in their creaky wooden bed, which my father had made with his carpenter's tools. That's what he was, a carpenter. When he was in bed with my mother, she moaned, making an awesome sound, and it was a bit of a while before I understood that her moaning had nothing to do with pain.

"Get out there and kill them dead," Barnum would say, as I pulled on my sailor suit for the three o'clock performance. At the piano, Old Tom, an African from Madison Street, banged away at the keys, and I jumped out from the wings and danced the hornpipe. Always, the crowd went wild. Applause, foot stomping. Shouts of bravo. They fussed over me because I was small and because I was perfectly formed, all the parts of me correctly proportioned—head, torso, arms, legs. But mostly, I think, they liked me because I reminded them of themselves. Looking at me, they knew that the self inside their bodies was something small, needing help. It could be hurt. It could be stepped on and bruised. So I was them, and they, in a sense, were me, all of us part of the same tongue-twisting song.

When Barnum thought I was ready, he took me out on the road for two- or three-day stints in New Jersey and lower Connecticut. It was a dizzying swirl—the faces, the people, the smiles and laughs as I sang and danced, and offered the impersonations that I learned from Barnum. I was Napoléon, wordless, brooding after Waterloo. I was Ajax, waving a sword, and Hercules struggling to lift an immense rock, which was papier-mâché, light as a feather. Or Samson in a ragged leopard skin, flexing my biceps—a joke, of course, because at fifteen pounds, what muscles did I have?

The ladies, they liked me best when I appeared in my flesh-colored tights and played Cupid, shooting toy arrows into the crowd—and how they grabbed for them, my little love darts. When my act was over, I walked among them, and they picked me up and hugged me, and passed me around.

It was a young dwarf's paradise. The rustling of their silks, the lure of their perfume, the heaving of their breasts as they breathed. Not bad, I thought, not bad at all. I could live with that. The only problem, since I was so short, just twenty-five inches, I wondered who in the world would ever want to marry me? And already, young as I was, I was thinking about that, and I was busy looking.

"Never talk dirty," Barnum said, cautioning me after hearing me pass a few foul words I'd picked up from the workmen who cleaned out the animal cages. "Think dirty all you want, but in public be polite."

"Do you think dirty?" I asked.

"All the time," he answered, gripping me with his dark gray eyes. "But I don't go around boasting about it."

He loomed above me with his great mop of swampy black hair. His face fleshy, the chin firm, the nose thick, lips wide and rubbery. He was under six feet, but there was so much fire and energy in him that he seemed taller than he was. He told me it would please him if I called him P. T. So I did. But in my thoughts, he was always Barnum—not Phineas, not P. T., not Mister Barnum, just Barnum, plain and simple. Because that's who he was. That one word, it summed him up, it defined him, it *was* him, the word and the person one and the same.

Occasionally we appeared together onstage, dancing side by side, in tandem, the same steps, each wearing a gray swallowtail and a high beaver hat, he twirling his big silver-topped cane, and I twirling my tiny one. And when the music came to a close, he would glide off the stage with me sitting on his shoulder.

So, yes, yes—I liked him, and still do. But hated him, too—because he took me, Charlie Stratton, and turned me into Tom Thumb, and there were days when I was never sure who I really was. Me—I—the one who thinks, who talks, who spits, who dreams. Was I, Charlie Stratton, pretending to be Tom Thumb, or Tom Thumb trying to remember I was really Charlie Stratton? Or was I simply the anger they both felt. The loneliness, the confusion, the bad mouth, a bit of steam coming off a hot roof after a summer storm.

My father had been a carpenter, but it was a hard way to earn a living—less than ten dollars a week, repairing porches and barns. When Barnum found me, good money started coming our way, and my father, little by little, quit hammering. He and my mother stayed with me when I was in New York, and Barnum brought them along when he toured me through Europe, since I was so young.

In London, huge crowds wanted to see me, especially after Queen Victoria invited me to appear at Buckingham Palace. Three visits I had with her, and on one occasion she kissed me on the cheek, and, in an overzealous moment, took a quick nibble at one of my ears. My performances at the Egyptian Hall drew overflow crowds, and it was soon apparent that a Tom Thumb craze was developing. Tom Thumb paper dolls appeared in all sorts of shops. And there was a new sweet, the Tom Thumb Sugar Plum, which sold wildly. Onstage I danced my own version of the polka, and it became the new dance sensation of the season, everybody doing it, the *Tom Thumb Polka*. Barnum was strutting like a peacock.

But my father, my father. In the halls and theaters where I performed, he sold tickets at the door and handled other small jobs, too—and it was, for him, a muddy time. In Liverpool his wallet was stolen. In Bristol he lost his watch, and in London a bundle of his favorite shirts went to the laundry and never came back.

And there was something else, too. On those many occasions when I was invited into the presence of royalty, he was never part of that, nor was my mother—and I now understand that he must have felt terribly put off. My mother did feel snubbed, and said so, blaming Barnum. "Him, that uppity humbug. Thinks we're not good enough for the high-and-mighty royalty!" She moaned and complained, and dealt with her frustration by rushing about from shop to shop and spending wildly.

But my father kept it all inside him. In London he took to the pubs, savoring the various brews, then he drifted into single-malt whiskies from the Highlands—and it became clear, even to my young eyes, that his drinking was becoming a problem.

During my busy days abroad, my sisters, Libbie and Frances Jane, were home, in Bridgeport, going to school and living with one of our aunts. I missed them. I remembered how they brushed their hair and talked endlessly about boys. And they sang—chirpy, zippy, rip-along songs that they made up, singing them into my ears while they tickled my feet and tossed me around.

Zootagataz, Zatagatooz—
Sometimes you win, often you lose,
But better to laugh, useless to cry—
Jump out of your shoes, leap high in the sky!

Sure, jump out of my shoes, that I could do. But the sky, that was something else. And Zatagatooz—I knew all about that. It was everything that was inside out and upside down, everything strange and hard to figure—things bent and curled, snarly and unexpected. Life is wrinkled, and it does confuse. Yet I came to see that sometimes, oddly, awkwardly, it could be fun—full of bonbons, galloping horses, cherry trees, and crowds of people applauding as if you were some kind of god, even though you were just you.

Toward the end of our first year abroad, Barnum took me off salary and made me a full partner, sharing equally in the profits. It was a windfall for my parents and they were more than pleased, as was I. But when we were alone in our hotel room, my mother nodded cynically. "See? See? He's scared to death some other agent will steal us away from him."

The money was bigger than my father had ever expected to see in his lifetime. But he was still drinking. There were days when he reached for a glass early, right after breakfast, and by noon he had an odd way of walking, as if afraid the floor might play a trick and suddenly leap up at him. But he stayed on his feet and went on drinking, sampling the different labels.

After a year in the British Isles, we departed in March and traveled to Paris. Barnum had brought my tutor along, Professor Kwink, mainly to prepare me for France. By the time we reached Paris, I could manage a bit of conversation in French, and was able to sprinkle my act with French jokes and French songs. The result was sheer magic. If the excitement in England had been a craze, what developed in France was nothing less than a mania.

I was *Tom Pouce*. On a busy boulevard in Paris, a new café opened, the Café Tom Pouce, with a life-size wooden statue of me above the door. King Louis Philippe invited me four times to the Tuileries and gave me a large emerald brooch encrusted with diamonds. In shop windows, there were Tom Pouce statues made of plaster—or of chocolate, or sugar. Someone wrote a play in which I performed, and I was made an honorary member of the Association des Artistes Dramatiques Française.

Barnum was ecstatic. My mother was happy. My father sampled all the French wines. Every night I went to bed exhausted. In many of my dreams, I spoke French, and often, when I woke, I wondered who I was, and where I was, and was afraid to close my eyes again.

After three months in Paris, I had long stands in many other cities across France. Then Barnum brought us down into the south of France, where we rested for a while and enjoyed the atmosphere—trees, orchards, vineyards thick with ripening grapes.

A week of that, then we crossed over into Spain, to Pamplona, where Queen Isabella was eager to see me. Three afternoons I spent with her. Beautiful brown eyes, she had. She was fourteen, and I was seven, yet we felt very comfortable with each other, as if she weren't a queen and I not a dwarf who was getting more than my share of public attention.

She showed me the palace, the large halls filled with paintings, statues, and wall hangings. And the chapel. Then she took me by the hand and brought me into her garden, to show me the camellias and the gardenias. And the flash of excitement in her eyes as she drew me farther along and showed me the purple rose that had been named for her, the 'Rosa Reina Isabella.' How does one forget such moments? How does one survive them?

On a Saturday afternoon she brought me to the bullfights, and, much to my astonishment, she picked me up and sat me on her lap. What an excitement that was, to be so close. "You will see much better from here," she said.

And for sure, I did. The picadors parading on their horses, then the banderilleros, and the matadors in their fancy costumes, embroidered with silver and gold. The matadors paused in front of us, bowing to the Queen. Three matadors, stern and ready, eager to go one-on-one against a bull. And the bulls, in a pen at the edge of the field, snorting and restless.

I enjoyed the pageantry, the colors, the brass band. But soon enough, when I saw the matador waving his cape, inviting the bull to charge, I felt the tension.

Many times it charged, and when it was worn down, in went the matador's sword, and the bull fell dead to the ground. The crowd crying *olé, olé*.

"Such a brave bull," Isabella said. "It knew how to die. And the matador, such courage—always an inch away from death."

That's what it was about, I realized—about death, and that bothered me, because then especially, as I sat on Isabella's lap, death was not something I wanted to think about. After all the traveling, and all the places I'd seen—palaces, cathedrals, bridges, rivers, thatched roofs, the different ways of talking and living, I had decided that I hated death, and wanted nothing to do with it.

While that lifeless bull was dragged from the arena, I felt that if death were something tangible, something I could see and walk up to, I would kick it in the shins and set fire to its underwear.

From Spain, we traveled back up to the north of France, then crossed the border into Belgium. We had a long stay in Brussels, where I met with King Leopold and Queen Louise. Then we toured through several nearby cities, and soon we were fully two years into our tour.

Barnum brought us back across the Channel, for another year-long sweep through the British Isles. He advertised it as my Farewell Tour. The crowds were still there for me, and since these were my final appearances, I concluded each performance with a song that was popular at the time—

When other lips and other hearts
Their tales of love shall tell,
There may, perhaps, in such a scene,
Some recollection be
Of days that have as happy been—
Then you'll remember me!
And yes—remember me!

After those three exciting years in Europe, my father found himself presiding over more wealth than he'd ever hoped to see. He set some of it aside for my future, and with another portion he built a new house for the family—a substantial three-story place with a garden, a veranda, and a high cupola from which you could look across the tops of the trees and see, in the distance, the schooners on Long Island Sound. There was a special apartment for me on the ground floor, with low windows and small furniture, and space for a dwarf piano and a dwarf billiard table. My two sisters had their weddings in that house, and those were happy times, full of excitement.

But my father, with his bottles from Scotland. My sense, always, was that he was openly proud of me, boasting that I was his son—but underneath, he was suffering. It must have been hell for him to see that I, so young, a kid, a singing-and-dancing brat, was able to pull in so much more money than he could ever make doing hard work with a hammer. It just tore him to pieces. What kept him going were those bottles from the Highlands, the morning nip and the evening sup, and the many swigs between. Too tipsy at times, shouting at the walls and quarreling with the furniture. But despite all that, he was a good father, gentle and always there for us. And still he sang, digging into the old tunes, "Annie Laurie," and "Rocked in the Cradle of the Deep." And his other favorite, "Comin' thro' the Rye."

Once, I remember, before I became Tom Thumb and before we had that spacious new house, he came home with a large wooden ball painted gray and blue. We sat on the floor, rolling it back and forth to each other. It seemed that he was a happy man that day, and I, too, felt happy, waiting for the ball as it rolled toward me. It was one of those special moments, a moment that is always there for me—just the two of us, rolling the ball back and forth.

The days and months flipped by, and suddenly, at seventeen, I found myself in a year that was like a box of broken crackers—and near the end of that year, at the bottom of the box, nothing but maggoty crumbs. That was the year my father's drinking became such a problem that his brothers, my uncles, gathered around and persuaded him to go into an asylum to take the cure. It would be months, we knew, and it wouldn't be easy, but he would come out a happier man.

That's what we thought, and hoped for. But only three weeks after he went in, his heart gave out, and we lost him. It was crushing. Impossible. Zatagatooz and Zootagataz wrapped up together in a lopsided nightmare. Why, I wondered. *Why?*

It wasn't just the suddenness that caught me, but the finality—the swift, irreversible shutdown. It had never crossed my mind, when he went into the asylum, that he might not come home.

My mother used to sing—old songs from long ago—but I haven't heard her sing for quite some time. She says the worst thing that ever happened was that Barnum brought us to Europe, because it was there, in London, in Dublin, in Paris, in Brussels, that my father quit drinking beer and started with whisky, and it ruined him.

She keeps a picture of him on the ledge above the fireplace, in an oak frame. He's standing beside an empty chair in a photographer's studio, one hand resting on the back of the chair. So young he was, so fine and good-looking, and when I think of that picture, I wonder what might have been running through his mind at the moment when the shutter clicked. Did he have even the faintest suspicion that he would someday afford the new big house that he put up for us? Could he possibly have foreseen that Queen Victoria, by having me to the palace so many times, would contribute hugely to my success? And, in his darkest imaginings, did he have even the vaguest notion that he would drink himself to death?

After my father passed on, Barnum, in a way, became my father, taking care of me, showing me how to handle money and property. But in fact he had been a father to me even before that, ever since he discovered me. He chose my clothes, and told me what to say when I met Queen Victoria and all of the other royals. He fed me the puns and jokes that I used onstage, and taught me the songs that I sang. And he showed me around, taking me to Brady's for the photograph exhibitions, to Brooks Brothers for my street clothes, to Genin the hatter, to the Park Theatre to hear Ole Bull playing his violin.

Sometimes I thought of him as a father, and sometimes I thought of him as God. There were times, too, when I thought of him as the Devil, and times when he seemed just an ungainly, overblown clown, eager for the day when every tooth in his head would be Tiffany gold. Somehow, all of those things were mixed up in him—they were part of him, braided into his personality.

"Life is a road," my father used to say, "you move from here to there, from yesterday to tomorrow. Hope for a good horse and a good wagon, and pray the damn wheels don't fall off."

A road, yes, that's what it was. And if you're a dwarf, twenty-five inches tall, and life, *your* life, is a journey, how do you make your way on this busy, bumbling, bombastic highway? How to avoid being trampled and crushed?

Day and night I was still out there, on the move, and wondering—what next? What lies in wait around the far bend? And where, where, was the woman whose perfume I caught a whiff of in a dream one night? I touched her and she was full of wild laughter, with liquid eyes and lips full of magic, and long fingernails that carved deep into my chest. Was she, too, out there on that same crazy road, searching, and waiting?

And the war that my father had talked about, the war that was waiting to happen—it was nowhere in sight, but you could hear it rustling around, grumbling in the grass, and you knew it was never far away.

~ PART ONE ~

THE BATTLE OF BULL RUN

CHAPTER 1

RIVERS OF REDEEMING LOVE

I was seventeen—then, too fast, I was twenty-three, in that Zatagatooz year of 1861. Toward the middle of April, after my evening performance at the Museum, I was in a state of complete exhaustion. I dragged myself to my room at the Astor, slipped out of my shoes, climbed onto the bed, and, still in my street clothes, sank into a deep, easy sleep. Not the flicker of a dream, as if my inner self had slipped out of my body and vanished—no sound, no color, no mood, no memory. An emptiness that was empty of its own emptiness.

I was awakened by cramps in my legs. I wriggled my feet, trying to shake off the tenseness. When the twinges persisted, I slid off the bed and did some stretching, which helped, but not much.

I paced around, back and forth, and soon, fully awake and restless, still with that tightness in my legs, I slipped into my shoes and went down for a walk in the night air.

I went along Broadway, past Barclay, Park Place, and Murray. It was after midnight and still a ripple of traffic, people in hackneys and broughams, heading home after the opera or a show, or a late supper at Delmonico's. The street resonated with the clip-clopping of horseshoes on the cobblestones.

When I reached Warren Street, across from the old Bridewell, I met up with a newsboy who had a stack of papers on the sidewalk. He was hawking an extra, shouting "The war is on! The war is on!" I handed him a coin and took a copy.

Under a streetlamp, I saw the headline—BOMBARDMENT OF FORT SUMTER. It had begun at four thirty in the morning, almost a full day earlier. So the war was on, and it had taken that long for the news to reach the city and get out on the street.

It was a heart-stopping moment. I remember the crinkly feel of the newspaper in my hands, and the clip-clopping sounds of horseshoes as carriages went by. And, on the other side of Broadway, the old masonry walls of the Bridewell, once a prison, now a hall of records.

And I? Who was I? A dwarf but still growing, all of thirty-two inches tall. And what I knew, and would never forget, was that the first shots in the war had been fired in the dark before sunrise, on a Friday—and as I stood there, under that streetlamp, it was already Saturday, and an odor of horse urine rising from the street.

A woman wearing a purple hat saw me with the paper and stopped. "Lincoln should kill them all," she said. "Every last one of them. Kill them all!" She was with a man in a black suit. He pulled her away, and they walked on.

After the fall of Fort Sumter, Lincoln issued a call for seventy-five thousand volunteers to put down the rebellion. The sign-up was for ninety days, and that, most of us thought, was how long the conflict would last. Quickly in—a speedy win—and quickly out.

War fever spread through the North, and in New York it was a full-blown mania. Instantly, now that shots had been fired, the city's bankers and businessmen plunged in, raising money for the war effort. For New York, which had long favored compromise with the South, this was an incredible turnaround—a Zatagatooz spin, a Zootagataz overnight reversal.

Huge numbers answered Lincoln's call for volunteers. People I knew at the barbershop, the corner newsstand—suddenly gone. At the Museum there were janitors and carpenters who went. Fritz, Tommy, Morris, Angelo, Bobby Cork. They signed with the German Rifles, or the Irish Sixty-ninth, or the Garibaldi Guard, some with the Fortieth or Sixty-eighth Infantry. I, too, wanted to go, but how? If you're as short as I was, less than three feet tall, how do you charge across a battlefield while lugging a knapsack, a canteen filled with water, a pouch filled with cartridges, and a musket that's bigger than you and impossible to handle?

The streets and parks were filled with soldiers marching and training. Flags everywhere—in store windows, on the horse-drawn omnibuses and the facades of churches. And Barnum, in his overblown way, went all out. He dressed Old Tom, the piano player, in a toga made from a flag, and he had a Stars and Stripes gown tailor-made for the Bearded Lady. Bihin, the giant from Belgium, wore an outfit that made him look like Uncle Sam. And Goshen, the Arab giant, sported a red-white-and-blue turban. We wondered about him. Was he truly an Arab? Some thought he might be Bulgarian, from Varna, with maybe a few drops of Sicilian blood. Or mestizo, from Guatemala. But wherever he was from, he was now in America, and if he were to volunteer, we wondered—would the army want him? Would a giant be an advantage during a battle, or just an easy target?

Up and down Broadway, there was fire in the air, and I, too, felt it. One day, after my midafternoon performance, I asked the doorman to hail a hackney for me. I rode up to Union Square, where the army had opened a new recruitment center.

As we made our approach, I saw a huge crowd lined up from Fifteenth Street to Seventeenth. The driver found a place to stop, and for a while I sat there, in the hack, gazing at the volunteers, most of them close to my own age, some older, some younger, eager to be in uniform so they could say, years later, *I was there—in it, part of it.*

And I knew—still know—that I wanted to be among them. And I hated my smallness, which excluded me from the one thing that seemed, at the time, truly important.

In the early weeks and months of the war, there were incidents, encounters, in places I'd never heard of. I wrote the names and dates in a notebook that I kept. Because all of this, every small scrap of it, was important—more dense with meaning, I felt, than my impersonation of Napoléon or my Highland fling.

At a town known as Fairfax Court House, Union cavalrymen were driven off by a mob of shopkeepers with rifles. It was a mud-in-your-eye humiliation. At Big Bethel, confused Union soldiers were firing on one another. They incurred a loss of eighteen dead and fifty-three wounded, against a Confederate loss of one dead. At Corrick's Ford, a Confederate general was killed. That was terrific for the Union, but it didn't make up for all the other bumbling, and it didn't bring anything like a quick end to the rebellion.

On a Saturday morning in July, when I arrived at the Museum, Barnum scooped me up, perched me on his shoulder, and carried me to his office. He stood me on his desk and looked me in the eye.

"How about it," he said. "The war, Charlie. The battle we've all been waiting for."

"Which battle?"

"The big one."

"Where?"

"Manassas Junction."

I offered a dumb stare. "Like—in Asia Minor?"

"In Virginia," he said, tapping a knuckle against my forehead. "Twenty-five miles out of Washington and ninety-five to Richmond. You don't think they'd be fighting the battle of battles in Chicago, do you? Horace Greeley gave me the route."

Horace, who else but Horace? Barnum's pal, Greeley himself, the Dalai Lama of the *Tribune*. Who else would know there was a battle brewing? He was a year younger than Barnum, had recently turned fifty, was wispy-haired, blue-eyed, passionate for all sorts of reform, and wore his spectacles low on his nose. Barnum described him once as having the face of a doting grandmother.

I was still standing on Barnum's desk. "We'll catch the ten o'clock at the depot," he said. "After the transfer in Baltimore, we'll be in Washington before midnight and grab some sleep at the Willard."

"Then?"

"Then it's a few hours out of Washington, in a rig."

"He's coming with us?"

"Horace? Of course not. At this very moment, Charlie, he's in my house, sipping milk sweetened with honey and writing his victory editorial, applauding the end of the rebellion."

"And if we don't win?"

Barnum leaned close. "Charlie—things get better, not worse. Don't be a dog-eared, seek-sorrow pessimist. Why do dwarfs see only the dark side?"

I had never thought of myself as a gloom-and-doom dark-sider. The plain truth is, there is winning, there is losing, and there are always surprises.

Barnum scratched his chin. "In your dressing room—you have a bag with a change of clothes?"

He knew I did. I always kept a satchel ready; there was no knowing when he might pop an idea for a trip to anywhere—but never before to a battle. He enjoyed the open road, the surprises, the adventure. He liked to be where big things were happening.

"But what about my morning show? And my afternoon show? And tomorrow? And the next day?"

He shrugged, waved a hand. "I already set it up for the Orpheon Sisters to go on. They're damn prettier than you and they are fizzing good acrobats. Why aren't you an acrobat? Those four girls in their short costumes, doing cartwheels and backflips, those are some legs they have."

"My breakdown dance isn't good enough?"

"Legs, Charlie. You don't got legs like they got legs."

But we weren't talking about legs—we were talking about the first big battle of the war, and maybe the last. He looked at me, and I looked at him—we had this way of talking to each other with our eyes. Manassas? Bull Run? All the way down there and maybe not even get near the battle? See only a few puffs of smoke and catch a stray bullet in an arm or a leg? My eyes and his eyes talking, thrashing it out, and I saw he was serious about this, dead serious.

I hopped off the desk and made my way to my dressing room, for my satchel. He followed with his suitcase and a lunch basket filled, I figured, with more than we could eat, and maybe a flask of brandy to celebrate the victory—even though he'd been a teetotaler, on and off, for thirteen years.

"This battle, Charlie—decades from now, you will be boasting about it to your grandchildren."

It was a warm day, the train grew hotter as the day wore on. I slept, or tried to. Barnum plunged through the seven newspapers he'd picked up before we boarded, then he promptly snored off and slept the sleep of a tired elephant.

Somewhere in lower New Jersey, he snorted awake, and I opened the lunch basket. It held bread, walnuts, fruit, a few large chunks of cheddar, and, yes, the brandy. I took a nip, but Barnum, mindful of his temperance pledge, resisted.

It was dark, well after ten, when we reached Washington. In the morning, after a quick breakfast, when Barnum approached the drivers lined up outside the hotel, one wanted a thousand, another asked for twelve hundred. A third was looking for fifteen. It was outrageous. I knew laborers who didn't make that kind of money in a year.

Barnum hurried me along to a livery a few blocks away, thinking he would rent a rig and do the driving himself. But the carriages were all spoken for. We went to another livery, farther off, where the owner asked five hundred for a barouche, and another five for the two horses. For yet another five, he offered to throw in his son as a driver. I could hear Barnum's exasperation in the way he breathed.

We returned to the hotel, looking for the driver who'd asked for a thousand, but he was gone. Barnum approached the man who wanted twelve and tried to bargain him down. He offered nine, but the man laughed. "This be a once-in-a-lifetime opportunity," he said. "Never agin you gonna see a thing like this—fifty thousand men doin' their damnedest to shoot each other in the face. It be now nor never."

"A thousand," Barnum offered. "Not a penny more."

They settled for eleven hundred fifty-five dollars and twenty-five cents. The twenty-five cents was for a salve the man needed for a rash on his backside, or he wouldn't be able, he said, to sit the long road, going and coming. I sensed a quiet hostility in him and figured he was a dyed-in-the-wool secessionist, born and bred in one of the small towns across the river, in Virginia. A long, narrow chin and dark eyes, and something in his manner suggesting that he resented Yankees in any shape or form, even when he had them over a barrel.

While he hurried off to a nearby pharmacy for his ointment, Barnum and I gathered our things, and when we were all put together, off we went, later than expected, and fully aware that the battle had to have already begun.

The carriage was an open four-wheeler, the driver on a high bench up front—and behind him, in the body of the carriage, two wide seats facing each other. A black horse and a bay pulled us, the bay restless, grunting, tossing its head and tapping a hoof when we stopped at the crossings.

We were soon on the Long Bridge, which took us across the Potomac. Then a bumpy, gibbering ride into northern Virginia, toward the town of Fairfax Court House, and beyond that to Centreville.

All I knew about the battle was that the Union troops were under McDowell, whom I'd never heard of, and the rebs were under Beauregard, who had fired the opening shots of the war when he bombarded Fort Sumter in April. The rumor was that the Federals had far more troops than the rebs, but it was expected that a pack of Confederate troops would be riding in from the Shenandoah Valley, and that could pose a problem.

What no one had to tell me was that it was a hot, sizzling day. July 21, 1861—everything limp, the entire landscape wilted. How anybody in that heat could dash around on a battlefield, load and shoot, and dive for cover, was beyond me.

Even from a distance, we heard the booming of the big guns, a mean, rumbling, thunderous roar. When we entered Centreville, we found a huge crowd of Union soldiers. Most of the villagers had locked their homes and left. They were Virginians, hardly thrilled about having a swarm of Yankees in town, and expecting, no doubt, that their village would become a battleground.

There was a road that led south to Manassas Junction, but a lieutenant told us to avoid that and stay with the Warrenton Turnpike, where the high ground offered a better view of the battlefield. That, he said, was where the congressmen and reporters and sightseers from Washington were heading. He thought Barnum was a senator, and Barnum made no effort to set him straight. God only knows what he thought of me. A dwarf prince from the Kingdom of Tonga? Or maybe just an undergrown orphan that Barnum had brought along for the show.

With a pencil, the lieutenant made a quick sketch of the turnpike for us. About a mile out of town, there was a bridge over the Cub Run stream. Some two miles beyond that, a heftier bridge known as the Stone Bridge, across the Bull Run, which flowed down out of the mountains. The opening cannon shot had been fired shortly after five in the morning, the lieutenant said, but the infantry didn't go head-to-head until sometime after ten.

Barnum thanked him for his help, and we made our way to the turnpike. It was a dusty road on high ground, with a far view of the sloping land on our left—a region of low, rolling hills, woods and gullies, with a number of farmhouses visible, and large open fields. The big guns were slamming away, and, in the pauses, when the guns took a rest, we heard the clack-clacking of musket fire. In the distance, flashes of sunlight glinting off the bayonets.

I was surprised at how many carriages were lined up along the edge of the turnpike, stretching out as far as I could see. Barnum knew several of the congressmen we passed. He lifted his hat and waved as we rode by.

Some of the onlookers sat in their carriages, using field glasses, others were on blankets in the grass beside the road, with picnic baskets and flagons of wine. A festive mood—this, the first big battle since the onset of the war, months earlier. High hopes for a quick victory, then a swift march to Richmond and a deathblow to the rebellion. The hammering of the artillery continued, shaking the air and sending great puffs of smoke up above the trees.

As we moved along, searching for a place to stop, I saw groups of infantry maneuvering on the slopes—so far off, they seemed smaller than the toy soldiers I played with when I was two or three years old. In those fields between densely wooded areas, they moved, they ran, they paused, they fired their muskets, a small puff of white from each shot that was fired.

We came upon a space where our carriage would have fit, but trees blocked the view. We moved on. The road descended toward the low bridge across the Cub Run, and as we lost elevation, the view diminished. We crossed the bridge, hoping for higher ground on the other side. Far along, we found a spot and pulled in, between a fancy carriage ornamented with silver cupids, and a carriage with gold lettering on one of the doors—BAPTIST CHURCH OF GOOD HOPE. We weren't as high up as we'd been on the heights at Centreville, but the view was as good as we were going to get.

I knew what the Baptist church was, but had no clue about the carriage with the silver cupids. Then, when I saw the women on the grass, I knew. Six of them, lolling about in frilly silks. Lotus flowers, *filles de joie*—parlor women, probably from one of the more expensive comfort houses in Washington, visited by bankers and politicians.

The driver secured the horses to a wooden post at the edge of the road, then he grabbed a blanket, curled up among the roadside weeds, and was soon asleep, though how he could sleep with the booming of the big guns, I hardly knew.

It was one o'clock, the sun high and beating down, baking everything. I was in a sweat. Barnum's shirt was soaked through. The horses were in a lather. With his field glasses, Barnum took a quick survey of the fields and slopes, the distant houses and dense clusters of trees—

and, sooner than soon, he was off, going up and down the line of carriages, glad-handing and digging around for information.

I remained in the carriage, standing on a seat to give myself some elevation, and used my spyglass. I was often not sure what I was looking at. A musket in the grass, or just a branch from a tree? A pile of stones, or a jumble of military gear? Here and there, glimpses of the Bull Run stream looping and turning as it carved its way through the hills. A few haystacks, a patch of wild roses.

Then, suddenly, off to my left, soldiers in an open field were being hit by volleys from the woods in front of them. The shots slashed right through them, and, one after another, they fell. A few fired back, though not for long. Some ran and got away, but twenty or thirty were down. It was weird and wrenching, to watch that, to see it through the spyglass. A wild, nightmarish moment, as in some crazy, upside-down dream. But I was awake, and those soldiers on the ground, they weren't moving.

I didn't know if they were Union or Confederate. With the drift of gun smoke between them and me, and the heat from the ground creating a shimmer in the air, it was hard to be sure of the color of their uniforms. I knew, too, that army colors weren't fully standard yet. The South wore mostly gray, the North was mostly blue—but the New York Seventh wore gray, and I'd heard of a Wisconsin regiment also in gray. And a Virginia regiment in blue. But, Northern or Southern, it shook my bones to see those soldiers down.

There was a lull, almost a silence.

Then, from another part of the field, the artillery acted up again. Shells were crashing into the woods from which those soldiers had been ambushed. Pounding and pounding, trees falling. If anyone was still there, it must have been hell.

I lowered the glass and gazed idly at the field, great clouds of white smoke from the cannons drifting, rising, here and there a patch of green grass visible. I looked, I watched. Then I sat and closed my eyes, numb, needing to pull away somehow, far from everything I'd seen.

But there was no getting away from it. Simply to breathe was to be part of it, the stink of gunfire high in my nose and deep in my lungs. And, much as I wanted to be somewhere else, there was, yet, a humming curiosity lurking inside me, a muffled desire to see, to listen, to know what was happening.

Then another lull, an easing off, the cannons resting, searching for other targets.

When I opened my eyes, the low ground toward the bottom of the hill was still a mess, clouds of smoke shredding apart and slowly lifting. I waited, then put the spyglass to my eye. To my left, again I saw those soldiers who'd been shot down. In the hazy air, they looked like clumps of dug-up soil. I tried to improve the focus, wanting to see a hand, a face, and searched around, slowly.

Then—*then*—I saw one of those soldiers moving. He slowly rolled over and, struggling, pushed himself up, onto one knee. After a time, he forced himself to his feet, and, limping, he moved off toward a thicket of shrubs and small trees.

But among the others there was no movement. As still as logs. And the night before, God knows, they may have been singing and whistling, cursing the salt pork and the hard tack, and picking lice out of their hair. I hated it that they were down, everything inside me rose up against it. And the sun, the hot, throbbing sun, like a drum beating in my head.

I searched the field, left and right, and again I spotted the soldier who had stood up out of the weeds. He had turned and was limping now in our direction, toward the lineup of carriages along the turnpike. I saw his face, a splotch of blood on his left cheek, and his left leg giving him trouble. He fell and was down a while, and when he was up, the limp was a little worse. If he wanted to reach the turnpike, I didn't think he would make it.

I left the spyglass on the seat and jumped down, out of the carriage and onto the grass, hurrying past our driver, still asleep on his blanket. Down the steep slope I went, into the high grass and weeds. Fast, running where I could, through swarms of mosquitoes and flies, and other bugs, fat beasty critters clinging to my skin.

The soldier saw me. He was waving me off, warning me to go back. "Get off the field—turn back! Go! Go!"

I glanced about, thinking there might be troops on the move nearby, but saw none. More weeds, more rocks, more bees and flies and mosquitoes. A clump of low trees not far off. And just then, from those trees, a volley of musket fire—minié balls kicking up dirt and grass not far from me.

It stopped as abruptly as it had started. One volley, that was all. I was still standing. But that soldier, he was down.

I didn't move. When I did, I was slow and cautious, walking toward him, past a blackberry patch, a rotting woodpile. When I reached him, he was on his back, not moving, blue eyes open but no life in him.

An envelope was sticking up out of a pocket. I took it with me and would put it in the mail. It was addressed to a woman in Pennsylvania. His wife, I figured, or his mother. The big guns were active again, the Parrotts and the Napoléons, and plenty of white smoke rising over the fields and hills.

I hurried back toward the turnpike, moving past a tall oak, half of its branches blasted away, and another oak felled by artillery. A white ambulance wagon was on its side, smashed.

I became aware, suddenly, that I saw no birds, and realized that even on the ride in from Centreville I had seen nothing on the wing, not a hawk, not a buzzard, not a sparrow. The booming of the batteries had scared them off. No deer bounding through the fields, no wild turkeys. I wondered why the flies and the bees and the mosquitoes were holding on so tenaciously.

When I reached the carriage, I climbed in and sat down. The driver was still asleep in the weeds. And Barnum, for all I knew, was in the thick of things, strolling around out there and picking up spent shot for the Museum. I was drained, sapped. The guns continued to pound, and I closed my eyes, trying to locate some inner silence—trying to empty myself and be, for a few moments, not me. Not thinking, not dreaming, not knowing. But how to do that? How not to remember?

A fly buzzed in my ear and I swatted hard. Missed the fly but hit the ear, and the ringing in my head yanked me away from the stillness I desired.

I sat facing the rear of our carriage, looking toward the one adorned with silver cupids. The parlor women were out on the grass, on brightly colored blankets. I had passed them when I rushed out to help that limping soldier, and passed them when I returned. I don't think they noticed me. They were drinking champagne, having a lively time. They chatted, they giggled. One had her skirts drawn up, her frilly red underpants descending to her knees. Another was flat on her back, with the top of her dress pulled down, letting the hot sun bake her breasts. The redhead was barefoot, massaging her feet. Three men were with them. Congressmen, I suspected, or lawyers, or bankers on holiday.

In the other carriage, the one in front of ours, the group from a Baptist church was singing. It had started with low humming, going on and on—then a woman's voice, near smothered by the rattle of musketry, but clear, a voice strong and tender at the same time.

Sweet rivers of Redeeming Love
Lie just before my eye—
Had I the pinions of a dove
I'd to those regions fly.

I'd rise aloft, beyond my pain,
And with joy outstrip the wind—
I'd cross death's cold and stormy main
And leave the world behind.

Her voice seemed a ribbon in the air, floating. I slumped down and again I closed my eyes, following the rhythm of that voice, the smoothness, which held and continued to hold, despite the fever of the guns.

Then Barnum was back, and, finding me sprawled on the rear seat, he bent close. "Charlie? Charlie? You okay?"

CHAPTER 2

THE HENRY HILL

My eyes snapped open. "Right . . . sure." I sat up, rolled my shoulders, and, swinging my head around, saw that Barnum had someone with him. I took a deep breath and hopped down out of the carriage.

The man's name was Sitwell, Tom Sitwell, a reporter from a London newspaper. I knew the name, I'd seen a story about him some weeks earlier. He'd covered the Crimean War, writing about the trenches and the hospital tents. He'd been in the thick of things at the Battle of Sebastopol.

He was a shade taller than Barnum and maybe ten years younger. Forty, I guessed. Thick-bodied, with large hands, and a bushy moustache. He wore riding boots and a khaki jacket with many pockets. He said he'd seen my show a few years ago, when I last toured England. He'd also seen me years earlier, on my first tour.

He shook my hand. "If all the world were as tiny as you, Little Tom, it would be a gentler place. The guns would not be as big as they are, and the *damage* would be less."

I wasn't too sure about that. "The guns would be smaller," I said, "but the shells might be deadlier—dwarf pellets that blow up whole mountains."

"You think so? Really?" There was an odd slant in the way he said that. Hard to tell if he thought what I'd said was ingenious or just plain crazy.

Then he surprised me. He told me that his father, during my first trip to London, had been one of the rope handlers when I was aloft in a hydrogen balloon, at the Surrey Gardens. It had been Barnum's idea to send me up, as a publicity stunt. But, on that particular day, a blast of wind tore the ropes from the fists of the handlers, and the balloon sailed off on its own, with me in the basket. My father ran like hell, chasing a rope that hung a few feet off the ground, and leaped to grab it as the balloon started to lift away.

"I was there," Sitwell said. "I saw it. That brisk, bright day, you were drifting, the wind had you. Remember?"

I clucked my tongue. Could I ever forget?

"My father was a wreck," he said, apologetically. "He was so upset."

"So was mine."

"That's what fathers are for," Barnum put in. "We are all a kind of wreckage." One of his daughters, Frances, had died young, not yet two, while he was away in Europe, and he never forgave himself for being away from home at that terrible time.

"I'll give you my father's address," Sitwell said to me. "Send him a nasty letter. I write nasty letters all the time. If it will be of any help, I'll lean on him and make him send his apologies to your father."

"My father is dead."

"Oh, sorry." He paused, gazing at the battlefield. "Someday, you know, we shall all be gone, every last one of us—and no one to do the mourning and the grieving. Nothing but the wind in the trees, and no one to hear it." Then, perkily, he stuck out his jaw. "I can hardly wait!"

He took three cigars from a pocket, and we lit up, but the aroma of Cuban leaf was smothered by the burnt-sulfur stink of the battlefield. From another pocket he pulled out a brandy flask and offered a sip to Barnum, who declined. With a wry glance, Sitwell extended the flask to me. "Is the lad snug for a quaff of golden Koktebel brewed near an ancient volcano on the coast of the Black Sea?"

"The lad," I answered, "will risk anything that goes down smooth."

I took a sip. It flamed my throat and sent my head swirling. I felt, for a moment, that I'd been launched toward the low ground between the hills, amid exploding shells and bursting canisters of shrapnel.

When I returned the flask to Sitwell, he tilted his head and took a gulp that would have sent an elephant reeling.

"A while ago," he said, "an officer rode by, shouting that the Federals were sweeping the field. But listen. You hear that racket? Does that sound like an end to the battle?"

There was a lot of musketry banging away out there. Not the end, no, more like a snarling, simmering rage.

"In my bones," he said, "I hope for a Union win. It would be utter hell if the New World's great experiment in democracy were to go smash. But a Union victory is not the story my paper wants from me."

The Queen's government was officially neutral, but his editor, he said, was pro-South, and Sitwell had been put on the carpet for some pro-North sentiments he expressed at a dinner speech in Boston. "I've been chastised, sanitized, and very nearly ostracized. So now I am officially neutral, though you know where my gut lies."

He'd arrived a few hours before we did, and had gathered a hoard of information from soldiers coming and going along the turnpike. The Union had already lost some officers, a major and a colonel, both wounded. The South, too—one general wounded, another dead. How Sitwell found out about the Southern losses, he never mentioned.

"The troops are brave, very brave," he said, "but they're green. On the march from Washington, they were romping around, raiding hen coops and chasing pigs. What should have been a one-day march dragged into two and a half." With his handkerchief, he wiped the sweat from his forehead and neck. "Not only that, but on my way in, I ran flush into a regiment that was marching home. The Fourth Pennsylvania. I spoke to an officer, he told me their ninety-day enlistment time had just expired. That's discipline? Walking away from a battle in progress? That's how to win a war?"

"They're *all* green," Barnum said. "North and South."

"That makes it better?"

"It makes it equal. Green against green."

"No," Sitwell answered. "It doesn't even things out. Green is not predictable—you never know which green soldier will turn and run, and which will leap with suicidal courage into a whole throng of the enemy. On a battlefield, unpredictability puts everyone at risk."

Barnum, too, was mopping his brow. "Yes, yes," he nodded, rocking his head from side to side, "and a shift in the weather can change everything. Don't we know." He leaned close to Sitwell. "You're worried, I see that. You're concerned. You want the Union to win, but you think we'll lose. I assure you—the Union will come out on top in this fight."

"You think so?"

"I know so."

"You're a man of instinct," Sitwell answered, "and I admire that. It has carried you far. And though my own leaning is toward logic and hard fact, trust me when I say that I hope your sixth sense proves right and that your army will carry the day."

He gazed far off down the turnpike, westward, toward the Stone Bridge and beyond.

"Out there," he said, "see that hill rising beside the turnpike? They call it the Henry Hill. There's a farmhouse up there, belongs to the Widow Henry. She's sick, and as far as anybody knows, she's still there. The whole battle has swung around, and right now, on that hill, that's where it's happening. That's where the battle may be won or lost."

I climbed up onto the carriage and grabbed my spyglass from the seat. There were two hills, one to the left and one to the right of the turnpike.

"The high one," he said. "To the left."

I fumbled around, then I saw it—the white farmhouse, two stories high, with a rambling fence cut from tree branches. A broad, open field up there.

"Look sharp, Tom—to the right of the house you'll see a cannon or two."

I saw them, sunlight glinting off the bronze, two of them, but the hill curved away and I couldn't see what else was up there. Nor did I understand the little that I saw—soldiers rushing about, the cannons not firing, drifting clouds of smoke obscuring the view.

I lowered the glass and looked to Sitwell, but he was silent. Something was boiling inside him. A need to know, a need to see for himself exactly what was happening up there.

He headed back to his gig and we went with him, toward the bridge over the Cub Run. He had a saddle horse hitched to the back of the gig, a chestnut stallion. "Gentlemen—it's time to ride into the field and see what's doing."

He reached into the gig and pulled out a red top hat, which he planted firmly on his head, then he unhitched the stallion and hoisted himself into the saddle.

"This is wise?" Barnum asked.

"Not to worry," Sitwell answered. "Nobody shoots at a man wearing a red hat. Not in Sebastopol, not at the Alma River, not at Inkerman. And not, I trust, at Bull Run."

He clenched the stub end of his cigar between his teeth, and off he rode, down a grassy slope at the edge of the turnpike, then quickly on his way to the Henry Hill. I watched through my glass, until the horse and the red hat vanished behind a stand of trees.

CHAPTER 3

THE WOUNDED SOLDIER

We made our way back to our carriage. Sitwell wasn't long gone, fifteen minutes or so, when a supply wagon came rushing from the direction of the Stone Bridge and rattled right past us, raising dust. Then an ambulance, and another supply wagon. And another, racing along recklessly. Moments later, a throng of Union soldiers came from the same direction, walking swiftly along the turnpike. Groups of ten or twenty, and smaller groups, three or four, and some alone.

Barnum approached a soldier. "What's happening?"

"Time to clear out while we can," the soldier said, not slowing his gait.

He kept moving, there were others hurrying behind him. It was four thirty.

Our driver was awake and on his feet, stepping out of the weeds, thin and wrinkle-faced, like an unfriendly dog. "Let's git the goddamn out of here," he said, stuffing his blanket into the box under his seat. "I heard what that fella said. This army's on the run. And we damn don't wanna git caught between an army on the run and the army what's chasin' 'em."

Others were already turning their carriages around, back toward Centreville. The Baptists, the congressmen, the senators, the fancy parlor-house ladies. Sitwell had mentioned a senator who brought along two carriages full of champagne, for a victory celebration. But not today, no, not if the army was quitting the field.

I climbed aboard the carriage, and, thinking of the dead soldier whose unsent letter I carried in my pocket, I wondered if he was still out there or if an ambulance had removed him from the field.

Barnum stood on the road, by the back wheel of the carriage, in a kind of daze. "Whipped?" he shouted. "Whipped? Who says? What kind of flumdiddling bamboozling craziness is this?" He was speaking to no one—to the sky, the road, to the Henry Hill where something had gone wrong. "I damn don't believe this is happening."

He was still on the road when the driver unhitched the horses from the post and led them, turning the carriage.

After a last, long look at the Henry Hill, Barnum climbed aboard and sat beside me. The driver, climbing to his perch, flicked the reins, and the horses were moving—but with the jumble of carriages and wagons up ahead, we went slowly downhill to the Cub Run bridge and crossed the sluggish stream.

We weren't far up the rise on the other side when a heavy gun opened up and shells landed not far behind us. I stood up on my seat and looked back. A white-topped ambulance wagon lay overturned on the Cub Run bridge, blocking the way and making it impossible for anyone to come across. Soldiers, trapped on the far side, were plunging into the waist-high water, and wagon drivers were cutting their horses loose. Men and horses splashed through the water and floundered up into the fields on our side of the bridge—the men stumbling, tripping on rocks and stubble as they raced for the turnpike, or any trail that would take them the hard mile back to Centreville. Horses, freed from their traces, roamed the fields, many of them wounded and bleeding.

Up ahead, the turnpike was a tangled mess. A few drivers, late to start, were still trying to turn their rigs. Horses reared and whinnied, and rigs locked wheels with other rigs. One of the army wagons that had sped by earlier lost a wheel and crashed into a few carriages, leaving wreckage that had yet to be cleared away. Two horses had to be put down, we saw them dead on the roadside.

The heavy gun stopped firing, and more and more soldiers came along from the fields to the right and left of us. Many had abandoned their rifles, and in the boiling heat more than a few had pulled off their shirts.

"Keep movin'," a sergeant called to us as he hurried by. "The enemy is on our back!"

But movement was near impossible, the road choked with carriages and army wagons. We inched forward, stopped, moved, and again stopped. Our driver, losing patience, swung the carriage off the roadway, onto the field at our right, and we bounced wildly across the knobby ground. Barnum kept a firm hand on my shoulder to save me from flying out.

We hit a bump that nearly tipped us over. The driver, coming to his senses, slowed the horses. But we were still moving, while the rigs on the road were barely inching along.

As we rumbled on, I spotted a soldier on his back, in the weeds—his shirt bloody, but I saw him move. He was alive.

"Stop for him," I shouted.

"He's a goner," the driver shouted back. "If I stop, we'll all be goners."

"He's alive," I yelled. "He moved his arm. Stop for him!"

"He's dead. We'll be dead ourselves if we don't git out of here."

"*Stop!*" Barnum roared, reaching up and grabbing the driver's collar.

"Then be it upon your head," the driver sneered, as he reined in the horses.

Even before the carriage stopped, I jumped out and ran back. The blood was by the soldier's left shoulder and across his chest. I leaned over him. His eyes empty, open but not seeing me. "It's all right," I said, wanting him to be okay, willing it, even though I doubted there was much hope. "It's all right," I told him.

His lips parted, but no words came out. I touched him, put my hand on his face.

Then Barnum was there, beside me, bending low. The soldier's eyes were moving now, from me to Barnum, from Barnum to me. Barnum grabbed hold of him and helped him to his feet, and led him to the carriage. He could barely walk, Barnum on one side of him, and I on the other, my hand on his forearm.

Barnum helped him into the carriage, and settled him into the seat across from us. His eyes rolled and he slumped off to the side, his tongue out at the corner of his mouth. I thought he had passed out. But as the carriage moved along, his eyes opened and he was talking, the words slow and slurred, pulled up out of a deep well of pain. Those eyes, they were a rich, bright hazel, yet they seemed, somehow, to be fading into a blur.

"We was damn near winnin'," he said. "Had 'em by the throat. But they took out our artillery, and that killed it." He paused, seemed about to fade, but again he was talking. "A regiment in blue uniforms . . . blue. They come out of the woods and we're thinkin' they was ours. But they was rebs. They blasted away at our men and it was bloody slaughter. Up there on the Henry Hill. Ten of our cannon they took. In the fightin' that followed, we took 'em back, but they overwhelmed us and took the high ground. Nothin' to do but fall back and the day be lost."

He fell quiet for a while, eyes closed. Barnum put his hand to the soldier's forehead, feeling for a fever. After a long moment, he nodded in an uncertain way, more yes than no.

Then the soldier spoke again, rambling, with long pauses. "This day, what a nightmare it were. Places where bodies be piled two and three deep. . . . At the edge of a thicket, a man not six feet from me was hit by a shell. Tore him to pieces. . . . My regiment, we was told to cover the retreat—but an officer gallops through, shoutin' the enemy be on us, and it all falls apart like broken glass. Bullets rainin' down on us, and it's run and panic. Every man for hisself. . . . Hard to believe. On the long march in from Washington, we was pickin' blackberries."

He fell silent, and for a while his eyes were blank, staring emptily.

"What's your name, soldier?" Barnum asked.

"Jesus, do it matter? When you be dead, you be dead. A name don't matter no more. Was a sick old widow in one of them houses on the hill. Snipers in the house were shootin' at us, so our artillery sent a few shots their way. One smashed into the woman's bedroom—when we reached the house, she was hurt bad. If she ain't dead yet, she will be by tomorrow."

Barnum leaned forward and gripped the soldier's knee. "You're not going to die," he said. "They hit you in the shoulder. We'll have you in a hospital soon as we're in Centreville."

"Them doctors with their pliers and saws. What do they know?"

"You'll be all right. You will. If you believe you will, it will happen. You can make it be."

All his life, Barnum had been making things be. Willpower, that was his way. I think he was expecting that he would will his way past death itself and live forever.

The soldier had fallen silent, and again his eyes were closed.

Then, of a sudden, his eyes were open, staring. He was shivering, shaking with fever chills and hugging his arms to himself.

Barnum moved across and sat beside him. He took off his jacket, hung it over the fellow's shoulders, and put his arm around him, holding him. "It's all right," he said, holding him close. "It's going to be all right." He stayed that way, holding the soldier until we reached Centreville.

The sun was still up when we arrived, though it was slanting away. That mile and a half on the turnpike, from the other side of the Cub Run, had taken almost two hours. The driver called to some soldiers, asking for the nearest surgery. They pointed us up a side road, to a stone church where they'd been putting the wounded.

We turned onto that road, and when we drew close, what we saw was sickening. Along the outside walls of the church, corpses were stacked up like cordwood. And piles of amputated limbs, great heaps of them, five feet high.

The driver pulled up in front, behind a hospital wagon. I went inside with Barnum, and there, too, what we saw was unnerving. The church benches had been removed, and all across the floor, wounded soldiers were lying on blankets. A surgery table was set up by a window, with racks of candles to enhance the light.

The soldier on the table was awake and howling, in terrible pain. Two attendants held him down while the surgeon examined him. His pants had been cut away, and I saw that both of his legs were shattered. He was struggling to stay alive, panting heavily and groaning. He made a brief effort to free his arms from the attendants who held him. Then, with a great shudder, the grunting and groaning stopped, and it was over.

A male nurse, in army uniform, approached us, and Barnum told him of the soldier in our carriage. He came out with us for a look at the injury, and, finding no exit wound, confirmed that the bullet was still inside. His name was Frank Thompson. I remember him because I was struck by the almost womanly gentleness with which he handled the soldier, careful to avoid adding to his pain.

"I'll send a surgeon to sedate him," he said, "and we'll see what next."

A moment later, a middle-aged man with a bloodied apron over his uniform approached the carriage. He gave the soldier a gulp of whisky from a flask, then put an opium tablet into his mouth. He drew Barnum aside, and I went with them. He said the wisest move would be to drive the soldier straight on to Washington, and the soldiers at the bridge would get him to a proper hospital.

"The plain truth," he said, "is that we don't know what's happening. Right now, if the enemy moves against us, we don't have enough ambulances to evacuate all the wounded. It already happened in Sudley, the other side of the Bull Run—most of the wounded were left behind. A few surgeons stayed, and God knows what the rebs will do with them."

Barnum's eyes were focused in a way I'd never seen. "He'll be all right? He'll make it to Washington?"

The surgeon stared at his boots, then looked up. "The opium will blunt his pain. The ball is still in him, and he'll be better off having it removed in a proper hospital. Beyond that, nobody can say. We worry about infection. Some get it, some don't, and we don't know why. If he makes it through the first week or two, he'll likely be all right. But I don't like that fever."

He seemed exhausted. He'd been probing wounds and cutting off limbs all day. He rolled his head from side to side, relieving a kink in his neck, then pulled out a handkerchief and blew his nose.

"Life's a crapshoot," he said. "Trust to the future, and steer clear of mad dogs."

Barnum thanked him, and off we went, hoping the road to Washington would be faster than what we'd just experienced.

We passed a livery, a tavern, an inn, and a general store where there was a post office. All were shut down tight, nobody there. At the livery, even the horses were gone, driven off to safe pasture, away from the possibility of bombardment.

The sun went down, but we had the benefit of a long twilight, then a bright moon. We weren't galloping, though our pace was hardly a crawl.

It was almost eleven when we reached the Long Bridge, where a detachment of soldiers stood guard. Word of the retreat had reached Washington by telegraph, and, though it was far too early for any of the infantry to arrive on foot, a flock of ambulances and wagons were lined up and waiting.

Our wounded soldier barely opened his eyes when he was put on a stretcher and carried to an ambulance. He seemed unaware of what was happening.

As we crossed the Long Bridge, heading for the Willard Hotel, it began to rain. Barnum raised the leather canopy, but still the rain blew in on us, barely more than a drizzle, and it was welcome, blowing in our faces, washing away the dust and the grit of that hard, hot day. The army was on foot, far behind us on that long road, and if Beauregard had been able to organize a pursuit, God knows what may have become of them.

The driver dropped us on the corner of Pennsylvania Avenue. When Barnum paid him the balance that we owed, the man pocketed the money and leaned close, peering into Barnum's gray eyes.

"It were worth the price," he said. "Weren't it? A once-in-a-lifetime miracle show. Won't nobody see nothin' like that agin—not never." He was dead sure the war was over, and made no effort to conceal his delight that the Confederates had won.

Barnum offered a piercing stare, then grabbed his luggage and the lunch basket, and we headed for the lobby.

Inside, there was gloom and confusion everywhere. People hovering in groups, shaken by news of the defeat. Reporters, businessmen, army officers, congressmen and their wives. And others, like us, who had come a long way to witness the battle.

We moved quickly past them, eager to change out of our wet, muddy clothes. We left our luggage at the desk, for a bellboy to bring up, and made our way toward the stairs, passing several of the many sitting rooms. As we neared one of the parlors, we heard a booming voice speaking out about the war. We paused at the door, the room crowded with officers and well-attired gentlemen. The man talking was an army colonel with a black handlebar moustache, which gave him a remarkable resemblance to a walrus.

He was saying it was time to make peace with the South. They had made their point on the battlefield, and it was time, now, to give them what they wanted. And if it meant that Lincoln had to pack his bags and depart, then let it be. No one in the room seemed unhappy with that notion. Several grunted in agreement, and the colonel went on with more of the same.

I sensed something like rage rising in Barnum, and thought, for a moment, he might plunge into the room and trade words with the man. Instead, he put his hand on my shoulder and led me away. "Before I punch the bastard in the face," he said. "It's idiots like him that handed us this defeat today." As we passed a bellboy, Barnum asked him to have a bottle of bourbon sent up.

One room, that was all we could get when we arrived the night before. Washington was that crowded. There was a four-poster for Barnum, a cot for me, and a window that looked out on Pennsylvania Avenue. Our luggage had already been sent up.

We changed out of our wet clothes, washed, and were in our nightshirts when the bourbon arrived. I took half a glassful and sipped it slowly. But Barnum, in a rage about the handlebar colonel, tossed off a full glass. And another, then more, leaving the bottle near empty. Then he hit the bed and in a moment he was asleep and snoring—and tomorrow, if he remembered anything at all, he would be cursing himself for having violated his temperance pledge.

I, too, was tired, ready for sleep, but before I fell off I was thinking again of the black woman from the Baptist church, singing in that carriage, and the others humming along. The plain, simple faith glowing in the way she sang. I admired that, the sureness, the confidence, and was even jealous of it. *Sweet rivers of Redeeming Love* . . . My own faith was not that simple, not that sure. I had doubts about everything: the future, the past, the present life, and the afterlife. Even, at times, doubts about doubts.

I wondered about the wounded soldier we took home. After that long ride, he was part of us, as we were part of him. If he died, what sense was there in that? He *had* to live. I *wanted* him to live.

I had a broken sleep that night—odd, distorted images of the battlefield drifting in my dreams. In one dream, I was aloft in a hydrogen balloon. The wounded soldier with the hazel eyes was with me. He said nothing, simply stood there, beside me, looking toward an approaching cloud. And the dead soldier in the field, the one I had tried to help, the one with an unsent letter in his pocket—he was alive and with us, keeping his eye on that same cloud. Suddenly we were in it, an enormous fluffiness filled with strange, glimmering colors. Birds with glowing wings soared all about us, and somewhere in that cloud a woman was singing. *Sweet rivers of Redeeming Love* . . . *I'd cross death's cold and stormy main, and leave the world behind.* The birds continued to soar, and it seemed that the wings of the birds and the streams of color, and the voice of the woman, were all, somehow, one and the same.

In the morning, I was up early and went to the window. It was daylight but dim, a lazy drizzle falling, the sun hidden behind a blanket of clouds. And there below, coming down Fourteenth Street and turning onto Pennsylvania Avenue, were the retreating soldiers, limping along in random groups, three, ten, seven, a dozen. Or alone. Some with their muskets but most without. All the way from the Bull Run they came, marching through the night.

Men from the houses were setting up plank tables, and women were bringing out bread, cakes, coffee, using oilcloth to protect against the rain. Some of the soldiers slumped down in doorways.

I woke Barnum, and, snorting, he came to the window. "My God," he said, when he saw them. "They're just getting in!"

I can't say how long we stood there, watching. Thousands of them, disorganized, dragging themselves along, on their way to Camp Clark and the other Washington camps. Some regiments were based on the other side of the Potomac, in Arlington and Alexandria—we couldn't see them, but we knew they were there, arriving, weary but alive. A day and a night, that's what it had been. A day of battle, and a night of tramping along on the desperate road back. And now another day.

Barnum took a fresh set of clothes from his bag and began to dress. "Let's go, Charlie. Time to go home."

Right. Sure. Out of here.

I pulled myself away from the window and dressed quickly. The envelope that I took from the dead soldier in the field was folded in my jacket pocket. I put it in my satchel, safer there during the long trip ahead.

As I dressed, I wondered. Home? What was home? My father was dead, my sisters were married, and my mother sat by a window browsing through old copies of *Godey's*. I'd spent more time in New York and on tour in Europe, and in many parts of America, than I'd ever spent in the big house my father built for us.

Home, for certain, was Barnum's American Museum. The Bearded Lady, the Egyptian mummies, and Ned the Seal, who could balance a big red ball on his nose. And magical Mary Darling, who could pull white mice out of my pockets and make cocker spaniels turn into pumpkins. She and I, we could eat ice cream in the roof garden of the Museum, talking about the ways in which things were more inside out than anyone had ever supposed.

"Home," Barnum said throatily, tightening the strap on his bag. "*Vamos!* Let's go. *Andiamo! Beeilen Sie sich!*"

And off we went. First to the kitchen downstairs, where the chef filled our lunch basket with plums, grapes, peaches, cheese, and chunks of roast chicken, and Barnum tipped him handsomely. Then off to the depot. And when we arrived late that night in New York, I slept in a guest room in Barnum's city house on Eighth Street, because that night, after everything that had happened and everything I'd seen, I didn't want to be at a hotel, among strangers.

As I fell off to sleep, I was thinking of Sitwell with his red hat, on his horse, riding into the thick of things. I wondered if he was still alive.

~ PART TWO ~

THE BIG
AND
THE LITTLE

⁓ CHAPTER 4 ⁓

A WAR OF ATTRITION

The defeat at Bull Run killed the dream of a quick, one-battle end to the rebellion, and both sides settled in for a long, slow, massive war. Lincoln asked for half a million volunteers with three-year enlistments. In the South, Jeff Davis called for four hundred thousand.

Union soldiers, putting their own twist on the war, were using "John Brown's Body" as their favorite marching song. They threw in a few new lines with some extra bite in them—

> *And we will hang Jeff Davis*
> *From a sour apple tree—*
> *As we . . . go . . . maaaar-ching . . . on!*

But Jeff Davis was prevailing. A week after Bull Run, the entire Seventh U.S. Infantry—seven hundred men—surrendered in New Mexico, without a shot fired.

In August, there was fighting at Wilson's Creek in Missouri, and later in the year at Ball's Bluff in Virginia, both with bad results for the Union. The war was grumbling along, bleating, and whimpering—and sometimes, it seemed, just blowing its nose.

I wondered about Lincoln, neck-deep in this muddy mess—what kind of headaches and bad dreams was he having? Should he have pulled the troops out of Fort Sumter before it was fired on? Could we have skipped the war? Let South Carolina and the other bad sheep go their way, as Horace Greeley had more than once suggested? If so, some of the states that had been slow to secede might still be in the Union. Yes? No? Maybe? The whole thing just another Zootagataz whirl inside a Zatagatooz swirl.

And in such messy, stormy times, what kind of climb-the-mountain madness had made Lincoln want to be the President anyway? I had never met him, but had seen him once when he spent a few days in New York while on his way to his inauguration. He went to an opera at the Academy of Music, and Barnum brought me that night, as much for the chance to see Lincoln as for the music.

It was Verdi, *A Masked Ball*, about a king in love with the wife of his best friend. They're inflamed and passionate, yet they do no wrong. But the friend, imagining the worst and obsessed with his suspicions, kills the king at a masked ball. Plenty of strong, poignant arias in all of this—but afterward, all anybody talked about was that Lincoln wore black gloves at the theater instead of white, and how could a man who made a dumb mistake like that be qualified to run the country?

I liked the black gloves. Why not? He had won the election and was on his way to the White House—the Chief, the Boss. Top Man. He can set the style and wear anything he wants. But no, not so easy. Now that we had this war that we weren't winning, people were remembering those black gloves. Many who voted for him were scratching their heads, and the ones who had voted against him found more bad things to say, and it was all there in the penny papers. They called him a wet rag, an uneducated imbecile, a Simple Susan. They cartooned him as a Kentucky Mule.

About a month after the defeat at Bull Run, Barnum heard that some French Canadian fishermen had captured a white whale at the mouth of the St. Lawrence, and he thought it would be a fancy thing to have a few white whales in the Museum, to lighten the grim mood that hung over the city. He took me along and we went by rail to Quebec, then off to the Wells River, where he chartered a sloop to Elbow Island in the St. Lawrence. There he hired a group of fishermen to catch two whales.

After a week of near misses, the first catch was made, and then a second. The whales were good-looking things, white and handsome, and Barnum was all lit up, gloating, saying they were just what people needed, a stunning aquatic distraction from the war. These were beluga whales—not very large, in the world of whales. In fact, it was fair to say they were a species of dwarf whales, and that made me especially fond of them. They would grow only to ten or fifteen feet—but whales they were, with flukes, a blowhole, and flappers.

They were shipped in open, copper-lined boxes, with seaweed and salt water. Barnum had an attendant caring for them on the five-day journey, sponging them to keep their mouths and blowholes moistened. When they were in their new home in the Museum, Barnum brought in Professor Agassiz of Harvard to verify their authenticity. *Delphinapterus leucas*, that's what he called them, and Barnum put those words on a big poster at the main entrance to the Museum.

Those two whales, they were unmistakably white, as white as Herman Melville's famous whale, which was just a thing in a novel. When that book first appeared, I was maybe twelve or thirteen. Barnum sprinted through it, then passed it over to me, urging me to improve myself by reading. But I was hardly ready for a book like that. I skipped to the end and read only the part where they harpoon the whale—but it turns on them, it sinks the whaling boats and the ship itself, and everyone is dead except Ishmael, who stays afloat on a coffin and lives to tell the story. Good for him, I thought. Smart. Don't drown. If he doesn't live, how would we ever know what happened?

Well, Barnum didn't sink, but his whales did. As the Christmas season drew near, there were signs that they were ailing, and in the first days of the new year, 1862, they were floating lifeless in the forty-foot pool Barnum had built for them in the huge basement menagerie—the Room of Living Animals.

Barnum immediately sent for another two whales, and built a new tank on the second floor, with plate glass from France, an inch thick—an imposing thing with four glass walls, each twenty-four feet long. He ran seawater through underground pipes, pumping it in from the bay, and he changed the water every week, keeping it fresh.

Thousands flocked to see the new whales in their glass home, which made them visible from every angle. Cornelius Vanderbilt came. Mrs. Belmont came. Charles Tiffany brought his wife and his son. There was a rumor that Lincoln would come, but it was just talk. He had his hands full and never saw those two whales wriggling around in their fanciful way.

Someone else who never saw them was the journalist we'd met at Bull Run. He was no longer in the country. Before he sailed home to England, he sent a large, bulky package—it was waiting for me at the mailroom in the Museum. When I tore off the wrapping, I found a hatbox containing the red top hat that he'd worn at Bull Run. There was a bullet hole in it, and a one-line message. "Even Sebastopol was safer!"

*   *   *

After the winter lull, the war was sparking up again. In February, Ulysses Grant took Fort Donelson, and then, in April, he made a big name for himself at Shiloh. But he lost so many men, there was a flap about whether he was fit to command.

That same month, New Orleans fell, and not long after that, there was action east of Richmond, at Mechanicsville and Savage Station, and Malvern Hill. I was still jotting names and dates in a notebook that I kept—because all of this, every ounce of it, was more real for me than anything I knew. More true than the songs I sang and the jokes I told, and my impersonations of Ajax and Samson and Hercules and Napoléon—all of which amused the crowd, but for me the stage was becoming tiresome. I no longer had my heart in it.

Because how could I take myself seriously anymore, strutting around in my Napoléon costume, or singing "Yankee Doodle," when so many were dying? At Shiloh alone—on those two days, April 6 and 7—the Union lost over seventeen hundred, and the Confederates roughly the same, with more than eight thousand wounded on each side. Men losing arms and legs, a hand, a foot, an eye. This was smart? This was how to bring a quick, clean end to the war? When I pondered the numbers, I felt queasy and unbalanced, as if everything inside me would rise up and spill out. My liver, pancreas, spleen. All the hidden dwarf parts inside me.

I was a performer, appearing onstage—but more and more, I realized, I was becoming a witness, looking on as the country tore itself apart. If there was anything to hold on to, it was the names of the battles, and the places where they were fought. And the people. I knew some. Billy Cork, a janitor at the Museum, killed at Ball's Bluff. And Angelo Speranza, lost both legs. Moses Scheinen, who built stage sets for the theater, dead at Shiloh. The places and the people, nothing was more rock-bottom real.

If the war kept on like this, both sides would run out of men. But the South had fewer and would run dry long before the North did, so the North wins. That's what Isaac Sprague said. "Men and horses, wait and see. It's a war of attrition." Skinny Isaac, he was of normal height, not a dwarf, but his weight was down to a mere fifty-five pounds. Barnum's Living Skeleton. You could almost see right through him. "Attrition," he used that word. It was the first time I'd ever heard it. I remember his face when he said it, his paper-thin lips puckering and unpeeling over the word, caressing it, as if the word were a woman's finger in his mouth and he was too delighted to let it go.

Thousands continued to visit the whales in their huge glass aquarium—but again it was bad luck, the newest pair dying on a warm day in May, within hours of each other. Barnum, relentless, sent off for yet another pair, and, while the war bumbled on, he waited impatiently for their arrival.

These were the days when Stonewall Jackson was romping around in the Shenandoah Valley, showing up unexpectedly and snarling Union movements. At Front Royal he hit the Union hard, inflicting nine hundred casualties while losing only fifty of his own men. Already, even to us in the North, he was a legend, this strange ascetic warrior who didn't smoke, didn't drink, didn't curse, and prayed with his men before going into battle. Could any of that be true?

Barnum wanted to recruit him for an appearance as soon as the war was over. He also wanted to bring Brigham Young to New York, with a dozen or so of his many wives. He had even tried to land Susan B. Anthony and Elizabeth Stanton, offering them the Museum's large theater for a discussion of their views about women and the right to vote—but they went elsewhere, to the Mechanics' Institute, and to the

Tabernacle on Worth Street, maintaining a cautious distance from for-tune-tellers and bearded ladies.

The third pair of white whales were slow to arrive, but they lived longer than the others, and displayed remarkable energy as they cavorted in the big glass tank. With their heads down toward the bottom and tails toward the top, they would bend and weave, circling each other in a lopsided, upside-down underwater dance. Crowds of soldiers came to see them, and quite a few officers—even some generals.

Herman Melville, in from the Berkshires, seemed satisfied with the whales' whiteness, though he did express disappointment with their small size. But Walt Whitman, the newspaperman-turned-poet, was completely delighted with them, as he always was with all of the crea-tures in the Museum, stuffed or alive. I liked Walt, his down-to-earth plainness. And I liked his poems. A lot of energy in them, the lines coming at you like rolling waves at the seashore. The first edition of his *Leaves of Grass* had been published several years earlier, in 1855. I remember that year because it was the year my father died. It was also, by a weird coincidence, the year when Walt's father died.

I had first met Walt before his book appeared, by the Egyptian mummies, and again, weeks later, by the Anatomical Venus. Once, we went down the back stairs and hurried off to the Fulton Street terminal, where we boarded a ferry and sailed to Brooklyn, and back. What a fantasy—my first ride on a ferry!

But that was then, and this was now. Here I was, twenty-four years old and still growing, about an inch a year since I turned fifteen. I stood at thirty-four inches, no longer the smallest-man-in-the-world phenomenon I once was, though I still drew a crowd. But I was appear-ing fewer times than in the past—in part because my Highland fling and my breakdown dance were hard on my legs, but also because I was less enchanted with the stage than I'd been. Twenty years at anything is a long time, and Barnum never complained about my cutting back. He had an overflow of performers in his stable—the stage always occupied, and the theater always full.

So I settled into a relaxed schedule, though I still spent a great deal of time at the Museum. When most of the patrons were at a show in the theater, I wandered through the galleries, enjoying the many birds that were begging for attention—parakeets, cockatoos, macaws—and had great fun chatting with the animals in the basement menagerie.

When the theater emptied out and the crowds in the galleries thickened, I retreated to the private parlor reserved for performers and staff, and met up with old friends, and new friends, too. We relaxed over coffee, tea, imported wine. Mary Darling, still magical, still looking younger than when I first met her. And the new singer, Dora Dawron, famous for her ability to sing in two registers, a deep tenor and rich soprano. Barnum put her onstage dressed half as a man, half as a woman—and now that the war was on, she wrapped herself in a flag and sang "Viva la America" and "The Flag of Our Union." She had a wonderful voice, and a good sense of humor, too.

I always enjoyed the company of skinny Isaac Sprague. He was a few years younger than I, but relatively new, having arrived shortly before the war began. When he was twelve years old, he had started losing weight, and was now skin and bones, scary to look at, yet a very pleasant fellow, gentle and thoughtful. Barnum hired a trainer who taught him how to juggle—three apples, or three bananas, or three dishes. Isaac told me that the juggling made him feel better about himself—giving people some entertainment, instead of being just a freak to be gawked at.

Occasionally I met up with Nellis, the man without arms. He traveled a lot and was many times off on his own, disappearing into far-off countries. But always he returned to the Museum, and Barnum always had a spot for him. With his toes, he used to draw pictures, and those same toes could load and shoot a gun. Now, amazingly, he could use a bow and arrow. Even more astonishing, he could play short selections from Bach and Beethoven on a violoncello. We spoke of old times, the people who were no longer around. And he always teased me about the time he wanted to shoot an apple off my head, but Barnum wouldn't allow it.

When I wanted to be alone, I retreated to my dressing room. It was my den, my lair, pictures on the wall and costumes in the closet, my hideaway where I could relax, and even take a nap. When I was ready for the world again, I stood in front of the big mirror, combed my hair, and off I went, wandering through the galleries, saying hello to Ned the Seal and the noisy cockatoos, and pausing by the many images of Italy and Egypt in the Cosmorama Room.

But nothing, of course, is ever as cozy or rosy as it seems. A few months earlier, in February, while I was comfortably settling into my semiretirement, something happened that turned me upside down and inside out. I heard of it not from Barnum, nor from any of his assistants. I saw it in a newspaper. There it was, staring me in the face: Barnum had just hired a new dwarf, and was promoting him as a major star.

I went right in to him, and put the paper on his desk. "Why?" I said. "I'm not good enough anymore? If you think my act needs juicing up, you could have said something."

He leaned back in his chair, with that beguiling Barnum smile that he has. "Charlie, Charlie, this isn't about you. It's about business, about the future. You have nothing to worry about. Nobody can replace you. There is only one Tom Thumb in the world, and you will never be forgotten."

That's what he said, *never be forgotten*, as if I was already in the past. It made me feel old—in my twenties but already over the hill, passing the baton to the younger generation. What kind of hippopotamus dung was this?

But Barnum was Barnum, there was no stopping him. He was racing into the future, grabbing for anything new, a fresh face, a different voice, a new name to draw the crowds and maybe create a craze, a mania. After all the things we'd been through together, I took it as a personal betrayal. He was grooming my successor, pushing me off the scene.

This new dwarf was younger than I, shorter than I, and very filled with himself, imagining he was going to be the next Tom Thumb, and hating me because I *was* Tom Thumb. His name was George Washington Morrison Nutt, from New Hampshire. With a name like that, he was everything you'd expect him to be, a bit snobbish, hopelessly self-centered, and often hard to live with.

Onstage, he delivered a capable act—a snappy breakdown dance, a few songs in a squeaky voice, and a few somersaults and acrobatic twists. For a tense moment or two, he walked on his hands. Bravo. And he had a quick, glib way of turning out the puns that Barnum, or Sylvester Bleeker, scripted for him.

But offstage he was saucy and a bit of a snob, God's gift to the universe. His biographical pamphlet, prepared by Barnum, said he was eighteen years old, born on April 2, 1844. But knowing the way Barnum played with the ages of his performers, who could say?

Barnum billed him as Commodore Nutt, and that, too, rankled. I was General Tom Thumb, and by making Nutt a commodore, Barnum seemed to be suggesting we were on an equal footing. I didn't like that at all. Before long, I figured, we would have an admiral aboard, and Barnum would be hiding me in a closet.

In August, there were reports that a battle was again shaping up at Bull Run. Barnum had an odd expression on his face, as if tempted to ride down there again. But one battle at Bull Run was more than enough for me. He must have sensed that. After floating the idea, he backed away, and the three-day battle, at the end of August, was fought without us.

It was Robert E. Lee against John Pope, and the outcome even worse for the Union than First Bull Run had been, a year earlier. The retreat to Centreville was orderly, not a rout, but the Union lost more than seventeen hundred dead and over eight thousand wounded.

Headlines flamed with words like carnage, slaughter, crushing defeat, and everyone in a fret about how poorly the war was going. Again those landmarks that I'd seen were a fever in my brain—Centreville, the Warrenton Turnpike, the Bull Run stream carving its way through those low hills like a curse.

Barnum thought Lincoln had the wrong generals. Tony Sarto, performing taxidermy on a gorilla that was to be mounted near the ticket office, thought the generals had the wrong horses. Skinny Isaac Sprague watched the whales in their second-floor aquarium, and still he was saying *war of attrition, war of attrition.* "The army with one man still on his feet beats the army that has nobody left at all."

Fat Boy said nothing. The Bearded Lady combed her beard. Lena Serena twisted her double-jointed body into more complicated shapes than ever, and, as happened more and more often now, she became stuck and needed help before she could untangle herself. Fat Boy helped her. He liked her. There was talk that they were becoming romantically involved.

"War of attrition," Isaac Sprague said again, juggling that phrase the way he juggled three dishes. But one day he fumbled, and all three dishes crashed on the floor. After that, he kept to apples and bananas.

"Wars are boring," Commodore Nutt said, as he slid off his chair. "I'm heading for the toilet."

Zobeide Luti, who shared my feelings about the Commodore, gave

a knowing glance. I knew what she was thinking. Maybe he'll fall in
and we'll never see him again.

The Snake-Charmer, scratching her ankle, looked at me and
winked—thinking, I assumed, much the same thing.

Meanwhile, the third pair of whales were very much alive, enjoying
themselves, entertaining their audience with dramatic twists and turns,
and sudden dives to the bottom. They seemed as delighted with the
spectators as the spectators were with them.

~ **CHAPTER 5** ~

THE WAR,
THE WHALES, AND ANNA SWAN

The Astor House was on Broadway, across from the Museum, but up a block, between Barclay and Vesey. It was showing its age, but in its day it had been the best hotel in the city and was known as one of the finest in the world, with running water even on the top floors.

I slept there, ate there, and drank there, usually gin but never more than a jigger because, small as I was, my body couldn't absorb it. As I learned the hard way, it could knock me on my head. I liked a gin and pine, which was gin in which a freshly cut piece of pinewood had soaked for a few hours. But sometimes I settled for a rum shrub, or a sleeper.

A few days after the second battle at Bull Run, I lunched at Mulray's, and when I returned to the Museum, I waved to Sam, at the ticket window, and, heading for my dressing room, I made my way to the wide oak staircase that led to the second floor.

At the foot of the stairs, I paused, catching my breath. When I was much younger, Sam or one of the doormen would carry me up—but now that I was old enough to vote and had grown a few inches, I handled the stairs on my own, and considered it good exercise.

Standing there, readying myself for the long climb, I glanced up and saw a woman of remarkable stature, descending toward me. Tall, exotic, with an abundance of auburn hair tumbling down over her shoulders. A giant—an authentic, genuine, true-as-rum giant, with such eyes, such a face, and her long, flared, organdy dress, pink and red, ballooning toward me. I stood dead still at the foot of the stairs, gaping. When she reached me, she leaned down with a smile as vast as a canyon, saying, "I'm Anna. Anna Swan. And you must be—Tom Thumb?"

All I could do was stare. Her eyes had an otherworldly softness, each of them a blue pool, warm and inviting. I felt I could dive in and swim around until my arms fell off. Giant eyes, giant lips, giant arms and hands, and, God save me, breasts more ample than the plump pillows on my bed at the Astor. And her hair, so much of it, silken tresses tumbling down to me, touching my face, my hands. I could have climbed around in her hair, lived in it, nested in it, talked to the birds in it.

"May I pick you up?" she asked. My bones turned to water at the mere thought of being close to her. Lilacs, she smelled of lilacs. Why hadn't Barnum told me about her? Why hadn't he given me a warning?

She lifted me, held me in her hands, then cradled me in the crook of her arm and carried me down a hall, past the diorama of the Creation of the World and the mural of the Garden of Eden, to a bench strong enough to support her. She sat me down beside her. Across from us, in a case filled with old Indian bones, a yellowish skull grinned from behind the glass, as if amused to see us—Anna so big and me so small.

"I'm from Nova Scotia," she said, and with an easy smoothness she told me about herself. She had grown up on a farm in New Annan, and this was her first time away from home. She was half an inch shy of eight feet tall. And Barnum—she referred to him as *Mr.* Barnum—wanted her to wear her hair piled on her head so he could advertise her as eight and a half feet. But from the way she said that, it was clear she was going to wear her hair the way she wanted. And as I sat there, close to her, listening, I was dizzy with desire.

In my travels, I had met only two other women giants. It's a weird fact of nature that giants are rarer than dwarfs, and female giants are rarer yet. The two I had met were sad-looking creatures with nothing to recommend them other than their height. One was as giggly as a gull, and the other was droopy-faced and maudlin, a ton of unhappiness.

But Anna—she was radiant, so refreshing and alive, and already, in my shameless way, I was imagining her stretched out on a bed. I wanted to walk barefoot across her naked body, across the acres of her flesh, exploring every crease, every crevice, every tender, ravishing nook, every luscious cranny.

And in this delirious moment, drowning in a sea of lust, I was completely perplexed. Because suddenly, as I sat there, feeling her warmth, I was thinking about God, and had no idea what he was up to. What was happening here? Was God being generous, doing me a favor, bringing this gargantuan woman into my life? Or was he just playing a practical joke—teasing, tempting, torturing, setting me up for misery and despair? How could I, a mere dwarf, have the audacity to even think of tangling with such an abundance? I wanted to kneel on the floor, abasing myself to her. I wanted to play with her toes. Wanted to reach my arms around one of her legs and hold it, kiss it, bite it.

And her voice, rich and strong but tender, honed by the weather and winds of Nova Scotia. "This is so wonderful, meeting you this way," she said. "But do I have the right person? Are you sure you're Tom Thumb?"

"I'm really not," I said. "That's not who I am. But sometimes, you know, I pretend."

"You're saucy," she said, putting a finger on my chin. And what a finger it was, long, and almost as thick as my forearm.

That evening, in my hotel room, I ordered a bucket of ice and dumped it into my bath, and sat there, in the tub, cooling myself until I was numb.

But then, in bed, when I fell asleep, I had a powerful dream about her. We were together, on the grass in a sloping field, and I was climbing all over her. What a delight, what an easy happiness it was. There were birds in that dream, flying all around us. And flowers, a powerful aroma of flowers. But suddenly everything changed. Anna was gone, and I was again in that old nightmare that continued to plague me—falling, plunging helplessly in a gaping hole that opened underneath me. As I fell, I was reaching out for anything I might grab on to, anything that might slow or stop my fall—and what I caught hold of, this time, was a thick clump of roses. They were giant roses, Anna Swan roses. But they were slipping away, the thorns tearing at my hands, making me bleed—and as I fell, I heard the long scarf of my voice trailing behind me, calling to her, echoing her name in the immense darkness of that bottomless hole. *Aaaannnnnnnaaaaaaaaaa* . . .

This was no good. I knew. No good at all.

The next morning, I saw Barnum in one of the third-floor galleries, near a caged parakeet.

"Why didn't you say something," I said.

"About Anna? Isn't she marvelous? My greatest find ever—except, of course, for you. Just sixteen years old, Charlie. Amazing, yes? Eight feet tall and all the right equipment. Makes you want to climb aboard for a long, wild ride, doesn't it?"

He said it with a devilish gleam, as if he'd been reading my mind and knew my thoughts. Or, more likely, he was having some ideas of his own. He had an eye for women. When we were on the road, it was easy to see—especially in Europe—how he gazed, stared, turned his head. During my first performance in London, at the Princess's Theatre, I well remember how his eyes lit up when he saw the near-naked ballet girls who were part of the entertainment. And on a later tour, in France, on the street, how his head turned, how he glowed.

So here we are, with the parakeet still looking on and listening, and he says, winsomely, that he wants me to appear onstage with Anna. The Immense and the Infinitesimal, the Wee and the Wondrous, the Tremendous and the Tiny. "She could pick you up and walk around with you onstage, hugging you to her breast. If that's what you'd like."

Sure, why not. Her breast. He was mocking me.

I tossed my head jauntily. "Which one, the right or the left?"

"Don't be smart," he said, and started off, heading for the stairs, on his way to check on the whales, which had suddenly lost their zest and seemed to be ailing.

"Forget it," I called after him, in a moment of pique. "Let the Commodore go on with her." Because, at that moment, something inside me, the Charlie Stratton part of me, still had enough sense to pull in the reins. If somebody had to go over the cliff, let it be Commodore Nutt, that priggish, egotistical piece of puff. With any luck, Anna might fall on top of him and blot him out of existence. Thoughts like that, yes, that's how worked up I was. My father dead, and Barnum, my surrogate father, abandoning me in favor of a snooty prig. And taunting me with his own thoughts about Anna. *Makes you want to climb aboard*, he'd said.

So with all this gnarly dwarf resentment twisting around inside me, there I was, next to a caged parakeet, and when Barnum offers to put me onstage with Anna, I tell him to go fly a kite. Cutting my nose to spite my face, though I didn't immediately think of it that way.

"Good enough," he answered as he hurried off. "Nutt's the one. His gain, your loss, and don't complain when you have second thoughts."

I could have quit, then and there. Good-bye, Barnum, good-bye,

New York. Grab the next train home to Connecticut and spend my days riding my ponies and pondering the clouds. I could have done that. Could have.

But, despite my better judgment, I was unable to tear myself away. I kept my room at the Astor and continued to spend much of my time at the Museum, hoping to catch a glimpse of Anna. When I saw her, I followed at a distance, watching as she mounted the wide staircase, as she walked the corridors, as she bent and turned, bowing as she passed through doorways that were too low for her.

A towering bunch she was, yet there was an ease and a grace in the way she moved. My rage for her boiled up again, and I knew it had been a horrible mistake, in my haste, in my fit of high dudgeon, to reject Barnum's suggestion that she and I perform together. The Lofty and the Low, the Too Little and the Too Much. But no, she could never be too much, because how could there ever be enough of her?

Twice a week, in the morning, she stood for half an hour on a platform, and the patrons walked around her, gawking at her huge dimensions. Afternoons, on the same platform, she offered dramatic renditions of speeches from Shakespeare. I saw her doing Ophelia's mad scene. "Come, my coach! Good night, ladies; good night, sweet ladies; good night, good night." And Lady Macbeth—"Out, damned spot! Out, I say! . . . The Thane of Fife had a wife: where is she now? What! Will these hands ne'er be clean?"

A tutor helped her with her piano playing and her singing, preparing her for a performance in the theater. Her voice was strong and vibrant, and she was wonderful at the piano, playing selections from Chopin and Schubert, with great feeling. She was so tall, they had to put the piano high up on stilts so it would be the proper height when she sat to play.

I heard her, one afternoon, practicing a medley of songs by Schubert. She sang in German, each word neatly turned, with warmth and emotion. From the time I'd spent in Hamburg, a few years earlier, I knew a bit of German, though not enough to catch all of the words that floated up from deep inside her. Still, from the pathos, the deep-felt tone, it was clear that these were songs of loneliness and loss.

And loneliness was what I felt, a kind of helplessness. More than ever I wanted to speak to her—but how? How to begin? How to say anything to her at all? How to tell her about the urgent feelings she inspired, the desire, and the raw need? Did she feel it, too, the same heat and passion? And how to explain that it wasn't the Chopin she played on the piano, or the songs she sang, but simply her—her body— that I craved. Not her mind, her heart, her soul, but her sheer physical abundance, legs, long arms, lips, and all the secret parts of her hidden beneath those dozens of yards of silk and lace. How to explain all of that? How to tell her that it was the very difference between us, she so large and I so small, that stirred me, and the name for that, when you come right down to it, is lust, plain and simple. The lust of the tiniest shrub wanting to sink its root into the flank of a mountain.

This will never do, I realized. And only then, in the grip of these fantasies about Anna, did I understand that all my life, from the time I was a child, my thoughts and feelings had been for women who were taller, much taller, than I. And now, hopelessly, a giant. So, yes, something unusual in all this.

Realism, I told myself. Feet on the ground. No more floating, drifting. To live deliberately, to see life for what it really is. Thoreau? Was he the one who said that? Something in that vein. The Walden Pond book. He was at the Museum once. He saw me perform and shook my hand, said he enjoyed the show. My puns, my songs, my Highland fling. *To front only the essential facts of life*, that's what he wrote. And the important fact for me was that I was a dwarf, and a short one. So be a dwarf, dammit. Little people fit with little people—and it had never been, and was never to be, any different.

But such nights I had, so many, thinking about Anna, and such tormenting dreams. Rifts of fog folding and unfolding, and somewhere in the darkness a faint light approaches, blue and glimmering. I reach for it. But nothing—nothing there.

How long had it been since I first saw her? Two weeks? Three? I hardly knew. How long does a fever last? How long is a dream while you are still dreaming it?

Eventually, despite my better judgment, there came a time when I went up to her room.

She lived on the top floor of the Museum, in a spacious room that Barnum had prepared for her. It would have been more than difficult for her to fit comfortably in a rooming house, or in a standard hotel room.

The fifth floor held several storage rooms and a small public gallery with displays and exhibitions. There was a bird that could talk, a dog that could walk on its hind legs, and a monkey that ate anything you fed it, even your shoelaces. The most popular exhibit up there was the Happy Family: a crowd of cats, pigeons, porcupines, white rats, and small monkeys, all living peacefully together. This was Barnum's contribution to the idea of utopia. The secret, he told me, was to keep the family members so well fed that they were simply too full to eat each other. He thought the same should be done with people—overfeed them, and there would be less crime and fewer wars.

Up the many flights of stairs I went, and even in the early morning, on the top floor, I felt the heat. It was never cool up there, under the roof, especially when a heat wave hung over the city. And here we were, autumn only two weeks away, yet for several days we'd been roasting.

I went past the room with the Happy Family, and the room with the talking bird, then down a long corridor, past a storage room, a linen room, another closet, and at the end of the corridor I arrived at

Anna's room, the door left ajar for any cooling draft that might whisper through.

Slowly, I pushed the door open, and there she was, on her bed, in her night shift, propped up on a pile of pillows. It was shortly after seven, morning light spilling through the window. The sheet was turned down, her knees drawn up, and she was reading a book that was perched on her thighs, as on a lectern. The book seemed so small against the sprawling acres of her body. Her bare feet protruded from under her shift, and, in their enormity, they were an inspiration. I found myself struggling with an impulse to bite her toes.

"You can't come in," she said, lowering her knees flat against the bed and adjusting her shift.

"Why not?"

"I'm not dressed, is why not. And I'm not awake yet."

"What's the book?" I asked.

It was *Gulliver's Travels*. I knew something about that one—restless Gulliver always sailing off and landing in trouble, shipwrecked in all the wrong places. Among the tiny Lilliputians he's too big, a giant, and among the Brobdingnagians he's too small. In the end, he was an unhappy man.

Through the thin white linen of her night shift, I saw the fullness of her breasts and the outline of her nipples, large as Spanish plums.

"Are you a virgin?" I asked, surprised at my own boldness.

She leaned up on an elbow, her breasts shifting voluminously. "You can't ask a thing like that," she said.

"Why not?"

"Because it isn't proper. Not proper at all."

"Are you a Presbyterian?"

"I'm not sure what I am," she answered. "What are you?"

"I'm a thirty-second-degree Mason."

"What's that?"

"It's—too complicated to explain," I said, then added, "When I go to church, I'm sometimes an Episcopalian, and sometimes a Congregationalist. Next week I may try the Seventh-Day Adventists."

"And Mr. Barnum? Is he a Mason?"

"He's a Universalist. He believes everything is good and everybody goes to heaven."

"Even the humbugs?"

"Especially them. And since he prides himself on being the prince of humbugs, he'll be first on line."

"I think you should leave now," she said. From her tone, her attitude, the way she looked at me, it was plain that she would give me friendship but nothing more.

"I'd rather stay," I said.

"Charlie—"

"Don't call me Charlie. Call me Tom."

"That's silly," she said. "Everyone calls you Charlie. Isaac Sprague, and Nellis, and Mary Darling. Sylvester Bleeker. Everyone. That's who you are, aren't you? Charlie Stratton."

"Tom," I said. "I'm Tom Thumb." And at that moment I really was Tom, because Charlie would never have done a thing like this, barging in at seven in the morning, she in her night shift, lying there, her long, meaty limbs stretched out upon the bed.

"And never call me silly," I said. "I'm older than you are."

The expression on her face was soft and sympathetic, and I resented that, because if there was anything I didn't want, it was pity.

"You really shouldn't be here," she said, drawing the sheet up, covering her feet, her legs, her hips, right up to her chin. "You know that, don't you?"

"But I *am* here," I told her—and with that I leaped onto the bed, wanting to touch her, grab her, nibble at her lips, and rove downward across her body.

"Don't," she said, reading my thoughts, and as I closed in on her, she pulled back sharply, the book slipping away and falling to the floor. With her wide, gentle hand, she pushed me firmly away.

I retreated toward her feet, and came up at her from the other side, and along the way, I gave her leg, through the sheet, a quick bite, which made her flinch. She was on her back, flat down, and I was quickly up onto the vast, tender softness of her belly, moving up, and I nestled between her breasts.

As I lay there, feeling her warmth, my whole body rising and falling with the rise and fall of her breathing, I pondered the unfairness of fate, the bruising inequity. How I, as a person, was made for her, and she for me, yet we were cursed to be in incompatible bodies, thwarted by the absurdity of physical size. And, stranger than strange, it was this very difference in size that was, for me, the source of her appeal. Because opposites do attract—the small yearning for the large, as the finite aspires for the infinite. If God created me as an oddity, why shouldn't everything in my life be uncommon and unimaginable, including my dreams, my hopes, my desires, and the woman I adore?

Tall women do link up with short men, I knew that to happen. But never, to my knowledge, a giant and a dwarf. It flew in the face of common sense. Yet that also, the unreasonableness, was part of it, sharpening my appetite. And, oh, the softness and the warmth, the heat of her immense, mythic body!

The war raged on, and still it was not going well. The first reports of the fighting at Antietam began to appear in the papers, a horrible battle with high casualties, more brutal than Second Bull Run. Lee had crossed the Potomac, eager for a victory on Northern soil, and the North turned him back, but at enormous cost.

The fighting took place near the town of Sharpsburg, in Maryland, with Lee's troops lined up along the winding bend of Antietam Creek. The Potomac River, which they had crossed, wasn't far behind them. Newspaper sketches gave a good sense of where things were—and as I pored over them, as I imagined and visualized, it was as if I was actually there. I saw it all and became part of it, gunfire and exploding shells, smoke from the guns clinging to the landscape. September 17, 1862, a Wednesday morning.

The first rough estimates of the dead and wounded were staggering. The Union lost over two thousand dead, and close to ten thousand wounded. Southern losses were fewer, but almost as bad. It was horrific—so many, so fast, in one day. Nothing could compete with that. Not all of the wonders in Barnum's American Museum—the sword-swallower, the Bearded Lady, the contortionist, the jugglers, the grizzly bear. The paintings in gold frames. Everything suddenly irrelevant, nothing but this unbelievable catastrophe. It was a Union victory, Lee was forced to retreat back into Virginia. But with so many dead on both sides, how could anyone speak of winning and losing?

For three days I didn't leave my room at the Astor. I had my meals sent up, along with the newspapers. I sat by the window and watched the movement along Broadway—the wagons, carriages, the crowded horse-cars running on rails set in the cobblestones. Women strolling, in rainbow silks and hoop skirts, with parasols. Shouts, calls. An Irishwoman selling vegetables from a cart. A boy hawking newspapers. The constant clatter of horses' hooves on the cobbles. A shrill whistle. I was on the third floor, above Broadway. To my left was Barclay Street, to my right was Vesey, and below me a constant flow of gigs and phaetons. Two Negroes on a wagon loaded with furniture. Carts with pineapples, melons, blocks of ice. A dog darting through the traffic. Immigrants lugging bundles. Quakers with wide-brimmed hats.

To look at them, it was hard to know there was a war on. Yet the war was in the air, you could feel it, taste it, everybody thinking *Antie-*

tam, thinking of the dead, the wounded, and Lee pushed back across the Potomac—but what a price. Too many killed, too many hurt and broken.

Three days in that room, then I went back to the Museum. I had a performance scheduled for that afternoon. I lingered on the ground floor, idling by the dioramas, pausing by the Creation of the World and the Garden of Eden. Then I went up the grand staircase to the second floor, heading for my dressing room, and was surprised to see Anna standing by the large glass tank that held the beluga whales.

I drew close. One of the whales was on the bottom, barely a flicker of life in him. The other stayed near the top, drooping.

Without looking down at me, Anna knew I was there.

"So sad," she said. "They're dying."

Her hands were clasped in front of her, as if in prayer. Her clothes had the scent of lavender, and, looking up, I saw she was weeping, tears sliding down her cheeks. Such a face, such a vastness. How could I, so small, a mere pebble, say anything that might console her? She, too, knew of the battle that had been fought, so many lives snuffed out so quickly, dawn to dusk. Everyone knew, there was no avoiding it. Close to four thousand soldiers killed in one day. But she was transmuting it, turning all of her grief into a sorrow for the dying whales.

I slipped away and went quietly off, leaving her by the bulky glass tank. In the spacious corridor, which smelled of perfume and old wood, I walked past glass cases containing dead butterflies and moths, past the marble Venus, the wooden Indian, past Barnum's office, and the room filled with trick mirrors. I turned off into another gallery, passing stuffed birds and living anacondas, and Ned the Seal, then I swung around into the wax gallery, and came full circle back to the main staircase.

At the top of the stairs I paused, feeling something odd, a vague dizziness. As I put a foot forward, my legs folded and down I went, rolling and thumping, nothing to catch on to—bouncing off each oak step and feeling the pain. I was conscious and aware. But then, before I hit bottom, it all swam away from me. I heard a dim hum, a buzz, but saw nothing, only the darkness.

When I came to, Barnum was bending over me, passing a vial of smelling salts under my nose. "It's all right, all right," he said in a consoling tone, touching my forehead. His face was a smudge in a sea of faces, and his voice, too, was a blur, blending with the hum. I was on the floor at the foot of the stairs—and behind Barnum, all those faces crowding around, strangers, men and women, kids. And though I was accustomed to crowds, though I liked them and needed them and wanted them, I felt, at that moment, naked and exposed. My body raw, full of pain, and more than anything I wanted to be somewhere else, hidden and unseen.

CHAPTER 6

THE DOOMSDAY HUM . . .
THE PENCIL IN THE EYE

That day in the Museum, when I took the long fall down a flight of stairs, I was bruised, but no bones were broken.

"Give yourself a rest," Barnum said. "Go home for a while and roll around in the grass. Play solitaire, it's calming."

Solitaire? That's what I needed? I was four years old when Barnum first put me onstage, and then, in the blink of an eye, I was twenty-four and weary of all that, and plain exhausted. Tired of impersonating Hercules, Ajax, Napoléon, and Charles the Bald, sick of singing the songs I sang and dancing the Highland fling and the hornpipe. One of my fantasies was that I might slip away on a small boat, alone, and drift in strange waters for the next twenty-four years and maybe meet up with a sea nymph on a small island on nobody's map.

I took the train to Bridgeport and parked myself in the big house where my mother lived. I slept, I ate, and played a few tunes on my piano. Retirement, this was it—for a month or two, or three. Maybe forever. I would figure out another life for myself. I drank a short portion of gin every day, practiced my carom shot at my dwarf billiard table, and took long walks in the woods. In the years since my father died, my mother spoke less and less, but she still made fabulous pies, and I ate everything that came my way.

The gin was to suppress my growth. According to popular lore, if you were a dwarf and wanted to stay profitably short, drink gin.

It was early autumn, a chill in the air, but the water on the sound was warmer than the air and reasonably calm. I went out on my boat, the *Angel X*, with Ned Blossom, a runaway slave from South Carolina. He had spent some time in New York, then landed up here in Bridgeport. My uncle Seth hired him to do carpentry work, building barns and houses. And a few years later, when my father died, Uncle Seth passed Ned over to me, as a caretaker for the big house and the horses.

I liked Ned, we had good times together out on the sound. He handled the sail and the tiller for me, things I couldn't handle by myself. We cruised along the coast, to the Thimble Islands, or in the opposite direction toward Norwalk, to Sprite Island and Little Ram. A few times we sailed clear across the sound to Port Jefferson. There were warships on the water, and freighters carrying war supplies.

I liked it out there, skimming along, weaving in and out among the other boats. Any pretty-eyed young female dwarfs on those boats? Any on the Thimble Islands? Any dwarf mermaids romping in the waters off Little Ram? I was looking, but mostly I just lazed around on deck, gazing at the clouds and waiting for a little bit of excitement—like a squall, or sudden fog, or a near collision with a swift-moving schooner.

Ned was ten years older than I and more than twice my size, hard and bony, with muscled arms and dark caramel skin, the backs of his hands blackish brown but the palms pink. He was a fine sailor, he got us where we wanted to go. But he sang, and he had no voice at all, squeaking on the high notes and groaning on the low, invariably off-key, and when he forgot the words, he faded into a tuneless hum. He rambled through the old spirituals, "Down by the Riverside," and "Roll, Jordan, Roll." Sometimes I sang along, trying to keep him on key, but I found it more interesting to gaze at the clouds and the gulls, the fast-flying flocks of ducks and geese.

One Sunday, aboard the boat, we were hit by a squall that slammed into us out of nowhere. It tipped the boat far over on its side, putting the mast at a sharp angle and the sail nearly down into the water. Ned was at the tiller, and I had a firm grip on a safety rope that ran along the gunwale—and that fierce blast tossed us hard before it moved on.

Slowly, the boat righted itself, still rising and falling on the rolling swells. When I looked again toward the tiller, Ned wasn't there.

I scanned the water, but nothing. I groped my way to the other side of the boat—but nothing out there either, and I felt a shiver of panic rising inside me. I returned to the other side, and suddenly there he was, his head breaking water.

With great difficulty, I grabbed hold of the lifebuoy and flung it overboard. He saw it and swam to it, and after several tense moments he was aboard.

"Thank the Lawd," he said. "Thank the Lawd. And thank you, Mistah Charlie."

I thought he was about to burst into one of his favorite spirituals. But no, too wet and worn down for that, and God knows what desperate, end-of-it-all thoughts he might have had when he was underwater.

That night, at my mother's house, Ned and I sat on the veranda, in sweaters, drinking beer, and I learned more about his past than I ever wanted to know. He told me about the Carolina plantation he grew up on, and the thing that happened down there.

After his father was sold to a plantation in Mississippi, and after his mother died, his life, he said, was flipping around like crazy. By the time he turned fourteen, he was tomcatting around, and on a rainy afternoon he was caught in the hay with a kitchen mulatto that his master had taken a fancy to.

The master, a burly man with a red beard, leaped at him and beat him hard, right there in the barn, the girl screaming, snatching up her dress and fleeing barefoot to the house. And Ned, pummeled and knocked around, reaches wildly and puts his hand on a sickle that's hanging on the wall—grabs it and swings wildly, slashing the point hard into the man's belly, in and up. And the man, ripped bad and bleeding, staggers back, and drops.

"Don't know if I never kilt him," Ned said, "but I sure wanted to, an' hope I did. After dat, I skips out fast and goes north, sleepin' in cornfields and thick woods, eatin' melons and raw taters I grab from the farms. In Virginie, I kilt a dog someone put on me, and when a posse come searchin', I be hidin' high up in a tree an' they passin' right below an' nobody get even a sniff of the cow dung on my shoes. Runnin' through fields and woods, keepin' off the roads, is how I done it, clear up to New Jersey, where my good luck become bad luck. I be grabbed by two slave catchers what tries to bring me back down south."

He rubbed the back of his hand across his forehead. "They be punchin' me aroun' and brings me as far down as Baltimore, where we spendin' the night in an inn what calls itself the Euphoria Hotel, a crummy run-down place wid mice runnin' aroun' all night—one of 'em come onto my pillow an' be checkin' me out, givin' me the sniff test an' not happy wid what he find, so off he go.

"In the mornin', cockcrow, them slave catchers plannin' to move out early. One of 'em goes to the outhouse and I be on the bed, left wrist cuffed to the bed frame, wid a night table close by dat have a pencil an' a pad on it, an' I be wonderin' who in dis godforsaken hole be needin' a pencil? An' dat person, I figgers, mus' be me.

"So it were now or never. And I do it. I fakes a sneezin' fit, keep sneezin' and wheezin', and when dat bounty bastard, gnawin' on a piece of beef jerky, come close to see what be happenin', I grabs the pencil wid my free hand and stabs him in the eye. Then I be snatchin' the pistol from his belt and bashin' him in the head, knockin' him into sleepland. But he be hard to reach now, so wid my free hand I grabbin' at his ankle and pullin' him close and be into his pocket for the keys—and go fumblin' through most of those dumb keys before findin' the one dat unlocks the cuff on my wrist. Quick then, I takes a match from the man's jacket an' sets fire to the mattress, an' I be off an' runnin' like hell, and keeps runnin' till I reaches New York."

A pencil in the eye. It was a long brown thing, he said, with a sharp point, beside a pink pad on the little table by the bed.

"You must have been pretty sore at those bounty hunters," I said.

"Madder than mad," he says.

"I hope you never get mad at me."

"You? Worst I ever does to you is tuck you in my back pocket and sit on you."

"Just try," I said.

In New York, he had hung around in the Five Points district for a few weeks, sleeping in the Old Brewery. He earned some money delivering ice, coal, and newspapers, and stole coins out of the pockets of drunks who passed out on the street. He shared food with an over-the-hill prostitute who took a liking to him. Then he moved on and found his way into Connecticut.

He was the only person I ever met whose birthday fell on the same day as mine—January 4. Maybe that's why I felt close to him, even though he was ten years older and our lives were so different. We traded jokes, puns. We bantered. Sometimes a hand of poker, or some silliness with three-card monte. And he did like to sing. He favored the dark, lonely spirituals, but there was, too, a stubborn, itchy humor in him that would gush up out of nowhere. Lips wide and white teeth flashing, he belted out the words—"Dem bones, dem bones, dem dry bones," and we sang it together, beating out the rhythm with our feet. "The thighbone connected to the knee bone, the knee bone connected to the leg bone, the leg bone connected to the foot bone"—and his right hand swiftly to the back of his neck, swatting a mosquito.

In the weeks and months while I was living at home, browsing around during my long vacation from the stage, I visited my sister Frances, and we sang some of those old Zootagataz songs that she used to sing with Libbie. Frances had two children, a boy and a girl. I romped around on the floor with them, and with malicious delight they spilled milk all over me.

When I visited Libbie, she wanted to know if I was ever going to marry. I hated being reminded of that. Who would marry a dwarf? I gave her a blank stare. "You have someone in mind?

"I was hoping *you* did," she said.

I didn't tell her about Anna Swan—no, never, wouldn't dare. Nor did I mention Mary Darling, or the African Earth Woman. Or Lena Serena, the contortionist who had never interested me anyway. I ate another of the blueberry crumpets Libbie had made. And another. She had three children, a boy and two girls—they thought I was some kind of toy, a walking, talking toy that could turn somersaults, eat crumpets, and sing. They looked in my mouth, to see where the words came from. They took off my shoes and socks and counted my toes. They took off my shirt and wanted to see if I had hair under my arms. They tried to take off my pants—but hey, hands off, forget it. I distracted them by standing on my head.

Back at my mother's house, I climbed the pine tree in the front garden, and, up in the branches, ate one of the ginger cookies she'd recently baked. I took long walks and talked to the butterflies. Stray dogs liked to lick the top of my head.

In the dwarf apartment my father had created for me on the first floor, I banged away on my dwarf-sized piano, competing with my sisters by composing a few Zootagataz songs of my own.

> *If your dreams are filled with rusty old screws,*
> *Talk to the sparrows—what can you lose?*
> *Talk to the mouse that's eating a prune*
> *And the midnight owl that hoots at the moon.*
> *Zootagataz, Zatagatooz—*
> *Talk to the toads and the kangaroos.*
> *To the skinks and the snakes and the muddy worms,*
> *To the cranky raccoon that twists and squirms—*
> *And ask around for scraps of news,*
> *Who's happy, who's sad, who's down with the blues.*

I also played solitaire, but at that game, again and again, I was a loser.

∼ CHAPTER 7 ∼

IN THE ROOM
OF LIVING ANIMALS

The war was still blustering along, with staggering losses on both sides. Even in nowhere Bridgeport it was never a surprise to see a veteran with a foot missing, or a leg cut off at the knee, or a hand or an arm gone. And, everywhere, people were unhappy about how long and drawn out the war was, and so many dying.

In the first week of December, Barnum sent a telegram, summoning me to the Museum. He had a surprise, the telegram said, and I wondered about that. Maybe another pair of white beluga whales to replace the ailing pair that had died. Or a crocodile. Or a new contortionist to fill in for Lena Serena, who could perform no longer because she was pregnant, though who the father might be, she wasn't saying. Fat Boy, I assumed. And if not Fat Boy, maybe the German janitor, who, despite his years and his scrubby gray beard, continued to do a thriving business on the couch in the storeroom.

I packed my small bag, and the next morning took a train to the terminal in New York. Then by horsecar to the Astor.

Aboard the horsecar I met two nuns, Sisters of Charity who worked uptown at St. Joseph's, the military hospital at McGowan's Pass, caring for the wounded. This was their day off and they were on their way to the Museum, which they'd heard about but had never visited. They had no idea who I was, and that, for me, was a novel experience—to be unknown. As the horsecar rattled along, passing the shops and emporiums along Broadway, I savored my anonymity, delighted to be nobody, nameless, a private citizen. Zero.

The taller one did most of the talking, and when she leaned toward me and asked where I was from, I said Connecticut and left it at that. The shorter one, who had a shadow of hair on her upper lip, seemed rather withdrawn. When she did speak, she mentioned that she had lost her brother in the first battle at Bull Run. Then she surprised me, saying she was from Virginia, and her brother had been in the Confederate army.

She was plainly upset, feeling the loss, yet she took comfort in the thought that he was out of pain and at rest in heaven. In a war, she said, God doesn't take sides, because God is large, very large, above any kind of pettiness. Her dark eyes were tranquil, with a peaceful confidence, and I thought how lucky she was to feel so good about God, and about life.

When I thought about God, I was glad he was up there, keeping an eye on the store. But there were a few things I didn't understand. Like toothaches, earaches, broken bones, hives, cramps, headaches, sore throats. Or why Anna should be so tall and I so short, and never the twain shall meet. And now this pious nun's brother, killed at Bull Run. Why? Why did that have to be? I was thinking that if I ever had the good luck to meet up with God—over a plum cordial, or a brandy flip—there were a few questions I would want to ask, and I looked

forward to that. Though I wasn't at all sure that I would understand
the answers.

The streets and parks were crowded with soldiers—if not for them,
it would have been hard to know there was a war on. After the fall of
Fort Sumter, many businesses had been hit hard—but now, with the
war industry steaming ahead, the markets were booming, and money
was changing hands fast. Cotton, in limited amounts, was still coming
in from the South. Plantation owners sold to merchants who smuggled
the bales up North, and there were colonels and captains on both sides
making a handsome income by looking the other way.

And if you were short on cotton, there was always that flimsy, infamous substitute known as shoddy. You could take bundles of old rags,
shred them, cook them into a thick, gluey stew, then roll the pasty
muck into a cloth that could be cut and sewn and worn. But God help
you if it rained, the stuff would simply fall apart.

The kings of shoddy pawned off all sorts of stuff on the army. Not
just shoddy uniforms and shoddy underwear, but a whole new kind of
shoddy. Rifles that didn't shoot straight, saddles that fell apart, boots
that had soles made of glued-together wood chips that fell apart in the
mud and the rain. And shoddy horses, too, horses that were half blind,
sold to the cavalry for better-than-ever prices, while government inspec-
tors blinked and took their commission. And if you were a soldier in
the field on a long march, your boots went to pieces, your knapsack
split open at the seams, and if you sweated too much or were caught in
the rain, your pants shredded, and before you knew it you were naked
as the day you were born.

The nuns on the horsecar, they too had been the victims of shoddy.
The hospital where they worked had received a shipment of shoddy
sheets, which shredded and came apart. And shoddy bandages too, they
said. All useless. The hospital's Mother Superior was furious and tried
to have the manufacturer arrested. But he was untouchable—he had

contributed to the governor's election campaign, and was considered a patriot.

But those two nuns, what a pleasant surprise—they had no idea who I was! I liked that, being anonymous. In the wax gallery, they would linger long before Jesus and Moses, and never notice me nearby. So different and exciting—to be unknown, not to be fussed over.

And what would they ever make of Anna Swan, nearly eight feet tall and all that lush auburn hair cascading down to her waist, and those blue eyes. Happily, on that day when I tumbled down the stairs at the Museum, smack to the bottom, those hard oak steps knocked some of the silliness out of my head and jerked me loose from my reckless infatuation—those too many days and nights that I'd spent yearning for Anna, dreaming of her, following her about. Imagining, crazily, that there was some kind of a romantic future for us. It took a whole flight of hard oak stairs to bounce me back to the clockwork world of reality.

But reality—my reality—what was that? I was thinking again, as in my earlier years, about Zootagataz and Zatagatooz, and other such fanciful explanations of life that I had grabbed on to. But explanations, I knew, were things that come and go—and now, as I listened to the clip-clopping of the horses' hooves, I was musing, wondering if my silliness about Anna was, in fact, truly gone.

The nuns and I left the horsecar when it stopped in front of the Astor. The Museum was across the street, and before they crossed over, we made our farewells. They said they would keep me in their prayers. That was kind and generous, though I later wondered how it was possible to pray for someone if you didn't know his name. They would pray for the dwarf, the dwarf on the horsecar. But would God know they were referring to me, or would he make miracles happen for some other dwarf who'd been riding the horsecar on a different day? I've heard preachers say that God knows everything, and there are never any mistakes. But I also heard a preacher in London, once, who said God gave us free will, and if we are truly free, even God can't know what we'll choose to do next. If he did, wouldn't it be immoral of him if he knew a murder was about to be committed but did nothing to stop it? That's what the preacher said.

But, truly, I don't know about such things, and it's especially confusing when preachers start quarreling with other preachers.

Before they made their way across the street, the short one, the nun with a hint of hair on her upper lip, gave a big smile. I think she liked me. I made a mental note to visit the hospital and put on a show for the wounded soldiers. And who knows? Maybe one of the nuns up there, at St. Joseph's, would tear off her wimple and run away with me.

After I checked in at the Astor, I had a cheese sandwich sent up, ate half of it, and gave myself a few minutes of rest on the bed. Then, eager to see what Barnum had cooked up for me, I made my way across Broadway.

A doorman from the Astor helped me through the thick traffic, lifting me at one point to get me past a particularly large heap of horse droppings. Straight ahead, on the Museum's facade, huge banners fluttered, depicting some of the current attractions—an acrobat, a singer, a giraffe, and Anna Swan holding that obnoxious shrimp, Commodore Nutt, in the palm of her hand.

Inside, by the ticket office, there were write-ups about the new performers—with pictures. Addie LeBrun, a singer just ten years old, and a Russian sword-swallower from Petersburg. Also an Ethiopian fire-eater, and a boy named Young Nicolo, an eleven-year-old aerialist touted as a magician on a trapeze.

And a large poster for a new dwarf, appearing soon: LAVINIA WARREN, SMALLEST WOMAN IN THE WORLD. Was she, maybe, possibly, the reason why Barnum had summoned me back to New York?

I left my coat in the cloakroom, then went upstairs. I found Sylvester Bleeker at Barnum's desk, searching impatiently for a schedule of theater performances. Years earlier, Bleeker had worked with the acting troupe connected with the Museum—he still did some acting, but now he was Barnum's factotum, handling details like newspaper ads and performance schedules. He also accompanied some of the performers when they appeared in other cities.

"He's not here?"

"Gone for the day," Bleeker said. "Won't be back until tomorrow."

Well, just like him. Send a telegram, come quick—and when you show up he's out of town.

While Bleeker rummaged through a stack of papers, he mentioned, in a meaningful way, that the new dwarf was in, learning her way around. Lavinia Warren. He told me to keep my eye out for her. She was going to appear two weeks from now and that's what the fuss was about, Bleeker had to find a spot for her and scratch somebody else.

Right, fine. Sure. Why not? It piqued my curiosity—a new dwarf. We chatted a while, then I left him, with his mess of papers and his frustration.

I wandered about, gallery to gallery, and despite my annoyance at having missed Barnum, it was a good feeling to be there again, because in so many ways, the Museum had been as much of a home as I'd had anywhere. The rooms, the galleries, many of the walls lined with glass-door cabinets that were stuffed with curiosities. I knew them all, since my earliest days, and had many favorites. Cabinet number 242 holding an Indian peace pipe, along with a blue mask from the South Sea Islands and a jade Buddha. A shoe from Turkey. A buckle that had been used by Peter Stuyvesant.

The wide halls, big windows, balconies, the oak and chestnut paneling. And the large room next to Barnum's office, with the trick mirrors that made you look like nobody you've ever seen.

I prowled from gallery to gallery, greeting old acquaintances. Isaac Sprague and Madame Clofullia, Fat Boy, and sultry Zobeide Luti. I saw the snake-charmer. But some—the dancer Celeste, the Albino family—were no longer around. And others, too—Betty Madagain, gone, and the Swedish fire-eater. I did not run into Anna Swan, and resisted an impulse to seek her out in her fifth-floor bedroom. Impossible Anna. Yes, I still thought of her, but there was such an enormous gulf of size between us, and down that road naught but madness lay.

I headed for the basement, which housed the enormous Room of Living Animals, lit by gaslight, the walls lined with cages, tubs, warrens, and dens—home for Barnum's living menagerie. In the center of the room was the forty-foot brick-lined pool where Barnum had put his first beluga whales, before he installed the large aquarium on the second floor. The pool was now occupied by a hippopotamus, the only one in America, taken from the Nile and shipped from Egypt.

It was dank and humid down there, with a distinctive odor, the fumes from the gas lamps mingling with the smells coming off the animals and their cages. It was the smell of the jungle—jungle darkness, jungle heat, jungle rot and decay.

Barnum had tried many times to get rid of that smell, with little success. He brought in sandalwood, cedar, camphor. Pots of incense purchased from a merchant on Mott Street. But the jasmine incense made the macaques sneeze, and the eucalyptus irritated the eyes of the Bengal tiger. The Egyptian musk was fatal, killing off three of the dingoes, all of the rabbits, and the sole anaconda, which had seemed a lonely thing and likely to die anyway.

In the end, there was no remedy and the odor persisted. It was a darkness you inhaled, a fetid, gray-green dream of struggle and loss, beginnings and endings and other beginnings. And you knew this was where you belonged, because somehow, in some distant, mysterious way, it was out of that rank jungle odor that you were born. And despite the smell, or perhaps because of it, I always felt that this huge room, home to so many living creatures, was in many ways the best in the entire five-story building.

Down I went, cautious on the stairs, remembering the fall I'd taken when I was last at the Museum. Slowly down, then into the wide corridor that led to the big room. At the entrance there was a viewing platform, then a few more stairs before you were fully down. I paused on the platform. Except for the animals, the place seemed deserted. The mountain lion asleep, the hippopotamus lazing in the pool, the bearded Barbary sheep swinging his neck restlessly. And the chimpanzee making clucking sounds, wanting attention but getting none, because a show was on in the upstairs theater and that's where everybody was.

But—*then*—there she was, stepping out from behind a potted myrtle bush near the turtles. Barnum's poster princess, Lavinia Warren, his new dwarf, pausing before a large glass terrarium that held a python from Burma.

She was something, I saw that right off. In her dove-gray dress with pink ribbons at the shoulders and waist, and dainty purple shoes. I descended the remaining stairs and came up beside her. She was a few inches shorter than I, her hair done up and the back of her neck showing prettily. Bleeker had told me to keep my eye out for her—and sure enough, my eye was out, both eyes, because in that dress, with the bustle and the embroidered bodice, and her hair piled on top of her head in the way that it was, she gave me something to think about.

She was interested in that python—stood close up to the glass, studying the intricate color patterns. I knew that snake. I, too, had paused and studied its strangeness, many times.

"So what do you think?" I said.

She glanced up with her dark, sumptuous eyes. "About?"

"About anything."

"Well, I hardly know," she said, pulling her eyes away from mine and looking again toward the python.

"You like snakes?"

"They make me feel—creepy. Is he poisonous?"

"It's a she."

"How do you know?"

"You have to have keen eyes," I said.

"Are your eyes keen?"

"More or less," I answered, laying my eyes on her in a way to make her feel just how keen they were. Then, glancing toward the snake, "No, it's not poisonous. Pythons just wrap themselves around you and squeeze until you're dead. Then they unlock their jaws, open wide, and swallow you whole. This one can swallow a hundred-pound dog."

"You're making that up," she said, unwilling to believe that a snake—any snake—could swallow something larger than itself.

"Well," I said, with a bright, brassy look, "maybe not a hundred pounds. But I know it could swallow you."

"Or you," she answered with a brassy look of her own.

"No, not me," I said. "A snake like this, if it came at me, I would talk to it. I would say the secret words, and it would slither away."

"And if it didn't?"

"I would punch it in the nose."

I tapped the glass. The snake, rousing itself, uncurled with a sensuous slowness.

"They're deaf, you know, can't hear a thing. But they feel the vibrations."

I was feeling some vibrations myself. Just catching the scent of Lavinia's perfume did that to me. Her eyes, her hands, her gray dress with the ribbons. In some ways, she reminded me of Isabella of Spain, who was fourteen when I met her in Pamplona, and already a queen. The same appealing fullness in the face, and dimples when she smiled, the same dark fire in the eyes. Nothing shoddy here, nothing fake or make-believe.

Like Isabella, maybe, but the opposite of Anna Swan. Anna overwhelmed with her startling immensity, but Lavinia enticed with her smallness—the intriguing simplicity of a periwinkle.

And I? What was wrong with me, swinging through such extremes—my compass spinning, a few short months ago so passionate for a giant, and now for a dwarf. Charlie, go home. Shoot pool, play solitaire. Talk to your fingernails. But Lavinia, Lavinia . . . it was a name that clings.

"You may call me Vinny," she said.

"Oh? That's what you use? Really? Fine, okay. You can call me Charlie."

She seemed surprised, embarrassed. "I'm sorry, I thought you were—Tom. Tom Thumb."

"I am. But my mother keeps reminding me that I'm Charlie Stratton."

She pursed her lips. Then, shyly, "Someone should have told me."

She looked again toward the big glass terrarium. The snake was moving again, looping and turning. It put its head close up to the glass, staring at us with great deliberation, as if considering us for lunch.

"I like your earrings," I said. She wore one small pearl on each of her ears.

"I like your moustache," she answered, returning the compliment.

"Do you? I put it on last year. Barnum hates it, he wants me to shave it off."

"I think, in a way, it's—very becoming."

"Do you?"

"I do."

"You dance?"

"Sometimes," she said.

"So? Onstage? You play a banjo?"

"I sing."

"Really? Go ahead," I said. "Sing."

She looked at me as if I were loony. Then she took a step back, putting some space between us, and she sang, a soft, sweet voice, surprisingly warm.

> *Thou art dearer than the dewdrop*
> *To the dry and parching flower;*
> *Or the sound of soft sweet music*
> *At evening's twilight hour.*
> *Thou art dearer! Thou art dearer!*
> *Than the moonlight to the sea.*

There was a delicate sadness in it, a bittersweetness. The python was perfectly still, and the chimpanzee stopped clucking and fell silent. So pretty she was, and such a voice, she was going to be a big success. They would be coming to see her in droves.

But she was nervous, frightened to death, she said, because here she was, just learning her way around, and Barnum—Mr. Barnum—was rushing her into things, with a reception at the St. Nicholas, for the press, then two days in Boston at the Parker House, and back to New York for a reception at the Fifth Avenue Hotel, and then her stage debut at the Museum.

"You'll sail right through," I said.

"But, you know, it scares me. The Vanderbilts, the Belmonts. And all the reporters."

"You'll bowl them over."

"You think so?"

"I know so. And I bet you like syllabubs."

"I adore syllabubs," she said. "Strawberry, it's my favorite."

Syllabubs were the thing of the moment. In fact they had been the thing of the moment for quite some time—a mix of sweet cider and milk, with a fruit flavor added and plenty of sugar and nutmeg. And if you were really serious about it, a dash of whisky.

"Strawberry?" I said. "Myself, I favor lemon. Barnum takes a syllabub now and then but never without a splash of brandy. Used to drink like a fish, you know, a bottle of champagne with his lunch every day. But he took the pledge, so now he drinks iced water when he's out, and sneaks wine in his office. The last time we toured England, one night he was so wallpapered he fell into the Thames and had to be fished out."

"I can juggle eggs," she said.

"Who taught you that?"

"A juggler on a riverboat. We sailed the Mississippi, town to town, a whole year. Then the war started and the boat shut down. I met Ulysses S. Grant when he was just a billing clerk in a shop in Galena, and now look where he is." She paused, her eyes bright with the memory. "Real eggs," she said, "three at a time."

"Someday you'll show me."

"Maybe," she said cheekily.

"I bet you cook, too."

"Only on special occasions, for special people. I do embroidery."

"Really! My mother does embroidery."

I didn't tell her about my father, who had died young from an unquenchable infatuation with single-malt whiskies. Nor did I mention young Isabella, Queen of Spain, who held me on her lap at a bullfight in Pamplona and whispered rapturous intimacies in my ear.

Vinny gazed at the python, the way it was coiled and twisted. Then, somberly, she mentioned that she had a brother in the war—Benjamin, the second of her four brothers. He was based at Arlington, close to the fighting in Virginia, and it was a worry for her. It troubled her, too, that she was here, at the Museum, getting all this attention and a shockingly big contract from Barnum—for what? For being a dwarf and singing a few songs, while Benjamin and thousands of others were risking their lives.

She was upset, I saw that. And I understood. I'd been worrying my way through some of the same confusion, feeling guilty about being safe and well paid at home. But a dwarf is a dwarf, and one learns how to live with that—though, in truth, the bad feelings never entirely vanish. You are guilty because you are the person you are. People see you and they want more and more of you, and the more you give, the less you have, and no one understands how empty you are. Guilty because you're alive, because you are you, with your own thoughts and imaginings, your own dreams, your own fears, your own loneliness, your own desperation.

I told her what Barnum had often said to me. "Give them a good song, it eases the way. Life is hard, we inch forward—a good song is a big part of every inch."

He was a relentless optimist, convinced that life was always taking a turn for the better, even when things were at their worst. I liked that idea, the notion of infinite progress—but somehow, like Vinny, I couldn't get past all those thousands who were being shot to pieces, and so many killed.

I took a cigar from my pocket, and with my nipper I cut off the end. I handed her a match.

"Where do you get them?" she asked.

"The cigars? A guy on Pearl Street rolls them. Calls them John Brown Freedom Sticks."

I put the cigar to my lips.

She hesitated, holding the match, studying it, as if making up her mind. Then she scratched it across the stone wall by the terrarium, and held the flame to the tip of the cigar.

I was thinking of the hills back home in Connecticut, the grass and trees, and how the hills flatten out toward the shore, with the blue waters of Long Island Sound wrinkling and swelling in the distance. And flocks of seagulls, weaving and dipping in the green air. That's what she did for me, she made me feel that good. We stood a long moment, hanging on each other's eyes, nothing between us but a few wisps of cigar smoke. If this was realism, well, it wasn't bad, I could live with it. Not bad at all. The chimpanzee was clucking again, begging for attention.

"Come on," I said. "I'll buy you a syllabub."

"Strawberry," she said.

"With a twist of lemon."

"Maybe," she answered. "We'll see about that."

The python was writhing and turning, showing off its fancy, intricate markings. And who could say what secret meanings might be lurking in those eye-catching designs?

As we started up the stairs toward the lobby, the two nuns I'd met on the horsecar descended toward us, on their way to see the hippopotamus. The short one with hair on her upper lip looked daggers at Vinny, and the tall one, angling her wimpled head in my direction, offered a complicitous grin. "You devil," she said.

When we were past them, still climbing, Vinny grabbed my arm. "What was that all about?"

"Oh, just a couple of old friends, " I said, glancing back. The nuns were off the stairs, on their way to the menagerie. "When times are tough, I hire them and they pray for me."

"Are they any good?"

"At praying?"

"At anything."

"The short one said she'd iron my underwear if I deliver it to the nunnery."

"That's outrageous."

"I agree, and that's what I told her. But, can you imagine—the last time I saw her, she blew a kiss."

"I don't believe a word," she said, not believing a word.

"Right, of course," I answered. "I understand. I do. But tell me, would Tom Thumb lie about a thing like a kiss?"

At the top of the stairs, she hung uncertain, then faced me squarely. "You're an adventure," she said. "You know that, don't you?"

"Is that what you think? I thought I was a delusion."

"That, too," she said. "And if that nun, that holy woman of God, actually did throw a kiss, I bet you enjoyed it."

"I did. I confess, I did."

"In that case," she said, "maybe I'll change my mind about that syllabub."

"Don't you dare," I said.

"And what if I do dare?" she answered. "What then?"

Yes, I thought, with terrible remorse. God help me, what then? Those eyes, those brown eyes, they had a way of grabbing and taking hold.

We took our coats from the cloakroom, and as we stepped onto the street, a low, sagging cloud released a gale of snow flurries that swirled crazily and blew across the cobblestones. I had always liked snow, white flakes driven in the wind. And I did wonder if the nuns—those two nuns—had snowball fights when no one was watching.

At the press reception in the St. Nicholas, Vinny wowed the reporters. They wrote her up in the local papers and in plenty of out-of-state papers, too. Boston, Philadelphia, Chicago, St. Louis. And, despite the war, she made it into quite a few Southern papers as well.

> A very pretty and intelligent little lady . . . a
> full, round, dimpled face . . . dark, waving
> hair . . . brilliant and intelligent eyes that fairly

> sparkle . . . the grace and dignity of a queen . . .
> an absolutely choice specimen of feminine
> humanity . . . and she sings excellently well—
> what more could we desire?

With everyone applauding her like that, it made me nervous. In the fluster and excitement, was she even seeing me? Noticing? Understanding that I was more than just a guy with a cigar, who takes a twist of lemon in his syllabubs.

I fretted, and wondered. Did she understand the deep, serious feelings I had for her? There were no words for those feelings. The being together said it all. To be near her, with her. To hear her voice, her thoughts, what she liked and didn't like. The being together, that's what mattered.

I didn't return to Connecticut as planned, but kept my room at the Astor. I gave Vinny flowers and a box of chocolates. I brought her to the Rotunda Bar in the Astor for the stuffed partridge, and Delmonico's for the Cornish hens. We went to A. T. Stewart's, and she picked out a silk scarf that matched her coat. I brought her over to the gold necklaces, but she was reluctant, she didn't want me to spend that kind of money. Still, I insisted, and the one she chose, she wore it everywhere. And wherever we went, people were always watching. The knowing nods, the glimpses—and that, all of that, was more than annoying. When you're with someone for whom you have powerful feelings, your emotions are deep and private—you don't want to be stared at as if you were two caged cockatoos.

We went to the Academy of Music for an opera, to hear Clara Kellogg in Gounod's *Faust*—and even then, when we took our place in Barnum's box, even then so many eyes were upon us. If you're a dwarf, everybody looks. If you're a famous dwarf, they look twice. At Vinny, they were looking five and six and seven times.

That Clara Kellogg, what a voice she had. The newspapers were saying she was the best in New York that season. They called her the "flower prima donna" because of the hundreds of bouquets thrown onstage after each performance. I brought a bouquet of red roses, but when I tossed it, it fell short, into the orchestra pit, hitting a bassoonist in the face.

Another day, I took Vinny to Trinity Church, and St. Paul's. And to Fraunces Tavern, where George Washington gave his farewell speech at the end of the war.

I did not bring her to the noisy, crowded saloons where there were cockfights and battles-to-the-death between rats and terriers, and boxing matches in which bare-knuckled bruisers bloodied each other until one, or both, couldn't get up off the floor.

Nor did I take her to Dr. Coffin's Museum of Anatomical Health and Enlightenment, on the Bowery, with its chamber of horrors and the skull of a local gang member, one of the Daybreak Boys, hanged for robbing the harbor boats and killing a watchman. And in an eerie corner by a purple window, seven large jars containing fetuses preserved in formaldehyde. And in a larger jar, the preserved remains of conjoined twins born dead in Mogadishu. Did Vinny want to see any of that? Did she? Did I?

And I did not—not—bring her into the Five Points district, where there were pigs and cows and dead horses in the street, and prostitutes lolling about on street corners, some leaning out of second-floor windows, half-naked. Drunks sleeping in the alleys, and the Dead Rabbits and Bowery Boys mixing it up, tearing at each other with eye-gougers and knives.

It rained, then it snowed. The snow melted, and for a few days we had clear, brisk weather. I hailed a hackney and we rode to the Battery, where we strolled and took in the view to New Jersey, across the river. Great chunks of ice on the Hudson, drifting down from as far away as Albany. We paused by one of the piers, where stevedores were unloading a big clipper ship home from China—plenty of muscle and sweat and energy, great rumbling sounds as huge kegs and crates were hauled across the dock. Thumping and pounding, squeaking of wheels and pulleys. Men shouting and bending and lifting and cursing. More rumbling. More pounding and thumping.

And, farther down, to our left, a clear view of the bay, the sun blazing, flinging light upon the water. We stood there a while, taking it all in. Hundreds of gulls circling and dipping, many squatting on the ice floes. Whole flocks of pigeons raced overhead.

She was something, the way she studied the birds and the river ice. Definitely something. There were moods in her eyes, and in the way she moved her arms and her shoulders, and in the way she breathed.

"Love is a devastation," she said. "Isn't it so?"

"Why a devastation?"

"Because it turns, it twists, it bends you around until you forget who you are."

I didn't, at that moment, feel bent or twisted. I liked us the way we were.

I put my hand on her hip, and she leaned into me. I liked that. Even the gulls out there, they were eyeing us, and they understood—not everybody had it this good.

She was right, of course, about love, it twists you around. But twist, maybe, is not the right word. It pinches, it pushes. It stands you on your head, and you have to relearn everything—how to walk, how to breathe, how to blow your nose. And you're never sure, when you turn the corner, if this is the right street that you're on, taking you to the right address, or if you are hopelessly, helplessly, lost. Love keeps you guessing all the time.

She told me about her large family, four brothers and three sisters, but mainly she spoke of Benjamin, who was in the army, and her sister Minnie, youngest in the family and, like Vinny, a midge, a little person. And her two older sisters, Sarah and Caroline, both tall and both with children. I told her about my two sisters, who had children, and we talked much about Barnum and the Museum, and about traveling and touring, and some of the things that she and I might do together onstage.

I had been weary of performing, thinking of quitting, getting into something else. But she was pulling me back, drawing me on, her head spinning with fresh ideas. We could sing duets—sure, why not? We could do scenes from plays—something, maybe, from Shakespeare. I could be Hamlet, she could be Ophelia. Or *A Midsummer Night's Dream*—we could be Oberon and Titania, or Pyramus and Thisbe.

Or a bit of silly, crazy, nonsensical buffoonery, for a quick laugh. I could be Satan, chasing her with a pitchfork, and she escapes on a trapeze and vanishes into the scenery. Or she could be a witch, chasing me with a broom, but I snap my fingers and she disappears into a puff of smoke. Then reappears as the Queen of Sheba.

"See?" she said. "Anything. It's easy. Anything at all. If it doesn't work, skip it and try something else."

PART THREE

LAVINIA REMINISCES— FROM MIDDLEBORO TO BROADWAY

CHAPTER 8

LAVINIA
THE POWER OF EMBROIDERY

What do I know, and what's to do? Where to go? What's happening? Young, I worried myself with such questions, because things weren't right, not right at all. I wasn't growing. Or rather, I was growing but too slowly, and when I turned ten, I stopped altogether, stuck at twenty pounds and only twenty-four inches tall. To my brothers I was a joke. They teased and poked fun and tossed me around, though they were careful not to break my bones, or our father, who was six feet tall, would have broken theirs.

My father built a pair of portable steps for me, to help me reach the things that had to be reached, and that was a great help. And my mother, she did the most sensible thing of all. Even though I was so tiny, she treated me as if I were completely normal, and she showed me how to do the necessary chores. I learned to cook and set the table and wash dishes, and how to keep things in their place.

And, better than anything, she taught me how to do embroidery. I loved that, making fancy designs with pretty-colored threads. We sat together by the window, she working on hers and I on mine, embroidering trees and flowers and leaves and vines. I still do some, now and then. It calms me. Pushing the needle in and drawing the thread through the cloth and watching the design as it grows and develops. The shape of a leaf, the slant of a branch. The yellow center of a daisy.

At school I was smart but mischievous, crawling about and pinching the other kids, driving the teacher to distraction. But my pranks were tolerated because of my ridiculously small size. When my schooling was over I was at home for a while, idle and restless. Then, when I was sixteen, there was a need for a teacher at the schoolhouse and I was asked to fill in for a term. I had great fun doing that. My students were all taller than I, and they took good care of me. When there was snow on the ground, they came to my home and brought me on a sled to the schoolhouse. When it rained, they carried me, to keep my feet from getting wet.

Then, in the spring of '59, my mother's cousin brought me to the Midwest, where he had a river showboat. Everyone called him Colonel, though I never found out why. I don't think he'd ever been in the army. The boat was his *Floating Museum of Curiosities*, filled with minstrels, acrobats, a sword-swallower, a giant, a snake-charmer, a fortune-teller, and me.

It was moored at Louisville, on the Ohio River, and soon enough I was having my first taste of river life, chugging from port to port, through fog and mist, and when the fog lifted, the sun was a yellow blister above the trees. Dogs barking from the shore, and cocks crowing, birds darting, hammers hammering. And the constant groan of the paddle wheels, pushing us sluggishly along.

From Louisville we came down the Ohio, through all the bends and angles, with Kentucky on the left bank and Indiana on our right, the captain tooting his foghorn on the blind turns, and some close calls we had with boats coming in the opposite direction. We traveled from town to town, offering our showboat performances.

Some of the towns were mean places—more than once, our people were assaulted and beaten. One night, after a show, three of the minstrels went ashore to see the town. They came racing back, pursued by a band of ruffians. The minstrels boarded safely, pulling the plank up behind them, and the captain, alert to what was happening, called to the crew to release the mooring lines. As we pulled away, the toughs, frustrated, pelted the boat with rocks. One of the toughs took out a gun and fired a few shots—a bullet whizzed past my head and smashed a mirror on the wall behind me.

We made stops at Brandenburg and Cloverport, Tell City and Evansville. Then Paducah and on to Cairo, where the Ohio merged with the Mississippi, and we turned north. Long stops we had at some of those Mississippi ports—three nights, sometimes four, or five. St. Louis, Hannibal, Quincy, Rock Island, and many whose names I hardly remember. Far up we went, all the way to Galena, in the northwest corner of Illinois. It was there that I met Ulysses S. Grant. He was, at the time, just an ordinary citizen, working at a business in town, and when he came aboard and saw me, he took an interest in me. We sat on a bench on the upper deck, talking. He wanted to know how tall I was, and how long I'd been with the showboat. He asked about my family, and where I was from.

"Middleboro," I said.

"And where is that?"

"In Massachusetts."

"Oh," he answered, as if he had an opinion about Massachusetts. But all he added was, "Is Middleboro near Boston?"

"Well, in a way," I answered, "but it's closer to Taunton."

He nodded, but I had a feeling that he'd never heard of Taunton and had no idea where it might be.

There was wine and whisky aboard, but he settled for a glass of Rakoczy Wasser, with ice, and I took a lemonade. I told him about my two older sisters and my brothers, all tall, and my younger sister, Minnie, who was shorter than I, and he found that amusing. "Sounds like the two last-born in your family were blessed with the shorter end of things."

He was in his late thirties, thin and stoop-shouldered, with gray eyes and a full beard of chestnut brown, neatly trimmed. While he stuffed his pipe with tobacco, I noticed something asymmetrical about his face, the left eye slightly lower than the right. And as we spoke, I sensed a hidden energy simmering inside him, a need to be busy and make good, but no clear sense of what he should be doing, and how to make the leap forward.

He had a quiet manner, and in his pleasant way he told me about his family—two boys, then a girl, then another boy. He'd grown up in Ohio, he said, and had been at West Point. The best part of that, he told me, was the time he spent on his own, reading novels and doing drawings and sketches. He'd read Cooper, Bulwer-Lytton, Walter Scott, and Washington Irving. I'd read some Irving but favored Scott, and had never heard of Bulwer-Lytton. And Cooper, those adventure stories in the woods, with Indians—I never got very far into any of that.

He hadn't been a whiz with the regular class-work, he said, but he did have a way with horses, and had jumped the bar higher than any other cadet, to this day. He was very proud about that.

It surprised me how personal he was, speaking easily, saying things I wouldn't have expected him to tell, given that I was a perfect stranger. I imagine it was the oddness of the situation, I so small, barely thirty inches at the time, and he never having met a little person before.

After West Point he was eleven years in the regular army, and rose to the rank of captain. Then he resigned and became a private citizen again, and was having a hard time. He had tried real estate, but that didn't work, and he'd tried chickens, and that failed. He'd done some farming, but prices fell, and even though he had a bumper crop, he took a heavy loss and had to give up the farm.

He was now working as a billing clerk at his father's leather business, on Main Street in Galena. From the tone of his voice, it was hard to tell which he hated more, being a billing clerk, or working in Galena. But at least he was earning his way and able to live with his wife and children. What he'd hated most about the army, he said, were the long periods away from his family.

The day was sunny, we sat under an awning on the upper deck. Below, on the main deck, the minstrels were doing their usual routine, running through "Oh! Susannah," "Listen to the Mocking Bird," and "Jeanie with the Light Brown Hair." They had a banjo, a fiddle, a tambourine, and a drum. And strong, hearty voices. A river breeze was blowing. A line of willows beyond the wharf sifted lazily in the warm air. I sipped my tall glass of lemonade, he smoked his pipe—and on that dreamy summer afternoon, neither of us could have imagined the way in which his life, so simple and ordinary, would in a few short years be completely transformed—that he would, in fact, be in the army again and would rise so swiftly to become not just a general, but the top one, a general among generals.

Time is a blessing, my mother always said. And a blessing it is. Often, as I do my embroidery, I think how odd and wonderful life is, so filled with unusual things. Even in those random moments when my back hurts, I think of the pain as part of life's wonderful strangeness. The pain is something I have a color for. I stitch it into the pattern, and the pain, in its subtle way, is there among the flowers. Green for the leaves, yellow for the sun, blue for the stream. The blue of the stream is the blue flow of time, running endlessly. And dark purple for the pain—sometimes it mingles with the stream, blending with the blue, and you hardly notice.

That day on the riverboat, before he left, Ulysses stopped at the concession stand and bought my photograph, a *carte de visite*. I signed it for him, and he put it in his wallet. Maybe I would bring him some luck, he said.

What I didn't know then but learned later was that he had a low tolerance for alcohol. One glass of whisky slurred his speech, and two made him tipsy. The rumor was that it was a problem with whisky that had caused him to leave the army when he was a captain—and the rumor came back strong after his big victory at Shiloh, when he was a brigadier general. He was a hero for winning the battle, but when it was seen how many men he lost, some newspapers ran a cartoon that showed him with a whisky bottle in his tent. Well, I have always hated rumors, they are so spiteful. Even if he did go off the deep end now and then, I've heard again and again how much he was admired by the men who served under him. And I like to think Lincoln really did make the remark he supposedly made when he heard complaints about Grant's drinking—"If whisky makes him win, find out his brand and I'll send some to my other generals." So clever, Lincoln was.

When we left Galena, we didn't travel any farther north. Our Floating Museum of Curiosities turned south, moving downriver and heading for New Orleans, with plenty of stops along the way.

But before we were very far along, it all went bad for me. I fell ill with a fever, and it was a horrible time. When we pulled into port, the Colonel sent someone off to fetch a doctor, and when the doctor examined me, his conclusion was that I was afflicted with typhoid. Three or four weeks, he said, the fever would last that long.

It was a dreadful time, the fever, moments of delirium, and times when I was sure I was sinking and would never survive. Lizzie Edmunds, the wife of one of the minstrels, kept me alive. She did everything she knew, sitting up at night and putting wet cloths on my face and forehead to lower the fever, and moistening my lips, which were dry and cracked. So good to me she was, she kept me alive.

Toward the end of 1860, when Abraham Lincoln was elected, our showboat was far down the Mississippi, in the South, and there was a great stir in the towns where we tied up, everyone talking about secession. It was happening, we could see it forming and fermenting. They wanted their own ways and didn't want to be bound to the North anymore. And we on the boat, we were all from the North, worrying that if war broke out, we might be stranded there, in the South, and impossible to know what might become of us.

Already, militias were moving around. We saw riverboats and trains loaded with crates of ammunition and other military stuff. My mother's cousin, aware of the danger, sold the boat, and we trained to Vicksburg, where, with considerable difficulty, we found a steamboat that brought us to Louisville. From there we had railroad service to most of the northern cities, and my mother's cousin brought me home.

I spent the following year at my parents' house, in Middleboro, with occasional visits to friends in other towns. And still I wondered— what to do and where to go? Doubting, seriously doubting, that anyone would ever want me, love me, marry me. Would it happen? How good, I thought, to be settled and have a home, and a child of my own. That's what I thought about. Could it happen for me, small as I was? But how? And when? Life kept its secrets, and nothing to do but await the unfolding.

Shortly before I turned twenty-one, Mr. Barnum heard of me—my smallness—and he invited me to make appearances at his American Museum. "It will change your life," he said. "In ways you can't imagine."

"Will it?"

"Be sure it will."

He offered a remarkable amount per week for my appearances at the Museum, plus an audience with Queen Victoria and appearances in the major cities of England. With a new wardrobe for the stage, and jewelry to go along with all of that. Rather much, I thought, for simply standing onstage in pretty clothes and singing a few songs. And very hard to turn down. But I felt not right about it because the war was on, and young boys who had never earned any kind of money at all, nothing like what I was about to receive, were struggling and suffering in those terrible battles. My own brother Benjamin, three years older than I, had volunteered, and I was so fearful for him. It didn't seem right.

I thought, too, of the people who would see me at the Museum—what kind of money did most of them have? The mothers and children, the store clerks, seamstresses, laborers, farmers who came in from out of town. The immigrants, spending the little money they had so they could hear me sing a song. Those were my thoughts, my hesitations.

Nevertheless, Mr. Barnum was so right when he said it would change my life—though I don't think even he could have foreseen the dramatic change that lay just ahead. In my first week at the Museum, while I was learning my way around, not yet performing, I met Charlie—Tom Thumb—and it was a head-spinning time for both of us, he looking at me and I looking at him, all eyes for each other, gluttonous and unashamed.

One day, he hired a carriage and brought me to the Battery, where we strolled by the river, admiring the great slabs of ice floating on the water. Charlie loved the seagulls, and who wouldn't—the way they circled around, dropping low then soaring again, performing for anyone who cared to watch. The sun bright but the day cold, too cold to linger there very long.

And many times, those first weeks, we rode the ferries, back and forth to Brooklyn, to Staten Island, and New Jersey. He did love his ferries, especially the ones with musicians on deck—banjos and guitars, and strong hearty voices. He always dropped a bunch of coins in the hat.

His instinct for ferries was something he caught from a newsman, Walt Whitman, who was also a poet. I had never heard of him, but if Charlie thought so highly of Whitman, yes, I would give him a try. On one of those ferry rides, he told me Whitman had gone down to Washington to see his brother, who'd been wounded. And he was still there, helping out at the hospitals.

"He writes to you?"

"Sometimes," Charlie said.

"And you write back?"

"Never. He doesn't send a return address. He imagines if I send to Walt Whitman, Anywhere USA—or Anywhere in the Universe—the letters will find him. He's a bit strange, you know. He has an odd way of seeing things."

"But you like the poems."

"I do, I do. But it's—different, you know. No rhymes, no regular beat, just a lot of lines that sprawl and spill over into other lines. So not for everybody, I suppose."

He mentioned that Barnum hated the book. As did John Greenleaf Whittier. He told Barnum that when he read Whitman's book, he was so annoyed he tossed it into the fireplace.

"He did that? Burned the book?"

"Did that," Charlie said. "That's how it is, I guess. You like him or hate him. There are parts, sure, that aren't my piece of meat, or just boring. But when he's on, he's on—the lines come rushing in at you like rolling waves."

He looked away, toward a small, low cloud, and suddenly the words were pouring out of him, flowing from memory—

I hear the bravuras of birds, the bustle of growing wheat,
    gossip of flames, clack of sticks cooking my meals.
I hear the sound I love, the sound of the human voice,
I hear all sounds as they are tuned to their uses . . . sounds of
    the city and sounds out of the city . . . sounds of the day and
    night . . .

I liked that. "Nice," I said. "Lovely—*the bravuras of birds, the gossip of flames.* You use that? Onstage?"

"Barnum would kill me."

"Why? It's beautiful."

"I know, I know." Then, with a grin, "I'll lend you the book. I marked the dirty parts."

"Well! I can't wait," I answered, lifting an eyebrow. Dirty parts? In a poem? "Can I show them to my mother?"

He gave me a hard, slanting look, and I gave him the same hard look right back.

He brought me to Trinity Church and St. Paul's, and the park by City Hall. When we left City Hall, we stopped in a shop and he bought a copy of *Leaves of Grass* for me, and promised to get Whitman's autograph on it if he ever returned to New York.

Every evening, after my final performance in the theater, Charlie walked me home. I stayed at a rooming house on Fulton Street, a short walk from the Museum. Three others lived there. Zoupetta, known as the Gypsy Fortune-Teller, and two of the Circassian women, Zalumma Agra and Zobeide Luti. They were friendly and we got along well together, but with our busy schedules, we rarely saw one another. Zobeide Luti was on the sultry side, always in tight-fitting, low-cut dresses when she appeared onstage. She was the oldest of us, but still stunning. She remembered when Charlie first started, what a sensation he was—women young and old grabbing for him, picking him up and giving him a hug. She recalled that Mr. Barnum used to charge extra for a kiss. Well, Charlie had never mentioned any of that, and I would certainly ask him about it, at a proper moment.

The other person I became friendly with was Anna Swan. I loved her piano playing, so rich, so sensitive, and the wonderful pieces she chose to play. Often we went to the coffee lounge on the third floor, where we sipped tea and nibbled on cookies, and many times she brought me up to her spacious bedroom on the fifth floor. She showed me her books—so many, I was amazed. I, too, enjoyed a good novel now and then, but was hardly the reader that she was. I wondered where she found time for that, given the many hours she spent at the piano, working on new pieces, selections from Schubert, Beethoven, Brahms, and interspersing them with a variety of songs that she sang.

Once a week she appeared on the main stage, and four times a week she offered hour-long performances in a large room on the third floor. It was hard work, but she enjoyed it—the practicing, the performing, the two hours every week with a piano tutor that Mr. Barnum hired for her.

What she did not like—indeed what she hated—was the clause in her contract that had nothing to do with music. Twice a week, for a half hour each time, she was required to stand on a low platform in one of the galleries—simply stand there, while people looked at her and gaped at her bigness. She didn't like that, not at all, and who could blame her?

There was a very large closet in her bedroom—she showed me her many dresses, one by one, wanting my advice about which looked best for a performance. Mr. Barnum had hired a couturiere who made many dresses for her, but she felt uncomfortable about them, didn't feel they were really her. She worried, too, about her hair—to wear it long over her shoulders or pulled back with a clasp. Or pulled back on one side but long and loose on the other.

I was older than she by about five years, and felt she was relying on me as if I were her big sister—which was amusing, given the immense physical difference between us. And, I confess, I rather enjoyed that role, a big sister to a giant! Sometimes we read to each other, short poems that we found in *Godey's*. But many times we were quiet and said nothing, she studying the score of a Chopin piece she was adding to her repertoire, and I doing my embroidery. Or I reading, glancing through a book from her shelf, while she wrote to her mother, who had never left Nova Scotia. And times, too, when we sang together, harmonizing.

Meanwhile, the war tumbled along, and my mother was worried out of her mind for Benjamin. Whenever I saw her, she kept a firm front, pretending everything was as it had been, yet I knew how terrified she was. My brother Sylvanus wanted to go, but with Benjamin already gone, she positively forbade it.

Back in August, while I was still at home and my parents were fussing over the contract Mr. Barnum offered, I wrote to Benjamin, telling him what was happening. And in his reply, I saw, in the way his pen met the paper, how eager and excited he was.

Dear Star-of-Heaven, Shedding Your Light on Broadway—

Fantastic! I like it! The Prince of Humbug is going to make you rich and famous? Grab it. Do it. Shine your teeth. December? That's when you start? I'll put a gun to my sergeant's head and will have the whole platoon up there for your debut—war or no war!

Nothing terribly dramatic in this neck of the woods. On reconnaissance last week, had to rough it in the wild. One night a cannonball smashed into a clump of trees—a guy in the tent next to mine was bashed by a falling branch. We had to carry him home. Happy to be telling you this from the velvet-lined comfort of our base, where the paths are lined with gold nuggets and the meals are cooked by a chef we abducted from Delmonico's.

And there, with that, with Benjamin at risk that way, I should be in New York, parading myself onstage?

But my mother, she said never you mind. Make good, do it for the family. So I did. Because how else to support myself and not be a burden, being as tiny as I was.

Still, something so terribly wrong in it all. Benjamin and thousands of others out there risking their lives. But in New York it was all restaurants, factories, hotels, and the big glittering stores—Lord & Taylor, A. T. Stewart, R. H. Macy, Arnold Constable. Tiffany, Brooks Brothers—as if there were no war at all. Even Mrs. Lincoln came up here to shop, and the prices were soaring. But the girls who sewed for Brooks and the others, what kind of a pittance were they making while their husbands and brothers were lugging rifles and being shot at?

"Be proud of yourself," my mother said, that day in December when I left for New York. "You're a little person, but look what you have—you'll have more than your brothers. Be glad for what God gave you. And look after your sister Minnie," she said. "Think of her. Take care of her."

I saw what she was saying. She had two of us on her hands, Minnie and me, and if this good fortune had not come my way, what a burden I would have been. She was hoping the same good things would happen for Minnie—and I had to push that, urge it, do my best to make it happen. What an odd, awkward world God put us in, I thought. Sunrise peaceful, full of promise, and evening rich and restful—but all the long day between, nothing but noise, hurry, drive, push and rush, buy and sell. Alarms on the hand-pulled fire engines ringing wildly, and the fierce clatter of horses' hooves. And what, in the end, will ever become of us?

Happily, happily, I had found Charlie. He was courting me, wooing me, impressing me. Wherever we went, people gazed at us. We were a

couple, a tiny couple. A couple in miniature. Eyes pondered us as if trying to touch us—trying to imagine miniature life and miniature sleep,
miniature meals, miniature walking and running and eating and laughing, miniature tears, miniature male and miniature female, she and he.
The knowing nods, the smiles. Waiters and servers giving us special
attention at the Astor House, at Niblo's, at Delmonico's.

Life is good, I thought. Bad, but good. I stitched many new colors
into my embroidery. Dresden blue, cerise, madder, sienna, topaz, all of
them mixing and blending. The threads came on small spools, I had
dozens of them in my embroidery sack. And I no longer needed to
work with a pattern. I threaded my needles with different colors, and
my fingers flew. I created my own designs as I moved along—a leaf,
a stem, a butterfly, a bird, though often I wasn't sure what the image
would be until it began to take shape.

And how I do remember that first day when Charlie and I met at
the Museum, in the menagerie, by the python from Burma. We strolled
for a while along Broadway, bundled against the cold, and had an early
dinner at the Astor House, where I'd never been—that vast, lovely hotel
with the bar under the rotunda and the walls adorned with paintings. I
can't remember what I ate, but do remember, while we were dawdling
over coffee, I showed Charlie the latest letters from Benjamin, which
I carried in my pocketbook. He wrote once or twice a week, but with
delays in the mail, often there was nothing for a while, then a whole
bunch at once. These had reached me while I was still in Middleboro,
just before I left for New York.

Dearest Younger Sister—

*A stray dog hung around with me for a week but the no-account
thing went off with somebody else that fed him better. How's that for
a thank-you? . . .*

Dearest Tiny One—

Lost my toothbrush, can you believe? Send when you can. Lost my watch, too, but still have my nose and fingers, and my ears that hear the damn sergeant shouting like doomsday, telling us where to be and when. . . .

Everlasting You Learning All Those New Songs—

The big guns shot up the sky like fireworks last night but nothing fell close to anybody hereabouts. My tent buddy slept right through it. . . .

Dear Tiddlywinks—

Can you knit me some wool socks? My feet get cold at night. . . .

Charlie read them all, smiling and nodding. "Nice, nice," he said. "He hates the sergeant and wants a dog. Can we send a Saint Bernard?" He reached across the table and touched my hand. "How long does it take to knit a pair of socks?"

"Oh, God, I haven't started yet. There is so much to do," I said, full of remorse. "But I will get to those socks. I will!"

Charlie bought a watch to replace the one Benjamin had lost, and we sent it. He was dead serious about the Saint Bernard, but did finally understand it might not be a terribly good idea. And those socks— to my shame, they lingered on my guilt list, because where, with the receptions and press interviews and my first performances—and with Charlie, forever lingering Charlie—where was the time to even think of shopping for a pair of knitting needles and a hank of yarn?

CHAPTER 9

LAVINIA
A QUARTET OF DWARFS

When I was living at home in Middleboro, there had been moments, many moments, when I felt there would never be a man for me—no man, and no family of my own. And when I was on the showboat, my fears only intensified. Every day aboard that boat, the *Floating Museum of Curiosities*, I was face-to-face with the fact that I was one of those curiosities. What man would ever want me? Me—so small, a freak of nature. I was overwhelmed by self-doubt.

But then, at the Museum, much to my astonishment, I was confronted not with one but with two suitors—Charlie, but also, hard to believe, Commodore Nutt.

He was shorter than I and younger, a cute little fellow, and I liked him. But what a problem he suddenly was. Mr. Barnum had given me a pretty ring with an emerald on it. The ring was too small for me, and, promising to buy another, he suggested that I pass this one over to the

Commodore. I did that, but the poor boy somehow took it into his head that the ring was a love token. What a flood of attention he gave me, and, though I offered no encouragement and did my best to shrug him off, he was a constant annoyance. Whenever he saw Charlie near me, he would puff up and strut around like a bantam rooster spoiling for a fight.

Well, one day it happened. The Commodore stepped right up to Charlie and punched him in the face. Isaac Sprague saw it. He said the Commodore stepped up to Charlie and just walloped him, and Charlie went down. This was in the corridor outside Charlie's dressing room. And Charlie just sat there, hand on his jaw, looking for all the world as if he might rouse himself and leap at the Commodore. But he was much the gentleman, Isaac said. "Brave fellow, he took it and let it pass. And the Commodore walked off in a huff."

So sad it was. All because I made the mistake of giving the Commodore that ring. I was annoyed with him, angry that he hurt my Charlie, yet I pitied him, too. Poor little fellow, he was suffering. But what, really, had he been imagining? I was, after all, older than he and inches taller—and, alas, heavier too. And Charlie, much taller and much heavier, could have really hurt him. It was so good of Charlie to have backed off the way he did.

Nevertheless, I confess that when Isaac told me, despite my surprise and anger, I did feel the faintest quiver of delight. Two dwarf bucks were fighting over me. Amazing! Over *me*. As in some silly fairy tale.

I found Charlie on the third floor, by the alcove that honored an ancient Greek philosopher, Heracleitus. It held several of his famous sayings, neatly framed. When Charlie saw me, we looked long at each other.

"Isaac told me," I said. "The Commodore? It's true?"

Charlie nodded vaguely. He touched a finger to his left cheek, the slight bruise there. "Oh, it's real, it's real." He nodded. "We meet tomorrow—pistols at twenty paces, first light of dawn. On the grass in front of City Hall."

Well—it was a bit of a relief to see him taking it so well, turning it into a joke.

"Tomorrow?" I said. "Will everyone be there? The Soothsayer? The Living Skeleton? The Snake-Charmer you were in love with when you were seven?"

"Everyone," he said. "Even the African Earth Woman who used to let me play with her tom-toms. And famous Caroline Howard, who played Topsy in *Uncle Tom's Cabin*, right here at the Museum. She was twenty-three and I was fourteen. She wanted to run away with me. But her husband found out and gave her a black eye."

"Did she kick him in the shins?"

"She put roaches in his stew and for a week he was afflicted with stomach pains."

Charlie looked away, briefly—then he touched the tip of my nose. "Tomorrow, at the crack of dawn. You'll be there?"

"I wouldn't miss it for the world."

He gave me a firm, steady, dead-serious stare. "Which one of us will you be rooting for?"

"I'm in a bit of a turmoil," I answered, mustering my best coy manner. "I'm sort of . . . thinking it over."

"Well, don't think too long," he said, putting both arms around me and pulling me close.

Less than a week later, we made our big, earth-shaking decision. Because where else were there two little people as happy about each other as we were?

He brought me to Tiffany's for an engagement ring, and he spent more on it than I would have wished. But that was his way, he liked to spend. He gave me a pair of earrings, too, with my birthstone in them.

The next morning, my ring at Tiffany's was ready. After we picked it up, we spoke to Mr. Barnum and told him our good news. I showed him the ring. He was quiet for a moment, withdrawn, then a slow smile crept across his face. "Wonderful," he said. "I suspected something, but not this soon. Magnificent! I assure you, you will have the most splendid wedding this city has ever seen."

The words hung in the air, in the late-afternoon sunlight that sifted through the window. I was glad he was pleased, but his mention of a big wedding sent a shiver through me. I'd been imagining a small, private affair in a local church at home, in Middleboro. But here, a big thing in the big city, it would take some getting used to.

"Blessings," Mr. Barnum said. "Double blessings upon both of you."

Then he leaned toward me. "And now that you've come this far and are a bride-to-be, may I ask if you've had any thoughts about who your maid of honor will be?"

In fact, I had not. But in the suddenness of the moment, I found myself saying, "Yes. Yes. My sister Minnie, of course."

He smiled. "Wonderful—little Minnie. Three dwarfs at the altar. And if there are three, symmetry demands that there be four. Two men and two women." And, leaning back in his chair, he proposed that Charlie invite the Commodore to be his groomsman. "A quartet of dwarfs," he said, beaming.

Well, that was a hard one for Charlie to swallow. Commodore Nutt as his best man? Nutt, who had punched him in the face? They were on speaking terms again, but to go beyond that, to choose him as his groomsman, would be asking too much, and Charlie simply walked away from it.

It took him two weeks. Then, reluctantly, he agreed. What changed his mind, he never said—though I'm sure he did it for Mr. Barnum. They had been through a great deal together, for so long, all of twenty years. The first European tour had brought a certain amount of wealth to Charlie's family. And years later, when Mr. Barnum went into bankruptcy, Charlie suggested a second tour of Europe—he was seventeen when they sailed, and the three-year tour proved so successful that Mr. Barnum's share of the earnings made him solvent again. They owed each other, in so many ways.

Symmetry? Was that the word he used? If symmetry was important, we would be symmetrical. Four little ones at the altar, a quartet of dwarfs. Give us each a harmonica or a kazoo, and we'll make dwarf music. A dwarf fandango, a dwarf gavotte. If necessary, a dwarf rigadoon. And how I do hate the word "dwarf." That day in Mr. Barnum's office, I said so. Whenever I hear it, I think of the twisted, mischievous creatures that appear in fairy tales. Hobgoblins, leprechauns.

"But my darling Lavinia," Mr. Barnum said, "'Dwarf' is the correct word. Everyone uses it. Newspapers, magazines, Horace Greeley. There are those that are perfectly proportioned, like yourself and Charlie, and then the other type, unfortunate people with legs too small for their bodies, with head and limbs and torso totally out of proportion. You are not that. You are beautiful, everyone says so. As a dwarf lily is beautiful. But both types are dwarfs, you see. Variations on the same theme."

Still, I thought, find another word. Sprite, pixie, sylph. Whatever. A variation did he say? On a theme? Well, I had never thought of myself as a theme, and I certainly did not want to be a variation. On that day when Charlie and I told Mr. Barnum of our engagement, he said he would take it upon himself to tell the Commodore, before he heard it from someone else—and he asked that I be present, as a gesture of goodwill, assuring the Commodore that we were all friends. It was difficult to say no to that, and I reluctantly agreed.

The following day, in his office, Mr. Barnum spoke to the Commodore, and it was a difficult time. Awkward, to say the least. The poor little man, he stuffed his hands in his pockets, and he just filled up. "I hope you will be happy," he said, without looking at me, and left the room.

Charlie wrote a handsome letter to my mother, asking for her consent to our marriage, and I sent a letter of my own, telling her how happy I was. The letters were carried by George Wells, an assistant at the Museum. Mr. Barnum authorized him to speak on his behalf. When he returned the next day, George said my mother had objected strenuously, fearing the marriage was a promotional stunt concocted by Mr. Barnum. But when she read my letter and Charlie's, she was much mollified. George did say, though, that my parents spent much time discussing the matter privately, in an upstairs room, and in the end my mother relented and offered her blessing.

Not long afterward, she visited me in New York to discuss the wedding, and was delighted that I had chosen Minnie as my maid of honor. "She needs it," my mother said. "She adores you and is so jealous of you. It will do her a world of good to have a place of importance."

Jealous, I knew. She watched me, studied me, she wanted to *be* me. And I told her, always, that she must be herself. To read and learn as much as she could, and have a wonderful life of her own. She was thirteen, with all of the future waiting for her.

I knew, too, that she was unhappy about her breasts. They had started to develop almost two years earlier, but after all that time, they were something less than she'd expected. On my last visit to Middleboro, she was stuffing things into her dresses. She said she once tried two apples, but they slipped around too much.

She fussed, she fretted. "Is this all I'll ever have?"

"Be patient," I told her, aware that it wasn't just her breasts she was worried about. "Good things will happen for you. They will." But she was too eager. What good things? When? And there I was, years ago with the teaching job, then the showboat, and now the Museum, and the many important people I'd met. I knew what she felt—she would never catch up. Torturing herself, wanting too much to happen for her too soon.

Shortly before Christmas, Charlie brought me to Connecticut, to meet his mother. She was a quiet woman, a widow. She prepared a small lunch for us, chicken sandwiches, with pickles and olives on the side, and tea.

While we ate, she asked me about my family. I felt a loneliness in her, a sadness. When we were done eating, she withdrew to the living room and sat in a rocking chair by a window, and did some knitting.

Charlie toured me through the house and showed me everything, all of the rooms. Then he led me into his own little apartment on the first floor, where everything was appropriately small—small chairs, small desk, small sofa, but the cabinets tall and wide, holding the gifts he'd received from the kings and queens he'd met abroad. The gold chain from Queen Isabella, the emerald brooch from Louis Philippe, a gold watch from the Dowager Queen Adelaide, a gold pencil case from Victoria—and all sorts of elegant little gewgaws and curiosities, from dukes and earls and mayors. Even something from a matador, from the time when he was in Spain.

Then he surprised me, opening a cabinet filled with strange-looking objects that I hardly understood. Not a clue.

"Matches," he said. "The earliest practical—or impractical—matches."

One by one, he tossed them onto the bed, antique devices from around the world, things used before the invention of the strike-anywhere match, which we now have. They were complicated things, mostly glass tubes containing chemicals. If you were to break the tube and expose the chemicals to air, they would burst into flame. I touched them, picked them up, and he named them all. The phosphoric candle made in France during the last century. The pocket luminary from the Italians. Latour's phosphorous bottle and things with names that I hardly remember. Somebody's electropneumatic fire producer. And so many others. In their strangeness, they were fascinating—you might almost call them works of art. He had found them in curiosity shops, mostly in Europe, during his second tour abroad with Mr. Barnum.

There was one I did recognize—the instantaneous light box, which was still around when we were children. He had, too, some of the first friction matches—the Walker matches, made in England. And the American lucifers, in a box that seemed brand-new, but the box and the matches were over thirty years old.

He also had some self-lighting cigars from Austria, made a few years before he was born. He said he tried one, but it blew up in his face and burned his nose.

Fire, that's what these things on the bed were all about. And as he showed them to me, I remembered, in the restaurants we went to, how he would pause in front of the fireplace and gaze at the burning logs, as if he were seeing something deep and meaningful in the flames. Reading his past and his future, I suppose. Or just forgetting, emptying his mind, mesmerized. I do the same, now and then. Just stare and forget.

But fire and matches were nothing wonderful to me. When I thought about fire, I found it hard not to think of the people who die when their houses burn down. And the workers who make the matches, the phosphorus-tip matches we have today—so many of those workers develop a thing called "phossy jaw," and a great number die.

"Yes, yes," Charlie said, "all of that, I hate it. But fire—think—without it, how would we live? We cook with it. It keeps us warm in the winter. And the sun—the fire of the sun—without it, nobody would be alive. None of us would ever have been born."

Then he was talking about those Heracleitus sayings in the exhibit at the Museum. About fire, about the universe, how the universe itself is fire. Well, all of that, those Heracleitus things—*The way up and the way down are one and the same. . . . You can't step twice into the same river*—they are clever, in their way, and people do admire them. But I'd still like to know—if everything is fire, the entire universe, then where, where, are all the ashes?

And my Charlie, three inches taller than I—did I love him? Oh, I did. I did. I knew it whenever I was near him, when he held my hand, when he pressed close and I felt his breath on my face. That day, in that room, with the lunatic fire-making things scattered across the bed, he drew me close and we kissed. What a good feeling that was, as if we were melting, and it seemed for all the world that we were one person, floating, lifting off the rug—and in that long moment, it might be said that we were, in the strangest of ways, yes, very much on fire. And despite my skepticism, that old Greek, Heracleitus, may not have been so dumb after all.

The weeks flew by, and as the wedding date drew close, Minnie was in New York, getting fitted for her gown. She stayed several days, still fretting over her small breasts.

"If they don't get any bigger," she said, "I'll never have anything I can pull out of my dress and show the boys. Can I show my belly button? Do boys like belly buttons? What about toes—does Charlie enjoy it when you show him your feet?"

"That," I told her sharply, "you will have to ask him yourself."

And, brazen little thing that she was, she did—she went right up to Charlie the next day and asked if it sent him flipping when I showed him my feet. And when all he offered was a shrug, she slipped off a shoe and wiggled her toes at him.

"She didn't," I said.

"She did," he answered, laughing because I wasn't amused.

The silly, reckless hussy—stealing my Charlie, giving it a try. I had a mind to put her over my lap and spank the dickens out of her.

~ CHAPTER 10 ~

LAVINIA
TIME WAS RACING—
THE GOOD AND THE BAD,
THE BAD AND THE GOOD

Charlie and I had met in December, and the wedding was booked for February, at Grace Church, on Broadway. Mr. Barnum announced it in all the papers, and we were quickly famous as the "Little Couple."

We went to Brady's for a photograph, and Mr. Barnum set aside a parlor in the Museum where Charlie and I signed copies of our picture for the crowds that came to see us. Thousands came, from as far away as Pennsylvania and Maryland.

It was a windfall for the Museum. Tom Thumb actually going to be married! And the bride-to-be (*me!*) advertised everywhere as "the Queen of Beauty."

Proceeds at the door were running so high that Mr. Barnum offered us a considerable amount of money if we would agree to postpone the wedding by a month, to take advantage of the public interest. A bonus of fifteen thousand dollars. It was a handsome sum, more than my father made as a farmer in an entire year. And more than Charlie's father had ever made as a carpenter. But—postpone the wedding? I put my foot down about that, and Charlie stood by me. I said no, flat no. And, in his genial way, Mr. Barnum smiled and backed off.

But a week later he cornered Charlie, saying he had arranged with Sam Lord, of Lord & Taylor, that we would go on display—Charlie and I—in one of the store's windows. Lord's idea was that we would wear our wedding clothes, I in my gown and Charlie in his swallowtail, and we could lie side by side on the wedding bed that Mr. Barnum was giving us as a gift.

When Charlie told me, I was aghast.

"I know, I know," he said.

"Not in a store window," I said.

"Lord told him we wouldn't have to hold hands, just lie there and smile at the passersby."

Well, there was no way. No way was I going to lie in a bed in a window at Lord & Taylor's and have every passing shopper thinking smutty, prurient thoughts about us. Even if we inspired beautiful, gorgeous, uplifting thoughts, the answer was no. And Charlie agreed.

But when he passed that along, Mr. Barnum suggested a compromise. Instead of us, they would put just our wedding clothes in the window, and a few small items—a brush, a comb, our little shoes. The jewelry I was to wear—the bracelet, necklace, earrings, the diamond star for my hair, all of them Charlie's personal gifts to me. The whole idea of a public display of our things, our personal things, was just too humiliating.

Charlie thought so, too, though he was doing his best to be conciliatory. "Barnum is paying for the wedding," he said.

"I know that. But it doesn't give him the right to trample on our dignity. And besides, he's paying for it out of the profits from selling our pictures. He told me that himself."

"The gown, the cake, the church, the reception," Charlie said. "Two thousand invitations. All of it. The whole thing."

"So?"

"He needs it."

"Why?"

"He made promises to Sam Lord. He's trying to save face. You know how it is."

"Save face? By putting our underclothes on display? He might at least have asked us first, before he made promises."

Charlie put his hand on my arm, trying to calm me. "Just the gown and the jewels," he said. "Not the underclothes."

"That's better?"

"No. But a lot better than us in that dumb bed in that silly window."

I was not happy, not happy at all. With gathering speed, the wedding was becoming a thing—a grossly public thing. A commercial thing. We were the little couple, the tiny couple, the about-to-be-married adorable small ones. Did I want this? Did I? Even the honeymoon—that, too. Plans were already in the making for a honeymoon tour through New England and Canada, and then abroad, from port to port, charging admission—and everywhere to do at least one song in our wedding clothes. That's a honeymoon?

I was beginning to feel I was in a tight closet and the walls were closing in on me. Not ordinary walls, but walls made of thick glass, and everyone watching, noses pressing against the glass as I twisted and turned and struggled with the door, which was sealed tight. This was the new world I was in. I'd had a small taste of it when I was aboard the river showboat, but never anything on this scale. It was my wedding they were talking about.

I looked at Charlie. "Will it always be this way?"

There was a vacancy in his gaze. "Sometimes I go home to my boat," he said. "And my ponies."

"But never for very long."

"No. Never for long."

Three weeks before the wedding, Lord & Taylor had our wedding clothes in the window, draped across a bed with a carved rosewood headboard, which Mr. Barnum had ordered from France, as a gift for us. Charlie's linen shirt and silk socks were there, along with my gown and veil, and my satin shoes.

Horace Greeley's *Tribune* considered the display dignified and proper. But Greeley and Mr. Barnum were old friends, very thick and loyal. No so, however, with James Gordon Bennett of the *Herald*—he thought it an embarrassment that in a time of war, with brave men dying, the country was doting on two dwarfs. Charlie told me that Bennett and Barnum were long-standing enemies, with Bennett never missing a chance to nip at Mr. Barnum, and that's all that was going on here. Still, I took Bennett's side, because it expressed my feelings perfectly. All those boys, so many wounded, so many dead—and everyone doting childishly on Charlie and me.

Mr. Barnum was so infuriated that he pulled all of his ads from the *Herald* and persuaded many of his Broadway friends to do the same.

I looked at Charlie. "That's how it's done?"

"That's how it's done. They do it to each other all the time."

Then, taking my hands in both of his, he told me, softly, calmly, not to be too upset by this Lord & Taylor stuff. It was the war, he said. The war had become an ugly beast, people were desperate for a diversion. "People can stare at bad news for only so long," he said, "then they need something else. And if my silk socks and your satin shoes do the trick, why not let them have that?"

And when he sensed I was still less than happy, he leaned close. "Look at it this way—they didn't display our underwear."

He brought me to Angelica's, where we had French pastries filled with cream, and fed ourselves fat. And I worried that I would never fit into my gown.

I am always struck by the way in which memory, in its ungainly manner, leaps about and catches you by surprise. A week before the wedding, I rode out with Charlie to Grace Church, on Broadway and Tenth, wanting to have a quiet look at it before our rehearsal. It was a handsome limestone building done in the Gothic style.

As we moved about, admiring the baptistry and the stained glass windows, I caught sight of a young mulatto woman in the east chancel, polishing brass candlesticks. Her face, the nobility of her features, so lovely—it lit a lamp inside me and brought me back some years. I was on that riverboat again, at a pier in New Orleans. Among the visitors was a mulatto girl of remarkable beauty, so soulful, I couldn't take my eyes from her. She was the property of a wealthy plantation owner who noticed my interest—and he, in turn, was so taken with me that he offered to give me the girl as a gift. "You may take her home with you," he said. "She will prove a fine servant."

But the whole notion of owning somebody was so abhorrent that, as politely as possible, I declined.

We were a whole week in New Orleans, enjoying the comforts of a hotel—and that poor girl, she had gotten it into her head that she now belonged to me. Every day she came to the hotel and I would find her waiting in the lobby, eager to help me in any way she could. But I would simply bring her to the dining room and treat her to ice cream, or whatever else caught her fancy.

And only now, watching this other girl as she polished the brass candlesticks, did I become aware of the wrong thing I had done. I should have taken that girl. I could have brought her with me, all the way home to Massachusetts, and could have set her free. Could have done that, taken her out of slavery. Why hadn't I thought of that? Such guilt I felt, realizing, too late, what I could have done. I simply didn't see. Did—not—see.

While Charlie roved about the church, I stood there, by the chancel, watching this other mulatto girl as she worked on the brass. I felt solemn and prayerful. I must do better, I thought. I will keep my eyes open and try never again to be blind, as I'd been in New Orleans.

Later, when I told Charlie about that girl in New Orleans, he was very comforting, reminding me that New Orleans was now in Union hands, and she was better off down there, among people and places that she knew. Not to worry, he said. Not to be upset.

But still, I thought. Still. What if she suffered terrible things in the time since I saw her, things she would have been spared if I had only been more thoughtful. Was she beaten? Abused? Maltreated? And even now, was that a good place to be, with all the turmoil and disruption from the war? Was she even still alive? I had simply been blind. Didn't understand. Did—not—see.

A few days after our visit to Grace Church, Charlie brought me on yet another ferry ride to Brooklyn, in search of a restaurant he'd heard good things about, Peladio's.

A brisk, chilly day, clear and not a cloud. On deck, leaning against the rail, we had a wide view of the East River. Boats coming and going, schooners, sloops, tugboats pulling barges. Directly ahead, the hills of Brooklyn dotted with houses and farms, and, down by the docks, the gray granite walls of the storehouses. And the gulls, whole flocks of them, some swooping about, and others floating on the water.

It was a cutting wind, those few minutes on the ferry. We leaned close to each other, and Charlie kept one hand firm on the rail, as did I, lest a sudden blast send us sprawling.

When we reached the terminal in Brooklyn, we strolled, for a while, then went to Peladio's, and treated ourselves to clams on the shell.

I was troubled, yet, about that mulatto girl down in New Orleans. And I worried, too, about my brother Benjamin. I had more of his letters with me, and showed them to Charlie.

Hey You, Beautiful Small You—

Thanks for the toothbrush, and for the licorice sticks! You can forget about the socks, though—my tent partner gets a new pair every week from his girlfriend. He now has more than he'll ever need, and throws the extras in my direction.

Dear Miss Know-Everybody—

If you meet Mrs. Lincoln, say hello. And if you see U. S. Grant, tell him I'm suffering from hives and still waiting for a promotion. If you run into Jeff Davis anywhere, that dummy, that flap-brain, give him a triple dose of those Kermott's Mandrake Pills that Pa uses when his bowels are stopped up. That gooseberry Davis, he is so compacted it's affecting his brain. Did you ever meet him when you were on the showboat?

Dear Miss Crazy-Dream—

For real, what you tell me? Thumb? Tom Thumb himself? That zingaling mini-dwarf you sent a letter to when you were a kid and he never wrote back? Did you tell him about that? Did you remind him and shame him? And now you are going to the altar with the

*guy? And me? You forgot about me? In the garden, by the roses, six
years old, you swore I was the only one you would ever marry. This is
faithfulness? This is till-death-do-us-part? Such, alas, is the fickleness
of women! Such! Such! Send a picture—caught his act in some ding-
a-ling town five years ago but I forget what he looks like.*

After the clams, we sat a long time over coffee. Our table was by a wide
window with a view of Manhattan across the water, the tall masts of
the ships ringing the shoreline. And, inland, the spire of Trinity Church
rising taller than anything around it.

"I want a family," I said, and was a little surprised to hear myself
saying that—it seemed to surface out of nowhere. "A boy and a girl."

For him, too, I saw, it came as a surprise. All his life onstage, rushing about on one tour after another, London, Paris, Cuba, Montreal, I
couldn't imagine he ever gave much thought to having a family of his
own, babies crying and screaming and waking him up at night.

"What if it's two boys," he said.

"I'll take what comes," I answered, with a shrug and a lazy smile.

"Or two girls."

"If they're as quirky and demanding as my sister Minnie, it will be
a trial."

And beyond all of that—boys or girls, and how many—was the
glaring thing we didn't talk about: Would they be tiny people like us,
or would they be normal, towering above us? And how would we quite
manage that? It was a doubt, an apprehension that hung in the air,
unspoken, like the gulls that we saw through the window, riding the
wind.

I mentioned the children my older sisters had, what fun they were.
And he told me about his sisters' children. He had seen them as babies,
he said, but when he next saw them, after his long travels, they were
taller than he and didn't know what to make of him.

The sun wasn't down yet, but it was on its way.

"A boy and a girl," he said, in a relaxed, welcoming tone. And I felt good about that. That hope, that dream.

On our return trip, the ferry wasn't crowded, and we found a seat by ourselves, near a window. Charlie had his Whitman with him—not the oversize first edition but a smaller, portable version. He flipped through the pages, found what he wanted, and, sitting beside me, so I, too, could see the page, he read. Quietly, with feeling.

Others will enter the gates of the ferry, and cross from shore to
 shore,
Others will watch the run of the flood-tide,
Others will see the shipping of Manhattan north and west,
 and the heights of Brooklyn to the south and east,
Others will see the islands large and small,
Fifty years hence others will see them as they cross, the sun half an
 hour high,
A hundred years hence, or ever so many hundred years hence, others
 will see them,
Will enjoy the sunset, the pouring in of the flood-tide, the falling back
 to the sea of the ebb-tide.

It avails not, time nor place—distance avails not,
I am with you, you men and women of a generation,
 or ever so many generations hence,
Just as you feel when you look on the river and sky, so I felt,
Just as any of you is one of a living crowd, I was one of a crowd,
Just as you are refresh'd by the gladness of the river, and the bright
 flow, I was refresh'd,
Just as you stand and lean on the rail, yet hurry with the swift
 current, I stood, yet was hurried,

Just as you look on the numberless masts of ships,
 and the thick-stemm'd pipes of steamboats, I look'd.

I too many and many a time cross'd the river of old,
Watched the Twelfth-month sea-gulls, saw them high in the
 air floating with motionless wings, oscillating their bodies . . .

He stopped there, his eyes gazing at my eyes, and mine at his.

"Worth the trip?"

I nodded. Yes, indeed, worth the trip.

PART FOUR

THE CELTIC FERTILITY CROSS

∾ CHAPTER 11 ∾

THE GRAND PIANO
AT THE METROPOLITAN HOTEL

The wedding was a large, ambitious thing, but elegant, not the circus Vinny had feared—and, despite all of her earlier misgivings about the way Barnum was handling things, she was really pleased. And that, for me, was what mattered.

Grace Church was packed, with an enormous crowd outside waiting to catch a glimpse of us. It was the second week in February, the day splashed with sunshine. When I stepped through the big front door and looked into the church, into that huge space with the high, Gothic vaulting and the long aisle leading to the altar, I felt, for a moment, that I was being swallowed by a whale. The big organ booming with lively selections from Rossini and Mendelssohn, making the floor vibrate, the notes rumbling through my feet and shaking my bones.

After a long, meaningful pause, the organ bounced into the wedding march, and that was our cue. With Minnie and the Commodore ahead of us, Vinny and I began our long walk toward the altar. Flowers and white sashes everywhere, the pews filled with smiling faces, one blurring into another.

Reverend Willey, who had baptized me in Bridgeport, was at the altar, along with Vinny's pastor from Middleboro, and the rector of Grace Church. Everything smooth and solemn, until the part where Reverend Willey asks the congregation if there is any reason why this man and this woman should not be joined in matrimony. Audible titters rising from the pews, a ripple, a rush of amusement, and we too, all of us at the altar, smiling, though for all the world I still don't know why. Why the laughter? Given our small size, was it a joke to think of us as a MAN and a WOMAN? Or were they imagining I was a hopeless rake, and it was hilarious to think I was a safe bet for an innocent bride—I who had kissed so many thousands of women as part of my act, for a shilling, a sou, a dime, or nothing at all. Such a tittering there was, some sort of massive nervous release, everybody a little thrown off to see four dwarfs not in a dime museum but in a church, at the altar.

At the reception, it was a hell of a crowd, with white-jacketed waiters rushing about, serving drinks and hors d'oeuvres. Barnum had rented the main ballroom at the Metropolitan Hotel, and invited two thousand guests. February 10, 1863. Lincoln was facing his third year as President. The war was not going well, and he was restlessly switching commanders. McClellan, sacked in November, replaced by Burnside, who was sacked in January after a bad time at Fredericksburg. So now it was Hooker's turn to try his luck, with everyone wondering, waiting. And what I noticed, in the grand ballroom at the Metropolitan, was that the wedding cake was twice my size—a tall, eighty-pound concoction from Barmore's, with an Egyptian temple on top, and angels playing harps.

The band rolled out the latest hits, "Sweet and Low" and "When Johnny Comes Marching Home," and some oldies too—"Flow Gently, Sweet Afton" and "Green Grow the Lilacs." And, the favorite at weddings, "Open Thy Lattice, Love."

Vinny, in white satin and lace, wore orange blossoms in her hair. We stood on a grand piano, which put us at a comfortable height for receiving our guests. They were smiling, chirping, smoking cigars, an immense, long line of them, all wanting to put their fingers on us, as if we were magical, a mere touch would bring luck, happiness, and long life. Sure, why not—touch a dwarf, live forever! Grab my arm, shake my hand. Grab Vinny's arm, snatch a kiss. The band played on, and the line of well-wishers continued to grow. Vinny rolled her eyes. I wiggled my toes. Barnum hobnobbed with the bankers and the politicos. Commodore Nutt was on top of a table, standing on his head.

It was a sea of faces out there, the gowns, the pearls, the dress suits, the stickpins and tiaras. I was wondering—all these people? For us? Because we're small? That's it? Tiny is good? Dwarfs matter? Not for the Bearded Lady, anything like this, nor for Fat Boy, or the Living Skeleton.

Nor for the giants, Goshen and Bihin—those two cranky giants. They performed together, but there were times when Barnum had to step in to keep them from coming to blows. I spotted Goshen far down the line, on his way to greet us—hard to miss him, so tall and fat. He was alone, I didn't see Bihin anywhere.

Then, as I stood there on that big piano, beside Vinny, amid the chatter and the tinkling of glasses and the strains of "Listen to the Mocking Bird," I was suddenly aware that she was slipping away, falling. It was Tiffany who caught her, Charles Tiffany, the jeweler.

"Have to take better care of your bride," he said. "We don't want nothin' terrible to happen, do we? Not to her!"

I put my arm around her waist. She leaned into me, and I knew how exhausted she was, worn down by the weight of the gown, and the endless nodding and smiling as the guests filed by.

The band was playing "Long, Long Ago," a song flavored with sadness—and that, for a while, was how I felt, standing on that piano on my wedding day, not unhappy but touched by a wisp of melancholy, though I hardly knew why.

Vinny sighed. We were a long time, up there on the piano.

George Opdyke, the newly elected Republican mayor, was there, and plenty of other Republicans, too. Barnum was a Lincoln Republican, but when he prepared the guest list, he threw his net wide and invited many Democrats, who were, at the moment, riding a high wave that was anti-war, anti-Lincoln, and anti-emancipation. Governor Seymour was there, and August Belmont, who was pushing General McClellan to run against Lincoln in the next election.

And, from the various districts, there were Democrats of many stripes and colors—Tammany Democrats, Mozart Democrats, Independent Democrats, Peace Democrats, and War Democrats. Fernando Wood, the ex-mayor and congressman-to-be, who had started with the soft-shell-hard-shell faction and evolved into an anti-war and pro-slavery Mozart Democrat, squeezed my arm so hard he nearly broke it.

They were all there, touching my hand, patting my shoulder, giving a nod, a wink, a gust of whisky breath. Grabbing at Vinny's arm and snatching a kiss. The governor of New Jersey, and his wife. The governor of Massachusetts. A Sioux chieftain from the Dakotas. A bahadur from Bangalore.

Even Mary Darling was there, the Museum's longtime magician, looking younger than ever and flaunting her magical powers. She carried a purse made of gold mesh. Not enough room in that purse for much of anything—but every time she opened it, a white dove flew out. Soon there was a whole flock of them, soaring about and delighting everyone. But they quickly became a nuisance, and the waiters were opening windows and shooing them out. Mary was at a table with a group of old Hunkers and Locofocos, who were gray, wrinkled, and out of date politically, but having a roaring good time.

I looked for Anna Swan, but never saw her. Nor did I see Isaac Sprague, the Living Skeleton. I had wanted Walt Whitman to be there, but Barnum struck him from the list and instead invited William Cullen Bryant, who didn't come. I looked for the Bearded Lady, Josephine Clofullia, but she wasn't there, either. When I was young, she used to let me comb her beard.

Then, towering and obese, casting a huge shadow, Routh Goshen, that aging giant, stood before me, like an image of death from one of the ancient manuscripts on display at the Museum. Unlike the other guests, he didn't touch me, and I was glad of that.

"Bihin?" I asked, wondering if he'd be arriving later. Barnum had invited all of the old-time performers.

"Him? Luckier than us all," Goshen said. "He has packed his bags and gone to God."

"Dead?"

"The same. It's a gift that awaits us all. Nevertheless, that was some act we had when you was a boy—me tryin' to catch you, and you escapin' between my legs. *Fun-ny*. Made people laugh. And now you—a married man. Someday we got to perform again."

He gave a big wink to Vinny, and swept away, plowing through the crowd like a rhinoceros plunging through a field of grass.

And I in my wedding shoes, on that piano—over an hour already, and more to come. Offering my dwarf hand to a bearded old man with one ear, to a gray-eyed woman with earrings that hung down to her shoulders. To a man with gold teeth, a woman with white eyebrows, a woman with no teeth and a hook nose—when I glanced over the shoulder of that woman, I saw, in the middle distance, a man standing alone, looking toward me. There was a mole on his left cheek, above his neatly trimmed beard. Of the two thousand guests in the hall, I knew at most only a few hundred—and this person, giving me a long look, was a man I'd seen before. But where or when, I couldn't imagine. It was, for sure, an uneasy feeling, knowing but not knowing.

After those few attention-getting moments when he stood on his head, the Commodore seemed to have settled down. He sat out most of the reception at a table with his parents, looking bored and thoroughly lost.

Minnie, all rouged up and wearing a wreath of roses in her hair, did a lot of moving around, meeting people. She spoke to General Burnside and Mayor Opdyke, and Governor Seymour. Bright eyes she had, full of life and eagerness, and a wry humor, too, a crisp irony in the way she looked at things. Poor kid, her breasts were still less than what she'd been hoping for, and when she saw how the dressmaker had padded out the gown on top, she said, "My, my, seems like they sewed just about everything in there except the nipples."

She was thirteen, but Barnum had put it in a news release that she was sweet sixteen. Then he did what was, I thought, a very wrong thing. Before the wedding, he brought Minnie and the Commodore to Brady's and had them photographed together—the Commodore, rejected by Vinny, now on bended knee, suing for the hand of the younger sister. It was a joke, a humbug. It sold well at the Museum, but for Minnie it was a bad thing, because she came out of it with a crush on the Commodore. And he—older than she and soon to turn nineteen—he wasn't seeing her at all.

Talk to her, I told Vinny. Don't let her go down that road. But Vinny had already spoken to her, and there was no way Minnie was going to get past this without being hurt.

During the reception, the gifts we'd received were on display in a parlor off the ballroom. Everyone had been so kind to us. Lincoln sent a set of Chinese fire screens inlaid with gold and mother-of-pearl, and Queen Victoria sent an ermine cape for Vinny. There were earrings, candlesticks, crystal bowls. A necklace of Tuscan gold from Mrs. Belmont, a porcelain dinner set from Mrs. Roosevelt, and a silver-plated sewing machine from the Wheeler and Wilson Company in Bridgeport.

Barnum gave us a Swiss music box with a feathered bird in a spun-silver nest, the bird warbling as if it were alive. Vinny was enchanted, I think she had more pleasure from that bird than from anything else.

Edwin Booth, the Shakespearean actor, as famous as his father had been, sent fancy slippers, ornamented with gold and silver, for each of us—his way of acknowledging our own small success as theater people. In ancient times, high-heeled buskins were the footwear for tragedy, but low slippers for comic actors and entertainers. It was a handsome way of saluting us. And how could any of us on that happy day have foreseen the hateful thing his brother John Wilkes Booth would do only two years later. How it shook us, and took the heart out of everything.

I kept those slippers, and have never worn them. They're in a drawer, for the memory. And whenever I catch sight of them, I am always amazed how two brothers, actors from a family of actors, could be so unlike, one loyal to the Union, the other an assassin.

After the reception, there was a dinner party with our families and with Barnum's family. Later, at ten, after Vinny and I had gone up to our room, a band and a chorus stood under our window, on Broadway, and serenaded us for an hour.

The street was so crowded with well-wishers that traffic had to be detoured on to other streets. A raw February night, yet all those people turned out for us, faces lit by the gas lamps. And the band tireless, play-

ing "Beautiful Dreamer," "Summer Longings," "Kissing in the Dark,"
while stray dogs were romping around, having a wild time.

Vinny and I watched from the balcony, wearing coats against the
cold. I knew what she was thinking. She was worrying about her brother
Benjamin, down there in Virginia. Even Greeley was complaining now
about Lincoln—too many dead, too many yet to die.

"Let's go inside," Vinny said. "I'm freezing." So was I, it was bitter
cold. We lingered a moment on the balcony, waving to the crowd and
the chorus, and as we turned to go, I realized that the tall one out there,
among the singers, was Anna, with a scarf around her head, singing her
heart out. I lifted my hand again, waving, and still the band played, and
we went inside.

And, in that room where Washington Irving had spent a night,
where Robert E. Lee, Harriet Beecher Stowe, Henry Thoreau, and
Susan B. Anthony had each spent some time—in that very room with
its enormous four-poster bed and a log burning in the fireplace, I
reached out for Vinny but she slipped away, rushing to her luggage,
and after rummaging briefly, she pulled something out and, facing me,
held it aloft.

"What in the world . . . ?"

"My sister Caroline gave it to me. It's a Celtic fertility cross. It's been
in the family a long, long time. My mother gave it to my sister Sarah,
and Sarah gave it to Caroline."

It was tarnished silver, with engravings on it—nothing enormous,
but large for her little hands. She went to the bed and, reaching up,
slipped it under the pillow.

Then she had her hands on me. She opened my shirt and slipped
her hand down into my pants, eagerly. After a few moments of that,
touching and holding, and kissing, her tongue in my mouth and mine
into hers, after some of that, we were hurriedly pulling away our clothes,
and I almost tore her gown trying to help her off with it, and the pet-

ticoats underneath. She kicked off her shoes, one hit the ceiling. And there we were, the first time that way together, all of her and all of me, so hot for each other, grabbing and holding and clinging and clutching.

And then the great challenge, to climb onto that high, lofty bed, a four-poster with a silk canopy. Even for normal people it was high— there was a wooden step-up on each side. I helped her, gave her a boost, both of us suddenly giddy, and when she was there, she pulled at my arms and I clambered up, and was aboard.

Then the giddiness was gone, and there was only the eagerness, the hunger. So ripely sensual she was, so urgent, and I the same, my skin on hers, hers on mine, and moments when it seemed there was no skin between us at all—we were merging, she needing me and I needing her, feeling the warmth, the heat, the pulse, as we thrashed about, roving from top to bottom of that immense bed.

The Celtic cross that her sister had given her moved around that night, like everything else. Pillows on the floor, sheets torn away, logs gone to embers in the fireplace, and when we awoke the next morning, dreamy and slow, after very little sleep, I found the cross wedged between her back and my chest, sticky and warm, a kind of blessing.

Then the struggle to move down off that high bed, onto the floor, harder than the climbing up had been.

~ **CHAPTER 12** ~

ON THE BONY LAP
OF LANKY LINCOLN

Three days after the wedding, Lincoln hosted a reception for us at the White House.

I had been there once before, many years earlier, invited by President Polk. Poky Polk, Barnum dubbed him, because he seemed plodding and dull, and gave no hint at all of being capable of a laugh.

And now, a few Presidents later, instead of Poky Polk it was Lanky Lincoln, about whom countless jokes were told because of his stovepipe hat, which he wore cocked at the back of his head, and his wrinkled black suits, which hung loose and shabby on his bony body. But I liked the carelessness, it showed there was more on his mind than the color of his socks.

We were in the East Room, chairs and sofas covered with damask. A large, long table held candied fruit and sugar confections, and a multilayered white cake with a bride and groom on top, bearing a striking resemblance to Vinny and me.

The guests were mostly members of the cabinet and their families. Gideon Welles, with his bush of white whiskers, and the war secretary, Edwin Stanton, long strands of his woolly beard rippling down across his chest like a gray waterfall. A few senators, Sumner and Trumbull, and some generals—Fry, Hooker, Banks, and Crook. And General Butler, known as Beast Butler because of his rough hand when he governed New Orleans after it was captured. So rough, Lincoln had to have him reassigned. He was known, too, as Spoons, having been spotted slipping off with a pocketful of silverware one evening, after dining at a French restaurant in the Vieux Carré.

Also at the reception was George Custer, then a captain, an aide-de-camp to one of the generals—trim and thin and young, two years younger than I, and who could have imagined that within a few months he would be a general? When that happened, I was astonished, and not a little jealous. A general at twenty-three, the youngest in the army. If I weren't a dwarf, could that have been me? In charge of my own brigade? With a bushy moustache and long, curly locks and shiny buttons on my shirt?

Mary Lincoln wore a pink silk gown, off the shoulder and low, with pearls around her neck and roses in her hair. She had been wearing black ever since her son Willie died a year earlier, of bilious fever, but now she was wearing colors again. She was a bright, vivacious woman, quick and sparkling, with blue eyes, glints of bronze in her hair, an energetic smile, and long eyelashes that she knew how to use.

But you could feel the strain, the tension. Two of her four sons were dead, and one of her half brothers, Sam Todd, had been killed at Shiloh, fighting for the rebels. Her family, the Todds, were slave owners from Kentucky, and, even though Kentucky had declared itself neutral, the Todds fought for the South. She had a brother-in-law who was a Confederate general. It must have been hell for her, two of her children dead and the political split in her family, with Southerners thinking of her as a traitor, and not a few Northerners suspecting she was a spy for the South.

She was more than a foot shorter than Lincoln, who towered above everyone in the room. The top of my head reached just above his knees. He wore a black suit, a black tie knotted into a bow, and moccasin slippers that bore his initials in beadwork, *AL*. His nose and ears too large for his head, and his bronze face crisscrossed with wrinkles. There was a glimmer in his eye, a shrewdness. His nose straight and long, and a prominent vein looping across his forehead. On the right side of his face, a warty growth that vanished when his face crinkled with a smile, but when he wasn't smiling it was visible to the point of distraction. I couldn't take my eyes off it, watching as it appeared and disappeared, and reappeared.

He showed me his watch, taking it from his vest pocket—a large, silver thing on a gold chain. It told not just the hours but the date as well. "See? See what it does? The only thing it does not do is tell me where I am and what in God's world I should do next!"

His youngest son, Tad, ten, the one born with a cleft palate, was puzzled that Vinny and I could be so short. And Lincoln, nodding, says, "The simple truth, Tad, is that Dame Nature is a quirky lady who enjoys doing strange things. And here," pointing to himself and to me, "here you can see the whole story, the long and the short of it."

Well, he was a punster. He had a gift. It was an age of puns, puns popping like grease in a frying pan—and Lincoln, in his way, was a better-than-average chef.

I'd been a bit crampy earlier in the day, something I ate, a smidgen of gas squirreling around in my intestines. And I felt crampy again just then, but I was managing.

Seward drank whisky, Stanton took rum. General Butler, who had taken both whisky and rum, was slumped in an easy chair, dozing. Gideon Welles smoked a cigar, as did Custer and Chase. Lincoln ate an apple, long teeth biting crisply through the skin and carving into the white. When he was done, he dropped the core into a saucer and, rising from his chair, he approached the table where the tarts and sweetmeats were spread out. Tapping a spoon against a glass, he summoned everyone's attention.

He offered words of welcome to Vinny and me—then, drawing from his pocket a clipping from a newspaper, he read, for our amusement, the latest description of himself that his secretary had clipped from a Richmond newspaper, written by an author who remained anonymous.

> Mr. Lincoln stands six feet twelve in his socks, which he changes once every ten days. His anatomy is composed mostly of bones, and when walking he resembles the offspring of a happy marriage between a derrick and a windmill. His head is shaped something like a rutabaga, and his complexion is that of a Saratoga trunk.

He hung silent for a moment, then he broke loose with deep, rumbling laughter, which was joined by ripples of amusement spreading through the room. He turned sharply and pinned me with his quick gray eyes. "General Tom Thumb, tell me—what do you think of that?"

"I think," I said, "I think, perhaps, the rutabaga was not entirely fair."

"Just so," he answered. "My head is not a rutabaga. It's more in the nature of a cauliflower not yet ripe for picking."

"And most days," his wife chimed in, "most days, it's an overripe pumpkin that has baked in the sun too long." And with that, amid a storm of laughter, she took hold of Vinny's hand and led her away, to show her about the house. They had met before, in Kentucky, when

Vinny was performing on a riverboat, the year before the war, and now they were getting on very well together, enjoying their memories of a better time.

I was alone on the small couch, with Lincoln across from me in a rocker, and Seward, Welles, and Stanton nearby. There was some talk about the new conscription law that was in preparation. At the start, both sides had gone to war with volunteer armies, but now the losses were so great, from casualties and desertions, that some form of conscription had become necessary. The South was already using a draft, and Congress was working on a conscription act for the North.

Seward, speaking to Lincoln, bent his eyes in my direction. "What do you think? Shall we draft him?"

"I don't see how," Lincoln replied. "How can we draft someone who already holds the rank of general? And for the time being, the only service this young officer will be performing will be on the home front—of the matrimonial kind."

This drew a lazy guffaw from General Butler, who had roused himself from his slumber and was working again on a glass of Kentucky bourbon. Seward smiled, Stanton grinned. Welles scratched an itch at the back of his head.

And I, squirming around, readjusting myself on the couch, even to me it came as a surprise—I passed gas. Audibly. A skimpy little breezer, a tiny piccolo squeak—and Lincoln, fixing me with his piercing gray eyes, leaned back and erupted with floating folds of laughter.

"If you want to defeat the rebel army," he said, "you will have to shoot with a bigger gun than that." Then, as if to reward me, he plucked me from the sofa and, returning to his rocker, he sat me on his lap.

And I, a connoisseur of laps, having sat on countless laps in many parts of the world, understood that this moment was indeed something special. This was not the tired lap of the old Duke of Cambridge, or the gunmetal lap of Wellington, the Iron Duke who had crushed

Napoléon. Nor was it the despairing lap of Louis Philippe, who saw the end approaching and fled Paris for the safety of England. This, the Lincoln lap, was a lap that knew loneliness, doubt, persistence, and hard times. In its raw boniness there was no fakery, nothing but rock-bottom truth. Flinty, tough, solid as brick, and hard on my ass. There was a leathery smell to him, as if, in some mysterious way, his body had been constructed out of rawhide.

Seward gazed at the ceiling. Stanton studied his fingernails. Chase, seeing me on Lincoln's lap, seemed subtly jealous. He was always submitting his resignation, needing to be coddled and loved and persuaded to stay on.

Lincoln, his mouth close to my ear, asked if I had ever read the dialogues of Plato, and I confessed I had not.

"Read him, read him—he has little to say about marriage but much to say about love. *Eros*, Mr. Stratton. It drives the stars, and it is, you realize, a powerful aid to digestion."

Mrs. Lincoln returned with Vinny, and moments later a bevy of waiters delivered a late-evening snack of oysters and canvasback duck. The guests lined up, serving themselves from large, gold-rimmed platters. Some stood about in groups, eating from their plates, others sat on settees and chairs, or on the floor. Mary Lincoln chatted with Sumner in French, and with Secretary Seward she spoke not at all. It was well known that she disliked him, and it was impossible not to notice that she deliberately avoided him.

Custer, on his feet near the middle of the room, was surrounded by a crowd of young ladies—daughters of senators and cabinet members—all pressing close, lusting for a touch of him, wanting to smother themselves in the long blond locks that tumbled in curls down to his shoulders.

In the rumbling hubbub, while waiters brought more platters to the table, Vinny drew me away and we slipped off, finding our way to the cloakroom—and there, amid the tunics and coats and capes suspended from hooks and hangers, she put her mouth on mine, and with a delicious, ferocious suddenness, we were into the throes of lovemaking, hungry for each other, gripping and clutching, leaning into those heavy garments that smelled of tobacco and wool and perfume. She was so wrought up that she let out a high-pitched squeal of delight—then a yelp, and another.

The door snapped open and a skinny butler with a candle poked his head into the room, to see what the noise might be. We froze and held our breath, hidden among the coats and scarves. When the butler departed, we were at each other again, and she bit me, hard, on my neck.

Not till the next morning, at breakfast, in the dining room of the Willard Hotel, did I think to ask her where Mary Lincoln had brought her when she took her by the hand and led her out of the East Room.

"Upstairs," she said, "to her bedroom. She opened her chifforobe and showed me her gloves."

"Gloves?"

"Hundreds of them. She took them from the drawers and tossed them onto the bed. Suede, leather, cotton, wool, calfskin. Imported from—everywhere."

Those were the days when women dined, in public, with their gloves on, and if you were often in public, you needed, obviously, many pairs, a fresh supply while others were being cleaned. But a hundred?

"More than that," Vinny said.

"Two hundred?"

"I suspect—more."

Gloves! Such an obsession. This need to ornament her hands, to hide them, keep them warm, protect them, make them fancy, stylish. We all knew of her shopping trips to New York, her odysseys to the palaces of fashion along Broadway, and the many on Sixth Avenue. Even when she wore mourning for Willie, she made the trip from Washington. At the White House she had her own seamstress, a black woman, Elizabeth Keckley, but always this craving for the latest fashions from abroad. Buying dresses, scarves, coats. Sometimes she stayed at the St. Denis and sometimes at the Fifth Avenue—reporters tracked her, watching her moves, her purchases. But no one had yet picked up on her passion for gloves.

"In her excitement, she wanted to give me a pair, telling me to take whatever struck my fancy—but as soon as the words were out of her mouth, she realized that none of her gloves could possibly fit my small hands. She was so embarrassed, she kept apologizing, and promised to have a pair made for me."

Vinny had quite a few gloves of her own, a dozen pairs, I'd say. It wasn't a hundred, but enough.

"You need more gloves?" I said.

She lifted her face in a quiet, urgent way that made her look prettier than pretty. "A woman always needs more of everything," she said.

Before we left for home, we crossed over to the military encampment on Arlington Heights and met up with Benjamin, Vinny's brother. Lincoln had signed a pass for us, and we rode across the Long Bridge, into the sprawling camp, where over a hundred and fifty thousand soldiers were living in tents and wooden huts. Some had seen me before, and some had seen Vinny, but this was the first time they saw us together. They cheered, saluted, and shouted, wishing us happiness. Threw their caps in the air. "Saw you in Boston, General. . . . Saw you in Hartford. . . . Saw you in Scranton. . . ." And shouts for Vinny, too. "Saw you on the showboat. . . . In Paducah . . . In Galena . . . In St. Louis . . . In Hannibal. . . ."

Benjamin was just back from the front, arriving the previous afternoon, and was waiting for us at a central post. He was tall and lean, just over six feet. When Vinny saw him, she ran to him and he picked her up, and she threw her arms around his neck and clung to him. He swayed from side to side, cradling her, and she pressed her face against his.

For a stark, empty moment, I felt abandoned, even jealous, seeing how attached she was to him, and how deep her emotions ran. She worried about him, I knew. But only now did I begin to understand how intense the worry was, and how powerful the attachment.

He'd been granted a leave of a few days, and we brought him to Baltimore with us, where we stopped overnight. We rented a swanky room for him, where he was able to take a hot bath and get into fresh clothes. Late in the day, we sat a long time over dinner, wanting to hear everything—where he'd been and how he was doing, and what the fighting was like.

What he said, though, was that army life was basically boring. "Mainly you just sit around waiting to be sent out somewhere. When you get where they want you, they don't need you, and they march you right back to where you were in the first place." So far, he hadn't even seen a graycoat, much less shot at one.

"In camp, you gamble, sleep, booze, and sing old songs. You roll a cigarette, write a letter. Write one for a guy who can't write. Two tough bruisers wrestle and you bet on who will win. You bet on the rain—will it or won't it. A fat fly settles on your arm—bets go down as to whether or not you will get him with the first swat of your hand. You pull some lice out of your hair, set them on an oilskin, and everybody puts up money—which louse will be the first to get off the oilskin."

I looked at him across the apple crunch we were having for dessert. "Are you winning or losing?"

"Near breaking even," he answered, "though I am sometimes on the shy side."

Vinny gave him a hard study. She was filling up, emotion getting the better of her. "You don't have lice, Ben."

"Well, now and then. But this kid from Brattleboro that I tent with, he's got so many, he plucks them out and eats them."

"Oh, go away," she said, shaking her tiny fist. "Just—go away."

There was something of a family resemblance, the high cheekbones, the forehead, the upper lip, but with Ben everything was long, there is no other word for it, long arms, long legs, long jaw, long and lean.

After dinner we went outside, onto the veranda, and suddenly Vinny was weeping—because who really knew if Benjamin, my age, twenty-five, bright-eyed, tall, growing hair on his upper lip, would get through it all safely and make it back home?

Again he bent down and picked her up, and she had her arms around his neck, crying like a baby.

"See what you married?" he said to me. "She's my little sister. She always was a crybaby. Now she's gettin' me all wet up with these salty tears."

She clung to him as if she would die if anything happened to him.

The next morning, Benjamin headed back to Arlington, and Vinny and I trained back to New York and checked in to the St. Nicholas. We visited with the Barnums, then made an appearance at the Museum in our wedding togs. Anna Swan wasn't there, she was on tour up in Buffalo. Vinny was disappointed to have missed her. In Vinny's short time at the Museum, she and Anna had struck up a friendship. They saw each other over tea in the third-floor lounge, and I cautiously avoided them when they were together—trusting, hoping, that Anna would have the good sense never to mention the way I had doted on her.

Barnum told us Anna had been ill with cramps on the day of the wedding, and that was why she skipped the reception.

"I'll have to write to her," Vinny said. She wrote a seven-page letter on her lavender stationery, and signed it from both of us, "with love."

We stayed at the St. Nicholas, and when we weren't making appearances at the Museum and at other venues, we wandered around. A full afternoon up in Central Park, and another afternoon strolling around Washington Square. We also went to the Croton Reservoir on Fifth Avenue, that huge four-acre supply of city water contained by thick forty-four-foot walls. On top of the walls there was a walkway, and what a good feeling to stroll there, high above the street traffic and close to the water, with sunlight glimmering off the surface, and a few puffy clouds wandering across the sky.

On a Friday, much to my surprise, there was a package for me at the Museum, from the White House. It was a copy of Plato's *Symposium*, in the translation of Friedrich Funke, sent by the President, with a brief note pointing me to the passage where Plato brings Aristophanes into the dialogue, and Aristophanes explains his theory of love and sex.

His notion was that human beings originally had four arms, four legs, and a large, round body. And they were happy—no bad moods, no aches and pains. But Zeus, in a cranky moment, split them apart into separate halves, with only two arms and two legs, and, ever since, the halves have been suffering from headaches and trying to get back together.

In his note, Lincoln said he'd never found a more sensible explanation for all the zigzagging tomfoolery that sends people into mad spasms for each other, to have and to hold, for better and for worse.

Well, cockadoodle. Sugar and cream, and gooseberry pie. And for them, the Lincolns, you do have to wonder what kind of a marriage it was anyway. He talking about Plato and Eros, and she running up to New York, buying not just gloves and clothes, but anything else that caught her fancy—chinaware, goblets, gold-handled cutlery. Nothing serene about this union, if you listened to the press. He from log-cabin poverty, inward, with a casual manner and a rich sense of humor. And she from a wealthy, slave-owning family, fussy, demanding, given to outbursts, and a bit of a hellcat.

There was a story in the paper once, about a farmer who remembered a time when he delivered some vegetables that were a little past their prime. She berated him so fiercely that he went to Lincoln and complained about the treatment he'd received. Lincoln listened, then said, "My friend, I want you to know I truly regret this. But in all candor, can't you take for fifteen minutes what I have taken for fifteen years?"

True or not, it was exactly Lincoln—witty and wry. But when I told Vinny about it, she wasn't amused.

"I don't care if he *is* our President," she said. "He never should have said that. It isn't funny. Not funny at all." There was fire in her eyes, a firmness in her jaw. "If you ever talk about me like that, I'll slit my wrists. But not before slitting yours."

I'd never seen her so upset. For her, that story struck a nerve.

After our few weeks in New York, we had a week with her family, then a week at my mother's house in Bridgeport, where we mainly strolled and wandered about. The forsythia were in full bloom, and daffodils and hyacinths were beginning to appear, sprinkling the neighborhood with color.

My mother liked to sit by the window in the living room, browsing through a newspaper, or simply gazing at the road, watching the wagons and carriages that passed.

She was thinking of leaving the house in my hands and moving to West Haven, to live near her sister. As to the house, it was pretty much in my hands already. I had Ned Blossom taking care of the grounds and doing house repairs.

"You trust him?" Vinny asked. "When you're away?"

"Ned? He's good with a hammer and saw, I'm lucky to have him. The only problem with Ned is that he can't sing but thinks he can, and he's a little mad at me for not using my influence with Barnum to get him a spot in a show. But I make up for it with little gifts that I pick up for him when I'm on tour."

"You're pampering him."

"Not the way I'm pampering you."

"I don't want to be pampered."

"What was that line Lincoln found about you in the paper? *A dictionary of beauty and sweetness*?"

"Charlie—"

"I should shut up?"

"Yes."

"I'm no good?"

"You're good, but sometimes good is bad."

"What does that mean?"

"Don't you know?"

Of course I knew. My old friend Zootagataz—up is down, bad is good, and the layer cake stuffed with cherries and whipped cream and chunks of chocolate, which you gobbled up, gives you a bellyache. Zootagataz, Zatagatooz. But cake, at that moment, was not what I was thinking about.

I was thinking about Benjamin. He could pick Vinny up off her feet and swing her around, and that was something I could never do. It made me feel less than adequate, and again I hated the smallness of my body. How to compete with your wife's older brother who is six feet tall? How do you do that? And what good to be adored by all the royalty of Europe if you can't pick your little woman up and lift her to the sky?

She smiled, she pouted, smart as a squirrel and coy. In the house, when my mother wasn't around, Vinny ran naked through the rooms, wanting me to chase her. Up one flight of stairs and down another, my dwarf feet chasing her dwarf feet. She glanced back at me and stuck out her tongue. In the bedroom, she allowed me to catch up with her, and she stood by the bed, waiting, breathing hard.

One day, thinking my mother gone, we ran about wildly—but there she was, my Ma, my Mum, in the living room, sitting by the window, gazing out at the road. Right past her we ran, but she never noticed, never turned her head. We stopped short and tiptoed off, wearing our bare skin, Vinny pink and glowing, as if she'd come to life out of a painting in a museum. Through the kitchen we went and back to the dwarf apartment my father had designed for me when the house was built.

My poor mother, she spoke less and less, and now she was going deaf, too. She enjoyed sitting there, in her own silence, by the window.

The next day, Vinny and I were in the garden, just the two of us, on the wide wooden bench my father had made. We were sipping apple cider.

"Is that really true about Lincoln," she wondered, "what he said about Mary?"

She liked him and was trying her best not to think ill of him. Her eyes soft but skeptical, mixing doubt and confusion. "Did he really say that awful thing to that stupid vegetable man? And why was the man selling rotten vegetables anyway? Why didn't Lincoln tell him off, instead of making that mean joke about his wife?"

What could I say? *Ask him? Send a letter?* If I dared her, she would do it, I was sure she would.

A cardinal, bright red, was moving around on the big forsythia bush. Vinny saw it and gasped. "Oh, look," she said. "Look—so red!"

That bird, he was studying the bush, measuring it, checking it out, branch to branch, wondering if he should buy this bush and live in it, or look for another in a different neighborhood. Then, in a blink, he darted off and vanished into the trees—that fast, changed his mind about the bush, couldn't afford it, too much upkeep, too many repairs, and he wasn't ready for any of that.

"Silly bird," Vinny said. "Why'd he fly off like that? So pretty. But God, too jumpy and skittish. Out of his mind. That bird, it's—just a mistake!"

"Life's a mistake," I said. Then I sang for her, yet another song about Zatagatooz, my old nemesis, this one brand-new, bubbling up spontaneously, out of nowhere.

Zootagataz, Zatagatooz—
The world's a wild bird that's always bad news
It flutters and flies
And tells bitter lies—
That slimy deceiver will give you a fever,
It bends and it rips and it tears and it rends,
And gives you this war that never ends.
Zootagataz, Zatagatooz—
Who needs a red bird that wears dirty black shoes?

Vinny listened with a hint of disbelief in her eyes, as if uncertain—having doubts, regrets, second thoughts and even third and fourth thoughts about the man she married.

CHAPTER 13

THE HOT DAYS OF JULY

April, May, and June slipped away too quickly. We were suddenly into a hot July, and the departure date for our honeymoon tour was fast approaching. Barnum was sending us up into New England and beyond, to the nearby provinces of Canada. Then home for some recovery time before sailing off to Europe.

While readying ourselves for all that, Vinny and I were in New York, at the St. Nicholas, newer and bigger than the Astor and farther up on Broadway, a few blocks above Canal Street. Vinny liked it there, and why not, with the fancy rugs and vast stretches of walnut wainscoting, and frescoed ceilings in the parlors and dining halls. Six hundred rooms in that hotel, and a telegraph in the lobby.

But it was a bad time to be in the city. The new draft law was about to go into effect, and there was a lot of restlessness, a mean spirit brewing among low- and midlevel wage earners—street cleaners, factory workers, repairmen, bricklayers, garbage collectors.

Married men between twenty and thirty-five were eligible for the draft, and unmarried men between twenty and forty-five. No dwarfs, for sure. No albinos, no pinheads, no living skeletons, no armless men who could write with their toes.

A lottery was established to determine who would be called, and that seemed fair enough, except for the buyout provision. If you preferred not to go, you could pay someone to take your place—or you could give the government three hundred dollars, to be used as a bounty to induce someone else to go in your stead. Three hundred was a chunk, not the kind of cash a common laborer could easily come up with. And, as might have been expected, there suddenly was a furious antagonism toward men of the moneyed class, who were reviled and sneered at as the "three-hundred-dollar men."

"They're all so unhappy," Vinny said in her understated way. You could see it, almost taste it. Everyone just a bit off center, and some on the brink. Hotel clerks, waiters, deliverymen, people on the street. The working class and the poor, furious because if their number was called they had no choice but to go. And the rich out of joint because their high hats and gold-handled walking sticks were now a stigma. You could feel the steam building. And the blacks nervous, because they saw what the laborers saw. If the laborers were drafted, the blacks were there to take their jobs, and who would love them then?

Day by day the mess grew, and the governor, Horatio Seymour, a Peace Democrat, raising the specter of mob violence, almost sounding as if he were inviting it when he gave his Fourth of July speech at the Academy of Music. I was there, I heard what he said. He was playing to the bad mood in the crowd. And the crowd was right to be angry, because there was, plainly, an inequity in the law. It did favor the rich, and it put a huge burden on the working class, making it especially hard on the wives who were left behind with young children. The whole idea of putting up money for a substitute was plain wrong.

At the Museum, Vinny visited Anna and they had coffee together. They shared things—talk, bits of gossip, poems they found in the weeklies. Vinny gave Anna a piece of embroidery, and Anna gave her a copy of *Ivanhoe*. They were friends, giant Anna and little Vinny. I liked that. And their being friends somehow confirmed for me that I was past the madness I had been through about Anna. And what, I wondered, had produced it, that strange phase I had been in? Something I'd eaten? Too much celery? Too much salt? Too many macaroons? Could an honest, decent, well-meaning macaroon make a young dwarf dizzy and push him over the edge?

But still, strangely, she lingered, hovering in the folds and creases of my dwarf brain. She was hard to get rid of, that Anna Swan, a faint but lingering glimmer.

In the gallery of stuffed animals, amid lifelike zebras and coyotes, Isaac Sprague asked, in all seriousness, "Me—if my number comes up, you think they'll want me? Draft me? Give me a gun?" He, the fifty-pound miracle man, vanishing before your eyes. Everything he ate ran right through him. You could count his ribs, could see the outlines of his bones.

"Or me?" asked Fat Boy, who weighed three hundred and fifty pounds. No, they didn't want him. Nobody wanted him. Even Lena Serena didn't want him anymore. On most days, he didn't want himself.

"Or me?" said Madame Clofullia. "Will they want me?" She, the Bearded Lady from Switzerland, who, some years ago, had been accused of being a man in disguise and had to prove to a court-appointed doctor that she was not. No, the army would not want her.

Nor would they want Chang and Eng, the Siamese twins—they had fled the North and returned to their farm in North Carolina, where they owned slaves. The two sisters to whom they were married had given birth, so far, to a combined total of twenty-one children. The last I'd heard, Chang and Eng each had a son in the Confederate army—so better, really, if the twins did not show their faces around here anymore, ever.

One afternoon, after hiking back to my dressing room, I found an army officer waiting for me. A colonel with a long nose and intense dark eyes. "Like good wine," he said, "you improve with age. I saw you when you were ten. I saw you when you were fifteen. Never so good as you were today."

We sat by my dressing table, in front of the wide mirror. "You're not here just to flatter me," I said.

His name was Nickerson. "It's a mean war, and growing meaner. I'm here, Mr. Stratton, because your country needs you."

Me? Needs *me*? Is that what he said? I was still in a sweat from my breakdown dance, and had a flash memory of the crazy deep-night dreams I'd had at the start of the war—me, a dwarf, waving a sword, leading the charge into battle, guns going off all around me.

"I need a courier," he said.

"Like—the Pony Express?"

"Not quite. I need somebody who travels widely, is well known, and would never be suspected. We have people out there, trusted people, who pick up information. If they come directly to us, their cover will be blown and they have to worry about being shot in the head by a copperhead as they come and go from the local army headquarters. So we've set up a network of intermediaries, people like you, passing through town and not seen there again for a while, if ever. Simple enough, and safe. Somebody named Greenwood approaches you for your autograph and gives you a sealed envelope—you slip it into your pouch. You hold on to the envelope until a person from Foxglove Collection appears. You hand him the envelope, and he delivers to the nearest Intelligence unit for assessment, or to a secret drop-off site. That's it. The Greenwood people are local citizens who've agreed to be part of our network—barbers, waiters, bartenders, cleaning women. Widows of dead Union soldiers. Foxglove is mostly people on the move—coachmen, railroad conductors, workers on riverboats, moving from port to port. In unusual circumstances, we use locals and arrange a drop site."

As he spoke, I felt off-balance. Even, in a way, disappointed. He wasn't talking about going up in a hot-air balloon and spying on the enemy with a hand telescope. Nor was it the same as lighting the charge on a big Rodman cannon and hurling a two-hundred-and-fifty-pound shell toward a target three miles away.

"I know what you're thinking," he said. "You're wondering how important any of this can be. I assure you—some of the information that comes to us has already altered the course of the war. And as to safety, realize you're doubly insulated from detection, by Greenwood and by Foxglove. Just as they are insulated because you and others like you are acting as intermediaries."

But I was shaking my head. "Our upcoming tour—it's just through New England and lower Canada. Then home for a rest, and off to England. Not likely that we'll pick up anything about troop movements and other such stuff, if that's what you're looking for."

"I know that, yes. But you're aware there are copperheads everywhere, doing what they can to further the Southern cause. And what you may not know is that the South has undercover men in Canada, plotting sabotage in the big Northern cities. We keep an eye on them, to the extent that we can. Think of yourself as a drop site where information can be deposited—a *traveling* drop site, which makes it safer all around."

"Even in Canada? Greenwood?"

"Wherever you go, Greenwood and Foxglove will find you."

"War is too complicated."

"Because life is complicated. Worse than a nest of hornets drunk on bourbon."

"Zootagataz," I said.

"Zoota—?"

"A song I sometimes use. *Zootagataz, Zatagatooz—Don't walk in the rain if there are holes in your shoes.*"

"This war is giving us a lot of rain. And mud. Stay dry if you can. If anybody by the name of Greenwood approaches, you'll know what's happening. Greenwood—man or woman. And on all this, I don't want an answer now. In the morning, leave a message at the front desk—a simple yes or no and your initials, CS. Nothing more. I'll be out of here by ten. And do discuss it with your wife—she should know. Or she'll notice the envelopes and think you're in deep with some femme fatale. But important—tell no one else, not your most trusted friend. Secrecy is essential."

I looked at him straight on, then our eyes slid away and met in the mirror, eyeball to eyeball. "It's a good plan," I said. "But in my case, not realistic. When I'm on tour, we follow a loose schedule. If one town loves us, we hang in and give them more. If ticket sales are sour, we move out fast. If somebody is sick, we sit where we are. Maybe we all get sick, and we cancel out like crazy. One of your Greenwood people might be waiting for me in a city ninety miles away, and I never show."

"But your name is always in the newspaper," he answered. "People know where you are. If you're far away, my Greenwood person will make the trip—or find some other courier who is closer. In fact, the randomness of your tours is an advantage—it adds to your cover. No one in his right mind would imagine you could possibly be of use as a go-between."

Again I looked at him in the mirror. "What's the risk? I can't endanger my people."

"Right now," he said, "the way things are, you and your troupe will be a lot safer on the road than hanging around like sitting ducks at this Museum."

"You know something?"

"If I did, I would tell you. I know the possibilities and the probabilities. The vulnerabilities. The weak spots where a desperate enemy might take advantage."

"I'm a weak spot?"

"Hypothetically. If a Confederate agent were to grab you, Lincoln would free a hundred war prisoners to get you back."

I didn't like being a hypothetical. "That's all I'm worth? A hundred?"

"A thousand. Or maybe none. One way or another, when a hypothetical turns into a fact, there is no happiness in Eden."

He was turning up the heat, trying to scare me. I didn't like that, not at all.

At the hotel, before Vinny and I went to dinner, I told her about Nickerson. She'd spent most of the day shopping, preparing for the tour, finding new dresses to wear onstage. She was exhausted, but eager to hear about this strange person who had approached me in my dressing room.

I told her what Nickerson had asked of me, and that I was less than enthusiastic. Working in the shadows, dealing with people whose names I'd never know, being part of a process but having no information about the process itself—the details, who was reporting about whom. And the consequences—who would live, and, if it should come to that, who would die.

She listened, and understood. She, too, was troubled by the cloudy nature of it all. The strangeness, the passing of information without knowing what the information was—what would happen or not happen, and to whom.

We thought about it, and wondered. Then she leaned close. "But if it shortens the war by a month," she said, "or only a day, it will have been worth it. Do it for Benjamin," she said. "And for everyone else who has a brother in the war."

For Benjamin, that was worth thinking about. Easier, yes, if you're doing it for someone—even if you don't know what, or why. Still, I was troubled.

We had dinner at the hotel, and I was glad to have a reason not to think about Nickerson for a while. But it wasn't one of the better meals we'd had that week. The succotash overcooked and mushy, the chicken undercooked and unappealing, and the ice-cream dessert melting away into a sloppy soup when it arrived.

On the way back to our room, I stopped at the desk and left a message for Nickerson. A simple yes or no, he had said. Nothing else. A no. Or a yes. Or a no.

~ CHAPTER 14 ~

RAGE AND
SCREAMING MADNESS

In New York, the first lottery for the draft was held on a Saturday, the eleventh of July—and that, as it happened, was about a week after Meade stopped Lee at Gettysburg. It was a major victory, and, as we later understood, the big turning point in the war. But we didn't think of it that way till much later. There were many more battles ahead, and pain for both sides.

News of Lee's defeat had trickled in by telegraph on July 4, and there was an enormous sense of relief. With thousands of New York's troops pulled out to meet the emergency at Gettysburg, the city was defenseless. If Lee had managed to push past Meade, he would have been into New Jersey and upon New York in less than a week. So this was, really, very good news, about Lee's defeat. Yet there was no great joy in it because, as the names of the dead came in, so many were local boys from Manhattan and Brooklyn, and nearby towns in New Jersey.

At the lottery, two thousand were to be selected. On the first day, Saturday, some twelve hundred were chosen. The remaining selections would be made on Monday.

But Monday morning, before the lottery could be resumed, all hell broke loose. While Vinny and I were at breakfast, the concierge came into the dining room and announced that word was coming in over the telegraph about disturbances in many parts of the city. A crowd of laborers had marched up the West Side, on Eighth and Ninth Avenues, beating copper pots and shutting down shops and factories along the way. They were workers from the railroads, shipyards, and machine shops. They swung east and met up with other mobs, all converging on the Ninth District Headquarters on Third and Forty-Seventh, where the lottery was due to restart at ten thirty.

Vinny was eating a poached egg. I was working on sausages and toast. Before I had my second cup of coffee, the concierge was back with word that a group of volunteer firemen had stormed the district headquarters. They destroyed the lottery wheel and set fire to the building.

The hum and clatter of the dining hall subsided into a mystified silence. Firemen? Firemen did that? Burned a building?

Later, additional details filtered in. The volunteer firemen were in a rage because the new draft rules took away from volunteer firefighters their usual exemption from military service. These were members of the "Black Joke" Engine Company No. 33, and when other fire companies arrived to fight the fire, the Black Jokers threw rocks and drove them off.

At the desk, waiting for us, was a hand-delivered message from the Museum, telling us it would be closed for the day. From the clerk we learned other establishments were closing as well. Genin, Knox, Lord & Taylor, and dozens of others. Groceries, butchers, and barbershops, all shutting down. The violence was spreading.

We spent some time in one of the frescoed parlors. While I glanced through the newspapers, Vinny wrote in the little diary book that she keeps. People coming and going, a lot of restlessness, uncertainty, and soon enough we returned to our room.

Vinny was on edge, I could feel it. Not nervous, just wary, troubled. We were due to depart the next day for our tour of New England. Everyone had been gathering at the Astor. The Commodore, and Sylvester Bleeker and his wife. And all our people. Jerry Richardson, our pianist. Harry Nobbs, our advance man, and Ken Keeler, who guarded our money box. And the baggage boys, Aaron and Forbus. And Minnie, who had been brought in from Bridgeport by Barnum's daughter Helen. This was to have been our last day alone before linking up.

So, with the mobs and the violence, Vinny was upset, and who could blame her? I was not just on edge but fidgety, eager to know more. Things were happening, and I was itching to have a look.

"I'm going for a walk."

She gave me a lopsided glance, as if to say I was out of my mind.

"It's all right," I said. "The trouble is up in the Ninth District. Down here, there's nothing. In any case, they're not mad at me. They're angry about the draft."

"Don't go," she said, shaking her head, frowning, trying to dissuade me.

But I had this urge, this need to stretch my legs, and a hunger to find out more about what was going on, without getting too close to the trouble. I planted a kiss on her forehead, then grabbed my jacket and went.

It was a warm day, the air hot and syrupy. In the street, on the cobblestones, clumps of horse dung were baking in the sun. I wore a light jacket over my linen shirt, but quickly slipped it off, and was still too warm.

I went north along Broadway, past Spring and Prince, and was struck by the small amount of traffic. A few broughams and phaetons, a couple of hackneys, nothing like the usual crowds. I kept walking, and soon enough I heard them, the noise and the shouting, and at the next corner I saw them, a great mob of men in working clothes, coming down Houston and heading for Broadway, moving toward me with their NO DRAFT signs.

They were throwing rocks at stores and houses, smashing windows. Plenty of women with them, too, as fierce as the men. They hated Lincoln, hated the war, hated the draft, hated the rich, and hated the idea that, if their men went off, the blacks would be replacing them, taking their jobs, and what would there be for the men to come home to? It was a raging anxiety.

I ducked into the recessed entryway of an antiques shop and tried the door. It was locked. Still, I thought I was small enough, in that alcove, to go unnoticed.

Three of them had a black man, dragging him by the heels toward an alley. Another bunch were beating a white man—one grabbed the man's top hat and waved it about, shouting, "Kill him, kill the rich bastard!" Men in twill work pants and grease-stained cotton shirts, red suspenders and black suspenders, and caps, many caps, white caps, blue caps, checkered caps, the women in long, loose, homespun dresses, hair bedraggled, a few bonnets, hands grabbing at rocks for their men to throw. I felt the whole world had turned upside down.

Then one saw me, and seemed not to believe his eyes. "Hey, lookee the midge. A fuckin' dwarf, dat's what."

He was tall and stout, a roll of fat under his chin. He came close and picked me up, wrenching hard with both hands, twisting the breath out of me. Not a thought inside me, just the pain and the awareness. The madness was real, here and now. Happening. To me. The darkness. The pain. The dizziness. He held me aloft and I felt the big fingers squeezing my bones. "Lookee the midge," he shouted—and those moments, while he held me, were a blur, a wilderness of jerking and bending, yanking and joggling. He tossed me in the air and caught me, then threw me to a fat towhead in a red shirt, who tossed me to a blue shirt that smelled of grease.

"'Ey, it's Tom Thumb," someone shouted. "Tom Thumb hisself." They threw me back and forth, high in the air, and I knew—if I hit the ground, my head would crack open. The going up was good, a release from the crushing grip of hands and arms. But then the downward plunge and the pain as hands snatched me out of the air and thumped me against the hard bone of a shoulder, a chest.

They were amusing themselves. They knew who I was. They weren't going to beat me the way they beat the Negro and the white man.

Up and down, up and down in the hot July air, my breath knocked out of me. Then a gravel voice roaring, "If it's Tom Thumb, kill him, kill the little freak! He belongs to that bastard Barnum who big-mouths for fuckamuck Lincoln. Kick him and do him the way we did that other one!"

Through the glare of my pain, I heard police whistles. Shots were fired. As the mob scattered, I was up in the air again, and came down into the arms of the gray shirt with the gravel voice. He was running, tucking me under his arm as if I were a package.

"I got ya now, I got ya—gonna bash your dwarf brains outa your dumb dwarf skull. But first I'm gonna bugger you, then I'll send ya to the devil."

Hustling, moving fast, agile and quick on the cobbles, away from the police whistles, away from the crowd and the gunshots.

I glimpsed his face, wide and plump. A scar on his cheek, a smear of saliva down across his chin. His shirt damp with sweat, the smell of his body like the stink of dead weeds rotting in a quagmire. Running, still running.

He turned down an alley, and the sharp edge of my pain faded into dull resignation. I closed my eyes, and still the gravel voice ran. When I opened my eyes, we were in a courtyard. He went up over a fence, still holding me, then through another alley toward another clot of rioters. They had a Negro on the ground and were kicking him. Kicking hard.

Blood spurted from his mouth and ears, his body dumb on the ground like a near-empty sack of beans. A wiry, short-haired tough bent with a knife and slashed away at him, then stood up, holding the bloodied genitals. There was a hush. He reared back and threw them, hurled them in a high arc, a murky glimmer soaring far off. I never saw where they fell.

The gray shirt, holding me, went close to the corpse. I saw the face, one eye gone, the other open. I knew him. He was a waiter at Croft's, on Sullivan Street. He had thin lips and a firm chin, in his early twenties. A week ago I'd been at Croft's with Vinny, he took our order. But now gone—that sudden. Dead on the ground.

The gray shirt was shouting. "I say fuck Lincoln! Fuck the coons! Fuck the three hundred men! Fuck the fucking draft and the fucka-muck army! Fuck Barnum and his fucking dwarf!" He lifted me high above his head and shook me fiercely, as if to shake the life out of me.

Then the whistles again and more gunshots, and again the running—left, then right, into another alley. He stopped running and held me in front of him, his face close to mine. "You saw it? What they did to the nig? Just wait, you dwarf freak. Get ready for yours."

I was numb. I heard the words, but they were water running down a drain. He tucked me under his arm and we were on the move again, through crooked alleys, puddles of black water, past a shed, a dog, loose garbage, a pile of wagon wheels.

Suddenly, it stopped. A shot rang out, and in the instant that I heard it, I felt his grip loosening. I slipped from his arm and fell to the ground. When I looked up, I saw him standing with a puzzled expression on his face, as if trying to figure something out. Then he turned, pulling a gun from his pocket—but before he could fire, another shot rang out and he slumped to the ground, one of his legs hooking across my chest. I lay there a moment, catching my breath, then crawled out from under.

His eyes were open, in a fixed gaze, like the one eye of the dead black waiter. There was a twitching at the corner of his mouth, as if he was trying to say something—but he was vacant, gone. His lips were parted, a front tooth missing. He was nothing, nothing at all, not mud, not dust, not the croak of a frog.

Then I bent and did an odd thing, and even as I did it, I felt it was a weird thing to do. I reached down and touched his lips—knowing, as my fingers grazed across his skin, that I was touching death. What a strangeness that was, to be alive in this world and to reach across and touch that other world where nothing breathed.

It was a soldier who had shot him, one of the few still in the city. He searched the shirt and the pants, took the money pouch and pocketed it, then lugged me out of the alley and handed me to a policeman, who brought me back to the hotel—carrying me, though I insisted on walking the last block on my own.

I was a mess. Shirt torn, pants with a hole in the left knee, jacket lost. I looked at myself in the lobby mirror and saw a bruise on my left cheek.

Upstairs, when Vinny saw me, a shadow slanted across her face.

"I fell," I said. But she knew that wasn't true.

"You had to? You had to go out there?"

She was angry, mad that I'd put myself in danger that way. She washed the bruise, and wiped away some dirt on my forehead. While I was gone, she'd ordered a bottle of soda, which had arrived in a bucket of chipped ice. She brought the bucket over, to apply some ice to the bruise. But the bucket slipped from her small hands, and ice chips scattered across the floor. She was so provoked, she kicked at them, slivers and chunks of ice flying everywhere. Then she picked up the bucket and threw it against the wall. This was new to me. She had a temper. I liked it, it was a spark in the dimness of a bad day. She made a fist and swung at me, punching me in the arm. Real hard. She loved me that much.

"I'll buy you some coffee," I said.

She frowned and turned away.

What she was really upset about was that she wasn't pregnant yet. We'd been married five months, and still no hint, no sign. A baby, that's what she wanted more than anything, and hoped it would be normal, not a dwarf. She never said it in just so many words, but I had picked it up in her reactions to my sisters' children. She wanted it normal, and wanted it soon. And a restlessness, a disappointment that it wasn't happening.

For me, the thought of a pregnancy was terrifying, because she was so small. I couldn't imagine how an infant could pass through. Dwarf women did have babies, I knew that, and often the babies were of normal size. Still—the risk, the danger. None of this was anything I was eager for.

While I was thinking about all of that, a dizziness swept through me, and the room swayed, heaving like a ship in a storm. I thought I would fall, but managed, somehow, to reach the bed. As I stretched out on the coverlet, everything around me seemed in motion, rising and falling. And Vinny, by the bed, saying, "Charlie? Charlie? What is it? What's happening?" Her voice fading, and I went swirling off into a darkness. I was falling, turning, and reaching out, trying to catch hold of something—but nothing, just the turning and the dizziness, and the dark.

Then I was in that alley again, held by that goon, that lug, that kiss of death. The odor coming off his body was a sewer smell. He was talking to me, saying something, throaty and hoarse, but I couldn't make out the words, they vanished in a low grumble.

Then nothing, nothing, and eventually I woke up.

Vinny was beside me on the bed, close to me, the room warm with the heat of the long day. My clothes soggy with perspiration.

"Charlie? Do you feel better now? You slept. Are you all right?"

"I don't know," I said fuzzily.

"You're hungry. You haven't eaten."

I wasn't hungry. Food, at that moment, was of no interest to me.

She ran her fingers across my forehead. "Don't ever leave me," she said. "The way you did this morning, going out there without me. Do you hear, Charlie? Don't ever leave me like that again."

Downstairs, the lobby was crowded with police and military people. The mayor had left City Hall and had set up headquarters in the hotel, so he could be in immediate conference with General Wool, who was also headquartered there.

Vinny and I took a table by the bar, we needed more than coffee. She ordered a glass of Madeira, and I took some eight-year-old Amazon bourbon.

We spoke a while with a major at the next table. He'd been out on the street, reconnoitering, and now he was eating. Things were getting worse, he said. He was long-jawed, with sunken eyes and a thick moustache. One of his earlobes was chopped away—an old combat wound, I assumed.

"They tore up the Fourth Avenue tracks, near Forty-Second Street," he said. "A mob ripped them up with crowbars. It was mostly women, as wild-eyed as the men."

Vinny was alarmed. "The tracks? The trains are not running?"

If the trains were down, it wasn't likely we'd be setting off on our tour in the morning. But with the lumps and bruises on my body, I wasn't eager to be on the road anyway.

"They're trying to isolate the city," the major said. "Stop the trains, stop the ferries. Already they've set some of the piers ablaze."

The battle at Gettysburg had siphoned off all of the city's regiments, and what was left, he said, were a few hundred men from the harbor forts, and some marines from the Brooklyn Navy Yard.

He bit vigorously into his sandwich, and on he talked, telling of small groups of policemen overwhelmed by the mobs, beaten, stripped, some of them killed. "I saw one with his face smashed. One with his hand turned to mush."

Then, his head at a slant, he studied the bruise on my face, as if noticing for the first time.

"What happened?"

"I fell down the stairs."

"Sorry to hear that," he said.

I was going to ask what happened to his ear, but he was talking again, talking and eating. A mob on Broadway had sacked the jewelry shops. Another crowd raided the armory on Second Avenue, took the rifles, and burned the place down. "Some of their own were killed in that blaze, ten or a dozen, caught on the upper floor. I was there, saw them trying to get out."

In many neighborhoods, men on rooftops hurled rocks at the police and the few troops from the harbor forts. Shooting, too. Along Third Avenue, some fifty thousand were swarming, all the way to Forty-Fifth Street.

Again he studied my face. "Fell down the stairs?" he said, skeptically. The words hung there, out of context. Then he was into the riots again.

A black man was beaten and strung up on a lamppost. They burned a black boardinghouse on Roosevelt, and black houses on Carmine.

They attacked the Colored Orphan Asylum on Forty-Third, but a brave fellow, McCafferty, got the kids out of there, more than two hundred. The mob wrecked the orphanage and put it to the torch.

"I really don't want to hear this," Vinny said.

Nor did I. Yet we listened, and the major rolled it out like a doomsday litany—mobs pulling furniture out of rich homes and making bonfires in the street . . . smashing, killing, burning. Negro neighborhoods burning. The mansions of rich whites on Fifth Avenue—some of those too, burning.

And through all of this, Vinny and I thinking, wondering—how to get out of New York tomorrow? She finished her wine, I finished my bourbon. The major still talking when we left, still eating.

Vinny wanted to go to the Astor, to be with Minnie. It was more than a dozen blocks away. We spoke to the concierge, but he warned against leaving the hotel. "Why take the chance," he said. "They're stopping everything—the gigs, the coaches. Robbing and beating. You don't want to be out there."

While we were still in the lobby, McKenzie, one of the ticket men from the Museum, arrived with a message from Bleeker. He was shabbily dressed, blond hair tousled, a smudge of ash on his cheek, deliberately messy so he would pass, on the street, for just another rioter. "Hope you appreciate how I risked my life," he said. "It's a jungle out there, a devil-to-hell wilderness. I wouldn't have chanced it, but Bleeker would have kicked my ass if I didn't."

He said Greeley at the *Tribune* had barricaded his people behind bales of printing paper. And Raymond, who ran the *Times*, managed somehow to get hold of some Gatling guns. They were mounted in the windows.

"And the Museum?"

"So far, untouched. They hate Barnum for boosting Lincoln, but they still love the Snake-Charmer and the hippopotamus."

I did appreciate the risk he'd taken, and tipped him well. The message from Bleeker alerted us to be ready to go at four in the morning, before the beasts were loose on the street again. The plan was to travel by coach and wagon, up into the Bronx, beyond the troubles. At the Melrose station, we would catch a train for Connecticut. So—four a.m. at the front door, with luggage.

Through the early evening the rioting continued. There were reports about the neighborhoods where the mobs were concentrated. We went upstairs for a while, to get away from the crowd in the lobby, and the tension.

I was still thinking of the one who ran, carrying me, swearing he would kill me. I remembered the face, the mouth, the missing front tooth.

From our window we saw smoke rising in the distance, and heard, far off, the noise of the mobs—the shouting, the chanting, the dry popping sounds of gunfire, and saw the red glow of fires. It was dusk out there, a deeper dark coming on, and no way of knowing how bad things would be in days to come.

That night, only a few hours of sleep. Four in the morning, Bleeker was in front of the hotel, his eyes alert and worried. He was a slight man, thin and angular, his beard cut close at the cheeks and descending in a long V under his chin. He came with three carriages, each handled by a hackman.

We were a crowd, eleven of us: the pianist, the treasurer, the baggage boys, Bleeker and his wife, Julia, who carried the medicine kit and handled all sorts of odd jobs. And Harry Nobbs, our advance man and ticket salesman. And Minnie, little Minnie, excited to see us, clinging close to Vinny. And the Commodore, in a world of his own.

Off we went, into the early-morning darkness, the streets dead still, everything shut down. Straight north we went, the long, steady ride to the river, then across the bridge and into the Bronx, to the Melrose station.

Bleeker paid the hackmen, and after a long wait, we boarded a train that brought us to Stamford, in lower Connecticut, where Bleeker arranged a four-night stay at a small hotel so we could get our bearings after all the turmoil.

It was a quiet, dreamy town, elm trees and peaceful streets. We didn't perform there, just rested, and waited for news from New York. But nothing—no newspapers, no telegraph, no trains from the Forty-Second Street depot. As Vinny put it, it was as if we were plunged into an enormous stillness, waiting for a pin to drop. All we knew was that something ugly was happening back there, and I'd had a taste of that, firsthand. We went to the water's edge, and, though we couldn't see the city itself, we did see smoke rising in the sky, veils and coils of black smoke quietly lifting.

Then, on a sudden, newspapers from New York finally arrived, with headlines saying the riots had been put down. Four days it had lasted, Monday to Thursday, and by Friday some sort of order had finally been restored. But the terror and the damage, and so many dead.

Among the papers deposited at our hotel, I found a copy of the *Times* that had appeared after the first day of the riots.

THE NEW-YORK TIMES

New-York, Tuesday, July 14, 1863, THREE CENTS

THE MOB IN NEW YORK.

Resistance to the Draft—Rioting and Bloodshed

A DAY OF INFAMY AND DISGRACE
Conscription Offices Sacked and Burned
An Armory and a Hotel Destroyed
Outrages upon Colored Persons
Attack on the Mayor's Residence
The Colored Orphan Asylum Ransacked & Burned

I saved the page with those headlines, because that day, for me, was realer than real, those fearsome moments when I was out on the street, in that wide-awake nightmare. And well I knew how lucky I was to be breathing and alive.

From Stamford we moved on to New Haven. Along the way, we met a young reporter who'd been working for the *New York World*, covering the riots—but right at the end he quit and left the city in despair. He was on his way home to Rhode Island, where his father farmed chickens. That, the reporter thought, was maybe a better way.

The riots were over, he said, but the city was a mess; it would be a long time fixing and healing. When the first day turned so violent, the Germans, who were mainly in it to protest the draft, pulled back and worried instead about protecting their neighborhoods from looters. There were priests and ministers in the street, trying to persuade the rioters to go home, with little success. The rioting continued, and part of it, the reporter felt, was the gangs, the Dead Rabbits from the Five Points, and gangs from other parts of the city—fanning the flames, turning anger and disorder into a bonfire of rage and violence.

People were angry about the draft law, the reporter said, but a lot of the violence was random. They burned the Five Points Mission, and what harm had that ever done to them? And they stoned the Magdalene Asylum up on Eighty-Eighth. That? To protest the draft? But smart—they stayed away from Wall Street, where there were people with guns at the windows, and with vats of acid to toss on the heads of any rioters who came close.

Late on Wednesday, five New York regiments arrived home from Gettysburg. That evening, and through the next day, they used howitzers loaded with grapeshot to disperse the crowds. Some of the rioters barricaded themselves in their neighborhoods, shooting from rooftops, throwing rocks and brickbats. The soldiers moved door-to-door, bayoneting anyone who opposed them. Many on the rooftops jumped, killing themselves rather than be captured. By Thursday night it was largely over, and by Friday morning the telegraph lines were being repaired.

"How many dead?" Bleeker asked.

"Too many. Haven't seen an official count yet, but I'd guess close to two hundred. Maybe a thousand wounded."

I was thinking, yet, not of the mob but of that bruiser who had carried me, running from the police and swearing he would snuff the life out of me.

It was over but not finished, the reporter said. Too much damage, too many wounds, and he didn't want to hang around for all the pain.

PART FIVE

THE HONEYMOON TOUR

CHAPTER 15

THE ROAD SINGS . . .
IT BENDS, IT CURSES

We launched our tour in New Haven. This was the first time all four of us—Minnie, the Commodore, Vinny, and I—were interacting onstage together, and we couldn't have done it without the help Sylvester Bleeker gave us. He knew a heck of a lot about theater and how to mount a show. And Jerry Richardson was a great help with the songs.

Three days we were there, with overflow crowds. People remembered the great fuss in all the papers about our "Fairy Wedding," as it had been called. And now, needing some diversion from the bad news out of New York, they leaped at the chance to see us in our wedding garb.

Vinny and I opened each performance with a slow walk down the main aisle, she in her gown and I in my swallowtail, while Jerry Richardson played the wedding music from *Lohengrin*. Then, onstage, along with Minnie and the Commodore, we danced a stately minuet.

After a quick costume change, Vinny and Minnie rotated through a few songs—"Listen to the Mocking Bird," "Merry Little Birds Are We," and several others. They vanished into the wings, and the Commodore, in a sailor suit, sang "A Life on the Ocean Wave," and followed that with his hornpipe dance. Then I leaped out in my Scots kilt and danced a Highland fling. More songs, more dances, and plenty of applause for all of us.

We finished our first act with Vinny asleep on a cushioned chair, and I, stepping close, sang some lines from a Longfellow poem that had been put to music—

> *Stars, stars of the summer night,*
> *Far, far in your azure deeps—*
> *Hide, hide your golden light,*
> *She sleeps, my lady sleeps.*

Then Vinny, rousing herself, leaps to her feet, and draws close to me, singing a piece by Bernard Covert—

> *Always look on the sunny side,*
> *There's health in harmless jest;*
> *And much to sooth our worldly cares*
> *In hoping for the best.*
>
> *Always look on the sunny side*
> *And never yield a doubt;*
> *The ways of Providence are wise,*
> *And faith will bear you out.*

We kissed, and while Jerry played a selection from Chopin, we drifted offstage.

In much of our second act we focused on the war, since that was the big thing on everybody's mind. Jerry, knowing that Vinny had a brother in the war, found this Stephen Foster piece, a perfect fit for her.

> *Bring my brother back to me*
> *When this war is done,*
> *Give us all the joys we shared*
> *Ere it was begun.*

> *Bring my brother back to me,*
> *From the battle strife—*
> *Thou who watchest o'er the good,*
> *Shield his precious life.*

Many such songs we had, the voices of mothers, fathers, sisters, and many in the voices of soldiers, both on and off the battlefield. We concluded this segment with a Stephen Foster piece that sounded an optimistic note about the future. The Commodore and I, each wearing a Union uniform, rotated our way through, singing one sentence apiece, and doing the final sentence together.

> *There's a good time coming, boys,*
> *A good time coming.*
> *We may not live to see the day,*
> *But earth shall glisten in the ray*
> *Of the good time coming.*
> *The pen shall supersede the sword,*
> *And right, not might, shall be the lord,*
> *In the good time coming.*
> *War in all men's eyes shall be*
> *A monster of iniquity*

> *In the good time coming.*
> *Nations shall not quarrel then,*
> *To prove which is the stronger,*
> *Nor slaughter men for glory's sake—*
> *Wait a little longer.*
> *There's a good time coming, boys,*
> *A good time coming.*

More songs, more dancing from all of us, then Vinny and I concluded with our Shakespeare thing, the balcony scene from *Romeo and Juliet*. We closed with Juliet's final words—

> *Good night, good night! Parting is such sweet sorrow,*
> *That I shall say good night till it be morrow.*

After New Haven, we trained to Hartford, for another three-day stand. Good crowds there, and good weather. The governor came, as well as a bishop and a group of rabbis. Plenty of soldiers, too. It was a stroke of genius when Jerry dug up those war songs. They were magical, drawing plenty of serious, heartfelt applause.

Then back to the hotel, and in the morning we had the long trip to Boston.

Trains, trains—if you have to travel, it's the best way. The train rocks and sways, it chugs, it rumbles. It lurches to a stop for cattle on the tracks, then clears its throat and moves on, passing trees and houses, fields and hills. You can stand in the aisle and stretch your legs, or stay in your seat and read, or doze. Or trim your fingernails, as the Commodore often did.

He was not a happy traveler. He hated trains almost as much as he hated horse-drawn coaches and wagons. He squirmed, he groaned.

Even when he slept he was miserable, startled awake by nightmares. He hated the less than first-class hotels we'd stayed in when we were in Stamford and New Haven, and was already dreading what was yet to come. "I should have stayed in New York," he said. And, hearing that, I wished he had. One way or another, he was always grabbing for attention—and Bleeker's wife, Julia, red hair drawn back in a long braid, was always there for him, caring, attentive, offering cookies, candy, jelly cakes. But I'd heard some of the rumors, and knew that the sweetmeats he wanted were sweetmeats of another kind. He was homesick for the off-Broadway saloons above Canal Street, which he'd been slumming in, barmaids fondling him, nibbling at his fingers and licking his ears. So of course—why shouldn't he be homesick for all of that?

On our way to Boston, while we were rattling along, twenty miles an hour, he was so itchy he stood up and did a breakdown dance in the aisle, his own special version, legs and arms flying, torso bending and twisting. But the engineer slammed on the brakes, and, as the train squealed to a stop, the Commodore was hurled down the aisle and his head went smash against the door at the front end of the car. Banged himself bad. I rushed to help him up and found him in a daze, eyes unfocused. Julia was quickly there, with water and her box of medicines. She rinsed the cut on his head and the scrapes on his arms.

Suddenly he was alert, and frantic. "My face! My face! Is my face cut?"

It wasn't. But the mess on his head, after the bleeding stopped, required a large plaster.

Julia gave him a dose of Dr. Mossgrave's, to settle his nerves, and a piece of chocolate to get his mind off of things. He loved the attention, wallowed in it. She held him on her lap and fed him chocolates from a box she'd picked up at Barmore's. She told him not to worry—when he appeared in public, he could hide the plaster under a hat.

That same day, on the train, I met a scratchy-voiced old man with bushy gray eyebrows. He was involved in the manufacture of artificial limbs. Right arms and left legs, that's mostly what he made, because the soldiers at the front were losing four times as many left legs as right, and four times more right arms than left. Nobody knew why, but that's how it was happening—right arms and left legs were being shot away by the thousands. The man had a flask of brandy and took frequent sips, saying it was the only thing that kept his old pump going. He gave me a copy of an ad he was running in several newspapers and magazines.

THE UNIVERSAL JOINT AND ARTIFICIAL LIMB

Weighs only 4 pounds

Soldier's price $50; civilians $75; silver-plated, $100.

Will lengthen and shorten—self-adjusting.

In Boston, the crowds were even larger than in New Haven and Hartford. To accommodate them we offered three performances on each of the days we were there.

After each show, the four of us usually sat at a long table in the lobby, autographing the pamphlets people had purchased at the door. There were individual pamphlets about each of us, containing pictures and a brief bio filled with the kind of wild exaggeration that only Barnum could conjure up. Our first day in Boston, while we were autographing pamphlets, it was there, on a warm evening, that I had my first Greenwood moment. After signing five or six pamphlets, I saw that the next person in line was a middle-aged woman with a studied look on her face. "My name is Greenwood," she said, as she laid the pamphlet before me—and, with it, a small sealed envelope.

It surprised me. There, in abolitionist Boston? Greenwood? Information about enemy activities? Would the South dare to send agents into that hotbed of anti-Southern sentiment?

"I adored your show," she said, tapping her finger on the envelope.

I thanked her for her kind words, and after slipping the envelope into my pouch, I dipped my pen and autographed her pamphlet.

The next person in line was a man with a mole on his cheek. I gave him a long, studied look—but no, not the man I'd seen at my wedding reception, whose face still haunted me. The mole, yes, but no beard on this one. He had a gold tooth up front, and a streak of white in his hair.

From Boston we traveled westward, though parts of Massachusetts and Vermont, toward Lake Champlain. Along the way, after our performances, I'd been handed several Greenwood envelopes, and it was becoming a bit of a nuisance, carrying those envelopes in my pouch and waiting for Foxglove to pick them up.

Across the border we went, up into Canada.

In Quebec, Vinny and I were invited to dine with Lord and Lady Monk at Government House. Lord Monk was, at the time, the Governor-General of Canada, a tall, stately man with a friendly manner. After dinner, Lady Monk strolled the grounds with us.

Lord Monk had sent a carriage to pick us up at our hotel, and the same carriage brought us back. As the coachman lifted me from the carriage and deposited me on the ground, he whispered in my ear, "Greenwood," and slipped an envelope into my hand. I was dumbstruck. In Quebec? At Government House? Incredible, the length and daring of Nickerson's reach. I wondered what he could possibly be learning. That Lord and Lady Monk had grapefruit for breakfast and boiled ham with chives for supper?

That evening, at the hotel, shortly after Vinny and I passed through the lobby and went to our room, a bellboy was at our door. "At your service, sir. Foxglove pickup. If you have anything to deliver." I gave him the envelope the coachman had handed me, along with the many others I'd collected before we crossed the border.

We were all of two weeks in Quebec, drawing huge crowds, thanks to the attention the lord governor had given us. While in Canada, we made one major alteration in our performance. Since Canada belonged to England, and since England had assumed a policy of neutrality in regard to our civil war, Bleeker thought it wise to cancel the war songs that we used in our second act, since they might not be received as sympathetically as they were at home. We had discussed that during our early rehearsals, and prepared a number of other songs that were popular at the time.

We moved on to Montreal, and by then invitations were pouring in from so many places, not just in Canada but in the American Midwest. With such a demand out there, Bleeker urged us to extend the tour for another few months and postpone our sailing date for Europe.

That was hard, really hard. We were all eager for Europe, especially Vinny. When Barnum hired her, he promised an extended tour in England and France, and she had her heart set on it. So we thought long about Bleeker's suggestion, and said no.

But he nagged, and nagged, and in the end, worn down, we agreed. When he wired Barnum for approval, an answer shot back within an hour. "My dear Bleeker—Go on. Your returns show it to be real cream and not skim milk."

I winced. "Skim milk? He sold the Museum and he's now a dairy farmer?"

"Where's the butter," Vinny said.

"And the Liederkranz," Minnie added. "And the cottage cheese."

"I ate the cottage cheese," the Commodore said sourly. "Every last curd."

Poor Bleeker, he had wanted to be onstage, playing Hamlet, or Lear, but this was what life handed him, a pack of noisy dwarfs aboard a noisy train, rattling along from city to city. He put up with us, though I wondered what went on in his mind, what tremors of hopelessness, what tides of desperation and despair. His gray-blue eyes hid everything. But he did his job, and was good at it. Diligent, prompt, professional, doing what he had to do, and always a spiffy appearance—thinning dark hair neatly combed above his high forehead, a thin straight nose, and tapered fingers that curled and uncurled in a variety of moves he'd picked up during his days onstage. And a way of gesturing with his whole body, tilting to the left or right and using his small shoulders to great effect, lifting one, dropping the other, or thrusting them forward or back.

His well-guarded secret was that his real name was Groesbeck, which he had changed to Bleeker when he was young, entertaining visions of himself as a success onstage. But the name change did nothing for him. In fact, as a name, I found Groesbeck far more interesting.

One afternoon, while we waited for a train that was more than half an hour overdue, it struck me, out of nowhere, that this business about extending the tour into the Midwest might have been, in fact, not Bleeker's idea, but Nickerson's. In a blink, it all fell into place—Nickerson throws the idea to Barnum, and Barnum, playing it close to the vest, tosses it to Bleeker in a telegram, telling him to sell the idea as his own. Clever Barnum, about as artful as a rainstorm, not wanting to take the blame if we were suddenly unhappy, screaming and jabbering like a gang of caged monkeys.

But why didn't I see it before? Nickerson, behind the scene, cagier than Barnum himself—manipulating, controlling. Even that one time when we spoke, when I emphasized we were heading into Canada but then directly home—even then he knew he wanted me in the Midwest, and knew how to make it happen.

After Montreal, we moved on to Ottawa and Toronto, with some lesser stops along the way. Then we crossed the border, back into the States, to Detroit, where we had a long stand.

It was Christmastime. Bleeker was Santa Claus. Vinny and I were his elves, along with Minnie and the Commodore. The crowds kept coming—as much, I think, for the tinsel and the sing-along Christmas songs as for us.

And in the midst of it all, I collected a surprising number of Greenwood letters, and I puzzled over that. Not till much later did I learn that the rail line running from Detroit into Canada was a favorite route for Confederate agents moving back and forth across the border. And that, I suppose, was what those letters were about.

We were still in Detroit when we welcomed in the New Year 1864. Then off to Grand Rapids, and eventually over to Chicago for a long engagement—and that, for us, was as far west as we dared to go, if we were ever to get home for that trip to England.

After Chicago, we spent a goodly amount of time in Indiana and Ohio, upstate and down, a week or two here, a week or two there, and who anymore, except Bleeker, knew exactly where we were? He was always there with a map, ready to show us where we were headed—but after a while, did any of us really care? The days slipped into weeks, the weeks melted into months, and we hardly noticed.

When we reached Columbus, Ohio, Bleeker wired Barnum, filling him in on our recent stops. An answer came back from Barnum's son-in-law Sam Hurd, saying Barnum had left a week earlier for Europe, with Anna Swan, Zobeide Luti, and a new contortionist, Maria Miralla. Not expected back till mid-July or thereabouts. We were on our own, and Sam wished us well.

When I saw that telegram, I was hauled back to the time when Anna first arrived at the Museum. The things Barnum said of her, the gleam in his eyes. "Eight feet tall and all the right equipment—makes you want to climb aboard for a long, wild ride."

As those words sifted up out of the past, the Tom Thumb part of me felt something surging, a wild flash of dwarf jealousy, dwarf possessiveness. Because she was mine. Didn't Barnum understand? *Mine.*

And while the Tom Thumb part of me was thinking those thoughts, feeling that rage, the Charlie Stratton part of me was telling me to cool down and come to my senses. What's happening? What kink in my dwarf brain was doing this? Frying my blood cells and turning the gray matter between my ears into cooked meat. *Charlie? Tom? Tom? Charlie?*

When we reached Wheeling, in West Virginia, we stayed at the McLure, which was filled with Union officers on their way to Washington. They sent champagne to our table and toasted us, and later in the evening they came to our performance at the Masonic Hall.

That champagne, it was the wrong stuff before a show. The girls sang off-key, the Commodore slurred his jokes and fell twice during his jig, and I, doing my impersonation of Napoléon—well, this Napoléon couldn't walk a straight line, and the soldiers loved it.

Afterward, while I was passing out signatures, signing our one-page program sheet, I was suddenly aware that my signature had reduced itself to a couple of wobbly squiggles. My last squiggles were for a woman in a nifty blue dress, whom I recognized as the waitress who had served our table at the McLure. A smile, and a friendly look in her beaming blue eyes.

"Foxglove," she said. And wasn't I glad to hear that, eager as I was to unload the too many envelopes I'd gathered since the last pickup.

Back at the hotel, as we relaxed in the wicker chairs in the parlor, something strange took hold of Vinny. We were close to the war, very close, and she wanted a closer look. "Why not?" she pleaded. "Why not?"

I shrugged. Bleeker lit his pipe. His wife, Julia, gazed despairingly at the slowly turning fan that hung from the ceiling.

"Would that be smart?" Bleeker asked.

"It would be very smart," Vinny answered. "My mother always said to see everything in life and learn all there is. And Mr. Barnum, too—he promised he would take me to Europe to see the world. But this isn't Europe, it's the war. So let's have a look."

I knew what it was. Her brother was in the war, and she wanted to see what it was like out there in the field, not far from the enemy—the camps, how the soldiers lived, what they ate. She was thinking of Benjamin.

Bleeker puffed on his pipe, worrying about the danger. He was looking at me, making a silent plea for help, begging, but I was of no use to him at all. It was, I suppose, my way of getting back at him for allowing him to persuade us to postpone Europe.

"Well, why not," I said with feigned enthusiasm. "We'll go close but not too close. We won't go near Richmond."

Bleeker was plunged into despair. His eyes slid away, gazing into an emptiness.

We stayed far from Richmond, but we did go into Kentucky, traveling by steamer down the Ohio River, to Louisville. By then, winter had melted away, there was no ice in the river, and many of the trees along the shoreline were coming alive with foliage.

What we learned along the way, talking with passengers who lived in the region, was that Kentucky was a sorry mess, torn apart with confusion. At the start of the war, it had hung neutral, but now, among the people, there were sharp divisions. Many of the young men joined with the Union, but others signed on with the Confederates, and it was not unusual to find brothers in the same family choosing opposite sides.

When we arrived in Louisville, the Union regiment stationed there was preparing to defend against an attack that was expected in about a month. A captain showed us around. He brought us to see the earthworks that had been thrown up on the outskirts of the city, then took us to a camp where prisoners were held. They were happy to see us. Many remembered Vinny from the time when she was on the showboat, and some remembered me from a tour I'd made years ago. We sang a few songs, and they joined in. "Camptown Races," and "My Old Kentucky Home." And "Dixie." Lincoln had told me "Dixie" was his flat-out favorite, and he was much put out when the South grabbed it as its own special tune.

When you're out on the road, there are moods, and moments. The road twists and turns, it sings, it bleeds. There are surprises, unexpected encounters that take on a special meaning only months or years later.

A few days after arriving in Louisville, unhappy with our accommodations, we moved to a different hotel, the Tobacco Leaf, where Vinny and I were lodged directly across from a room occupied by John Wilkes Booth.

We'd not met him before, though we had heard of him, and I did know his brother Edwin, whom I'd seen many times performing at the Winter Garden.

John Wilkes was now appearing at a downtown theater in Louisville. He wasn't the huge success that his father had been, or that his brother Edwin now was, but he was well on his way. I'd heard he was pulling in a solid income, about a thousand a week when he performed in the North. He wasn't tall, but not short either, and from the news items I'd read, I knew that he and I were the same age, both born in 1838.

He had vivid eyes, animated and flashing, and jet-black hair. I'd seen a piece in the *Herald* that said he was the handsomest man in America—which was a bit of puff, I thought. The article painted him as dashing, romantic, and adventurous, with attachments to a whole string of women. It did seem that women went for him in a big way. In some parts of the country, they followed him home after his performances—in New Orleans, they carried him off the stage and tore away most of his clothes.

We had coffee with him at the bar in the lobby of the hotel. The lobby was a long, rectangular space, with the desk clerk at one end and a small bar at the far end, tended by a gritty-faced, gray-haired man with a gold tooth. There were a few stools at the bar, and a few small tables nearby. We took a table close to a window that looked out on a rose garden.

Vinny took coffee with the merest dash of Amaretto. I took Amaretto with the merest splash of coffee. Booth took whisky with ice— Edradour, one of the labels my father had been addicted to, though he always skipped the ice. And Booth did something else. He stirred a dash of salt into his whisky. "It helps the voice," he said. "Deepens the timbre. I learned that from my father."

His father had been a legendary guzzler. I'd never seen him onstage, but often heard that he'd delivered some of his best performances when he was completely oiled.

John Wilkes studied his fingernails. He said that when he last played at Ford's Theatre, months ago, in *The Marble Heart*, Lincoln was there. "What a sorry piece of business that man is, causing all this death and ruin," he said. "Look what he's doing to the South— destroying a whole heritage, a whole way of life. Damn country will never be the same." And more, much more, in that vein, sounding like the copperheads we had up North—anti-Lincoln, anti-war, pro-South, and pro-slavery. And now, this being an election year, it was more than just the copperheads against Lincoln. All sorts of people, even many Republicans, were trying to dump him, and, wherever you turned, there was irony, sarcasm, a smirk, a sneer, open ridicule of his looks and manner. His jokes, his clothes, the stovepipe hat, and, above all, his handling of the war.

While Booth was going on about Lincoln, a fellow in a black broadcloth suit took a stool at the bar and ordered a brandy. I felt I knew him, but couldn't place him.

He sat with his back to us, arms on the bar, and he tilted his head, as if straining to hear our conversation. I felt uncomfortable about that. For a brief moment, when he glanced over his shoulder, I caught a glimpse of the right side of his face, but never saw him straight on. Still I was sure I'd seen him before.

I was uncomfortable about Booth, too—and not just because of his pro-South chatter. He gave Vinny his *carte de visite*, which he autographed, and she gave him one of hers. And somehow, deeply, it all didn't sit well with me.

Afterward, in our room, I was peevish. "You were flirting with him," I said.

She was huffy. "Charlie—go away."

"You were, I saw you. That gleam in your eye, the eyelashes going."

"Actually," she said, "I thought, for a moment, *he* was flirting."

"You were both doing it. He was batting his eyes and you were batting yours."

"Charlie, there is no reason for this. He's a very talented man, and except for the fact that he's against emancipation, hates the Republicans, despises Lincoln, and has a fondness for the old Know Nothings, I can't see that there is anything at all to be upset about. And as for batting my lashes, I had something in my eye. It's still there, and it hurts. There," she said, lifting her eyelid with a finger. "Take a look."

She's punishing me, I thought. That's what this was. Flirting with strangers and making me jealous, because we were now married more than a year and she was secretly suspecting it was my fault that she wasn't pregnant—my dwarf seed too dwarfish to do the job. Was that it? Was it? Disappointment made her contrary.

"I don't like him," I said.

"Well, he's a fine-looking man and everyone thinks so. Are we quarreling?"

"Are we?"

"You certainly sound that way," she said. "Just listen to yourself—accusing me of this, that, and the other."

"Of this and that, maybe," I said. "But I would never accuse you of the other."

She wasn't amused. "Charlie, why are you being so mean today?" She fell into a pout, drawing away and making herself inaccessible, and I knew that nothing I might say—for a while at least—would draw her back. It was the disappointment about the baby and the deepening worry about her brother Benjamin. With the casualties growing so hugely, there was reason to worry, and she was doing her best, steeling herself, readying herself for bad news.

"Let's be friends."

"No," she answered. "I don't want to."

"Never again?"

She lifted her face, so firm, so lovely. "Never again," she said, with reckless abandon.

We went on to Frankfort and Lexington, and many small towns in the region, performing wherever there was a hall, a church, a barn, or a tent. And wherever we slept, Vinny pulled out that Celtic fertility cross, putting it on the bureau or slipping it under her pillow. Still hopeful, believing in the power of that silver cross to work its magic. But that cross, it was taking its own sweet time.

Late one afternoon we arrived at a town by the name of Paris. While we were checking in, a cavalry officer rode in with news that a town just east of us was being raided by Morgan's cavalry.

He was something, that Morgan—wild, sudden, flamboyant. We'd heard a lot about his daring raids, and even though he was an enemy, it was hard not to be dazzled by his care-to-the-wind exploits. A year earlier, in July, when the riots were raging in New York, he'd been sent into Kentucky to destroy the railroad and capture Louisville from the Union—instead, he dashed through Indiana and tore into Ohio, raising hell in every town he passed through. After a long chase, he was captured and locked up in the Ohio state prison, a maximum security penitentiary. But he tunneled out, and was now in Kentucky, with his cavalry, tearing up rails, blowing up locomotives, and keeping everything off-balance.

That night in Paris, we didn't get much sleep. Vinny was a wreck, sitting up in bed and biting her fingernails. At every sound, she was up, looking through the window.

"You wanted a taste of the war," I said.

"I know, I know. But in the daytime, from a distance. I didn't think these nizzies would be riding in the dark."

I leaned my head back on the pillow and closed my eyes. "Vinny, after they raid one town, they need some sleep before they take on another."

"So? Maybe they've had their nap and they're on their way," she said, climbing out of bed for yet another look through the window.

The night was uneventful, but instead of feeling relieved, she seemed disappointed. And Minnie, at breakfast, she too—not just disappointed but vexed, because she'd been hoping Morgan would ride in and sweep her off her feet. "Since nobody else seems to be bothering," she said, aiming that at the Commodore, who was still looking past her, not seeing her. He too had spent a sleepless night, and seemed desperate to be out of Kentucky.

But Vinny, having survived the night, wanted more. She liked a bit of adventure, a hint of danger, and that too was something I was learning about her. Risky situations set her atingle, and then the pleasure of knowing she had passed through unscathed.

∽ CHAPTER 16 ∽

THE REBEL SOLDIER
WITH TOO MANY NAMES

We were longer in Kentucky than any of us had expected, performing in one town after another, with now and then a day off to relax and sleep. The expected attack on Louisville didn't materialize, and that was good news. The South had decided its manpower was needed in Virginia, to protect Richmond. We breathed easier, though we were much aware that Southern units were still around.

We moved on, traveling by rail. All the way down to Paducah, and spent two days dancing and singing there, not far from Tennessee, which was Confederate territory.

Then we traveled east, still close to the Tennessee border, passing farms, lakes, ponds, horses grazing in open fields. A long stop at a small town by the name of Vertigo, where the steam engine took on water. Most of the passengers stepped out to stretch their legs and buy snacks and newspapers from the vendors. Vinny went, and most of our people, but I stayed behind, just coming out of a deep sleep that had grabbed hold of me. I stayed aboard, too foggy to move, and gazed at the people milling about on the platform. A gray-haired man sold newspapers, a woman sold sandwiches. A bald man sold ice cream, scooping it out of an improvised icebox mounted on wheels.

And as I sat there, my face at the window, again I saw him—this fellow that I'd seen before. He came walking down the platform, close to the train. As he passed, he turned his head and looked straight at me, as if to say that he knew me—knew who I was and where I was.

He passed quickly, moving farther along on the platform, his left hand gripping the handle of his luggage bag, and a folded newspaper tucked under his right arm. On the other side of the platform, a few hackney cabs were lined up. He climbed aboard the first in line, and a moment later the cab moved off.

My head was swimming. Him—the same fellow I'd seen at my wedding reception, with the mole on his cheek. And at the bar in Louisville, when Vinny and I were at a table with Wilkes Booth. Could it be random? Sheer chance and coincidence?

As I sat there, by the window, it flashed home to me that I'd seen him yet another time—at the train depot in Bridgeport, a week before we set off on our tour. I had visited my mother, and while I waited for the train back to New York, I sat on a bench in the waiting room—and this fellow with the mole, he rushes in, buys a ticket, and heads for the platform.

So—in Kentucky, just then, during the long stop in Vertigo, while the steam engine took on water, I was more than astonished to see him again. How long had this fellow been around? And what in the world was he doing there, so close to the Tennessee border? He walks past the car I'm in, and through the window gives me a straight look, as if to tell me he knows who I am and where I am. That—what was *that* all about? Was it haphazard that our paths kept crossing, or was this something plain rotten?

When the train was ready, everyone aboard, we pulled out and rolled through one little town after another. We passed an encampment of Confederate soldiers, and, farther along, a few miles away, an encampment of Union soldiers. Eventually, we pulled in at Bowling Green, maybe twenty miles from the border. Three days we were there, appearing at the town hall, a hospital, an orphanage.

At the orphanage, a woman drew me aside, for my autograph. She seemed young, but her face was worn and troubled. She was a widow, her husband had been a Union soldier. "When I heard you would be passing through, I traveled a bit of a far way to see you. From Greenville. And, if you wish," she said, as she drew an envelope from her black satchel, "you may call me Mrs. Greenwood." The envelope surprised me. I took it, and felt humbled in her presence—a war widow, the pain of it visible in her eyes, in the expression on her face.

"You're very brave," I said, slipping the envelope into my pouch, and felt dumb for having nothing more comforting to say. Dumber than dumb.

Then on a train again, rumbling back up toward northern Kentucky—passing tobacco farms, horse farms, forests thick with poplar and oak. You could open the window, and if your arms were long enough you could grab a clump of leaves.

Between Horse Cave and Munfordville, we were held up about an hour. A section of track had been torn up. It was Morgan again, slippery and fast, doing damage, then vanishing. The conductor passed through, shaking his head as he gave us the bad news. We stepped off the train and stood around, waiting for the crew to hammer the tracks back into place. A sweaty day, hot and uncomfortable, everyone gathering in the shadow of the train, away from the sun.

"I have to pee," I said.

"I'll join you." Bleeker nodded, and we made our way through clumps of grass and low brush, toward a stand of trees on a low hill. Bleeker grabbed a stick and poked around, scaring off the snakes.

When we moved into the trees, we stopped short, startled. In front of us, close, in a tangle of sunlight and shadows, a rebel soldier sat on a large rock, with a loosely held rifle pointed in our direction. Pale, wispy eyebrows and gray eyes like small onions pickled in a jar. His nose bony, and his long, narrow chin thin and fragile, as if it might break apart if someone were to punch hard. He wore a gray rebel jacket and cap, and torn green pants that he'd probably pulled from somebody's clothesline.

And the rifle: a queer-looking thing with two barrels, one under the other. Barnum had one just like it on display at the Museum—not an antique but a recent invention. The bottom was a shotgun barrel, and the top fired bullets from a revolving cylinder. You could shoot nine bullets in less than a minute and finish it off with a shotgun blast. I knew there weren't many of these around, and it more than surprised me to see one staring me in the face.

"I don't want no trouble," he said with a languid drawl. "Just don't shout and scare up none of those others, and you will mebbe live to have your next bowel movement."

Hearing his voice, I felt a connection, something familiar. "I know you," I said.

"Well, maybe you do and maybe you don't. Knowin' somebody be only a make-believe thing anyway. Truth is, nobody never knows nobody."

I studied his face, his eyes, but still I couldn't place him.

"What you starin' at," he said, not so casual now with the rifle, the long barrel pointing straight at me.

"We just come here to pee," Bleeker said, adopting a friendly drawl, as if he were a Southerner, a neighbor.

"Well, be my guest," the fellow answered. "One at a time. The little one first."

I turned around and opened my pants, my bladder full, aching, and out it poured.

"Tiny fella got a lot of piss in him, don't he?"

Then it was Bleeker's turn, and already the reb was talking, the words spilling out of him, a lazy, uninterrupted flow. I had a sense that he'd been on his own a long time, separated from his unit, with nobody to talk to—and now, with us for an audience, he talked and talked, entertaining himself that way. In his easy, lackadaisical manner, he was a real gasser.

He talked about the roots he ate for supper and the salads he made out of the grass, and how he was smart with mushrooms, knowing which were safe and which would kill you. The lucky times were when you found melons in a field, or squash, or if you wandered into a swamp and caught an eel. And, best of all, a wild turkey, but hard to find. In this part of the country, most of the turkeys had already been eaten.

Still talking, talking, and the rifle swinging lazily, pointing in our direction. He mentioned his father, who was dead, and his mother who had quit the South and had gone off to Oregon, and he moaned about his sweet darlin', his woman, the girl that was his, but she took sick and died. She was in heaven, he said, and he couldn't wait to see her and be in bed with her again—but not too soon, because he was still hoping for a good long life in this vale of tears, and why shouldn't he get the full rich benefit of it, like the smart ones up North that have mansions and cash. "God be all good and Satan be evil," he said. "And the poor and the hungry will inherit the earth."

On and on he went, and it crossed my mind, dimly, that much of what he told us was sheer fantasy. He'd been a long time alone and there was this deep need that he had—to talk, to make words with his mouth and let them spill out on the air, saying the things that he said because somehow, in his odd-fangled way, he was trying to impress us.

Then, still sitting on that rock, still holding the rifle and swinging it lazily, he told us how they'd had conscription since early on in the war, and he'd been beating the system by volunteering as a substitute.

If you owned twenty slaves, you were exempt from the draft. But if you didn't have that many slaves and you still wanted out, you had to pay a substitute to serve in your place. And that, he said with a glimmer of pride, was how he'd been beating the system. He'd been offering himself up as a substitute for the easy money, then deserting, changing his name, and substituting all over again in a town where he wasn't known. A Confederate dollar, he said, wasn't worth near as much as a Union dollar, but a dollar in any shape or form was nothing to sneeze at. He was rattling on, spilling it out, proud of how clever he was.

"I ain't the only one," he said. "There be a big bunch just like me, playin' the same game. And Robert E. Lee and Jubal Early never be knowin' just how many men they has in the field. It be happenin' up North, too, in your neck of the woods, now that you got the draft. Us substitutes, North and South, when we vanish from the ranks, they puttin' us down as the ones that be missin' after a battle. And, you know, more than once I were listed as plain dead. And maybe I am."

In his underworld life of desertion and substitution, he'd run through a whole string of different names, and he smiled, remembering some. At one time or another, he'd been Solomon Stripe, Fred Chuckle, Judas Wrath, Goose Wrinkle, and Godfrey Worm. And he added, with an odd grin, that he was no longer sure which of those, if any, was the name he'd been born with. There were other names, too, others that he'd used. Snow and Mingus and Racine, and Tom Fanchoo. Maybe his real name was one of those.

"But what's in a name?" he said. "And what do it matter who you really be?"

He scratched his left ear, wincing, feeling an itch there. Then he was talking again. "There were a captain, once, caught on to what I was doin'. I fixed that by shootin' him in the face and quick hiked over to another town, where I took a new name."

"Which name are you using now?" I asked.

"None of them. I am goin' to be plain nobody for a while. Trouble is, Mr. Jeff Davis, he sign a new law abolishin' substitution, 'cause there be too many no-good unreliables like me around. So I be headin' north, to the bluecoats, to offer myself as a substitute—for those good Yankee dollars. It be no good down here in the South no more. Confederate money ain't worth dogshit. And the Yankee army got real food instead of roots and weeds, and a potato now and then."

He took a plug of tobacco from his shirt pocket, and for a few moments just sat there, chewing. Then he spat, and swung the rifle again, with a kind of lethargy. "And by the way," he said to Bleeker, "I be much obliged if I could borrow those duds you be wearin'. And in fair exchange you may have mine, what be left of them. I am goin' to keep the bandanna, though. It were a love token my pretty one give me. She be gone now, into the big beyond, though I still be dreamin' about her, yes I do."

Having no choice in the matter, Bleeker made the exchange, but nothing fit. The pants, torn at the knees, were too short, and the shirt too tight. The jacket, bereft of buttons, was worn through at the elbows.

"Now you two git on back to that train, and I be right here to shoot you dead if you raise the alarm. The dwarf gets it first. I got deadly aim."

As we emerged from the woods, Jerry Richardson, our pianist, came running to meet us. "What kept you?" he called. "Everyone's aboard. The train's ready to move."

Then, close up, his eyes scanning the rags Bleeker was wearing. "You were mugged?"

"Something of that," Bleeker said. As the words fell from his lips, the train whistle blew, three short toots—and, right after that, we heard the crack of the rifle, and a bullet whizzed past my left ear. Then another, and another, and everything inside me sank. Richardson fell to one knee, grabbing at his right leg. Then he was up and running, with a limp, but running. Bleeker whisked me off my feet and, gripping me with both arms, raced past Richardson. Another shot, and I heard glass breaking, then more shots and more glass. The reb was shooting out the windows. Bleeker scooted around the back of the train, to the safety of the other side, with Richardson behind us, and as we boarded, a conductor waved to the engineer, and the train moved.

I found Vinny, she was all right. Minnie and the Commodore, too, and the others. Richardson's right calf had been grazed by a bullet. Julia—Bleeker's wife—found her kit and washed the wound. She applied some iodine, not because she had any faith in it, she said, but because a friend of hers, a Southerner in Georgia, worked for a doctor who swore iodine could cure anything, including goiter and malaria. Well, maybe. She used iodine on Richardson's leg, and on many who had been cut by flying glass when the windows were shot out.

There was, too, a woman who'd been hit by a bullet high on the right side of her chest. She was in the car in front of ours. Two conductors did what they could to stanch the bleeding. She was breathing and conscious, when I saw her, but didn't look well, not at all. We were an hour away from the next big town that had a hospital. I still have a vivid memory of her, a small scar on her chin and a streak of white in her thick brown hair.

When things began to settle down, our people gathered in seats at the back of the car. They were eager to know what had happened in the woods, and what the shooting had been about. Bleeker, looking clownish in the ill-fitting shirt and pants, told them about the wily fellow we'd met, who was outsmarting the draft and making money in the substitution game.

While Bleeker was cursing the reb for shooting, and for taking his clothes and for simply existing, the train rounded a bend and leaned hard to the left. And suddenly it came to me—I did know that rebel soldier. The voice, the slant of the jaw, the eyes, the drawl. Years ago, before the war, he'd been one of the baggage boys when Barnum was touring me through the South.

"Ike Hokus," I said, realizing, as I spoke, that this, too, was probably just one more of his fake names. He'd been telling lies about himself ever since he was born.

"Hokus," I repeated—but Bleeker didn't know the name, and I remembered that Bleeker hadn't been with us on that tour.

It struck me too that if I knew Ike Hokus, he certainly must have known me, though he obviously didn't care to say so. He was deep in the mud, lost in his multiple identity deceptions—becoming one self, then another, and, in his mysterious way, he had become, it seemed, simply anonymous. And if he did know me, it made me doubly mad that he knew me and shot at me anyway.

Still, the multiple names and the confusion about who he really was. That was something that interested me, something I partly understood. Because there I was, assuming those many different roles onstage. I was Charlie Stratton pretending to be Tom Thumb, who pretends to be Napoléon, Hercules, Cincinnatus, and, in my younger days, Cupid. At any moment, who, in fact, was I? And where? And why?

Often, so many times, I too felt a craving for anonymity. As the train chugged along, I wanted to see Ike Hokus again, to tell him we were brothers under the skin, playing the same game, switching from one identity to another, and in this I knew him better than he knew himself.

But the sonofabitch had shot at us. And for that woman in the next car, it was a big maybe.

Vinny was gazing at me, troubled, upset that I'd been so foolish, going into the woods. Upset with Bleeker, too, but more with me—

didn't I know this was Kentucky? Didn't I understand the woods were full of treachery? She glared. "Didn't you *think*? My God, Charlie, what's happening? What's wrong with you?"

Something was, in fact, happening, though it was hardly something I could talk about, and it had nothing to do with my going into the woods.

For a time, even before I boarded that ill-fated train, I found myself, at random moments, thinking about Anna Swan and remembering the wild feelings I'd had for her when we first met, a short-lived infatuation that afflicted me like a fever. Not that I was unhappy with Vinny, or bored, or disappointed—no, not that at all. It was simply that Anna was out there and very much alive, all eight feet of her, too enormous to be blotted from memory, and my thoughts swam back to those large eyes, gigantic limbs, meaty lips, and the secret parts of her that I could only imagine. And imagine, I did. Her slopes, her valleys, the voluptuous hills. The caverns, the ravines.

This was, I knew, nothing less than wayward desire, and it came, I suspected, from the rocking and swaying as the train chugged along. I was married to Vinny, and didn't want a life without her. Still, my thoughts wandered into fantasies that bloomed like wild roses. Could I have Vinny and Anna, too? Would that be possible? Would Vinny object? Would Anna be agreeable? We could travel together, two dwarfs and a giant, Anna standing onstage, with Vinny reaching up, holding one of her hands, and I holding the other. And would the world be any the wiser? Would they have any idea of our glowing nights and sunsplashed mornings? We, a trinity of bliss, enjoying the comings and goings, the throb, the rhythm, the drumbeat of rapture.

And what a sweet revenge upon the entire world of normalcy—the world of average size, average dimension, average height, average hopes, average meanness, average hate and average pleasure, average dreams. The humdrum world that had delivered us into this endless war that was destroying the country. We three, each other's solace, getting away from all that, escaping the common run and leaping into some far beyond, toward something felt if not seen, some vague hint of an eternal flame.

But why, why was I thinking such thoughts? Was I, in my own small way, my dwarf way, simply depraved? Or was it truly something else, gleaming and necessary, beyond words, beyond size, and even, perhaps, beyond comprehension.

In any case, what still bothered me—what flipped me over and spun me on my head—was my awareness that while I was in Kentucky, Barnum, at that very moment, was touring Anna through the British Isles. It troubled me, touched a nerve. Barnum, Barnum, old master, mentor, friend, Prince of Humbugs, a father to me. He had discovered me, groomed me, taught me, made me the most famous dwarf in the world—and this, now, was what he was doing? Stealing Anna? Didn't he understand that she belonged to me? And didn't *she*?

Again, the Charlie Stratton part of me knew that the Tom Thumb in me was running wild, barefoot in tall grass, scaring the sheep, bothering the crows, terrifying the butterflies. And how, how, to get away from all that?

I left my seat and went to the washroom at the end of the car. I stood a long moment, studying my face in the mirror above the basin, this face that was me—but was it truly me or merely some sort of mask, a false image the gods had put there, teasing me, playing with me, hiding me from myself.

I washed my hands, using plenty of soap, then I soaped my face, washing away the woods that Bleeker and I had stepped into, the smell, the mood, the odor, last year's dead leaves rotting. And that crazy Ike Hokus, shooting and smashing the windows. He could have killed someone, could have and maybe did. That woman with the wound in her chest, not much hope for her. I dried myself with the towel. Then, unfocused, I was washing my hands again.

As the train struggled along, past farms and woodland, I sat across from Vinny. We were alone, nobody near us. We needed some of that. Aloneness, solitude. She was still upset, annoyed with me for having gone into the woods. And she was right—it was dumb. If Bleeker and I hadn't stumbled upon Ike Hokus, he might never have lifted that rifle and fired at the train.

"You don't love me," she said.

"Why are you saying that?"

"Because you don't."

"But I do," I said, wondering if she was guessing my reckless thoughts about Anna.

She turned away, gazing through the window. Old shacks out there, the ragged edge of some run-down village. Clotheslines. Broken wagons rotting on the embankment near the tracks. We were opposite each other, looking through the same window, she seeing the scene as it moved away, into the past, and I seeing it as it rushed toward me, out of the future.

"Have some chocolate," I said, reaching into my satchel, on the seat beside me.

"I don't think so," she said, still looking through the window.

"But you love chocolate."

"Not now," she said. I saw her withdrawing, pulling away into a middle distance, and heavy fog on the way.

"Here," I said, holding the chocolate out to her, a chunky piece, the smell of it mingling with the crisp smell of smoke wafting from the wood-burning locomotive. But she turned away, and I put the chocolate back in the bag. This is the way, I thought—how it is and will be. Good days and bad days, and the good make up for the bad. But the bad have a way of canceling out the good, and where are you then? Yes, where?

We went past a field full of cows, and I thought what a dreary life for them, existing solely to give milk, and when they're no good at that anymore, what then? Cows and more cows—trees, and a pond, and more trees, and who was still thinking about that rebel in the woods, or about the torn-up tracks that had held us up for an hour. Or about Morgan. Him? He was dust, coming and going on the wind.

The woman with the bullet in her chest was still alive when they took her off the train. Workers at the station brought her to a local hospital, but we never found out if the surgeons were able to save her. That's how it was, life was full of unfinished stories. You catch the story at the beginning, or maybe in the middle, but your train pulls out of the station and you never find out how the story ends.

CHAPTER 17

MORGAN'S RAIDERS/LETTERS FROM BENJAMIN

During our time in Kentucky, we heard much about Morgan but saw him only once—in a town named Lebanon, maybe twenty miles out of Liberty. We were in a shabby hotel on the main street, across from a barbershop and a general store that sold everything—nuts, fruit, meat in tins, shotgun shells. It also housed the post office and the telegraph. No federal troops in Lebanon, though there was a Union flag on the pole in front of the town hall, and another at the general store, hanging from an upstairs window.

Midafternoon, a warm, sunny day, Vinny and I were napping after a morning of travel, resting before an evening performance in the town hall. I had just slipped off into sleep when Morgan rode in with his cavalry. What a powerful sound, all those hoofbeats, a distant rumble growing into a thunderous roar that shook the building. We were quickly up, looking through the window, and Minnie came rushing from her room.

There were more than a hundred out there, filling the street—you could feel the power, the energy, all those horses, and so many men and guns. We were up close, on the second floor, a few feet above their heads, and could see the sweat, the strain in the faces, the alertness, the beards, the scars, the mud and dust on uniforms that were shabby and torn.

"We should move away from the window," Vinny said. "Don't let them see us."

But we were gripped. Something happening out there, big and real, and how to tear ourselves away?

On the street, two women carrying packages stood frozen, then bolted into a linen shop. Three boys, teenagers, lingered in front of the barbershop, jaws firmly set, hands in pockets. They turned their heads slowly, studying the men, the horses, watching as two wagons pulled up in front of the general store, and more men on horses.

Then we saw him. The tall one with the full black beard, quickly off his horse and onto the wooden sidewalk outside the general store, waiting and watching while his men went in and took what they needed, emptying the place of food and cartridges. We'd heard about this sort of thing, Morgan riding into a town and his troops grabbing what they needed, then riding out, never firing a shot. Gathering provisions, keeping themselves fed and alive so they could tear up more tracks and knock down some trestles, and maybe blow up a locomotive.

As my apprehension mounted, Minnie's subsided. She stood between us, and, far from frightened, she was awestruck. "He's adorable," she said. "I want him. Why can't I have him?" She heaved a long, warm, despairing sigh, and hung quiet, gazing.

Then she wriggled friskily and seemed, for a moment, ready to run out and throw herself at his feet.

"I'll be his slave," she said. "I'll make French toast and fritters for him. I'll sit naked on his lap and feed him marmalade."

Vinny put a protective arm around Minnie's waist and held her. Restraining her, holding her.

When the wagons were loaded, Morgan mounted his horse and, briskly, they all moved out. Big thunder again, swirls of dust rising from the street and hanging in the air. That fast, the swooping in and the taking, then quickly on their way.

Those three boys that were out there—they ran down the street, toward the rear of the column. Two were throwing rocks, and one had a pistol. He stopped running and fired off a shot. I couldn't hear it, the gunshot smothered by the roar of the horses' hooves, but I did see the gun jerk, and saw one of the riders at the rear stiffen in the saddle and lean off to one side. Maybe hit by a bullet, or maybe by a rock thrown by one of the other boys. He turned his horse and unlimbered his rifle, and the riders close by did the same, coming to a stop. They took aim and fired, then reloaded and fired again, and those boys, all three of them, they were down.

The soldiers galloped back to the column, and as the rumble of the hooves faded, there was nothing out there, only the street and the dust, and the three boys on the ground, and a gaping sense of an enormous emptiness. The owner of the store was still out there by his front door, dumbstruck, looking lost.

People came slowly out of their houses, cautious, looking up and down the street. Some went over to the boys.

Then I noticed that Minnie had grabbed hold of the curtain. She had the edge of it in her mouth, and was biting down hard.

We'd had our fill of close-to-the-war Kentucky, and Bleeker brought us back up into Ohio. We spent a few days in Cincinnati, where there were swarms of Union soldiers, and they were glad to see us. We entertained them, some songs, some dances. Vinny and Minnie sang a few of the new war songs, "Tenting on the Old Camp Ground" and "Tramp! Tramp! Tramp!" along with the old favorite from the start of the war, "John Brown's Body."

The best part of Cincinnati was the pouch of letters waiting for us when we arrived at our hotel—including several from Benjamin. He sent his letters to the Museum, and whenever possible, we wired Roth, in the mailroom, telling him far in advance of a hotel we were planning to be at, and the pouch would be waiting when we arrived. But because mail delivery was slow, and because it was difficult to know, weeks in advance, which town or city we would be in, and which hotel, it often happened that months went by with no mail at all. In fact, before the Cincinnati pouch, the last mail we'd received had been in Detroit, just before Christmas.

Poor Benjamin, when we had last seen him, at the camp in Arlington Heights, more than a year ago, he was complaining about the lack of action—but after we parted, they handed him more than he ever really wanted. They put him on picket duty on the Columbia Pike, and then, in April, he was sent to Norfolk, and the regiment fought against Longstreet's siege of Suffolk. Vinny saved every one of his letters and carried them with her in her luggage. Now and then, she pulled some out and we read them again, especially when we hadn't heard from him for a while.

When the siege of Suffolk was raised, the regiment was moved to Yorktown, and, in June, Benjamin took part in a raid on Jamestown Island. That was before the draft riots in New York and before Vinny and I had set out on our tour into Canada.

"It's a weird feeling," he wrote, "to hear bullets whizzing past and to know the person firing them wants to kill you. Something changes inside you. And even weirder to know that I, firing my rifle, fully intend someone else's death. This is not like throwing snowballs back home in Middleboro."

Vinny hated it when he wrote about the shooting; it filled her with dread because of the danger he was in. But she cherished the letters, couldn't do without them. They were with us wherever we went.

In the summer, about half a year after we'd seen him in Washington, there had been a letter that he wrote when he was on Folly Island, off the coast of South Carolina, preparing for action against the rebels on Morris Island and at Fort Sumter. There was still talk, he said, about the assault against Morris Island back in July, spearheaded by an all-black company from Massachusetts. After a heavy bombardment, the blacks stormed the fort but were driven back by heavy fire. They had many dead, including their officer, a colonel named Shaw, Robert Gould Shaw. "The men who saw it still talk about it," Benjamin wrote. "Those black fellows, they fought like hell. Lincoln should have thrown them in right away, first day of the war."

Then, early in the new year, 1864, his letters were from Florida, where he was involved in the fighting at Ten Mile Run and Barber's Place. And these, now, were among the letters in the pouch that reached us in Cincinnati. After Barber's Place, there was the big Battle of Olustee, where they took a beating.

Dear Vin and Charlie—

My lice are now known to be the smartest and fastest in my company. Our new way of racing them is to put them on the end of a log, tip it up at an incline, and the louse that makes it first to the bottom end is the winner. Some are too dumb for the game, they stay where they are, or they go round and round the log with no ambition to scoot on down. But my lice zip along, driven by an internal command from Destiny. So far I have won three hundred and thirty-three dollars this way and thirty-three cents. Should I quit while I'm ahead?

Dear Both of You—

We are a weird, wild bunch here but we hang together. Jed Leary has a furry mongrel he picked up as a stray and carries it around with him. Tim Belch keeps a rabbit on a leash. Carl Sloe has a canary in a cage that he takes everywhere—he swears it's the canary that keeps him alive. If the canary drops, Carl says he'll drop, too, and maybe the whole regiment. Fred Thorne plays a sweet harmonica, we sit around and listen. Sometimes the guys go a little crazy and dance with each other. But mostly we gamble, craps and poker, some faro, and always a jug of tar water to pass around. There are days when time is slow, thick as molasses—but then it's thin as vinegar, acid in your mouth, and you don't know how much more of this you really want.

Dear V and C—

Yesterday, at Olustee, the grays were all neatly entrenched, and our general, Truman Seymour, damn fool, sends us smash against the breastworks and we lost a lot of good men. That's how it happens, and it damn hurts. But the other side took a beating, too, and at the end of the day, even though we ran like hell, they were too much of a mess to follow and take their advantage.

Carl Sloe is one of the many who didn't make it back. Yesterday, February 20, 1864. A day to remember. I found Carl's bird in camp, in its cage, tweeting away and hungry. I guess the damn thing is now mine.

Dear Married Couple—

In answer to the question in your last letter—yes, we still are doing well enough in the chow department, though it is not Delmonico's. And I can tell you the fellows on the other side get less and less. They are full out of coffee and now make a substitute brew from boiled peas, or okra, or pumpkin seed. They're out of ink and write their letters with pokeberry juice. Some dig for worms and fry them. The lucky ones are the ones in the swamp areas, they get snails and sometimes a catfish.

And, yes, we do still have plenty of soap, but it ain't much use unless you are near a river or a creek. We suffer much from the scream-ers—which some call the quick step, or the runs—but at the moment I am fit as a fiddle. So far I have not come down with measles or variola or swamp fever, as some have, but expect I will have my turn. And no sign, yet, of yellow jack. They had an epidemic in North Carolina, it killed thousands.

I tell you all this because I have to tell somebody and I don't dare say any of it in my letters home. Mother would cry her eyes out. Vin, don't ever dare show her what I write! When all of this is over, I think I will become a gardener and grow roses. Hey, Vinny—remember those pretty flowers we had in the garden behind the house?

Hello, hello—

I am thinking today, don't know why, about that Homestead Act they put through back in 1862. If you go west, the government lets you pick out a hundred and sixty acres—and if you work on it, it's yours. Do I have it right? I think the two of you should make plans. You could set up a dwarf farm with dwarf apple trees, dwarf sheep, dwarf cattle, and dwarf potatoes growing in the ground. Little Minnie could be the maid. Sounds good to me. I think you folks could make a go of it!

Dear Fancy People in Your Fancy Duds—

I don't think I ever told you this. Some time ago, when we were on Folly Island, we were given an issue of fresh uniforms, which we were glad about, as most of us were wearing mud-caked rags with stains and holes in certain vital places. Well, those new uniforms lasted not nearly three days. We were hit by a heavy rain and the damn things shredded and washed away. So there we were, standing around bare-assed. Yes, we had heard about this sort of thing, but never thought it would happen to us. Some fuckle-brained lizards are making this shoddy junk and pawning it off on the army, and the men here are so mad, those bastards better watch their backsides when we get home.

Among the other letters in the pouch, there was yet another from Benjamin, addressed only to me, and lucky that I, not Vinny, was the one who had picked up the pouch at the hotel desk. In the letter, Benjamin asked that I not show it to her. "It would upset her awfully," he wrote.

He'd been at the Battle of Cold Harbor, where things went horribly wrong. Grant had sent his troops headlong into Lee's line, hoping to crash through and plunge straight ahead to Richmond, but all he got out of it was a lot of dead bodies to ship home.

We had already heard about the battle, which was fought at the start of June, in Virginia, while we were still in Kentucky, and it was a bit of a shock to learn that Benjamin had been there, at Cold Harbor. In less than an hour, thousands of Union soldiers were dead or wounded. Some of the papers said five thousand. Some said seven. Either way, it was a horrific loss.

. . . Bad, bad, bad. But my regiment, luckily, was to the rear of that crazy frontal that cost us so many. They say Antietam gave us the bloodiest single day in the war—but this now, Cold Harbor, handed us the single bloodiest hour. June 3, 1864. Remember that date, Charlie. And the hateful part is that it took a couple of days to arrange a truce so we could pick up our wounded. A lot of good men died that could have been saved if they'd a-been brought in sooner.

It was a hideous defeat for the North. Even in Kentucky, where opinion was so divided, pro-North and pro-South, there was, I remember, a general sense of horror that so many could be cut down so fast. Modern guns could do that, shoot down thousands of men—in what? Forty, fifty minutes? Less? Everywhere, a sense of overwhelming calamity, a feeling that the world had changed in some awful way, and how were we going to live with ourselves when such mad things were now possible?

Even Grant knew it was too much. He pulled out, swung around Lee's flank, and accepted the hard fact that he would have to go to Richmond the long way, by attacking it from the south, and to do that he'd have to fight his way through Petersburg first.

Horace Greeley's reporters in Washington dug it up that Mary Lincoln was hopping mad, calling Grant a butcher. Greeley didn't print it, though he did mention it to Barnum, who passed it to me in a letter that reached me in the same pouch that carried the last few letters from Benjamin. Vinny read that letter, and it upset her, because it was hard for her to put the two Grants together, the easygoing, down-to-earth, homespun man she had met before the war, when she was performing on a Mississippi showboat, and the hard, aggressive general who could send thousands to their death in battle. Him? The one who had been a humble clerk in his father's leather store? The one who couldn't make a go of it as a farmer, and then in real estate? And if this Grant, the warrior Grant, was a puzzle, an incomprehensible piece of Zootagataz, Robert E. Lee was no different—he of the noble spirit and generous heart, he too was sending thousands to their death.

Vinny saw Barnum's letter about Mary Lincoln, but not the letter from Benjamin to me, about Cold Harbor. As far as she knew, he was never near Cold Harbor and was tucked safely away in the big camp at Arlington, resting, playing cards, racing his lice, eating salted pork, and picking his teeth with his fingernails.

For quite some time, I'd found myself, in idle moments, thinking about Africa. It was calming, enchanting. Barnum's Museum was crowded with African things—not just the stuffed birds and animals, but ritual masks, carved wooden figures, garments, stone pieces used in cooking. So I knew some little about the Dark Continent, and had done a bit of reading, too.

We were aboard a train, leaving Ohio and on our way into Pennsylvania. I was thinking of the rosewoods, the cedars, the baobabs, the mangroves. Monkeys in the trees, birds with exotic plumage, and vast, open fields crowded with zebras and gazelles.

With the slave trade slowly stumbling to an end, there was a new Africa rising out of the old. Things to see there, things to learn. Satinwood trees and ebony, and long, braided vines with gigantic purple flowers. And the Pygmies, my dwarf cousins—I liked to imagine that in some ancient past, we were all one, arising from the same root. Dwarf zebras, too, and dwarf giraffes, dwarf elephants, all there in Africa, waiting to be discovered.

I was thinking, dreaming, and turned to Vinny, wanting to tell her how interesting Africa might be, the wonderful things to see there. "Vinny? Vinny?" But she was asleep, head leaning back against the cushion, her face serene. Gone, adrift in a dreamland of her own, her breasts rising and falling with the steady rhythm of her breathing, a rhythm that matched the rhythm of the train, and I understood that she too was the journey. The two of us one and the same, this shared life that we had, on the road. The road was home, and in more ways than one I was beginning to understand that the road was her. Her breathing so calm, so steady. Before long her sleep became my sleep, and I too was gone, wandering in the dream she was dreaming, a dream that brought us into a dark green place in a forest where neither of us had ever been.

PART SIX

BLACK SMOKE IN THE MORNING SKY

∾ CHAPTER 18 ∾

CHAMBERSBURG

On the last leg of our tour, Sylvester Bleeker brought us into Pennsylvania. We were moving fast, tired of the road and eager to get home. No more weeklong stays anywhere. Keep moving, that was the mood. After one-night stands in Pittsburgh, McKeesport, and Manns Choice, we arrived, on a Friday afternoon, in Chambersburg, and made our way to the Franklin Hotel. The day warm and uncomfortable, the hot end of a hot July.

It was a pleasant little town, a hundred years old, with handsome downtown buildings that sported fancy facades and stone columns. A large bank, quite a few churches. And rows of stores along Main Street, with colorful awnings.

Before the Battle of Gettysburg, Robert E. Lee had camped his army in the neighboring fields and hills, a sprawling corps of more than sixty thousand. The proprietor of the hotel, a stout, black-haired man with an egg-shaped growth on his forehead, told us what a mess it had been, soldiers swarming all over the town. He mentioned, too, that before the war John Brown had been in town, on East King Street, posing as a prospector, but in fact he'd been gathering guns, preparing for the raid on Harpers Ferry.

"You never know what's on the way," the proprietor said, sounding as if he was looking forward to the next bit of excitement. Very proud he was of the town's long history. He told us to stop in the cemetery before we left, for a look at the old headstones. And I'm thinking, sure, why not, just what I need. A graveyard.

That evening we performed at the Masonic Hall on South Second Street, and at the end of the long day, when we returned to the hotel, we were ready to drop. Keeler and Harry Nobbs shuffled into the bar, and the rest of us dragged ourselves up to our rooms. But when Vinny and I reached ours, she turned to me with a slow, needful look and said what she would really like, at that moment, was a macaroon.

I winced. "In this town? A macaroon?"

"Char-lie," she said, pleading.

"But nothing's open."

"Up the block," she said. "I saw a place, we passed it just now, coming back from the Hall."

So I went down into the night, big me, thirty-six inches tall. Looking around, I spotted a shop with its lamps lit. They sold crackers, bread, and incidentals. The girl behind the counter, mesmerized by my smallness, couldn't take her eyes off of me. Bright blue, those eyes, like the indigo-blue of forget-me-nots, and a sullen, mystified stare. She had no idea what a macaroon might be.

"We have lemon drops," she said.

"Nothing else?"

"Chocolate pound cake. But it's stale."

I bought the lemon drops.

Back at the room, Vinny's face sagged with disappointment. "I can't eat these," she said. "They'll ruin my teeth."

I took one. Not half bad, as lemon drops go.

"They had beef jerky. I should have bought some?"

"Don't be silly."

She took a lemon drop and said, after a moment, "They could have put more lemon in it."

I took another, and she took another. We did that for a while, sitting on the bed, she in her night shift and I in my street clothes. Before long, fatigue set in, sweeping through both of us. She leaned back on her pillow and, faster than I knew, she was swallowed up in sleep. And the same with me, so tired I slept in my shirt and pants.

I don't recall that I had any dreams that night, though I know there are people—Barnum is one—who say we always dream, and when we seem not to, it's because the dream was too deeply buried to be remembered. Well, what does Barnum know? In fact, what do I? What I do know, and painfully remember, is the thing that happened late that night, while I was far off in the dark spaces of sleep—I was wrenched awake by the sound of a big gun firing. Vinny, too—yanked out of sleep. And, no doubt, everyone in town.

It was half past three in the morning. A thin slice of the moon was up, the sky busy, full of stars. Again the roar of that gun. I stepped into the corridor. Minnie came out of her room, and some of the others, in night shifts. Bleeker was up and dressed already—or, like me, he may never have changed out of his day clothes. He hovered by the staircase, then rushed down to see what he could learn.

Moments later he was back, saying a Confederate force had arrived in the night and was bivouacked on the high hills two miles west of town. The firing was from a gun that General Crouch's men had set up on the Pittsburgh Pike, to hold the rebels off. But it was hopeless, because all Crouch had was fifty men. The regiments that were based in the town had been siphoned off to bolster the defenses around Washington, which was again threatened by a Confederate advance.

"Pack your things," Bleeker told everybody. "Better to be ready."

I went back to the room, and while Vinny dressed, I stashed our stuff into the luggage. Through the window I saw wagons and buckboards pulling up to the stores along the street, and gaslights coming on inside—shopkeepers rushing in and pulling merchandise out of their stores, riding off with as much as they could handle. A fabrics shop, a furniture store, the shop where I'd bought the lemon drops. At the bank there were two coaches and five or six guards with rifles—the bank people filling the coaches with sacks of money.

Vinny left to help Minnie, and I found Bleeker in his room, buckling up his bags. His wife, Julia, had gone to help the Commodore.

"What do you think?"

"I don't know." His mind was racing. So was mine.

We went down to the lobby, and the others followed—Ken Keeler, and Nobbs, and Jerry Richardson, and the baggage boys. The lobby crowded up, and the night clerk was telling people there was a room in the cellar—if they had any valuables, they could store them there. Luggage, too, and we knew what he was saying. The rebs would grab anything they could carry.

Ken Keeler had the box with the jewelry and the cash receipts; he went nowhere without it. Under his long jacket, he carried a pistol on his hip. "I'll keep the box with me," he muttered.

Bleeker was busy thinking—eyes darting, intense, fierce. Suddenly, he was all decision.

"I need a wagon and a coach," he told the night clerk, a slim, dull-eyed fellow with sideburns, thirtyish, in black pants, a blue vest over his white shirt, his necktie a black shoelace tied with a bow.

"Impossible," he said. "You see how it is. The ones with wagons, they're carting their valuables into the hills. It's routine, whenever the rebs come near. Some don't bother no more, but a lot do."

Bleeker took out a roll of bills, peeled off two fifties, and stuffed them into the fellow's vest pocket. The clerk nodded. "I'll see what I can do."

He darted out of the lobby, and while he was gone, we were out front, on the portico, waiting. When he returned, he pulled up with a wagon drawn by a scraggly old nag.

"That the best you can find?" Bleeker said.

"Beggars can't be choosers," the clerk answered, with a shrug. He had thin lips with an odd curl at the corners that seemed almost a sneer. "And you can forget about that coach you were hopin' for."

"Then find another wagon."

"Already paid everythin' you give me for this one, and offered my solemn promise you would bring it back," he said. "I don't think you understand the big favor I just done you."

Bleeker stared at the clerk, mistrustful. Still, he took out two more fifties.

"I'll be back," the fellow said with a slick nod, grabbing the cash, and he disappeared up the street. The sky was brightening, the faintest glimmer of dawn. The stars fading, the skinny moon paler than it had been.

Bleeker told the luggage boys to fetch the trunks and baggage from the rooms and load them onto the wagon. He told Keeler to stay by the wagon and guard it with his life.

We went inside to check on the women. They were already on their way down. The Commodore was fidgety, asking when and where to pick up some breakfast.

"Next week," I told him. "If you're lucky."

Vinny yanked at my arm and leaned close. "Was that necessary?" she said.

Julia rummaged in her carryall and came up with a muffin wrapped in a napkin, from last night's dinner. The Commodore took it and stepped away, not wanting us to watch as he ate.

Bleeker and I returned to the portico, keeping an eye out for the night clerk. But nothing. The boys had all of the luggage aboard the wagon. Bleeker checked everything, wheels, axles, and made sure the luggage was secure.

Still no sign of the night clerk. "I gave him too much," Bleeker said. "He never spent a damn nickel for the nag and the wagon—must have grabbed them from some back alley, and now he's pocketed the extra hundred I gave him and hiked his ass out of here, to the big city. Which for him, I suppose, is Harrisburg."

Still we waited, and before long the hotel proprietor rode up on a black mare.

"Looks bad, looks bad," he said.

Bleeker stiffened. "How bad?"

"They'll sack the town and do damage. Bastard rebs are hungry and they forage for what they can get. Better for you to get out while you can."

"That's what we're trying to do," Bleeker said.

It was half past five. Just then three cannon shots were fired into the town, one ball smashing into a shop just up the street. The proprietor rushed off, riding fast, and Bleeker, swiftly, like a man possessed, sent the two baggage boys off with the wagon, pointing them to the road that would take them to Fayetteville and then on to Gettysburg. "We'll catch up with you there, at the depot," he said, and sent Richardson with them, since there was room for one more. He kept Keeler and the cash box with us.

We were braced for more cannon fire, but there was none. Moments after the wagon was gone, a heap of cavalry came thundering in, arriving from different directions. Foot soldiers, too, appearing to our left and right.

"Inside, inside," Bleeker shouted, herding us back into the lobby.

Then we waited, and it seemed forever. A few Confederate officers stepped up onto the portico and stood there, on the other side of the glass-paned doors, talking animatedly. One pointed toward the bank. Another shook his head, and another pounded his fist into the palm of his hand. One, grim-faced, stepped inside, glanced about at the mob, then stepped back out.

"Maybe we should go up to our rooms," the Commodore said.

I didn't like that idea. Nor did Bleeker. "Better to be here," he said, "in case something happens."

"What could happen?" the Commodore chirped.

Bleeker didn't answer.

Julia took a bag of peanuts out of her mesh carryall and passed them around. We sat there for a while, cracking the soft shells and crunching on the nuts. A woman was humming to her baby. A bearded man paced by the door. A tall man blew his nose, the sound reminding me of my father, the deep bassoon resonance whenever he blew into his handkerchief.

When the proprietor returned, he was swollen with anger. He stood by the desk, and in a strong, tense voice, told what he knew. The officer in charge, he said, was General McCausland, with orders from Jubal Early to collect a tribute from the town or burn it to the ground. "They want a hundred thousand in gold coin, or half a million in Union currency."

A low moan limped through the lobby.

"Will they pay?" the man with the beard called out.

The proprietor rubbed his hands together and swung his head from side to side, as if struggling to avoid the bad news he was giving us. "It ain't likely or even possible," he said, and again the low, restless moan, folding and unfolding. "The town elders say there ain't near enough cash in the town, which is true. The bank moved its reserves up to Harrisburg soon as they learned of the troops on the hill. Right now the parties are still talking—but frankly, folks, it don't look good. People in town are gathering what they can and going off to the fields and hills. I would urge all of you to do the same."

None of this was anything I wanted to hear. I was shutting it out, pushing it off. Inside my head, I was humming, a silly rhythm flowing like a brook through my brain. Vinny too in her mind she was humming. I was holding her hand, and felt the humming coming through her pores.

And the proprietor—still there, warning us that looting and window smashing had already begun. They were breaking into homes and shops, grabbing whisky and whatever caught their fancy. Some were already drunk. He urged us to stay in groups because it was getting wild out there, soldiers snatching hats and purses, pulling rings off fingers. He told the women to hide their jewelry—and still, in my mind, I was humming, no words, just an easy flow of sound running through my head.

"Why?" someone called out, the woman with the baby. "Why are they doing this awful thing?"

"For compensation, that's what they say. They want compensation."

"For what?"

Again he swung his head from side to side, with obvious discomfort. "Well, it's tit for tat, you see. General Hunter, right or wrong, burned a bunch of houses in the Shenandoah. Local farmers were killing his men in the night, grabbing them, cutting their throats, and the big landowners and the governor were encouraging it. So Hunter announced he would burn any houses in the vicinity of the murders. He torched some big ones, a few belonging to folks with close ties to Jeff Davis. So it's tit for tat, you might say."

People were worrying now about their luggage, to carry it with them or leave it behind, though for most the luggage would be too heavy to carry anyway. There were no bellboys to help. None had yet arrived for work that morning, and it was unlikely that any would.

Bleeker, turning in on himself, sank into a dark mood. I knew what he was thinking. When those three cannon shots were fired, he should have abandoned the luggage and squeezed everyone aboard, the entire troupe—and could have driven off, away from the mess and the danger.

I should have thought of that myself. Because this was, after all, my troupe, we were Tom Thumb & Company. I was the one. Responsible for what we did or didn't do, and if Bleeker was in a darkness, I was in a messy midnight of my own. I felt a growing sense of panic for Vinny and little Minnie, and for Julia, and all of us. We were caught there with no way out, and no knowing how bad it might become.

And the bitter irony—this was happening not in dangerous Kentucky, where we had foolishly, carelessly, put ourselves at risk, but here in the North, close to the battlefield where Lee's invading army had been soundly beaten just over a year ago.

The proprietor told Bleeker to swaddle us in towels and carry us out as if we were babies. "Some out there are crazy drunk—you want nothing that will catch their attention. If they see the dwarfs, they'll be on you for sure."

In my head I was humming again, trying not to think, trying to shut it all out. Suddenly, from a corner of my eye, I glimpsed a man coming down the main staircase. He wore a black broadcloth suit, carried a hefty leather valise, and kept his eyes straight ahead. His black beard closely trimmed, and—yes—a mole high on his left cheek. The same fellow, the one I'd seen at the train station in Vertigo, during a long stop. And too many other times, even at my wedding reception. I stood rooted, watching as he stepped briskly from the stairs, past the front desk, then out the door, onto the portico, and gone.

I said nothing to Bleeker, nothing to Vinny, just stood there, baffled, unable to believe what I'd just seen.

Then it was all of a rush, out onto the street. Bleeker carried Vinny on one arm and me on the other, and Harry Nobbs held Minnie and the Commodore—each of us wrapped in a blue towel the proprietor had found for us, only our faces showing.

A soldier with a whisky bottle in one hand, and a pistol in the other, stopped Bleeker, wanting to know what he was carrying. When he saw our faces, Vinny's and mine, he laughed and stepped back. "Two of 'em, huh? Been keepin' your woman busy. Where is she? Got another in the oven?" He stepped away and urinated by a bunch of bushes—and Bleeker, seizing the moment, hurried on.

Soldiers were kicking doors down, entering houses, and smashing the furniture, creating piles of splintered wood ready to be torched. We saw them through open doors and windows, throwing clothes and mattresses into heaps, tossing them on top of smashed chairs and tables.

Some, though, were unhappy with the goings-on. One lugged an old woman's sewing machine to a safe spot away from the houses, so it would be far from the fire. Several were doing that, helping people to move their belongings, carrying lamps, trunks. Two soldiers carried a corpse out of a house where it was being waked, and buried it in a shallow grave in the small front garden. But many were looting, coming out of houses with things they'd taken—a copper kettle, a bearskin rug. One wore a calico dress over his uniform, his carbine in one hand, a bottle of rum in the other, and a cigar hanging from the corner of his mouth.

As we turned a corner, I saw a soldier knock a man down and take the satchel he was carrying—but it held nothing, only some clothes. He pulled them out and threw them on the street. Farther along, a woman screaming and wailing in front of her house—a soldier slapped her in the face and shoved her to the ground.

"Keep movin', keep movin'," a sergeant shouted at Bleeker, and soon we were out of it, away from the houses, stables, shops, brick buildings.

Bleeker carried us up a long hill and into the cemetery, where most of the townspeople were gathering, amid the gravestones.

General McCausland had the main body of his force on the western side of the town, about a mile off, on the fairgrounds by the Pittsburgh Pike. From the hill where we stood, they were faintly visible in the morning light, a dense crowd of gray uniforms. Somebody said it was two thousand troops out there, on the fairgrounds. Maybe more.

And, all around us, people murmuring, coughing. Sobbing.

We stood on dewy grass, looking down at the town. Vinny leaned against me, my arm around her waist, and Minnie leaned against her. A few feet away, the Commodore sat on a low stone that marked a grave.

People were scattered across the hill and in the neighboring fields—standing, sitting, holding each other, some just arriving out of the town, with satchels, knapsacks, baggage filled with the few things they'd been able to rescue. A bad mood, fear and anger in the air. People groaning. Where to go, what to do? The sun low and rising, a warm breeze, a few horses wandering free. We saw right down into the heart of the town—houses, shops, livery stables. The courthouse. The brick bank. The Franklin Hotel. There was an ache, a heart-wrenching astonishment—simple disbelief that all of this would very soon be gone.

Nine o'clock, people still coming from the town. Suddenly, a massive flash of flame from the town hall, then flames exploding through the windows of the courthouse. To the east and west of Main Street, shops and homes bursting into flames, soldiers using explosive devices to ignite the fires.

Long black columns of smoke rose in the morning sky, weaving and snaking about. The hissing and crackling of wood burning, the roar of roofs and walls collapsing. And the woeful moaning of animals caught in the flames and dying. It seemed, somehow, the end of the world. That's what it was for the people on the hill. That fast, their town was a bonfire. They had lost everything.

Minnie was still leaning against Vinny, frightened, withdrawn, looking away from the ruined town. Vinny stroked her arm, comforting her. Houses and buildings still burning, and, high above the town, clouds of smoke lingered.

By eleven o'clock, the fairgrounds to the west, by the Pittsburgh Pike, were deserted. McCausland and his cavalry had pulled out. A few soldiers were still in the town, some rambling through what was left of Market Street, inspecting the damage, others darting about, in and out of the few homes that had escaped damage, taking whatever they could carry. A birdcage, a picture in a gold frame. A violin case. A red umbrella.

All that was left of the bank were the blackened brick walls. Of the courthouse, only the columns and one wall, amid the scattered bricks and stones from the walls that had fallen. Where the homes and shops had stood, brick chimneys rose like long, blackened fingers. About two-thirds of the town had burned. It was worst in the downtown area, by the bank and the courthouse, the destruction spreading over some ten square blocks. The hotel where we slept, and the restaurant across the street, where we had eaten. The shop where I had bought lemon drops for Vinny.

It was Saturday, one day before the last day of July—and strangely, with a bleak sense of the emptiness inside me, what I felt on that hill, as I gazed upon the ruins, was that I was no longer young. All of twenty-six years old. In a few months, Vinny would turn twenty-three. It was 1864. Sherman was moving against Atlanta, and Grant was besieging Petersburg. And anything could happen, anything at all.

People began to move off the hill, back into town, for a closer look. "I hate all this," Vinny said. "I hate it." She was weeping. Minnie, facing the town now, was frozen, as in a trance, the knuckle of one of her fingers anchored in her mouth.

The Commodore seemed dazed and confused, and frightened. "I

want to go home," he said, looking down into the ruined streets and avenues. And only then, when he said that, did I realize I didn't know where home was for him. I knew he was from New Hampshire, but from a village or a city, in the mountains or by the ocean, I had no idea, and had never asked.

"Take me home—please," he said, to no one in particular, sounding not at all like himself. His eyes were still fastened on the devastation. He stood motionless, gazing like a lost child.

And I—I just stood there, holding on to Vinny. She was all I had. We were part of the same slice of time, caught in this bad moment, in a cemetery, and all that foul smoke hanging in the air.

∽ CHAPTER 19 ∽

ASHES AND CHARRED WOOD . . . THE JOURNEY BACK

When I turned, preparing to move down off the hill, I saw the proprietor of the hotel. He was lost in confusion, gazing at the wreckage. His hotel was gone, nothing left but the stone pillars of the portico, and the chimneys. Wherever you looked in the burnt center of that town, you saw chimneys. They were everywhere, stubby black fingers rising up out of the destruction.

"I don't know," he said. "Just—don't—know." He was worn down, with none of the strength and vigor that he'd had before the town was put to the torch. "This war, it's too much," he said, shaking his head from side to side as he moved off the hill, down into the desolation.

I heard the same from a widow who had stood near us during those many hours. She was one of the lucky ones whose home had been spared—but who was lucky, she said, when the bank, the town hall, the stores, and the stables were gone. And so many with nowhere to live? We were still on the hill. She pointed to her house, east of the burnt-out area, but I hardly knew which of those faraway houses she was pointing at.

"It never ends," she said, her voice drenched with despair. "Never. And now this—the worst."

Her name was Sarah Pyne, and she was good to us. She understood the distress we were in, and brought us to her little home, a far walk, the stink of ashes and charred wood everywhere.

She invited us to stay at her house, small though it was, till help arrived from the army, but Bleeker was eager to get out of the area as fast as possible, before more trouble developed. We'd heard that McCausland had torn up the tracks in the surrounding area, so we needed, at the very least, a horse and wagon to get us to Gettysburg, where Richardson and the baggage boys were waiting.

The widow gave him the name of a farmer who bred horses, about four miles out of town. "He's a friend," she said. "Be sure to mention my name. If he ain't there, keep walkin', there are more farms farther off." With a pencil she drew a little map.

It was shortly past noon when Bleeker went off. He took Harry Nobbs with him. They carried a few jelly sandwiches the widow made for them.

While they were gone, she shared with us the little that she had, some leftover turkey, boiled beets, bread, and the remains of a cherry pie. "Not to worry," she said. "I have a sack of potatoes, and a big bag of flour to make bread with. And plenty of carrots. Enough to keep me going till the army sends some supply wagons." And we dug in. We'd been awake since the wee hours of the morning, no food in us till now, and before long our dishes were clean.

We didn't expect Bleeker back till well after two, or later. But he surprised us. He was back in little more than an hour, with a horse and a dead-axle wagon, and Harry Nobbs handling the reins. Harry had done some of that when he was young, transporting kegs for a brewery. The horse looked strong enough, but the thought of riding on a dead-axle wagon was less than inviting.

"You're back early," I said to Bleeker.

"Luck was with us. We were less than ten minutes up the road when we met a fellow who was hitching his horse to a buggy. When I told him where we were headed, he said he knew the place and told us to hop aboard. We were spared the long hike."

I put my hand on the wagon and looked Bleeker in the eye. "How much?"

"Don't ask," he answered, making it clear that he'd dug deeper into our earnings than his self-respect would allow him to admit.

As we prepared to depart, he offered the widow some money, in gratitude for her hospitality, but she wouldn't take it. He passed the money to me, with a nod, and while she was at the wagon, making her farewells, I slipped inside and left it on the kitchen table, along with some extra from my pocket, knowing she would need it.

It was a rough, grumbly ride to Gettysburg, some twenty miles off. Even in a carriage with springs you feel the road, but when you're on a dead-axle wagon with no springs, the road kicks at you every inch of the way. Most of us suffered with varying degrees of impatience—Bleeker gritted his teeth, and little Minnie clenched her fists. There was a moment when the Commodore stood on his hands, but at the next bump he tumbled backward and his heels hit me in the head.

Vinny sang. She was joined by Julia and Minnie, and Harry Nobbs, whose voice should have been declared illegal. I gazed at the sky, searching for eagles, but saw none. Ken Keeler wasn't interested in eagles or anything else. He leaned over the edge and belched up most of what he'd eaten at the widow's house.

The sun was still up when we arrived in Gettysburg. Jerry Richardson and the baggage boys were waiting at the train depot, with their wagon. They had all but given up on us. Bleeker bargained with the ticketmaster, obtaining tickets to New York in exchange for the two wagons and the horses—he didn't come close to recouping the amount he'd paid for them, but it was something.

Bleeker had planned a performance in Harrisburg, but after what we'd been through, we were less than eager about that. While we waited for the train, he telegraphed the theater and canceled. He also telegraphed Sam Hurd, to let him know we had survived the trouble in Chambersburg and were on our way home.

And while we were in a canceling mood, we decided, yet again, to delay our sailing date for Europe. This was painful, but what was the point of rushing off to Europe if we were too dragged out to enjoy it? That's what Vinny said. And Jerry Richardson. And Nobbs. And Julia Bleeker. And Bleeker himself, reluctantly. He suggested we hang around till the election, since it was likely to be a cliff-hanger, and we might even think of lingering till Thanksgiving, which Lincoln had elevated to a national holiday.

Election Day—yes. We would stay for that. After the losses at Cold Harbor and elsewhere during the first half of the year, Lincoln was down, down, down. McClellan, running on the Democratic peace platform, was beginning to look like a shoo-in. Even though the South was low on food, low on manpower, low on all sorts of supplies, and trapped in a downward spiral—despite all of that, many in the North were vomiting over the high body counts and wondering if conquest of the South could be worth the price. Grant was denounced as a butcher—wasting his men and sending them to the grave. And Lincoln, backing Grant, was lampooned as a gorilla, a tyrant, an Illinois beast, a mule.

All through the war, he'd been on a seesaw. When the Union won a battle, he was up and applauded, but when the army lost, he was down and hated. Baggy-pants Lincoln, wooly-haired Lincoln, long-necked Lincoln, hat-cocked-at-the-back-of-his-head Lincoln. And skinny, losing weight. His own party wasn't sure they wanted him. At the June convention there had been efforts to dump him. So it was touch-and-go, and too many uncertainties.

When the train for New York arrived at the Gettysburg station, it was an hour behind schedule, and it gave us a slow, stop-and-go ride. Yet we were glad to be heading home. The bumps and bounces of that dead-axle wagon were printed on our bones, and the stink of the simmering ashes in Chambersburg was still with us. Where was there air clean enough and fresh enough to wash away the smell?

"I'm so tired," Vinny said, sitting beside me on that slow, cranky train, leaning her head on my shoulder. "Every bone in my body feels broken. Are your bones broken?"

My bones weren't broken, but they were bruised. My dreams were bruised. My memories. Everything I knew about life, what I had hoped for and imagined—bruised, and I felt the pain. I wanted to believe what Barnum believed, that things get better, not worse. For everyone. People helping one another, getting past the rough spots, and moving on to better things. But it wasn't happening, no. That wasn't the world we were in.

Of all of us, little Minnie was the only one who was undaunted. She wanted to go back to Kentucky and was still talking about Morgan, using words like "gorgeous, exotic, a tree, a wild hunk of a man"—though it was hard to know if she was really caught up in an obsession or just pretending, her way of trying to catch the Commodore's attention and make him jealous. What she saw in him, I never understood.

From a vendor on the train, we bought jam sandwiches, pickles, bottled soda, and a newspaper.

The news on the front page was a punch in the eye. The previous day, while we'd been at Chambersburg, watching the town burn, there had been fighting at Petersburg, with big losses for the Union. And that was a worry. The last we'd heard, Benjamin's regiment had been on its way to Petersburg—and no knowing, now, if he was okay.

It was hard on Vinny. She was stiff-upper-lip about it, hiding her worry, but she was bleeding inside. The paper carried lists of the dead and wounded, but only those from the Pittsburgh area, nothing about Benjamin's regiment, the Fortieth Massachusetts. That's how it was—you waited, and did your best to bury your worry and get on with the things that you had to do. But the worry was always there, nibbling away.

When we reached New York, it was deep into the night and we all put up at the Astor.

The next morning, early, the Commodore dashed off with a packed bag, saying he was on his way home to New Hampshire. I had my doubts about that. But off he went. After breakfast, Bleeker and I made our way across Broadway and found Barnum at the Museum, in his office.

He was back from his tour with Anna Swan, and not looking well—hair uncombed, jacket off, shirt open at the throat, a scrambled intensity in his eyes. With him in the office was his son-in-law, Sam Hurd, now his top assistant.

When Barnum saw Bleeker, he was less than happy. He had, on his desk, a stack of the more recent telegrams Bleeker had sent to Sam.

"Are you mad? Insane? What kind of an incompetent ninny are you, dragging four helpless dwarfs into enemy-infested Kentucky? They could have been abducted! Captured! Held for ransom! Killed!"

I had never seen him so wrought up. It was an un-Barnumesque bad moment, and I was as stunned by it as Bleeker was.

He stepped close up to Bleeker and put his finger on Bleeker's nose.

"Go to Smithers," he said. "Settle the accounts and collect your earnings. You're finished here."

It was cataclysmic, as if Barnum were God himself, an angry Jehovah, damning Bleeker to an eternity in hell.

I stepped between them and looked up into Barnum's eyes. "*I* made that decision," I said. "*I*'m the one who put Kentucky on our list."

"*You?*"

"Yes. Me." It had, in fact, been Lavinia's idea, but I wasn't going to say anything about that. "Sylvester had nothing to do with it."

"If that's true—and I don't believe a word—then *you* are the ninny, and Bleeker is an elephant's ass for listening to you. What in heaven's name is wrong with you? Both of you. Does riding the railroad joggle your brains? Enemy agents are everywhere. Right here in New York. But to go *there*, to Kentucky, with Morgan's Raiders doing damage at will—and then, in Pennsylvania, to put yourselves into Chambersburg, in a corner of the world where enemy regiments run around like rats in a country kitchen! Lee camped in Chambersburg on his way to Gettysburg—didn't you know? Didn't you?"

We knew. Yes, we knew. "*I*'m the one," I insisted, "Right or wrong, it was me. And we're back—with sore bones and road fatigue, but safe and alive. Even the Commodore, who would have been happier in another universe. He was cranky the whole trip. You should put him in a cage with the Madagascar monkey."

Barnum gave Bleeker a mean look, and the same mean glance for me. "I'm going to the toilet," he said, and stomped out.

I turned to Sam Hurd, wondering what all the anger was about.

"It's the tension," he said.

"What tension?"

"The house. Didn't you know? Ever since those draft riots last year, some mean threats have been floating around. There's an anti-war mob that plants rumors about raiding Phineas's house and burning it down."

I didn't know.

"You've been a long time away, Charlie. Threats against the house and threats against *him*. That's why he took Anna on tour, to get away from it all. Threats against other pro-Lincoln Republicans, too. Imagine, in Bridgeport. They want to kill Phineas and burn his house. Kill us all, I suppose. He has a warning system at the house—if there's trouble, he can fire off some rockets and the local regiment will ride in. While he was away, a few soldiers stood guard. Charity stayed here in the New York house, with the maid and a bodyguard."

Rough times, yes. I'd been nearly killed in the draft riots, so I knew how hot and mean things could get. And I knew, too, about the copperheads who hated Lincoln and wanted an end to the war. But Barnum mentioned enemy agents, as Nickerson did just over a year ago. And I wondered—where were they? If not planting bombs and blowing up ships in port, what were they doing? Playing pinochle? What *could* they do in New York where there was such a strong military presence?

But Barnum had insisted they were here, and Sam Hurd was saying the same. "Swarms of them in all the big cities," he said, "linking up with the radical anti-war groups. Doing bad and planning worse. Sabotage the docks, burn the hotels, kidnap people for ransom. Anything. Washington put out a warning to the governors."

Bleeker shrugged. "Kentucky was safer?"

"Could be, could be." Sam nodded.

I thought, just then, of that fellow I'd seen so many times—the one with the mole on his left cheek, and those sinister eyes. I was going to mention him, but it seemed far-fetched. If he was dangerous, he would have done something by now, and the world would know of it.

Sam lit a cigar and blew smoke toward the ceiling. I lit up and blew smoke toward the floor. Bleeker didn't smoke. Someone had told him smoking would ruin his voice, and he was still hoping, I suppose, for a career onstage.

Barnum returned from the toilet, and he, too, lit a cigar. "So tell me," he asked, looking at me and nodding, as if nothing had happened, as if he hadn't just flown off the handle and splashed the walls with rage. "Tell me—the tour? You found good accommodations? Good food? How are the pains in your feet? And how is young Minnie? She did fine, did she? I knew she would. And Lavinia? She still knits? Still does her embroidery?"

"Vinny sends her best," I said in a subdued tone.

"Ah, yes, such a fine little lady the Good Lord chose for you. You're a lucky man, Charlie, a lucky man."

What I knew, what I understood, was that it wasn't the Good Lord who chose her, but Barnum himself. I saw right through him. When he hired her, he was already making plans, designing the wedding and the incredible fanfare—completely confident that magic would strike for us. And doing the same, now, for Minnie and the Commodore. But about them he was dead wrong, nothing happening. And if he didn't know yet that he wasn't God, he would go to his grave imagining that he was.

"A plucky little lass, your brown-eyed Lavinia. Tell her I send my best, my very best. And to little Minnie, also." He glanced shyly toward Bleeker, in a vague effort to make amends. "And to Julia, of course," he said. "She's well, is she? Your Julia? Survived the journey? Happy to be home?"

His dark hair was thick and curly at the sides, but thin and receding on top. He'd been born in 1810—the same year, he liked to say, in which Chopin had been born. But Chopin was long gone, dead at thirty-nine, and Barnum was still going strong, though more than a little frayed at the edges.

*   *   *

Toward the end of the week, in my mailbox at the Museum, I found a letter from Benjamin, addressed only to me. It was about Petersburg, which we'd read about while training home from Gettysburg.

Dear Charlie—

This is about yesterday, which I have to tell about to somebody. And I guess, Charlie, you're it.

Some days ago they sent my regiment down to Petersburg, which our troops have had under siege since June. To get to Richmond, we have to pass through Petersburg—but it's armed to the teeth, and yesterday was sheer hell.

Our sappers had mined a tunnel under one of the rebel fortifications that blocked our way. They loaded the tunnel with a few hundred kegs of gunpowder, four tons of the stuff. When it blew, it created an enormous crater—bigger, maybe, than anyone expected.

It went off about five in the morning, a gigantic roar and a blinding flash, sending earth and sandbags and guns sky high, soldiers and pieces of soldiers. Some three hundred Confederates went to God or the devil in that blast. Nobody's measured the hole yet, but it's deep and big, I'd say two hundred feet long and maybe seventy feet wide.

The plan was for a division of our troops to rush in while the rebs were disoriented—they were to skirt the edges of the crater, then fan out behind the enemy line. Two more divisions were to follow and move against the city. With luck, my regiment was held in reserve.

But that first division—instead of skirting the rim of the crater, somehow they stumbled into the crater itself and got bogged down in there. Meanwhile, the rebs on the flanks of the crater made a quick recovery and poured a hell of a lot of gunfire into the hole.

My regiment was at a distance, over a hill, and we saw the hellish thing that unfolded. With the other divisions coming on, there was soon a whole mob of our troops down there, stumbling over one another. The rebs brought in some big guns, right up to the rim of the crater, and raked our men with canister and grapeshot. Shooting fish in a barrel, that's what it was.

I used the spyglass my pa gave me when they sent me off from home. I've lugged it with me everywhere and have seen some damn ugly things with it—but nothing worse than this. Men ripped apart by the guns at the rim, arms torn off, legs, dead and wounded piled on top of one another and blood everywhere, a muddy, bloody stew.

By God, I hope never to see such a sight again. Some in the regiment just turned away and puked, including yours truly.

Eventually, a fresh regiment charged forward onto the rim, and they drove the rebs back with hand-to-hand fighting. But that went back and forth, and finally the rebs charged into the pit with bayonets, taking prisoners and killing those that resisted. They were tough on the black soldiers, from Ferrero's division. I saw one, then another, trying to surrender, but they were shot dead.

It didn't end till midafternoon, under a blazing sun, and the talk today is that we lost close to five hundred dead and more than fifteen hundred wounded, with over a thousand unaccounted for—probably prisoners.

This thing about the crater, don't tell Vinny a jot of what I wrote. It would make her sick with worry. This is a dumb, doomed world we live in, Charlie. There are things I don't understand. Don't, and never will.

I will be stuck here, in the trenches, for the next three weeks. After today's disaster, it will be a quiet time. Then off to Bermuda Landing for provost duty at the prison, and none of those big guns shooting canister and grape at us for a while.

I lingered in the mailroom, then folded the letter and tucked it into a pocket. It was a great relief, knowing he was safe. I wanted Vinny to know, so she too could be released from the fears that she had. But how, how to do that without showing her the letter?

She was in her dressing room, going through her wardrobe, looking at things she hadn't brought along on our yearlong trip.

"He's all right," I told her.

"Benjamin? He wrote?"

"A three-line telegram. His regiment was on reserve, not in the fighting. He was nowhere near the crater."

She held out her hand, wanting to see the telegram.

I told her I'd opened it on the second-floor balcony and was so delighted by the good news that I stayed a moment, stupid me, gazing at the traffic. "And wouldn't you know, an updraft snatched the telegram from my hand."

"It's gone?"

"Gone."

"Maybe it's still there."

"Vinny—it blew away."

She was so mad at me. Just stood there in front of me and glared, in that fierce, corrosive way that she has. Nobody glares the way Vinny does, the kind of glare that could melt a foot-deep blanket of snow.

CHAPTER 20

HOME

The next day, we brought Minnie home to Middleboro, and stayed a few weeks, resting. We ate, slept, went on long walks, and played croquet. We'd earned a goodly amount from our tour, and Vinny was talking, now, of putting up a house close to her mother's. It seemed a bit of a stretch—Middleboro was far from New York, and if we continued to perform, Barnum's Museum would be our home base and the jump-off point for our tours. And we had, too, my mother's big house in Bridgeport, which I'd been supporting ever since my father died.

But Vinny had her heart set on having a place near her mother. It would make it easier, she said, when we visited. And we could build it in a way that would suit us. "We're tiny people, Charlie. Wouldn't it be delicious to have a low sink in the kitchen, instead of having to stand on a footstool all the time? And a low stove. Low windows so we could see out without standing on our toes. And stairs with low risers, so it wouldn't be like climbing a mountain every time we go up."

She'd been working on this, giving it a lot of thought—even had a plot of land picked out, on Plymouth Street, across from her parents' farm. "*Char-lie*," she pleaded.

Well, let's see, I thought. Which way the crow flies, which way the tree leans. A house? Another house to support? "Maybe after we do Europe," I suggested. Maybe.

But her eagerness for Europe seemed to be waning. It was being replaced by this new desire for a house in Middleboro, where she had grown up, and I suspected it was linked, somehow, to her simmering desire to become pregnant and have a baby. If we were off the road and no longer on tour, in a place of our own and close to her mother, perhaps that would turn the biological trick for her. She never said so in just so many words, but it seemed to be what she was thinking. Wherever we went, she always had that Celtic cross with her, hoping it would spread its blessings.

August passed, and if there really were Confederate agents in Canada, plotting mischief and ready to strike, they were being ultracautious. Or maybe they were just asleep. Barnum's house in Bridgeport didn't burn, and Barnum himself was untouched, though he was not without physical damage. He slipped one evening while stepping out of the bathtub and, with Barnumesque flair, broke his left arm. Entirely his own doing.

In September, we were back in New York, at the St. Nicholas, and appearing at the Museum. Some days we took the stage together, other days I was up there alone, while Vinny and Minnie were off on a shopping spree. I played around with a few off-the-hinges fancy dances that I'd picked up. A mazurka, a ziganka, a galliard. A few new puns, a few new jokes. *Question*: Why doesn't Jeff Davis throw in the towel? *Answer*: He's sweating so bad he needs the towel to wipe himself off. *Question*: Is it true Jeff Davis has a dress in his closet for the moment when he has to disguise himself and run? *Answer*: Not true. . . . He already ran. . . . That isn't him at his desk, it's a mannequin disguised to look like him.

Pretty awful, I knew. But people laughed. I stood on my head, turned somersaults, and scrambled around on my knees, then bowed my way toward the wings, flinging drops of sweat into the clouds of applause.

September vanished into October, and by then it was clear that the South could no longer stop the onslaught of the Union armies. Early in September, Sherman had captured Atlanta, and, by mid-October, Sheridan had scorched most the farmland of the Shenandoah Valley. He boasted that a crow would starve to death flying over it, unless it carried its own rations in a haversack. The South was short on food, short on munitions, and short on medicine. They were using thorns for pins and Spanish moss to make rope. Salt was precious—smokehouse floors were scraped for every ounce of salt that could be recovered. Women and men were asked to save their urine—the nitrogen in it was used in the manufacture of gunpowder. So if they were surviving on their own piss, how much longer did Jeff Davis imagine he could keep the show on the road?

Then, soon enough and faster than fast, election time was upon us. You could vote for McClellan, the peace candidate who had looked good when the Union was taking heavy losses, or for Lincoln, who was suddenly riding high because, with the victories in Georgia and in the Shenandoah, and with the noose tightening around Richmond, it was plain that the South would soon have to quit. With victory this close, why switch to McClellan and negotiate away the very things we'd been fighting for?

But at the same time that I was trying to figure it all out, I was thinking again about Benjamin, and wondered how long—two months, five months, or even a year—before the South surrenders, and in that time how many more would die of sickness in the camps or from gunfire on the battlefield? It sent a shiver through me, the thought of losing Benjamin, and thousands like him. Somebody's brother, somebody's cousin, somebody's son.

Benjamin must have guessed my thoughts. A week before the election, I had a letter from him, urging me to vote for Lincoln. "Better to get the job done," he wrote. "Whip the Confederacy, wipe out slavery, and move on." And Vinny, seeing the letter, gave it some thought and reluctantly agreed. It had to be Lincoln.

I voted in Bridgeport, where I was registered. But after casting my ballot, I strolled for a while in a small park near the polling station, and was more than half-wishing I could go back and change my vote. It wasn't just Benjamin I worried about, but the country itself, the strange, undefined future that lay ahead.

Because what did I know? What did anyone know about how and why and when and what if? In the end, after the war, how would it all spill out? What kind of a South would we have after all the destruction down there? Wherever I went, people were wondering, arguing, speculating.

Isaac Sprague, the Living Skeleton, was now as famous for his dire predictions as for his near-fleshless body. "A war of attrition," he'd said at the start of the war, and that's what it had become. And now he was saying that the South, for the next hundred years, would be terrorizing the blacks and hanging them from trees and lampposts. Crazy Isaac. If he weren't such a gaunt, ghostly skeleton, would he be as bleak as he was in his thoughts about the future? I had bleak thoughts, but his were bleaker than bleak, grimly apocalyptic and wrapped in black crepe. Sure, bad times ahead. But lampposts? Trees? Bonfires? A hundred years?

Nevertheless, despite his pessimism, he voted for Lincoln.

*   *   *

When the count was in, Lincoln was again a loser in New York City. The laboring class, especially the ones that had run amok during the draft riots, had never forgiven him for imposing the draft law, and the people in business and finance had never liked him, even though they'd profited immensely from the war. And you didn't have to be a banker or a shipbuilder to share in the wealth. Even shopkeepers and blacksmiths and coachmakers were wearing gold chains and gold rings, and their wives sported thousand-dollar camel's hair shawls, and were sprinkling gold dust in their hair.

I asked Vinny if she wanted gold dust. She nearly spat at me. There was a new movement, started by the Women's Patriotic Association—an effort to persuade everyone to reduce the use of luxuries while so many of our soldiers were being killed in battle. Vinny was all for that. She attended several of the rallies and even spoke at some. I'm not at all sure, though, that the movement met with any great success.

If gold was too fancy, I asked if she'd settle for silver dust. She didn't spit, but she did throw a shoe.

Lincoln may have lost the city, but when all the results were finally in, he won the state and took the national election by a wider margin than most had thought possible. He swamped McClellan, earning more than two hundred electoral votes against McClellan's twenty-one.

It was a triumph: Lincoln, the first President since Andrew Jackson to win a second term, and the Jackson thing had been long ago, before I was born. So this was a big YES, a mandate to push the war through to the only acceptable conclusion—an end to the Confederacy, and an end to slavery. And that, I suppose, was the way I'd been thinking when I cast my ballot, even though I had reservations, doubts, second and third thoughts, because of the too many casualties yet to come.

Already the number of dead and wounded—for the Union alone—was well over half a million, and God knows what the numbers were for the Confederacy. All of it too much, impossible to absorb. And the horror inside the horror was that some of the dead, on both sides, were boy soldiers, under the age of fifteen. I knew that the South was using boys, but had learned only recently that the Union had picked up a large number of recruits under fifteen. These were not bugle boys. Did Lincoln know about any of this? Did Secretary of War Stanton? Did Secretary of State Seward? I learned of it from Tim Riley, a janitor at the Museum, who was home from the army with one eye blind and two fingers gone from his left hand.

Ned Blossom, the caretaker for my mother's house, told me he would have voted for Lincoln, but the Supreme Court, in its wisdom, had ruled that African slaves were not citizens, and neither they nor their descendants could ever become citizens. So Ned went to the polling station before it opened, and carved a small *x* on the door. That, he told me, was his ballot. He said he voted for Dred Scott, who'd been manhandled, abused, and stomped on by the Supreme Court. And for Vice President he picked John Brown, even though he'd been, as some said, a little crazy.

"But they're both dead," I noted.

"And that be even better," he answered. "When you is dead, you got tricks up yo' sleeve that the livin' ain't never yet heard of."

~ PART SEVEN ~

NOWHERE
IS SAFE

CHAPTER 21

THE MAN WITH THE MOLE

Anna Swan had returned from her tour of England about a week before Vinny and I were home from the Midwest. Not long after the November election, she came down with a raging toothache in one of her molars, and took to her bed on the fifth floor of the Museum.

Vinny went up to her every day, and told me how miserable Anna was. "We should do something. We really should."

But what could we do? A cream-filled layer cake from Barmore's would be wrong. Candy would be worse. A white rabbit to amuse her? A talking macaw to annoy her? A new dentist to sit with her, giving her an opium tablet every hour?

It was a Friday afternoon. After a morning at the Museum and lunch at Bendo's, we were in our room at the St. Nicholas, taking it easy. Vinny in the plush comfort chair by the window, deep into *Gulliver's Travels*, which Anna had passed over to her. I was on the bed, browsing restlessly through *Leslie's Illustrated*—stuff about the war, about Lincoln, Robert E. Lee, Jeff Davis. And the many ads stacked one on top of another—for perfume, artificial legs, artificial arms, clocks, microscopes, a nostrum guaranteed to cure coughs, colds, and consumption.

"Come on," I said, slipping off the bed.

"I'd rather not," she answered. "Where?"

"For a walk. We'll buy flowers for Anna."

"Charlie—she has a raging toothache and a fever. You think she wants flowers?"

"We should buy her a new dentist?"

"Charlie—"

"Come on," I said.

"It's after three already. Before we get back it'll be long after four and dark. I don't like walking in the dark when it's cold."

"Which coat do you want? I'll get it."

"I hate this," she said, rolling off the cushioned chair and going to her trunk. She pulled out the wool coat with the wide collar that she could turn up around her ears.

I couldn't find my gloves and went without them. Chilly out there, but so what?

Coming out of the lobby, we headed down Broadway under a November sky, the sun low, in and out of small, puffy clouds. We crossed Broome and moved on toward Grand, the traffic slow, like a thick stream of molasses. Hackneys and horse-drawn omnibuses, barouches, cabriolets. But the sidewalk wasn't crowded and we were comfortable enough, moving at our own pace, with no fear of being trampled by some out-of-breath messenger hurrying with a telegram, or a red-hot gambler rushing to a backroom poker game in a Canal Street saloon.

Past a barbershop we went, a tailor, a tobacconist, a clockmaker.

We crossed Grand and strolled toward Howard, heading for a flower shop on the corner of Canal, where they sold exotic tropical blooms raised from seed in greenhouses in Brooklyn. I wanted something big and luminous, with a devastating fragrance that would wake Anna out of her fever and knock that toothache out of her head.

"We can't carry anything big," Vinny said.

"They'll deliver. Before suppertime."

On we went, past a bootmaker, a chandler, and a bakery, the warm aroma of fresh pastries drifting like an invisible cloud flavored with almond and chocolate.

"We'll buy some on the way back?"

"Maybe," she said.

Then—suddenly—I heard footsteps close behind us. Glancing over my shoulder, I saw him bearing down on us, and my heart sank—the same fellow, the one I'd seen in Chambersburg, and in Kentucky, and at a train station in Bridgeport, the one with the mole on his cheek. He rushed down on us, and, swinging low, he came between us and in a single motion swooped both of us up, one under each of his arms, and set off at a run.

Vinny screamed. I was wriggling, flailing with both arms and jabbing my elbow into his ribs. As he turned right onto Howard, away from Broadway, his grip slipped—I caught hold of one of his fingers and bent it backwards, giving him enough pain to make him loosen his hold. I slipped away and fell to the ground, and still he ran, with Vinny under his right arm. He didn't look back.

I was quickly up, chasing after him, knowing I could never catch up—yet I ran, and ran. I passed two men on a doorstep, they watched idly, sharing a bottle of rum. Up ahead, a woman came walking down the street and the man with the mole raced past her. As she approached, I called to her. "Find a cop," I shouted, hurrying along. "A cop! A cop!" I wasn't sure she heard—if she did, she pretended she didn't, and kept walking. Who needed trouble? Who wanted to be near it? And still I ran, knowing I could never close the gap.

At the next corner, the man turned right. When I reached the corner, he was already far up the block, opening a door. He paused, looking back, then vanished inside.

It was a street of row houses, all attached, three stories high.

I stopped running and approached cautiously. There was a FOR SALE sign on the door the man had passed through. The house to the left was boarded up—there had been a fire, the front wall badly charred. The house to the right held a ground-floor shop where chemicals were for sale, but the shop was closed.

I went up the steps to the door with the FOR SALE sign, it was unlocked. Inside, a long hallway with a door to the first-floor apartment, and at the far end an exit door. A narrow staircase led to the upstairs apartments.

I tried the door to the first-floor apartment. It was unlocked, I pushed it open. The dim light of late afternoon spilled through the uncurtained windows. The room empty, no furniture, and the same in the room on the other side of an archway. I moved quietly, room to room, my heart beating wildly, and found nothing, nobody there. No rugs, no furniture, a wall in one room burnt by the fire in the neighboring house, and a lingering stink of scorched wood.

It crossed my mind that the fellow may have come into the building as a way of throwing me off—he made sure I saw him go in, then he hurried through the hall and out the back door. Could be. Could be. But maybe not. I was in a panic to find Vinny, but thinking clearly enough to realize I didn't know what I would do if and when I found them. Small as I was, what *could* I do? Yet I kept looking.

The second-floor apartment was like the first—barren, not a chair, not a rug, no sign of life. Room to room. It was a mistake, prowling through this house on my own. I should have gone for the police. But if I'd done that, by now the man would be gone, off to another city in another state, with Vinny. And how, then, to find her?

By the time I reached the third floor, I was convinced I should have gone for help. Dumb. A mistake. The building empty, the man long gone. And had they been here, what good if I found them? Small me, I could only have compounded the mess.

I pushed open the door to the third-floor apartment and found yet another empty room, windows facing the same way as in the apartments below. I looked down into the street. Nothing but row houses, and the street empty, not a horse, not a buggy, not a person.

I turned away and opened the door to the next room, and, with heart-stopping suddenness, there he was, arms folded, in a black suit. Waiting. Him, the one who grabbed us. The same one I'd seen before, at Vertigo, at Chambersburg, a mole on his left cheek, the beard trimmed short.

"Sure took you long enough," he said, a low, growly tone.

"Where is she?"

"Ah, your bride. I knew you would come, damn sure I was. Knew you wouldn't leave her by her lonesome. Fuckin' dwarf, you nearly broke my finger back there. Are all dwarfs as bally mean as you?"

I looked about, there were two other doors. One, I figured, was a closet.

"In there," he said, pointing to the nearer door.

I sent a cautious glance in his direction, then went quickstep to the door and turned the knob.

That room, too, was empty—except for the maroon trunk that stood in the middle. It was open, the lid thrown back, and there, in the trunk, standing, was Vinny, her head and shoulders rising above the edge, her lush brown eyes more woeful than I'd ever seen them. I ran to her and put my arms around her, and she broke into heavy sobs.

The man with the mole allowed us that moment. Then I heard his voice, the sound of it rebounding off the barren walls. "Not to worry, not to worry. We're shippin' both of you safe and sound to a proper location, and your Mr. P. T. Barnum will be more than pleased to cough up a pile of crisp Yankee dollars to get you back. When you grow old you will tell your grandchildren how you helped turn this war around for the sufferin' people of the Confederacy. This puking, pig-shit war. And not to worry about air to breathe while you're in the trunk. There be three holes to let the air in, drilled 'em myself."

I remembered what Ned Blossom had told me, how he'd escaped from a slave catcher by stabbing him in the eye with a pencil. I had my fingers, my teeth, my toes, and my watch, which didn't always tell the right time. A cigar and some matches. What could I do? Light up and blow smoke in his face? Set fire to his hair? And my small nipper to cut off the tip of the cigar. But what good was that? A cigar up his nose might be better.

I slipped my hand into my pocket, and as the fellow bent to lift me, to put me in the trunk, I whipped out the nipper and, twisting around, stabbed, going for an eye—but he swung his head and the nipper went, instead, dead center into his left ear. The pain sent him yowling across the room, off-balance.

And—fast—I helped Vinny out of the trunk and we scampered off, down the two flights of stairs and out the front door, running—and, quicker than quick, swiftly back to Broadway, out of breath, panting. I glanced about and saw, a block off, to our left, a line of waiting hacks. Again we ran, and with a bit of a struggle, climbed into the hackney at the head of the line.

The traffic along Broadway had thinned, and I told the driver to get us double-quick to Barnum's Museum. As we moved off, I looked back and there he was, running and very much alive, racing for the hack that stood next in line. He pulled the driver down, jumped aboard, and, grabbing the reins, he was quickly after us.

I shouted to our driver, telling of the hack in pursuit. He saw it, and, swinging past an omnibus, he urged his horse into a trot, lucky to have, briefly, a clear lane.

But the man with the mole kept coming, lashing at his horse, a bay with a splash of white on its forehead. When the horse came alongside, our driver struck it with his switch, hitting at the nose and eyes, slowing him.

We hurtled along, down Broadway, and ripped a quick turn onto Franklin, away from the traffic. But the other hack followed, faster than sin, and again drew near.

There was a lap blanket in our hack. As the bay drew close, I flung the blanket over his head. That slowed him and he fell behind, swinging his head from side to side. When he freed himself from the blanket, he whinnied and reared.

The man with the mole lashed furiously, and as the horse twisted and pitched about, the hack tipped over, and the horse went down with it.

The man tumbled onto the street, yet he was quickly up, chasing after us. But impossible for him to close the gap, and he shrank in the distance.

Our driver took us back onto Broadway, and in minutes we were at the Museum. He dropped us at some distance from the front door, because of the long lineup of hacks. I tipped him well. If not for his skill with the reins, we would have been helpless.

The sun was down, but still some light in the sky. A long purple cloud, shaped like a whale, was fading to gray. A man on the corner of Park Row sold hot roasted chestnuts. Across from the Museum, at St. Paul's, people were gathering for a service.

And I? I felt a strangeness coming on. An oddness. As if, in a way, I was not the person that I was. Not Tom, not Charlie, not my Highland fling or my breakdown dance. How long would the strangeness last? Would it pass, as a mild pain passes? Would it melt away, as ice melts, as butter melts, as time itself melts?

It was a bit of a walk before we reached the main entrance to the Museum. Vinny held on to my arm, and I felt, in her, a confidence and a strength that surprised me—the way she moved, the firmness of her step, a remarkable vigor replacing the fear and terror she was feeling when I found her in that trunk, such a short time ago. While I was fading, she was recovering, growing in self-assurance.

We found Barnum in his office. He wanted to send us right off to England, to put us out of harm's way. But Vinny wouldn't hear of it. She was determined to have Thanksgiving with her family in Middleboro. And the day after, back to New York for the three Booth brothers in a onetime evening performance of *Julius Caesar*.

The play was a fund-raiser, the proceeds going toward the purchase of a statue of Shakespeare to be placed in Central Park. It was the first time all three brothers were appearing together, and, given the family friction over the war—Junius and Edwin firmly pro-North, and John Wilkes rabidly pro-South—it might well be their last.

"So you see?" Vinny said breathlessly. "We can't miss this. We mustn't!"

"Dwarfs," Barnum said, scratching the back of his neck. "I don't know who gives me more trouble—the giants, the acrobats, the dancers, the Sioux Indians, or you precious leprechauns."

"But you do know who pulls in the most receipts," Vinny answered sharply.

"Yes, yes." He nodded. "And for that we are all of us grateful and delighted. But—both of you—you were kidnapped. Grabbed off the street. Don't you understand? I'm trying to remove you from danger."

He put both hands to his head and ran his fingers through his hair, with restless desperation. "Look—if you won't sail tomorrow, we'll keep to the scheduled sailing date, ten days from now. I'll give you Harry Nobbs, he has a gun and knows how to use it. But swear to me—the two of you go nowhere without him."

Vinny looked to me—puzzled, uncertain. And I looked to Barnum. "He hates Shakespeare," I said. "He'll go crazy sitting through *Caesar*. And what if he's in the toilet when they come at us?"

"Sweet knees of Jesus, you are something, Charlie. A gift. Truly a gift." It wasn't anger, it was fatigue and weariness. His eyes flat, the keenness gone. Something was lost. I remembered how he had growled at Bleeker, the day we came in after the tour, how he had ranted and threatened because Bleeker had brought us into dangerous Kentucky. That wild anger wasn't him, and this, now, the dimness in his eyes, this wasn't him, either. In more ways than one, he was losing his grip. He needed a rest, needed to get away from it all. As, indeed, Vinny and I needed a rest, after this wild episode with the kidnapper.

So we would use Harry Nobbs to guard us by day, and Barnum gave us one of his custodians, a retired policeman, to sit outside our room and guard us through the night. He came with us in the hackney that took us back to the St. Nicholas.

Later, when we were alone in our hotel room, Vinny threw her hands up over her head, not in anger and not in despair, but with plain annoyance, impatience with the twists and turns that life was tossing at us. Harry Nobbs—we were to have him with us the next ten days, every waking minute, three meals a day. *With his gun!* And this retired policeman outside our door at night. Her hands flew into the air again, and I had a vague sense that she was beginning to understand something about the unfriendly intricacies of Zootagataz.

"Why is anything the way it is," she said, letting out a prolonged, world-weary sigh. "Tell me, Charlie. Why?"

What could I say? What did I know that she didn't know? "I have this awful itch between my shoulder blades," I said. "How about it?"

"Go away," she answered. But she did scratch. Not scratch, exactly, more of a rub. She knew that once you start scratching, the itch migrates and spreads, and there is no end to the need for more scratching. A quick rub and some pounding, then she returned to the blue-cushioned easy chair by the window and picked up an unfinished piece of embroidery she'd begun a few days earlier.

The police and the military investigators found nothing in the apartment where the kidnapper had taken Vinny, not even the trunk. They knew there was a group of Confederate officers, in disguise, working out of Canada, plotting all sorts of mischief—as Nickerson had told me, and as Barnum and Sam Hurd had mentioned when I returned from the Midwest. And from the things the kidnapper said, it seemed likely he was part of that group.

The afternoon after our escape, two officers interviewed us separately—Vinny first, then me. One was a police lieutenant with a small moustache, the other, a tall army captain with a scar on his forehead.

I mentioned that I'd seen the man before, and told them where. They listened and jotted notes, but suspected the earlier encounters may have been coincidental. He was probably meeting with other agents to exchange messages or money, or assessing a list of possible targets. In Bridgeport he may have been meeting with the copperheads who were threatening Barnum and other Lincoln Republicans. In Louisville, probably assessing Union military defenses prior to a Southern attack that never came off. In Vertigo, near the Tennessee border, he must have been meeting up with his Confederate contacts, delivering or receiving information. At Chambersburg, as I myself had suspected, he'd probably been an advance man for McCausland, confirming that the town was undefended and telegraphing an OK to move in.

They were speculating, guessing. The idea of a kidnapping had developed later, they thought, after he'd spotted me so often and realized how easy it would be.

They showed me photographs of men in Confederate uniforms. I eliminated some, was uncertain about others. Hard to tell, with the caps and uniforms. But the second time around, I spotted him, dead certain, though I saw the skepticism on their faces when I lifted the photo from the pack.

"I know," I said. "There's no mole on his cheek. And no beard. Simple—the mole is stage makeup, part of his disguise. The beard is something he plays with—grows it, trims it, shaves it, grows it again."

"No, no," the army captain said, "the mole and the beard are not the problem. The problem is—this man is in jail. He's in Johnson's Island Military Prison. Sandusky Bay, Lake Erie."

Again I studied the photo, and again I knew—this was the man. The eyes, the forehead. The nose. "If he was in jail," I said, "he's escaped."

"But your wedding, more than a year and a half ago. If he escaped that far back, we would have heard."

"Maybe you never had him. You have somebody else using his name."

The captain's face lit up. "But the picture you identified—it was taken in the prison. The man in that picture is behind bars."

"Don't be too sure," I said, and told them that after the Commodore was hired at the Museum, his picture and mine had many times been mixed up on the posters that Barnum spread all over town. "And this— if your man really is in prison, maybe he and the guy who grabbed us are just dead-ringer look-alikes."

"Twins?"

"Why not?"

The police lieutenant looked to the army captain and shrugged. "See? I told you. Dwarfs are smart. Should we put him on salary?"

The army captain rocked his head, side to side. "Stay out of bad neighborhoods," he told me. "Wherever you go, go with a crowd. Tell your wife—nowhere alone. And above all, don't get killed—my wife would never forgive me."

I asked if Vinny had picked out the same photograph. The army captain nodded sourly. Yes, she had.

Thanksgiving Day, we were up in Middleboro, a cold, brisk day, but no snow. When I was young, I don't think more than nine or ten states observed Thanksgiving, and they did it on different days. But now, with Lincoln issuing his Thanksgiving Proclamation two years in a row, it seemed a sure bet that Thanksgiving would become as rooted as Christmas.

At noon, Vinny's mother served an enormous stuffed turkey, with candied yams, creamed onions, butternut squash, and all the condiments.

"See?" Vinny said, whispering in my ear. "If we build a house on that plot across the road, you can eat like this every Sunday."

After dinner and before dark, Harry Nobbs entertained the children by shooting tin cans off the stone wall behind the house. He was good—tin cans kicking wild all over the place. The kids ran, grabbing them and lining them up again on the wall.

Not to be outdone, Vinny's oldest brother, James, borrowed his father's rifle and killed a woodchuck that had been haunting the field behind the house. The oldest sister, Sarah, gave him a smacking kiss on his lips. Caroline, the sister who had given Vinny the Celtic cross, threw rocks at the crows. The younger brothers, Sylvanus and George, threw rocks at each other.

Early the next morning, with Minnie, and with Harry Nobbs as our bodyguard, we boarded a train that brought us back to New York in plenty of time for the Booth brothers' performance. Vinny had insisted on bringing Minnie along, thinking it important for her to see the play. We would take her home the next day, and return to New York in the afternoon.

∽ CHAPTER 22 ∽

GREEK FIRE

At the Winter Garden, a crowd, every seat taken. We used Barnum's
box, and Harry Nobbs was with us, sitting behind me. Barnum was
home in Connecticut, visiting with his relatives.

Those three Booth brothers, if it weren't for their different costumes
and different ways of delivering their lines, it would have been hard to
tell them apart. All with the same long-jawed face, same high forehead,
and slender, arching nose, and all roughly the same height. Edwin was
clearly the most accomplished, though the youngest brother, John
Wilkes, had plenty of fire in his eyes, a bold, dashing manner, and
a vigorous way of swinging his body around. I wondered if, after the
show, the women in the audience would carry him away and tear off
his clothes, as happened, once, in New Orleans. Vinny and I had met
him at a hotel in Louisville, but the person onstage seemed someone
else entirely.

Everything smooth and flawless, right through the first act. Then, a few minutes into the second act, the clanging bells of fire wagons, and the smell of smoke, something burning. A great murmur and turning of heads in the audience, and the onstage action at a standstill.

"What the hell," Harry muttered, tapping me on my shoulder. "Be ready. For anything."

I was ready for nothing, just sitting there, my hand on Vinny's arm, with thoughts of Chambersburg spinning in my head. And now—here in the Winter Garden—everyone looking about and wondering. Smoke? Smoke? We were a lot of people in that packed theater.

Edwin, briefly offstage, returned in a hurry and, close to the footlights, raised both hands in a calm gesture that suggested everything was all right.

"Not to worry," he said. "We're fine, we're not about to burn up. The trouble is next door, at the hotel. The Lafarge House. They had a fire in the front parlor, off the lobby, but it's under control. So the play will go on! I wouldn't do this if I thought my life was in danger—and I certainly wouldn't do it if I thought there was a danger for any of you."

His words were reassuring—but still a restlessness, an uncertainty, a lot of tension, like a dry twig bent to its limit and ready to snap. I had a feeling that if one or two were to make a dash for the doors, hundreds would be leaping to get out, and many knocked down and trampled.

Someone in the dress circle—I knew him, Judge McClunn—stood up and said the very thing I was thinking. A rush to the doors would be disastrous. And uncalled for—the fire was in the hotel, not here.

Harry poked me hard. "Time to get out," he said in a harsh whisper.

I turned and glared. "No."

"Charlie—be smart."

"We're staying."

"Son of a bitch," he groaned.

Vinny's gaze was troubled, tense. Minnie seemed relaxed, enjoying the confusion that swept through the audience. I felt my heart beating in my chest, and, on impulse, stood up on my chair and, giving little thought to the words I would use, I spoke out, and the words were there.

"I think many of you know me," I said. "If there is one thing *I* know about, it's theaters. I ask you—would I, Tom Thumb, stay here for three seconds if I thought there was the slightest danger? With my beautiful wife? And her lovely sister? Would I risk their lives? I smell smoke and I hear fire engines—but if we're in danger, wouldn't the firemen be rushing in by now to lead us out in an orderly fashion? Wouldn't they?"

For a few moments, a restless silence. Then someone shouted, "On with the show!" But still a silence, and I saw a few in the back rows quietly leaving. Then another call—"On with the show, on with it!"— followed by a smattering of hand-clapping that was reassuring, though not altogether convincing.

Just then, a group of policemen, about a dozen, entered the theater and lined up along the walls—and that had an immediate effect. Clearly, they would not have come into the theater, intending to stay, if there were any real danger.

So the play went on, right through to the fateful moment of assassination—Caesar dead, and then the long, grim aftermath. And still the clanging of fire wagons, and that dim odor of smoke.

Not till we were out of the theater, asking around, talking with a newsboy, with a doorman, with people on a street corner, did we gain a fuller sense of what was happening. The city was under attack. Arsonists were going from hotel to hotel, setting fires in an attempt to burn them down, and the best guess was that they were Confederate agents.

But luckily, thus far, they'd been unsuccessful. Here and there, a mattress burned, a rug, a bureau, draperies—but whatever they were using to start the fires, it wasn't working. A policeman told us even the Museum had been hit—Barnum's Museum—with a crowd inside. That sent a tremor through me, the thought of the Museum going up in smoke. But the fire fizzled out, the policeman said. Some damage but no injuries.

"You're sure? Nobody hurt?"

"Nobody."

Vinny and I were both thinking of Anna. Her toothache had subsided, and she'd been scheduled to perform that evening. Vinny felt we should stop by the Museum to see her, before returning to the hotel, to confirm that all was well.

Harry Nobbs was scratching the back of his head. "The cop said there were no injuries."

"I'm sure he's right," Vinny answered. "But you never know. In any case, I want to see her."

I nodded to Harry, and reluctantly, he went to the curb and signaled a hackney.

Minnie looked tired. "Do I really have to go home tomorrow?" she asked Vinny.

"Don't you want to? Mom wants to see you. We were a long time away on that Canada tour, and we'll be even longer when we go to Europe. Don't you want to spend more time with her before we sail?"

"But I've been home a long time already. New York is more fun."

"Fire engines are fun? Minnie, you're bad."

"I'm not bad. You're bad."

"You hated the play?"

"I adored the play."

"Who did you adore most?"

"The one with the eyes. Marc Antony."

"John Wilkes," Vinny said.

"Yes. Him."

Vinny turned to me, rolling her eyes. "Let's sleep on it," she said to Minnie. "We'll see what tomorrow brings."

A hack pulled over. Harry helped us aboard, and it wasn't long before we reached the Museum. But what a shock, to see it totally unlit. Always, through the night, there was plenty of light inside, the janitors cleaning up and preparing for the early-morning crowd. But now, nothing. With Harry, I hopped out of the hackney and took a quick walk down Ann Street, for a look up at Anna's fifth-floor window. But not a hint of light anywhere. The building had been evacuated.

We returned to the St. Nicholas, and even there an attempt had been made. Just before nine, fires had broken out in four rooms, but all were quickly extinguished. It made us nervous about staying there. Policemen were on duty in the lobby, and the concierge gave us every assurance that people passing through were being scrutinized. But there was no guarantee that the arsonists wouldn't try again.

The retired policeman who guarded us at night was already on his chair, between our door and the door to Minnie's room. When I asked if he thought the arsonists might return, he shrugged vaguely and said anything was possible. But he was there, he said. If another fire broke out, he would hear the alarm and would get us out safely. A comforting thought, but not altogether reassuring. Something oblique about him. His left ear larger than his right, and his right eye larger than his left.

Minnie waved good night and disappeared into her room. And Vinny and I, in our room, changing into our night clothes, were wondering—what if the old fellow at the door were to fall asleep? What if an arsonist were to come along and hit him over the head with a truncheon? *What if, what if.* But we stayed, and despite our misgivings, we closed our eyes and slept the night, though we did get up early.

When I opened the door, our old fellow was dead asleep. I didn't wake him, not wanting to embarrass him—so I closed the door, then made some pounding noises inside the room, hoping that would rouse him. It did.

We took an early breakfast and left the retired policeman at his post, since Minnie wasn't up yet. Harry Nobbs hadn't shown up yet, but we felt secure enough in the crowded dining room, having pancakes and bacon. When we glanced at the morning paper, we saw how extensive the attack had been. Not just the hotels that we knew about—the Lafarge, the St. Nicholas, the Fifth Avenue, the St. James—but a long list, well over fifteen, including the Metropolitan, where we'd had our wedding reception, and the Astor, which had been, for many years, a second home to me. Attempts had also been made to burn a few downtown lumberyards and some barges at the docks, loaded with hay—but only minor damage.

If everything had burned as planned, there wouldn't have been enough firemen to handle it all, and with flames leaping from one building to another, and house to house, a huge portion of the city would have gone up in smoke.

Greek fire, that's what the arsonists used—a liquid mix of naphtha, sulfur, and quicklime, in a bottle. When the liquid is exposed to air, it spontaneously bursts into flame. It did ignite, but the flames sputtered out, and the theory of the moment was that the chemist who prepared the mix had made a mistake, either in the proportions of the mix, or in the chemicals. Greek fire—used long ago, one newspaper said, by the Byzantine Greeks.

THE NEW-YORK TIMES
DIABOLICAL PLOT TO BURN THE CITY OF NEW YORK

THE PLOT—FULL AND MINUTE PARTICULARS

HOW THE PLAN WAS CONCEIVED

HOW ITS EXECUTION FAILED

Names of the Hotels and Buildings Fired

Attempts to Fire Shipping in the Harbor

STRINGENT ORDERS FROM GENERAL DIX

For Barnum, enough was enough. Right after breakfast, when we were back in our room, Bleeker was at our door, with Julia and a luggage boy.

"We sail at noon," he said. "Boss's orders."

"Impossible," I answered.

"We'll help you pack."

I stared, amazed. Vinny glared, the barest hint of rage in her dark brown eyes.

"What can I say," Bleeker offered apologetically. "P. T. thinks it's too risky to hang around anymore. So what's the difference? We're departing a few days sooner than planned."

"He's here? In the city? I thought he was spending time with his brother Philo."

"True—still in Connecticut. We were half the night trading telegrams, back and forth, and again at dawn. Finding a ship and reaching our people. The telegraph, Charlie, it makes all things possible. And— sooner than you think—people will have machines they talk into, in their own homes, talking to people a hundred miles away. Are you ready for that?"

I was not. The telegraph had already complicated things enough. It made life move faster. Without the telegraph, we wouldn't be sailing that afternoon, nor could the long, bloody war, with its massive movements of troops, have been possible. And, in the Zootagataz mix of things, the telegraph, with its clickety-click dots and dashes, was contributing to the incredibly high numbers of casualties.

"The future, Charlie," Bleeker said, with an almost gleeful acquiescence. "It's our fate. Our destiny."

This was, I thought, a strange statement from a man who in the deepest chambers of his heart had wanted to spend his entire life onstage, playing Hamlet, Lear, Macbeth. Barnum was falling apart, and now Bleeker, too—no longer sure who he was or what he hoped for and wanted. It was the war, too long, too brutal, getting inside us and nibbling away.

Even me—I—myself—there were moments when I hardly knew

who I was anymore. Vinny was keeping me together. Were it not for her, parts of me would be falling off and flying in the wind. My toes, my fingers, bits and pieces of my dwarf soul—if in fact there was anything left of it still wandering around inside me.

"Whatever the case," Bleeker said, "look at it this way. We had Election Day, we had Thanksgiving. Last night you had the Booth brothers. Caesar is dead. And, though I hate to say it, P. T. is right. Time to get away from the lunacy. Sherman burned Atlanta, and now it's payback time, an eye for an eye. Imagine. They want to burn New York. Nowhere is safe. For all we know, they may figure out what went wrong last night and try again tonight. It's showtime, Charlie—come on, let's pack."

Vinny was still staring. She had never enjoyed this part of it, the way Barnum arranged and disarranged our lives, as if we were puppets on strings. Julia bent low and put her arms around her, comforting her. But Vinny wasn't looking for comfort.

"Let's help Minnie first," she said, turning practical. "She's not awake yet. I was supposed to bring her home today. We'll have to send a telegram, or Mom will think we were all killed in the trouble last night. And, yes—she has only her overnight bag with her. All of her stage wardrobe is in a closet in Middleboro. And plenty of other things that she'll need right away. Like underwear, for God's sake."

Bleeker was undaunted. "We'll send a telegram to your mom at the desk downstairs, and we'll buy a new wardrobe for Minnie in Liverpool. Right now, before we sail, we're all gathering at the Museum as a jumping-off point. While you and Charlie gather stuff from your dressing rooms, Julia will help Minnie pick up the immediate necessaries in the shops by the Museum. If she's still asleep, tickle her toes and tell her what's happening."

Vinny pursed her lips and glanced at the ceiling, then went off in a huff, to Minnie's room, and Julia followed.

I turned to Bleeker. "Harry Nobbs," I said. "He didn't show today."

Bleeker was taking my clothes from the closet, laying them on the bed. "He's at the Museum, sorting out stuff for the trip. Today, Charlie, I'm your protection. Where's that derringer you bought?"

"What derringer?"

"P. T. said you bought a gun. After that banana-brained idiot nearly killed you."

"He made that up, about the gun."

Bleeker tilted his head in a knowing manner, and nodded. "He makes everything up. That's how he's such a huge success. He lies his way clear through to the day after tomorrow."

It wasn't true, what I'd said about not having a derringer. I did have one, and wanted no one to know, because what would people think? WORLD'S MOST FAMOUS DWARF TOTES GUN. Barnum knew, and it was more than annoying that he told Bleeker. And Vinny, poor Vinny, she knew, and she was spastic, hopelessly upset, fearful that the gun would go off and hurt someone. The someone, in all likelihood, would be me.

The army captain who interviewed me after our escape was the one who suggested a gun. "In times like these," he said, taking me aside as I was on my way out, "a little fellow like you—you got to protect yourself." He gave me the address of a German gunsmith in the Kleindeutschland district, above Canal Street. I went there that same day, after taking Vinny back to the St. Nicholas.

The man had small ears, a long jaw, one eye, and a large assortment of single-shot derringers. I picked the smallest, and in his basement shooting gallery he showed me how to load and fire. Seven times I did that—bullet in the chamber, aim, pull the trigger—but hit the target only once, far from the bull's-eye. Even then I knew the gun was useless. If the target were a few feet away, maybe. But eight feet? Ten?

Hopeless. My hand and arm not steady enough, and that small gun not small enough for the smallness that was me.

Still, I bought it. And though I knew it was useless, I felt, strangely, a quiet confidence when I had it with me, a mysterious peace of mind. It was my talisman, my rabbit's foot. I kept it in my carryall pouch, which had a strap that I slung over my shoulder. The pouch held the gun, a few bullets, my wallet, a pencil, and the Kermott's pills that I sometimes used to calm my stomach. And a few Greenwood envelopes that Foxglove had never bothered to pick up. The pouch was on the night table by the bed, and with Bleeker rushing about, grabbing things to pack, I leaped for it and tucked it into my steamer trunk, lest he put a hand on it and discover my secret.

"Dress warm for the boat, Charlie. Everything else into the trunk. We're gathering at the Museum and will leave for the ship together. You and Vinny will want to sort through the stuff in your dressing rooms, for whatever else you need. Julia will help."

"The Commodore? You reached him?"

"The Commodore and the whole bunch. Ken in New Jersey, the baggage boys in Brooklyn. Even your Ned Blossom in Bridgeport."

"He can be here on time?"

"His train should be getting in just about now."

Ned had been doing a first-rate job taking care of my mother's house, and I knew of the hard life he'd had, growing up on a plantation. I wanted to give him something, the experience of traveling abroad, so I signed him on as a baggage handler, and found someone else to care for the house while Ned was away.

"In the Museum," I asked, "how bad was the damage?"

"Nothing a few coats of paint won't fix. No wonder those rebs are losing the war. They don't even know how to light a fire."

"Anna," I said.

"Anna?"

"Anna Swan. She okay?"

He pursed his lips and tilted his head. "She had a rough time. She was on the third floor, playing some piano pieces for the crowd. When she smelled the smoke, she went leaping down the stairs and out of the building—in a panic, flailing her arms wildly. She had to be sedated."

"And now?"

"Still under sedation, I guess. Sam set her up at the Pembroke House and hired a nurse to stay with her."

"Vinny will want to visit her."

"Charlie, I don't see how. We're running late already. Talk to her. She'll understand."

I wasn't too sure about that.

Bleeker took the last of my clothes out of the closet and I stuffed them into the trunk. Like Vinny, I, too, hated this part of it, the packing and unpacking and the packing up again. I'd been doing it since I was a kid.

And while I pushed some things around in the trunk, trying to make it all fit, what I learned from Bleeker was that the Commodore had been, as suspected, not in New Hampshire but at Amos Eno's Fifth Avenue Hotel, within reach of a swanky parlor house.

"Don't ask me how I found out," Bleeker said.

I didn't.

Before we left for the Museum, I drew Vinny aside and told her about Anna.

She was upset. "Sedated?"

"That's what Bleeker said."

"Charlie, we can't leave without seeing her."

"I know, I know. But how do we get over to the Pembroke, see Anna, then rush to the Museum to fetch what we need, and reach the ship before it sails. We'd probably find her asleep anyway."

"I hate this. Before the Canada tour, we had to rush off in the night because of the riots. No chance to see Anna before we left. And now this. It isn't right. Let's skip the ship and sail tomorrow."

"I thought of that. But Vinny—you. You and I. We're the show, we're what it's about. If we don't go, the others won't. You think they'll want to slum around in Liverpool, waiting for us? Meanwhile, I come down with measles, or brain fever, and can't make the crossing? What then?"

"Charlie, this is so wrong. I hate living like this. Hate it."

"I do, too. Always have. Ever since I was told I was not allowed to bite my fingernails while onstage." I took her right hand in both of mine. "Look. When we reach the Museum, jot off a note for Anna—we'll give it to Roth, he'll make sure it reaches her."

I dismissed the retired policeman who guarded us at night, and tipped him. He went limping down the corridor, toward the stairs, and I wondered if I'd ever see him again. People come and go like summer rain, that's how it is. There was a sadness in that, a strangeness, like the strangeness I always felt when I was in the Hall of Trick Mirrors.

When Minnie was ready and Vinny was finished packing, off we went to the Museum, with our steamer trunks and luggage bags. Minnie hadn't had breakfast, and as the carriage moved along on the slow ride down Broadway, she nibbled on a croissant that Vinny had brought along. Earlier, when Vinny woke her, she'd been having a dream about frogs, and it was still on her mind. "Why do frogs spend so much time in the water," she asked. "If they can't breathe underwater, why in the world do they keep jumping in and spend so much time down there? Are they just dumb?"

"But they *can* breathe underwater," I said. "They breathe through their skin."

She tilted her head and looked at me suspiciously. "No they don't."

"Yes they do. Out of water, they breathe with their lungs. But underwater they have this clever trick."

"Life is a trick," she said. "You're making this up." She turned to Vinny. "He's teasing, isn't he?"

"He's always teasing," Vinny said.

"No, not true," I said to Minnie. "And if you don't know it yet, this is something else you should know—underwater, not only do frogs breathe through their skin, but dwarfs, too. Us. You never noticed?"

"Never noticed because it ain't true," she said.

"But it is, it is. Tell her," I said to Vinny, "tell her how wonderful and calming it is." And, turning again to Minnie, "For hours on end, drifting around underwater, breathing through your skin. I'm amazed you don't know about that yet. I mean, you're fifteen, on your way to sixteen. It's time you understood about some things."

She wrinkled her nose and said, "Stick a cigar in your ear."

Which I did. Took a stogie from my pocket, stuck it in my left ear, and, with downturned lips, stared her in the eye. She was amused, I know she was, but never cracked a smile.

At the Museum, Minnie went off with Julia, for some quick shopping at the nearby stores, and Vinny went to her first-floor dressing room, to gather what she needed. I headed for my room, passing murals and dioramas, then up onto the wide oak staircase to the second floor.

On my way up, I caught a lonely smile from Zoupetta, the Gypsy Fortune-Teller, and a bright hello from Nellis, the Man with No Arms, who came light-footed down the stairs, weaving and bouncing like someone in a ballet.

On the second floor, as I crossed through on my way to my dressing room, I met Mary Darling. She was in the outfit that she wore for her performances, a man's black jacket and pants, and a red cravat—hovering by the large aquarium that held yet another pair of beluga whales, replacements for the previous pair that had gone the way of the others. I hadn't seen her since Vinny and I departed on our honeymoon tour to Canada and the Midwest. Mary, too, had been away—just back from a string of performances in New England.

"You're going to turn the belugas into sharks?"

"No," she answered. "I was thinking of turning them into daffodils. Or snapdragons. And you? You're about to perform your disappearing act? Into the cracks and crevices of Europe? Will you never come back?"

I would return, but hardly knew when. My two previous trips to Europe had each lasted three years. I knew of people who went and never returned, and others who came scrambling home after a week in Liverpool. I had no idea what might lie ahead. Two years, Barnum had suggested, if the crowds were good. A year at least, maybe three.

"Nothing is firm, we'll see how it plays."

"And we still have the war," she said.

"We do. We need another meteor."

"You remember that?"

Years ago, when Lincoln was making his first run for President, Mary and I were having ice cream at the refreshment bar on the roof of the Museum—and suddenly this raging meteor in the night sky. So long ago, already. Those flaming colors, purple and green, and as soon as it was out of sight, a big noisy boom, but we never found out what that was.

She asked about the honeymoon tour through Canada and the Midwest.

"Grueling." I didn't tell her we'd been shot at in Kentucky by a rebel soldier who had once been my baggage boy. Nor did I mention that we'd been at Chambersburg when it burned, or that a week ago Vinny and I had been abducted in daylight, on Broadway. But Mary, with her magical powers, probably knew about all of that, long before any of it happened.

I still had a fond memory of the trick she pulled off at the wedding reception, releasing one white dove after another out of her purse.

"But people were annoyed," she said. "They were opening windows and shooing the poor things out into the cold." When I was five, she was maybe twenty-one and I was infatuated with her. I thought with her magic she could stop having birthdays until I caught up with her, and we would marry. Well, she did stop, and looked as young now as she did then. Except that she had to wear spectacles when she read a newspaper, or a menu.

"Those white doves," I said. "I was impressed—still am."

"I can do better than that," she said.

"You can?"

"You know I can."

She reached her arm around me, and I felt her fist between my shoulder blades. Then a big, bulky thing back there.

When she withdrew her arm, she was holding a turkey by its legs, upside down. A big black-feathered tom, with a curved beak, tiny black eyes, and a big red wattle. She set him on the floor and he stared at me in an unfriendly manner.

"I don't think he likes me."

"He doesn't. He's smart. He has good taste." She nudged him with the toe of her shoe, and, with a noisy flapping of his wings, he flew off and settled on the head of the marble Venus, perching there as if he owned her.

When I reached my dressing room, I stashed a few things in a satchel, and for a few moments I amused myself, rifling through some of my old costumes. Bleeker poked his head in, wondering if he could be of any help—his way of hurrying me.

"Last night," I said, "where was the fire?"

"On the staircase, between the fourth and fifth floors."

"Let's have a look," I said, handing him the satchel.

"It'll have to be quick," he answered. I locked up, and followed as he hurried over to the staircase leading to the upper floors.

At the fourth floor, the stairs to the fifth floor were roped off, scarred from the blaze and needing repair. "There it is, that's where the fire-bomb went off. Not much damage, but a ton of smoke. Scared the hell out of Anna. She was on the third floor, playing her piano, and must have figured it was doomsday." He checked his watch. "Gotta run, time to round everybody up. Front door, Charlie." And off he went, quickly down the stairs and out of sight.

On my way down, I offered a quick farewell to Isaac, the Living Skeleton, and to Nellis, the Armless Wonder. I paused by the beluga whales and said good-bye to them also. And the Egyptian mummies.

Vinny was still in her dressing room. She'd written a two-page letter to Anna, with a promise to follow up with more from England as soon as we had an address there. We gathered her things, and on the way out I left the letter with Roth, who promised to deliver it himself.

Bleeker had three carriages waiting, and we were soon on our way to the ship. Cold weather moving in, a few snow flurries whirling around in a lazy wind. A briskness in the air that was hardly welcoming.

PART EIGHT

LAVINIA AND CHARLIE ABROAD—NEWS TWO WEEKS OLD

∾ CHAPTER 23 ∾

LAVINIA
THE HOUSE
ON BENNETT STREET

In London we took a house on Bennett Street, a stone house in a row of stone houses. We were all there, the usual entourage, with Sylvester Bleeker again managing the tour for us. We were a crowd, but we fit comfortably in that wonderful house.

This time Charlie brought Ned Blossom along, the caretaker of the Bridgeport house where Charlie's mother lived. Ned was an escaped slave from South Carolina, and he and Charlie got along very well. When Charlie went sailing on the sound, it was Ned who handled the boat. Charlie wanted to give him the experience of traveling abroad, so we took him with us, to handle the luggage and any odd jobs that turned up.

But what an unpleasant surprise, in London, that so many people assumed Ned belonged to us—our chattel, Charlie's slave. What a humiliation, and I was quick to strike down that notion whenever I encountered it.

Fourteen days upon the sea we'd been, and for Minnie it was not a good voyage. She suffered from the mal de mer, and after that she was grouchy for more than a week—because of the hard journey, yes, but other things, too. She still felt an impish rivalry with me, jealous that I'd been to the White House and had met Abraham Lincoln. And long before that, when I was singing on a riverboat, I had met so many who were now famous. Grant, Lee, Jefferson Davis, Stephen Douglas, and others. Once, in Kentucky, before Lincoln became the President, I'd had lunch with his wife, Mary Todd. Sixteen years old I was. And now Minnie, soon to turn sixteen, was beginning to feel there was too much catching up to do. She had a growing fear that, for her, the good things might simply never happen.

On top of all that, there was this thing with the Commodore. When she first saw him, at the wedding rehearsal, she immediately had eyes for him. But, poor Minnie, she was then just thirteen—and he, eighteen, never looked twice at her. It was, in fact, dreadfully ironic. When I first met the Commodore, I was twenty-one and he just eighteen. I learned, soon enough, that he'd set his heart on me, but I was looking right past him and had eyes only for Charlie. Well, the world turns, doesn't it, spinning on its axis, and it does put us in a whirl. How, I wonder, how do we ever keep our balance?

In truth, I must say I was rather glad the Commodore was not returning Minnie's attentions. There were things about him Tom had heard, unsavory things—rumors that he'd become, in New York, a bit of a rounder, wandering about in the bad parts of town and visiting unsavory women. So, not the right person for my Minnie, no. But how to convince her of that? How to explain it, and how to save her from this silly crush that afflicted her? The human heart is such a tricky, unmanageable thing. If I were to tell her of the rumors, I knew what would happen—she would scoff and react angrily, clenching her tiny fists and stamping her feet. Sweet and good-humored she was, but she did have a temper. And she would have hated me—scorned me—for trying to tamper with her feelings

During our first week in London, Charlie and I were summoned to Marlborough House, to dine with the Prince and Princess of Wales. Their wedding had taken place a month after Charlie and I were married.

She was lovely, the Princess, with thick, wavy hair and keen, friendly eyes—and proud, too, of her firstborn, Albert Victor, who had arrived in January. She was now pregnant with their second, and it did make me jealous. Because still, for me, there was no hint of a pregnancy, and I was beginning to wonder if it would ever happen. She had the baby brought in, and allowed me to hold him, though he was already ten months and quite a bundle. It meant so much, to hold that baby. Envious—so envious I was.

The Prince was almost four years younger than Charlie, and they had met many times. He was friendly and chipper, and recalled, with some delight, that he had already been put to bed when Charlie made his first visit to Buckingham—and when he discovered the next morning that he'd missed the famous General Tom Thumb, he went into such a tantrum that his mother was compelled to invite Charlie for a second visit, and a third.

Charlie and the Prince met again during Charlie's second tour of Europe, when they were both in their teens. And again only a few years ago, when the Prince was in New York. So now, during our visit to Marlborough House, they were quite chummy, bantering back and forth and smoking cigars. And Charlie felt very free about addressing the Prince by his nickname, Bertie, as he had done when they were children.

It has always struck me, in my many encounters with nobility and people of high station, that our tiny size does something to them. It breaks down the barriers, and they are quite themselves with us, with none of the airs and formalities, none of the pretenses.

So there are certain advantages to being a little person. Charlie often frets about being small, because there are things, physical things, that he can't do. But I always remind him there are things he would never have been able to do were he *not* a little person. But when I say that, he usually does a backflip and comes up singing one of his silly Zootagataz songs, like "Tall is bad, short is good—but maybe you'd rather be a piece of wood!"

Princess Alexandra told me she used the same obstetrician that Queen Victoria had used, Sir James Simpson. "He's wonderful," she said. "Just splendid." He was the first to use anesthesia in childbirth—he used ether, but then he came up with chloroform. And Alexandra, who'd had the chloroform, said it was just wonderful. "Like the warm, cozy air of a summer afternoon. You breathe deep and take it in, and it's marvelous, you close your eyes and the pain is gone."

At the start there had been a bit of a storm against Simpson, from the clergy and from other doctors, but that quickly vanished when Queen Victoria appointed him as her obstetric physician. I made a mental note to ask around in New York, to see if there were any obstetricians using chloroform. In Middleboro, where I grew up, most of the women used midwives. But a physician, why not. If I should ever need one.

"Chloroform?" Charlie said, when Alexandra spoke so glowingly of it. "Ether? Laughing gas? They kill the pain? Any pain? Can I pick some up at a flea market?"

Sure, Charlie. Buy a dozen. He'd had a whole goblet of wine and was beyond any need for chloroform. Feeling no pain, none at all.

*   *   *

Soon after that visit, we began offering performances for the public at the St. James Hall, close to where we lived.

We always started with the routine we'd established during our tour of Canada and the Midwest—Charlie and I, in our wedding garb, walking slowly down the main aisle while Jerry Richardson played the wedding music from *Lohengrin*. Then, onstage, Minnie and the Commodore joined us for a stately minuet.

After that, however, we were into new territory, singing songs that had a long tradition in the British Isles. "Greensleeves," along with "Scarborough Fair," "Barbara Allen," and many others. "O Dear! What Can the Matter Be?" and "Drink to Me Only with Thine Eyes." We used two religious songs, "Abide with Me" and "All Things Bright and Beautiful." And, as in Canada, we avoided the many Civil War songs that had been such crowd-pleasers in New England.

The one American song we used was "Where, Oh Where, Has My Little Dog Gone?" Jerry told us it was based on a melody in a Beethoven symphony. Beethoven had lifted it from an English traditional dance dating from the thirteenth century and still well known among the Brits—so it couldn't be more right.

The Commodore, in a sailor suit, sang his "Ocean Wave" song and did his hornpipe dance, then Charlie leaped out in his Highland costume and danced a fling. More songs, more dancing from all of us, then Charlie offered his famous impersonation of Napoléon in exile, without words, pacing back and forth, stern and somber. So perfect he was—the uniform, the Bonaparte hat, his right hand tucked into the buttoned jacket, and the fierceness of his gaze. He came to a stop at center stage and turned his head to the right, then to the left, giving us the profile. He had the look of Napoléon, the face of Napoléon, the eyes of Napoléon, the grim intensity. His Napoléon act had been a huge success in England when he first appeared here, when he was six years old. And it was still a huge success for the Brits. But he'd been doing Napoléon ever since he was a child, and, even though audiences still loved it, he was weary of it and was ever on the search for new figures to mime. George Washington? Thomas Jefferson? But how would they play in Europe? I suggested Ben Franklin—the French would love it, he'd been so popular with them. He of the kite and the lightning rod, and the irresistible charm that fascinated the ladies of Paris. But how, how to do Franklin? Where was the right gesture? The right attitude, the right moment? My Charlie, he was always thinking, searching.

One day, after a performance at the St. James, Charlie was approached by a middle-aged woman in a black dress. I was close enough to overhear. "Greenwood," she said, cautiously taking an envelope from her handbag.

Charlie was surprised. "Here? In England?"

"Wherever there is a need," she replied. And added that she was from Ohio but had been living here for several years, working as a nanny.

Charlie took the envelope and signed her program. Then she stepped over to me, for my autograph, and we chatted briefly. She said she missed Ohio, and asked wanly if it was still there. I said I was sure it was—but these days, given the uncertainties, it was hard to know if the moon was really the moon or just an optical illusion. She smiled, and as she went off, I saw that she walked with a pronounced limp.

Toward the end of January, we were summoned to Windsor Castle, to see the Queen. She wore black, still in mourning for Albert—but lively, I thought, and excited to see us. We were received in the Rubens Room, with its high, ornamented ceiling and its damask-covered chairs. And so many paintings by Rubens on the walls. The Queen's three youngest daughters were there, and a son, along with a handful of lords and ladies.

We performed briefly—while Minnie and I sang, Charlie performed a dance, bending and weaving and spinning on his toes, then the Commodore offered a dance that included several handstands and somersaults. Then the four of us sang "God Save the Queen." She seemed more than pleased, and signaled for Charlie and me to approach.

She took my hand and placed it upon hers, marveling at how small it was. "Smaller than an infant's," she said. She asked about my brothers and sisters, and my parents, and wanted to know what my father did for a living. She thought it remarkable that my mother had given birth to two little people, especially since some of the other children were on the tall side.

She spoke at length with Charlie, glad to see him again and eager to know how he was faring. Then she signaled for Minnie and the Commodore, and introduced us to her remaining unmarried daughters—Helena, who was eighteen, Louise, who was sixteen, and Beatrice, seven. And her son Leopold, eleven.

The Queen was not a tall woman, and that, I suspect, was what made her feel comfortable with us. I had read somewhere that she was a cold and indifferent woman, with something of a temper—but I saw none of that in her. She showed a great deal of personal warmth, and I sensed too that she had a keen, wide-ranging mind, and a gentle disposition.

After tea was served, and before I had quite finished with my glazed crumpet, the Queen took Charlie and me by the hand and whisked us away, out of the Rubens Room, to a smaller room lined with bookcases and tall cabinets. In the middle of that room, she turned and, leaning toward us, said, rather formally, there were two things that contributed to a happy marriage. The first, she said, is love, and she was sure we knew about that. "Love, in a marriage, is like a garden, rich and wonderful, but you must work at it, tend to it, care for it, and it's sometimes a struggle, with all of the weeding and trimming and transplanting, and the fertilizing. You must keep your garden well. Guard it and watch over it, because it is the only garden you have."

She tilted her head and ran her fingers through her hair, eyes glancing toward the high, coffered ceiling. "And the second thing," she said, in an almost whimsical tone, "is that you must have an interesting hobby. Life is too grueling. You need something to keep your mind and your hands busy. I had, I must tell you, a truly unpleasant childhood. If I hadn't had something of my own to do, I think I might never have survived."

She paused, hesitant, then leaped ahead. "And this," she said, pulling open the doors of one of the mahogany cabinets, "this is what kept me sane and sensible in those difficult days. And in days thereafter, too."

The shelves were filled with dolls, some sitting, some standing, each dressed in its own unique costume. She took several down and placed them on a settee, so we could examine them. They were remarkable, the great figures of history. So many. Alfred the Great, and Henry VIII with all his wives, all six of them. She gave us to understand that she had made all of the garments herself. Queen Elizabeth, and Sir Francis Drake, who had sailed around the world. Sir Walter Raleigh, who did much to popularize tobacco in England, but then had his head cut off.

And many characters from Shakespeare's plays. Macbeth and the witches, Antony and Cleopatra, Hamlet and Ophelia. She thought it so wrong of Shakespeare to have dealt with Ophelia as he did, letting her lose her mind and drown in a brook. And he really ought to have come up with a less dreadful ending, all those dead bodies onstage at the end of the last act. She sighed when she said that, and seemed forlorn.

She disapproved of endings in general, the notion that a play, or anything, had to reach a conclusion. There was always a sadness in that, a melancholy. Life, she thought, was more interesting when things were fresh and just beginning, or in progress, moving along, and the ending so far off that you don't have to think about it. "Is it not so?" she said, heaving another sigh.

When we returned to the Rubens Room, I found Minnie sitting on the lap of an old, white-haired woman, the Duchess of Roxburghe, and the young princesses standing about and doting on her, adoring her tiny hands, tiny fingers, tiny shoes. From the expression on Minnie's face, it was clear that she wasn't enjoying any of this, not at all.

Afterward, she told me how she hated it when people picked her up and held her on their lap. I hated it, too, people treating you like a child, instead of the adult that you are. Once, during a presidential campaign, Stephen Douglas took my hand and stooped to kiss me—something he would not have dared to do if I were a woman of average height. I drew back sharply, and I think he got the point.

"Nevertheless," I said to Minnie. "We must never forget—when we're in the presence of royalty, we take what comes." She wasn't entirely happy with that idea. Nor, I confess, was I.

"Actually," she said, "that burly Scotsman in kilts, who wheeled in the tea wagon—if he had put me on his lap, I wouldn't have minded at all. Wasn't he a handsome chunk? *Yum!* But that old Duchess, she smelled so stale."

The Scotsman in kilts was, I assumed, the infamous Mr. Brown, a servant to whom the Queen had become very attached after Albert's death. He'd been a favorite of Albert's, and she turned to him as someone she could lean on. He took her riding. They went on walks together, and it was mainly through him that she communicated with the other servants. As one might expect, their closeness did cause tongues to wag, and some even referred to her as Mrs. Brown. But I say if he was good for her, a sturdy support, why shouldn't she have her long walks with him? And whatever else.

When I told Minnie about the dolls, she stamped her foot in a flash of anger. "Why didn't she show them to *me*?" she said. "Instead of passing me off to that lumpy Roxburghe."

∽ CHAPTER 24 ∽

CHARLIE
THE SAGA OF COBB KENNEDY

We had set sail for England at the end of November. Then, with an eerie swiftness, it was suddenly April. We were still on Bennett Street, in that stone house in a row of stone houses. We liked it so much that we held on to it and paid the rent even when we were many weeks elsewhere.

One of the hardships, though—especially with the war on and our eagerness for news—was that the transatlantic telegraph cable had a break in it, so any news from America came the slow way, by ship. That usually meant two weeks, sometimes more, occasionally less.

It was certainly an odd sensation, reading about "news" that was already dusty and old. And an even greater strangeness when you found yourself reading Monday's news a day after you'd already read Tuesday's news, which had come in on a faster ship. So there you are in a foreign country, reading the *Times* or the *Tribune* over a cup of coffee, and you're tilted, off-balance, because time, your time, is all mixed up, and you know what's doing it. Your old friends, Zatagatooz and Zootagataz are up to their old tricks again.

On a cloudy afternoon, while browsing in a local magazine shop, I picked up a copy of the *Albatross Gazette*, a weekly based in downtown New York. I flipped through and was thunderstruck when I saw a picture of the man who had abducted Vinny and me. His beard bushy, not trimmed close—but clearly him, same eyes, same nose, same forehead, the man himself. No mole on his cheek, and I was surer than ever that the mole had been stage makeup, used as a form of disguise.

I paid the woman at the counter, hurried home to Bennett Street, and on the couch in the living room I sank into the story. His name was Robert Cobb Kennedy, an officer in the Confederate army, heavily involved in the November attempt to burn New York. After that night of Greek fire, he and the other arsonists fled to Canada. In February, he was captured aboard a train in Michigan, during a stop at the St. Clair station. He was brought to New York, put on trial, and found guilty. His picture was in the *Albatross* because he'd been hanged at Fort Lafayette, in New York Harbor.

He was the only one of the conspirators who'd been caught. He was born in Georgia, grew up in Louisiana, and had indeed been in the Johnson's Island prison, as the investigators said. But my guess was right—he had escaped, tunneling out with several others. Strange that the army captain who interviewed me after the abduction hadn't known about that. But there it was, in the *Albatross*.

Kennedy was the one who tried to torch Barnum's Museum. After starting fires in several hotels, he had a few drinks at a bar, then went to the roof of the Museum, expecting to see fires blazing all across the city. But nothing, though he did hear the clanging of the fire engines. On the way down from the roof, he cracked open his last bottle of Greek fire, doing it, he said, on a whim, thinking that with all those people in the Museum, it would be a bit of a lark to stir up a scare. All of that— that's what he said at his trial, apparently proud of what he'd done.

Somehow, I had missed the reports about the capture and the trial. Through February and March, we'd been making forays into other towns and cities, and there had been plenty of days when we never saw a newspaper from the States. Well, there it was, in the *Albatross*, the whole thing, with the picture of him in uniform. The same fellow I'd seen in Bridgeport, and at the wedding reception at the Metropolitan. In Louisville. At the railroad station in Vertigo. In Chambersburg.

He'd been hanged on March 25 of that year, 1865. A Saturday. By then, the Confederacy was in its death throes. Sheridan had already ravaged the Shenandoah—and Sherman, after burning Atlanta, had marched all the way to Savannah, his troops looting and burning along the way. But Jefferson Davis was still not quitting. Still waiting for Lee to do something magical on the battlefield.

It was astonishing that Lee, protecting Richmond, was able to keep his battered army alive—and even more astonishing that Jeff Davis, at this late date, still hadn't raised the white flag.

And Cobb Kennedy—before he dies, while he stands on the gallows with the noose around his neck, he sings. Yes—sings.

> *Trust to luck, trust to luck,*
> *Stare Fate in the face—*
> *For your heart will be easy*
> *If it's in the right place.*

Incredible. With a noose around his neck, his final moment before dropping into eternity—he bursts into song? He could do that?

He may have been a wild-eyed, reckless daredevil, as the *Albatross* reported, yet it gave me no special joy to know he was dead. If he had hurt Vinny—yes, send him to the devil. Or if the city had burned and people were killed, plunge him into an eternity of Zootagataz. But no one had been killed, the damage had been minimal, and by the end of March the war was all but over. His arsonist buddies had faded into the woodwork, and there had been no further attempts to torch a Northern city.

So I wondered—was his death necessary? What purpose did it serve? Especially against the background of what Sheridan had done in the Shenandoah, and what Sherman had done in Georgia. Or what the Confederates, on orders from Jubal Early, had done in Chambersburg. When we win the war, should we hang Jubal Early? And on the wild, crazy chance that the South wins, will they hang Sheridan and Sherman?

But things like this, the more I ponder them, the less I seem to know. What I did know about Cobb Kennedy was that I would always hear his voice, the words he spoke when I walked into that vacant apartment on Mercer Street. *"Fuckin' dwarf, you nearly broke my finger back there. Are all dwarfs as bally mean as you?"*

That voice was alive inside me, and though I couldn't say the ones who hanged him did right or wrong, I knew there was no stopping that voice, no way to smother it and snuff it out.

When I showed the story to Vinny, she drew back and didn't want to read it.

"Charlie, I don't want to go there. I just—don't." Then, a moment later, "He was the one? You're certain?"

"He was the one."

She looked through the window, toward a wagon passing by, loaded with stacks of kindling wood. "It's over," she said. "Let's just—put it behind us."

Behind us, yes. Though I did wonder, given the twists and turns of Zootagataz, if anything was ever truly over.

CHAPTER 25

LAVINIA
GOOD NEWS, BAD NEWS,
AND WHO KNOWS WHAT NEXT?

All in all, I must say I found Europe even more interesting than I'd expected. The cathedrals, the palaces, the kings and queens and many lesser royals that we met, and the parks, rivers, quaint neighborhoods. But, as with Charlie and many of the others, it was impossible to forget there was a war raging back home, and a constant irritation because of the long delay before any news could reach us. And what made it extra hard was that Benjamin was out there in the thick of things, and I did worry.

Somehow, we lived with all that. We performed at the St. James, and at theaters in nearby cities, and did whatever sightseeing we could squeeze in.

But then—then—the biggest piece of news ever, the thing we'd prayed for but had begun to lose all hope of ever seeing—Lee's surrender at Appomattox. April 9, 1865. What we'd been hungry for, and such a happiness when that news arrived. There were still some Confederate generals holding out in the South and the West, and there might yet be some fighting, but Richmond had fallen, and it was plain that the Southern cause was lost. How we grabbed for those exciting headlines from America!

> CHARLESTON—NEWS OF LEE'S SURRENDER
> The Old Flag Raised over the Ruins of Fort Sumter
> JEFFERSON DAVIS—THE TRAITOR—SEEKING
> TO ESCAPE—reaches Macon, on 10th instant. Guerillas
> found and killed in Lexington, Kentucky. Webster, the
> foremost guerilla, is expected to surrender his whole
> command to Gen. Hobson, whose forces are so arranged
> that the guerillas must surrender or be exterminated.

The war truly at an end. For months it had been close and within reach, only inches away—but the closer it drew, the slower it was. Suddenly it was upon us—those blazing headlines in the *Times*, the *Trib*, the *Herald*, each arriving on different days, and what a topsy-turvy feeling that was.

We celebrated with oysters and champagne. And caviar, too, imported from Russia. The men lit cigars. Jerry Richardson pounded the piano in our large living room and we sang our hearts out.

> *And the rockets' red glare, the bombs bursting in air,*
> *Gave proof through the night that our flag was still there.*

And all the other songs that celebrated America—we stretched our lungs with an excitement that rumbled through the stone house we were in. Our neighbors must have thought we'd gone mad.

More champagne, more caviar, and Jerry still pounding away at that tinkling, clinking, poorly tuned piano.

But. *But.* Less than a week later, all of the joy we felt was blotted out by the appalling news that Abraham Lincoln had been assassinated. Lincoln himself. The President—killed.

It was a wet, foggy morning. Even before we saw it in the paper, we heard of it from the maid. Baffling, shocking. Too horrible. And all the more unsettling because of the time gap we were living with—the awareness that at the moment when we were celebrating Lee's defeat, Lincoln was already dead. Shot on a Friday, April 14, and dead the next day.

We had seen him, Charlie and I, just two years earlier, at the White House. So full of life he'd been, telling jokes and making us laugh, though so burdened by the war. I will never forget his face—the lines, the wrinkles, the worry in his eyes.

And even more astonishing, the report that the assassin was John Wilkes Booth, that handsome young actor we had met in Louisville, when we were touring through Kentucky. He could do such a thing? Him? It left me breathless. I had liked him. I had.

He'd expressed some views, yes, that revealed a sympathy for the South, but I simply took him for another copperhead, one of those pro-slavery people calling for an end to the war and a negotiated peace. We'd encountered so many of those in Indiana and Iowa, and had more than our share of them in New York. But an assassin? No, couldn't be.

He had given me his photograph, a *carte de visite*, and signed his name on the back. I had it with me, in London, in a box where I kept some letters. When a reporter approached me, asking if I knew anything about Wilkes Booth, I happened to mention the photograph. He begged to be allowed to use it, and the next morning his paper was the first in London to print Booth's picture.

I still couldn't believe it. John Wilkes? Him?

And Lincoln, in his coffin—even in death they wouldn't let him rest. They put him on a train to carry him home to Springfield, and went the long way, stopping at eleven big cities and opening the coffin so everyone could have a look at him. Charlie and I followed the journey closely, and always that odd sensation, reading about events that were already much in the past. Things my parents knew twelve or fourteen or sixteen days ago. Things my brothers and older sisters knew, and the janitors and animal keepers at the Museum. And Anna. But only now, day by day, was it reaching us.

In Baltimore, it rained hard, but more than ten thousand made their way through the drenching rain to see him. He was in a mahogany coffin that was lined with lead, his head resting on a white silk pillow. In New York, at City Hall, more than a hundred thousand filed past the open coffin. Then an immense four-hour funeral procession from City Hall all the way up to the railroad depot at Forty-Second Street. People paid as much as a hundred dollars to view the procession from upper-story windows along the route. All of this, amazingly, in a city that had twice voted against him.

And still we couldn't absorb it. Lincoln gone, shot in the head by Booth. How could that be? Something inside me refused to accept it, and I wasn't alone. All of us feeling puzzled and a little off-balance. Even tough-minded Harry Nobbs. Even leathery Ken Keeler. Even Ned Blossom, who'd been through some brutal moments when he was growing up on a Carolina plantation.

I think we were all feeling the same thing—a tug, a loneliness, a need to be home, close to the sorrow. As if something terrible had happened to someone in your own family and you are far away, across the ocean, among strangers, and where do you turn? Every day we followed it—Lincoln's body carried on a slow train from city to city, people all along the route watching as it passed, waving farewell, throwing flowers.

And the reporters, relentless, digging up all of the gory details. Everything about the embalming—how the brain had been removed, and blood was drained from the body through the jugular vein. After an incision was made on the inside of one thigh, a chemical preparation was pumped into the blood vessels and they soon turned hard as stone. Who needed to know all of that? Was it necessary? Was it?

Lincoln embalmed. Old Abe. Beaver-hat Lincoln, wrinkled-clothes Lincoln, whose lap Charlie had once sat upon—and this, now, was what they'd done to him, turned his arteries into stone, to keep his corpse from rotting during the long journey home to Springfield. Did I need to know any of that? Did anyone?

What I did want to know was why they had removed the brain and what they did with it. I found no answer to that in any of the penny papers. Charlie thought someone must have slipped off with it and made a fortune, selling it for a few million to the khedive of Egypt, or to some bahadur in Bangalore, or to King Mongkut of Siam.

The embalmer went along on the two-week journey and prepared the body before each of the showings. In Harrisburg, the face was darkening and it had to be chalked so it would be presentable. In New York, the jaw had fallen, and parts of the face were black. One reporter thought the lips had been glued together. By the time the train reached Chicago, blackness had spread over the entire face and it had to be powdered many times.

In Springfield, after a viewing in the statehouse, he was brought to Oak Ridge Cemetery. His horse, Old Bob, cloaked in a mourning blanket, walked behind the hearse. The procession was the largest the city had ever known.

The coffin was placed in a receiving vault built into the side of a steep hill, with the expectation that an immense monument would be built above. And the son, little Willie, who had died three years earlier—he too was brought along, his coffin taken from a vault in a Georgetown cemetery so he could be with his father, the two coffins going into the limestone chamber side by side.

It was April 14 when Lincoln was shot. Not until May 4 did they put him in the hillside vault. Everywhere, in newspapers, magazines, there were stories about the dream that he'd had, in which he saw himself dead in a coffin in the East Room. And about the plainclothesman who had tried to dissuade him from going to the theater that night. And after he was shot, the things they found in his pockets—two pairs of spectacles, a linen handkerchief, a pocketknife, a pencil, a button from his sleeve, a leather wallet. The wallet held a few old newspaper clippings and, curiously, a Confederate five-dollar bill. What had he ever had in mind, carrying that Confederate bill with him?

And the watch in his vest pocket, the big clunky watch that he had shown to Charlie when we were at the White House. A big silver Waltham on a gold chain. Charlie was so impressed—it told the time of day, the day of the week, the month and the year. But for Lincoln, none of that mattered anymore.

When they laid him out in his coffin, they put white formal gloves on his hands. Wrong, wrong, he had always preferred black gloves.

"That matters?" Minnie said, glancing at me, then at Charlie. We were in Green Park, just around the corner from the house on Bennett Street, on a bench, close to a large patch of yellow daffodils.

"Well—doesn't it? If he preferred black?"

"But he's dead," Minnie answered, sharply. "I don't see what difference it makes."

She had, at times, an impish, irreverent way about her. Often it was charming, but sometimes, to annoy me, she could be prickly and provoking.

"In fact," she added, "I don't see why it's such a fuss that he's dead. Dead is dead."

I just stared at her.

"So he won this big, awful war," she said. "If he hadn't been the President, maybe there wouldn't have been a war. Even up North there were people who didn't like him."

I was so angry, I was at a loss for words. Finally, with grit, I blurted what we'd heard our mother say many times in that farmhouse filled with eight children—"Go scrub your mouth with soap!"

She was, for an instant, stone still. Then she stuck out her tongue, and, rising from the bench, she turned, wriggled her spine snakily, and went off toward a stand of trees in the near distance, to be alone.

∾ CHAPTER 26 ∾

CHARLIE
SOMETHING STRANGE,
SOMETHING DIFFERENT

Not long after we learned of Lincoln's death, Minnie started smoking cigars—small, modest-size things known as cigarillos, which she purchased from a nearby shop on Piccadilly. She looked devastatingly smart, holding a cigarillo between two fingers and putting it to her lips. But Vinny scolded her, telling her it was not a sensible thing to do. She'd been trying to get me to stop smoking, too, with no success. I was then in the range of three or four cigars a day, and saw no reason to cut back. Vinny had no luck with Minnie, either. Minnie blew smoke in her face, and there were times when, with a devilish twinkle, she blew smoke in my face too.

I liked her. How not to? There was a brightness in her eyes, a cleverness in the words that curled off her tongue. "Chew air," she told me once, when I'd said something she didn't want to hear. "Tell it to the geese. Tell it to yesterday."

She was fifteen, weeks away from turning sixteen, and more and more she was asserting herself—with Vinny, yes, openly, and occasionally with me, but especially with the Commodore. She was sick of his neglect and the way he ignored her, and she was striking back.

More than once, when she came upon his jacket hanging on a peg or draped over a chair, she slipped pins into the pockets. She put sand in his shoes, and worms in the drawer where he kept his underwear. He accused Aaron, one of the baggage boys, but Aaron calmly lifted a leg, passed gas, and walked away.

The Commodore carried a dwarf-size flask with him, filled with cognac. On a rainy day in Bristol, while he was onstage in his sailor suit, dancing his hornpipe dance, Minnie poured out half of the cognac and replaced it with urine, her very own, which she'd spiced with cinnamon.

I didn't know, at the time, that she'd been responsible for the pins in his pockets, and for the sand in his shoes and the worms in his underwear. Nor did I yet know about the urine in the flask—but I do still remember the twisted expression on the Commodore's face when he took his first sip.

"Something odd," he said. "Very odd," and took another sip. "Strange, strange. *Fleur de coeur.* They must have changed the recipe." He tossed his head back and took a slug—but gagged on it and went breathless. His eyes bulged, and he spun around. Then, after swallowing, he nodded slowly. "Interesting," he said. "Not bad, not bad."

Minnie couldn't resist telling me what she'd done, but only after making me swear I would tell no one—especially not Vinny. She told me too about the pins, the sand, and the worms.

"You're bad," I said. We were, at the time, still on our short visit to Bristol, on a bench behind our hotel, by a chestnut tree.

"I'm delicious," she answered. She took from her purse a blueberry muffin wrapped in a napkin, and while a warm breeze touched the leaves of the chestnut tree, we shared that muffin.

"Worse than bad," I said. "Did your brothers teach you to do things like that?"

She looked me in the eye. "I taught them," she said.

It was already May when Lincoln's coffin was put in the burial chamber. A week earlier, on April 26, long before sunrise, while the funeral train was still on its slow journey, a cavalry unit found John Wilkes Booth in a tobacco barn in Virginia. With him was David Herold, who had been part of the conspiracy. It was mid-May when this news reached us.

Herold came out of the barn with his hands up, but Booth did not. The barn was set afire, to smoke him out, and while the fire raged, a sergeant—Boston Corbett—raised his rifle and took aim through a chink in the barn wall. The bullet went through Booth's neck, and he went down.

He was dragged out of the burning barn and brought to the porch of the Garrett house, close by. "Tell Mother I die for my country," he whispered to the lieutenant who was searching his pockets, looking for weapons. His breathing was labored. Some two and a half hours after he'd been shot, he looked at his hands. "Useless," he said. "Useless." It was early daylight when he died, close to seven.

He had, on his person, two pistols, a knife, a diary, a candle, a compass, a map, and pictures of five women. One was Lucy Hale, the daughter of the abolitionist senator John Hale, named by Lincoln to be the ambassador to Spain.

All of that was laid out at length in the newspapers from America. And the Lucy Hale thing was a flat-out, beyond-the-pale puzzler. Booth is so pro-South and pro-slavery that he kills Lincoln—yet there he is, secretly involved with the daughter of an abolitionist senator from New Hampshire. How does that happen?

And still I remembered Professor Caso Capovolto's spinning planets, when he lectured years earlier at Barnum's Museum. And how could I ever forget my sisters' songs about Zatagatooz and Zootagataz—

> *Life ain't smooth, ain't comprehensible.*
> *Sometimes it tickles, sometimes it prickles—*
> *Sometimes delicious, more often pernicious,*
> *And never just plain sensible!*

Strange, yes. And part of the craziness was Wilkes Booth, spinning in his own orbit, smooching with the daughter of a pro-Lincoln senator on the very day when he will put a gun to Lincoln's head. Compared with that, my meandering fantasies about Anna Swan were child's play. So Professor Caso Capovolto wins. Life is a floating paradox—top is bottom, inside is outside, and the star you are gazing at, far off in the heavens, may be nothing more than an optical illusion. And my sisters with their Zatagatooz, they also win.

> *Life's a fat puzzle, not many clues—*
> *A box full of noisy cockatoos!*

And yet again I am there, in the long-ago past, with Frances and Mary Elizabeth—they have just tossed me, once more, high in the air, and I am descending, anticipating the moment when I will hit the mattress and bounce.

And bounce I did—bounce and flip over and land smash on my bum—when Vinny showed me the newspaper Bleeker had just brought in, with the big story on the front page:

GREAT CONFLAGRATION

BARNUM'S MUSEUM IN ASHES

∽ CHAPTER 27 ∽

LAVINIA
DOWN IN THE DEPTHS

I had been relaxing in the sunroom at the front of the house, on a cushioned chair, half asleep, gazing at the occasional passersby. Suddenly, I saw Sylvester Bleeker coming down the street with a newspaper under his arm. He came through the front door and, pausing in the vestibule, he saw me, and hesitated. Then, slowly, he stepped through the archway, and handed me the copy of the *Tribune* that he'd just picked up.

There it was, with its heart-stopping headline about the Museum. I gasped, wanting to believe it was a misprint, or some sort of hoax. But no, not so. Sylvester was so distraught, he settled into a chair close to mine and, elbows on his knees, he leaned forward and held his head in his hands, and said nothing.

That fire, so dreadful, as vivid and horrible as if happening that very moment.

Smoke was first noticed at noon, seeping through the floorboards on the second floor. The morning show in the theater was over, and most of the huge crowd had already departed. But a few hundred were still milling about, looking at the exhibits. Mr. Barnum was in Hartford, and Sam Hurd was filling in. He quickly sent word to the local fire companies, and went rushing about, telling the janitors to hurry everyone out of the building.

Firemen from several stations arrived quickly and helped the last few to get out. They broke open some of the bird cages, and the birds flew off though the windows. A few animals were released from their dens, but with the flames rapidly spreading, most were abandoned. The polar bears, lions, kangaroos. I assumed that the python from Burma was also gone, the one I'd been admiring when Charlie and I first met. A Bengal tiger found his way to the second-floor balcony and leaped to the ground. Three policemen shot him, lest he attack someone and do harm.

But the monkeys, the monkeys, a bitter time for them. A few found their way onto the third-floor balcony overlooking Broadway—frantic, desperate to escape the smoke and flames, but at that height they were too frightened to jump down to the hard cobblestones below. They went back in, searching for another way.

And Anna, dear, precious Anna—trapped in the third-floor venue where she'd been at her piano. Fire and smoke blocked the main stairway, and the only way down was a tight, narrow staircase where, giant that she was, she couldn't fit. Isaac Sprague, the Living Skeleton, was with her, staying as long as he could—consoling her, assuring her that firemen would soon be there. But as the smoke worsened, it became difficult to breathe, and she insisted that he leave and get out while he could. He lingered, then went.

Eventually, some Museum workers, on the street below, saw her. They quickly brought a tall ladder, expecting she would climb down.

But the window was narrow, she couldn't pass through. The men hurried off, and what feelings of helplessness and despair she must have felt as the smoke thickened.

The newspaper reported that men returned with a derrick equipped with a ball and chain. They smashed out part of the wall on both sides of the window, and shouted, encouraging her to grab hold of the chain and they would lower her down. She did reach out for the chain, and held it briefly, then let go and stepped back. She was a giant, with the weight of a giant, and must have felt she simply did not have the strength to hang on to that chain. She backed away from the opening, and with the flames drawing closer and the smoky air filled with the cries and moans of dying animals, one can well imagine the dark, desperate thoughts that overwhelmed her.

But the men below kept shouting up to her, and eventually she returned to the hole in the wall. After much hesitation, she reached out, grabbed the chain, and somehow managed to hold on while she was lowered to safety. When she was down, she was quickly brought to a hospital for care.

The reporter who wrote the story mentioned that the last people to walk out of the Museum were the Fat Lady, assisted by a fireman, and Isaac Sprague, the Living Skeleton. I assume it was from Isaac that the reporter learned that he'd been upstairs with Anna—and it probably was Isaac who told the workers of Anna's plight, and pointed out where her window was. Isaac, five and a half feet tall but losing weight, skin and bones, afflicted by some strange disease that was eating his life away. Still, so generous he was, so giving.

And I, sitting on that cushioned chair in the sunroom—how distraught I was, thinking of Anna. What a nightmare for her. The smoke, the fire, the moans and roars of dying animals.

What the paper didn't say, but what had to be true, was that Anna lost everything in that fire—books, clothes, jewelry, the sheet music for her piano performances. And all of her money, which she kept hidden under her mattress. How to get past all that? I wanted desperately to write to her, to offer whatever help I could—but with the Museum gone, where to send the letter? Wherever she was, I knew she must be suffering terribly. I would write to Mr. Barnum to see if he knew of her whereabouts—but where was he? In his home in New York or in the mansion in Connecticut? Or, after this huge catastrophe, he may have abandoned all hope and sailed for Paris.

The fire had started at noon, and by one the entire building was engulfed in flames. At two thirty, the walls collapsed and the Museum caved in on itself. Many neighboring establishments were also lost. A clothing store, a hat shop, a cigar shop, a restaurant, a bookstore, a liquor shop, a store that sold opera glasses. The only good thing in all this was that nobody died.

When I was finished reading, I folded the paper and simply sat there, in a daze. Sylvester was still in the chair beside me, leaning forward, his head in his hands. Eventually, he lifted his head and gazed through the window.

"Somebody has to tell Charlie," he said.

After a long silence, I pushed myself up off the chair, and took the newspaper with me.

Charlie was upstairs, in our bedroom, sitting on the settee beside the bureau. He was glancing through the little notebook that he'd kept all through the war. He still wrote in it, odd things that happened, things he wanted to remember. When he saw me pausing in the doorway, he seemed to sense something was wrong. I moved slowly toward the settee, and showed him the headline.

He said nothing, just stared. It was an awful moment for him. He took the paper and began to read, and I sat close to him, my hand on his shoulder. Not a word from him as he read those long columns, just a deep, troubled silence—and I knew, yes, knew, everything inside him was turning upside down. That Museum, he was four years old when he had first started there, and it shook him to the core to know it was gone. I saw something in his eyes, a darkness, that I'd never seen before. The rest of that day he seemed lost, in a kind of bewilderment.

And I—I was just heartbroken, because all of the future was suddenly so uncertain. While we were in England, on tour, we were earning our way and supporting our entourage—but we couldn't be on tour forever. Without the Museum to go home to, what would we do?

Charlie was so stunned, I don't think he was even thinking about the future. His father had died young, some ten years ago—and now this, losing the Museum. It was like losing another member of his family. The suddenness, the finality, the knowledge that there were rooms and whole galleries he could never return to.

On a Thursday it happened, the 13th day of July. Many times I'd heard Mr. Barnum joking about the number thirteen—but this, now, was no joke, and we wondered how he would ever get himself back on his feet after such a disaster.

I worried about Charlie, and was troubled, too, about the many people who were suddenly out of work—more than a hundred and fifty, the papers said, performers, staff, janitors, caretakers for the animals. And the people with us—the Bleekers, Jerry Richardson, and the others, no job to go home to when our tour was over. I was especially concerned for Minnie, because I'd been hoping she would have a place at the Museum as a new young star. But all of that was suddenly gone.

With so much disruption all around me, so much confusion about the future, I just didn't know anymore. What to hope for, what to expect next.

But what I did know, what I knew with every breath I took, was that time passes, yes it does. It moves, it trudges on. And I was thinking, beginning to think, maybe it was time for a change. Time to go home. To shut down the tour and sail off—and maybe, back home, it would be easier to sort things out and get back on track again. For me, and for Charlie. And for everyone.

~ PART NINE ~

As Real as Rain

CHAPTER 28

MAGICAL TRICKS, MARVELOUS TRANSFORMATIONS

On the day when Vinny showed me the news headline about the Museum, something inside me went dizzy—and worse. As if my brain had been ripped out of my skull, fried in oil, hung out to dry, and tattooed by a cross-eyed lunatic who was drunk on tequila.

The Museum? Gone? Impossible.

But there it was in the newspaper—within hours, the entire building gone, nothing but smoldering ruins.

From the time when I was a scrappy, overconfident kid, I had been tied to that building. It was my home base, my job, my carousel, my funhouse filled with a buzzing family of friends—acrobats, fire-eaters, dancers, sword-swallowers, and visiting professors who lectured about the planets and the universe. But suddenly the best part of my childhood and my growing-up days had just been wiped away in an enormous conflagration.

I used to prowl around, gazing at the colorful wings of dead butter-flies. I lingered by the umbrella cockatoo and the gang-gang cockatoo, admiring their plumage and listening to their noisy conversations. I spent time in the Hall of Mirrors, studying the garbled, zigzag images of myself that those trick mirrors threw back at me. The American Museum—it was my playground, and my school, the only school I'd ever known. I touched medieval armor and ancient copies of the Bible. Wigs and muskets from the time of the Revolution. Egyptian mum-mies. And learned so much from my tutor, Kwink. When I saw the buckle that had belonged to Peter Stuyvesant, Kwink explained who Stuyvesant was, and I never forgot. When I saw the jade Buddha, Kwink talked and talked—I not only learned what jade was, but found out more about Buddha than maybe Buddha himself ever knew.

And, best of all, in the basement, the huge Room of Living Ani-mals, with the crocodile, the zebra, the chimpanzee, the gnu. So many hours I spent there, talking to the cranky camel and the lonely giraffe. It was there, near a python with exotic brown, black, and yellow mark-ings, that I first met Vinny, on a cold afternoon in December. And two months later we were married.

But that marble-clad building, that treasure-house of relics and rare things—it was off the map. Gone. The Fejee Mermaid, the Anatomical Venus. The alcove that honored Heracleitus—that too up in smoke. Heracleitus, who believed the entire universe was made of fire. If he was still alive somewhere, in some ash-filled corner of the universe, was he gloating because, once again, he'd been proven right?

I thought of the two white beluga whales in the large tank on the second floor. They were the twelfth pair that Barnum had purchased. And now, like the others before them, they were gone from this world and swimming in some deep beyond.

And Anna—tall, indelible, inevitable Anna, trapped in a smoke-filled room on the third floor. What harrowing memories were drifting now in her midnight dreams? Those Museum workers with the derrick—they saved her, and thank God for that. God and Zootagataz, which is sometimes kinder than we think.

Many called it a miracle, and it seemed that it was—a miracle that Anna was saved, and that nobody was lost, none of the many hundreds who had been in the Museum when the fire broke out. And no one seriously injured. But the lions, the kangaroos, the polar bears—no miracle for them. The llamas and the bearded Barbary sheep.

That fire, it was hell for Anna and a bad time for everybody—but for Barnum it was catastrophic. What the papers did not report, but what I knew, was that the contents of the building were not insured for even half of their value. And the loss of so much had to be crushing. Years ago, when Barnum went into bankruptcy, he had stopped payment on many of his insurance policies, and that enabled him to get on his feet sooner than he might have. I often asked if he had renewed his coverage, but it was a question he always shrugged off. "Not to worry," he would say. "I'm putting the money to good use."

But this time he was deep under, and hard to imagine how or when, if ever, he would get back on his feet.

Vinny was troubled about all the Museum people who were suddenly out of work. Yes, a worry. Us, too—what to go home to? But somehow, despite my troubled feelings, I think I was a little less diffident about the future than Vinny was. I was content to rock my head from side to side, figuring we would deal with the future when it was upon us, come what may. And found it easy to sink into my memories. Those Museum memories, they were me, all the way back to when I was four years old. The galleries, the exhibits, my dressing room, the roof garden. And the stage, where everything, in those early days, came to life for me, as nowhere else.

While I drifted in the past, Vinny was suffering. Ever since the assassination, she said, things had been going wrong. The only times she felt good, she said, was when she was onstage—singing, or doing our Romeo and Juliet piece, the balcony scene. Or romping around in the little skits she created.

We were, at the time, appearing twice a week at the St. James, and interspersed that with appearances in nearby towns and cities. After the bad news from New York, I was barely able to paddle my way through—but for Vinny those performances were a godsend. Onstage, she let go of all the bad baggage and came alive in a different world. She was vibrant, transformed, singing, smiling, dancing, and darting about. But offstage, there was too much reality, too many bad things happening.

She said there were moments when she was tempted to ask Minnie for one of her cigarillos. I offered her a cigar, but she pursed her lips and waved me away. I was no good, useless. A pinhead. No help at all. And she was right. I drooped along, in the thick soup of nostalgia, swimming and near drowning in the sweet apple juice of the past.

Then, not quite two weeks after we learned that the Museum had gone up in smoke, there it was in Greeley's *Tribune*, fresh from across the ocean—a bold-print notice that Barnum was back in business. He was carrying on, temporarily, at the Winter Garden Theatre, and promising he would open a new American Museum as soon as he could find a suitable permanent location—within two months!

But how? How? I could only think that some of his rich friends came through, knowing he was a good investment and they would reap a bundle.

The Winter Garden was nothing near the size that the Museum had been—no space for caged animals, paintings, dioramas, rare old books and manuscripts—yet Barnum had most of his people there. The Bearded Lady, the fortune-teller, the acrobats, along with singers and dancers, young Nicolo on the trapeze, a dancing bear, and—yes—Anna Swan. Plus an orchestra playing popular tunes. And even a full-length play—

THE GREEN MONSTER
A Great Spectacular Fairy Show
Full of Magical Tricks, Comic Incidents
Marvelous Transformations

That, for sure, was the Barnum we all knew, full of magic and fantasy, and mind-boggling transformations. He loses the most famous museum in America, and in a blink he's up and running again. Doesn't have a proper five-story building yet, but it's soon to come.

Meanwhile, the show goes on and the performers perform. Restless, relentless, Zootagataz Barnum. I love him and hate him, curse him and adore him as a god. Push him, and he pushes back. Knock him down, and he'll kick you in the head with both feet. I understood why he didn't enjoy the usual parlor games, like whist or dominoes, or jackstraws. For him, life itself was the game, hot and heavy, and for real. You yourself are on the line. If you don't make the right moves, it's your blood that flows, your cash, your dreams, and even—it could happen—your life.

So—bring on the acrobats! Bring on the dancers! Bring on the clowns, the fire-eaters, the trumpets and drums! *BRING ON THE DWARFS!* Admission thirty cents—children under ten, fifteen cents. Good old Barnum, he believes in Providence, but he's a firm believer in himself, too. *God helps those who help themselves.* So many times I'd heard him say that. His motto, his mantra, printed on his forehead in invisible ink.

*   *   *

A few days after I saw the notice about the Winter Garden, I took
a short walk to a nearby shop to pick up a few cigars. The woman
behind the counter knew me from my many earlier visits. She was
short, approaching middle age, and from Ireland, with green eyes, and
black hair hanging down over her forehead. When we concluded our
transaction, she surprised me, handing me a Greenwood envelope.

"The war is over," I said. "Didn't you know?"

She gave me a blank stare. "It's never over."

I took the cigars and walked home in a heavy London fog, wondering why Greenwood was still active, now that the war was shut down.
And curious, too, about how and why Nickerson was allowed to func-
tion in England at all, given the crinkly posture of neutrality that England had assumed during the war.

In the ensuing days, I collected three more Greenwoods, and soon
enough there was a Foxglove to pick them up. I figured this would go
on and on forever, even if I sailed to China, to India, to Afghanistan.

For the longest time, there hadn't been any letters from Benjamin. We
attributed that to a simple delay in the mail, given that we were far
across the ocean. Still, it was troubling—the uncertainty, the not knowing. There were days when Vinny was beside herself, imagining the
worst. And who could blame her?

Then, the first week in August, we had a letter from Ben that he'd
written on the last day of June, telling us he'd finally been discharged
from the army and was on his way home. That was better medicine
than anything Vinny could have hoped for.

Dear Lucky Ones in London—

Here I am in Readville, Massachusetts, and I, too, today, am one
of the blessed—relieved of duty, discharged, mustered out of the Union

army. I have given up my rifle and am about to start for home, with both legs, both arms, both hands, both eyes, both feet, and some stale old hardtack in my knapsack. What a dream!

Some, I suppose, will say my unit got off easy, held in reserve at many of the battles and not in much of the fighting. But the truth is, we did our share of shooting and being shot at. If our casualties were low, it was because we knew what we were doing and had, for the most part, officers who were smart enough not to lead us through hell's door. Except, maybe, on rainy days. We also had good meat, good potatoes, and, when needed, good whisky in our bellies.

And I like to think Carl Sloe's canary had something to do with our luck. When we lost Carl at Olustee, I took charge of his canary and kept it alive, and will give it to his folks. I expect they will be glad to have it, as a memory of Carl, if they don't mind caring for the little beast. It eats a lot, shits like crazy, and doesn't sing very much. But Carl loved that bird. He was a good fellow, Carl. He used to hum, and whistle, too. Sometimes I still hear him whistling the old tunes, "Jimmy Crack Corn," and "Oh! Susanna." He could whistle like nobody I ever knew.

Vinny was so overjoyed to have that letter, she sat right down and answered with a long, five-page epistle, and then a note to her parents. She also wrote to her brother George, who was a farmer, and her brother Jim, who installed lightning rods, and her brother Silvanus, who milked cows. And her sister Sarah, married to a man who repaired church steeples. And her sister Caroline, who had passed along the Celtic fertility cross that Vinny still carried in her luggage.

She was half the day writing all those letters. When she was done, she looked at me forlornly and said she wanted to go home.

Home, yes. Why not? I knew, too, that some of the others felt the same way. Ken Keeler, Harry Nobbs, Julia Bleeker, Jerry Richardson. Ever since Lee's surrender, they'd been talking about cutting the tour short and going back. The burning of the Museum put an end to that kind of talk—but with the news that Barnum was muscling his way back and making promises to rebuild, the go-home talk was warming up again.

It would soon be four months since Lee's surrender. The long years of war were over. Zatagatooz was full of surprises, and this, now, was one of the better ones, the country at peace with itself, trying to put itself together again.

Many of the big cities in the North were thriving—but the South was a mess. The rebuilding would take a long time. A hundred years, Isaac Sprague had been predicting. Isaac, the Living Skeleton—he was wrong, *had* to be wrong. We would go down there, into the South, and sing in the hospitals, the orphanages. We would tour around, town to town. As Barnum always said, there is nothing like a good song and a laugh to help people along.

A new feeling, yes. A new mood. And, like Vinny, I, too, wanted to be there, part of this strange new world. To know it and smell it and feel it in my veins, before the ice cream melts and the beer goes flat, and the egrets fly off for the winter.

But how? How? We had our contract with the St. James Theatre, and appearances scheduled in Norwich, Coventry, and a few other places. And if we suddenly turned up on Barnum's doorstep, would he have room for us? Or would he fatten us up on lasagna and stuffed turkey from Delmonico's, then ship us off on a five-year tour of Australia, New Zealand, and the Kingdom of Tonga?

CHAPTER 29

A WALK IN THE PARK

In the evenings, after an early dinner, Vinny and I often went for a stroll. We had the two parks close by—Green Park, a few steps away, and the St. James Park, at the bottom of St. James Street, with Buckingham Palace not far off. Or, if we wanted, there was all of Piccadilly, with its shops and crowds. Westminster Bridge was a hefty distance for our short legs, going and coming, but when we had a free afternoon, we sometimes stretched that far.

It was the last week of August, a Friday. Vinny was suffering from cramps that day, so I took my after-dinner stroll alone. The sun low, on its way down, but I expected to be back while there was still plenty of light in the sky.

I went down St. James Street, passing Park Place, Blue Ball Yard, King, and Pall Mall, where the St. James Palace was. Then on to Marlborough Road and a snappy walk to the path leading into the trees of

St. James Park, one of my favorite spots. I took the path that led to the lake, then on to the small bridge, and lingered there, midway across.

A few ducks on the lake, and a pair of swans, large and bossy, like white battleships, and plenty of geese. Swallows were swooping down, diving low over the water, catching insects.

After a long pause, I moved on, off the bridge, and turned onto a narrow trail that cut into shrubbery and tall trees. Still enough light for me to find my way. But I wasn't far along that path before I was caught up short.

"Fuckin' dwarf," I heard, and immediately knew who it was. Him, nobody else. He wasn't dead. There he was, right behind me, same beard, same arched nose, same small eyes under bushy eyebrows, and it swept through me like a flash of light in a storm—I'd been wrong about Cobb Kennedy. He wasn't the one who tried to abduct us. It was this lump of pus. And on his left cheek, the mole.

"You."

"Yeah. Me."

"And the other one? Cobb Kennedy? Your brother? Your twin?"

"My cousin—and the bastards hung him from a rope. How many times I told him keep his dumb mouth shut, but he never learned. Boastin' to those blood-lustin' Yankees how he lit this fire and that fire and was expectin' the whole damn New York City to go up in flames, and what a lark it was. So they strung him up. And you—you friggin' cockroach, you deserve to have your nuts crunched for what you done. Near ruined my ear, damn you, with that devil-to-hell thing you stuck in. You fuckin' don't deserve to live—but I am lettin' you breathe, you no-account piece of puppy shit—lettin' you breathe till money-bags Barnum comes across with twice what I would've asked for your worthless ass when I last had you in hand. Twice as much. And more—plenty more."

By then, cautiously, I had worked my hand into my pouch, which held the derringer. I still carried it with me, it had become a habit. But I felt no great confidence, none at all. If I didn't hurt him bad enough, he'd grab me and kill me, or break my bones and keep me alive until he got the ransom. But while my mind was saying no, my hand, ready with the gun, was saying *yes*.

When he saw it, he laughed. "That tiny one-shot toy? Stop dreamin', little fella."

He stepped toward me, reaching to snatch the derringer. I fired. The sound of it in the calm evening air like a block of river ice cracking open.

He took another step, a ferocious meanness in his face—then he folded and went down like a pile of rags.

On the ground, in the shrubbery, he was faceup under the darkening sky. The bullet had gone through his left eye, a mess of bloody fluid leaking across his face. He was gone, not breathing. A swirling dizziness looped around inside me. Dead, and I was the one who did that—sent him off, for better or worse, to another world, or to nothing at all.

It was as if I had passed through a door—and, having stepped through to the other side, there was no way to return to where I'd been.

I lingered briefly, and in the strangeness of the moment I bent low and touched the mole on his cheek. It wasn't stage makeup. I had been wrong about that.

I looked about, confirming that I was alone, then hurried back to the main path. As I crossed the bridge, I dropped the derringer into the lake and hurried on, back up the path that brought me out of the park. I crossed the Mall, made my way along Marlborough, then across Pall Mall and onto St. James Street. Moving fast, quick as my legs could take me, past King Street and Blue Ball Yard and Park Place, under a half-moon rising. Then, out of breath, the left turn onto Bennett, and I was back at the house.

In the living room, Minnie was playing double solitaire with Julia, and Ned Blossom was deep into a poker game with Harry Nobbs and Ken Keeler. Jerry Richardson was at the piano, working on a new song he'd found at a shop on Piccadilly. Sylvester Bleeker was in an armchair, studying a newspaper.

In the dining room, the Commodore stood in a chair, by a window, having a conversation with a moth. I liked that. It was a side of him I hadn't seen before.

Vinny was upstairs, in our room, working on her embroidery, needing to be alone for a while. I hesitated, then told her what happened, let it all spill out.

"The one who tried to kidnap us? You're sure? Not Cobb Kennedy but someone else?"

I nodded. "Cousins. Look-alikes."

"Unbelievable," she said, staring at the ceiling, then at me. "You were alone?"

"On a trail, away from the main path."

"Nobody saw you?"

"I don't think so. No."

"You're all right? Are you?"

I nodded vaguely.

"Thank God. Thank God. But I hate it," she said. "That you had to go through this—this nightmare. But he didn't hurt you. And he's—dead?"

Again I nodded.

"I'm glad," she said. "I'd rather be dead myself than for you to be hurt. He was going to lock both of us in that trunk. I still have nightmares about it. That house, that trunk. *Him.*" She touched her fingers to her chin, and stared, briefly, at the wall. "So? He wasn't the one that was hanged."

"No."

"And he was still after us."

"It's over," I said, putting a hand on her arm.

She gave me a firm look. "But *is* it over, Charlie? Will there be others? Other madmen?"

"It's over," I repeated, though I knew what she was saying. This sort of thing, something like this, once it starts, you never know. There was too much out there, more than enough.

I drew her close and held her, and she held me.

And still, in a dark place inside me, while we stood there, holding each other, I was baffled, and couldn't understand. I had killed a man. Actually did that. In a weird, shadowy way, I felt altered, changed into a different person, with this grim secret squirming around inside me.

"Let's go home," she said. "I want to go home, Charlie. Everybody wants to go—so why not? It's nine months since we sailed."

She looked at me, and I looked at her, the two of us sinking into a long silence.

Then, on impulse, I went downstairs and drew Bleeker aside, into the kitchen. If everyone was still eager about going home, I said, this seemed, perhaps, as good a time as any.

He asked when.

"Tomorrow. We'll head for Liverpool and take the next ship."

He was aghast. "How? We have a commitment with the theater. There's a penalty clause in the contract."

"We'll pay it."

He let out a low whistle.

"First thing in the morning, get out on the telegraph," I said. "Lock in the next available ship. We'll leave for Liverpool before noon. Make it eleven."

There was a bottle of Glenlivet on the table. Bleeker grabbed a tall glass and more than half filled it—lifted the glass, eyed it, and swallowed off a big gulp. Stood motionless a moment, then huffed out a long, hot breath.

He set the glass down, then leaned down, close. "Charlie, it's a lot to do. We have to close out the house and settle with the landlord. And the manager at the theater—he'll never want to see us again. The train, the ship—if, in fact, anything's available this late. A place to sleep in Liverpool." He picked up the glass again.

"But you're good at this," I said. "Ken and Harry will help. Gather everyone and tell them what's up. They've been talking about cutting the tour short, so I assume they'll be pleased."

He gave me a straight look. "I think you should tell them," he said.

He was right. I should. But at that moment, did I really have the strength for it? I reached for a small glass and poured a splash of Glenlivet.

"They all love Julia," I said. "They'll agree to anything you say." I took a small sip, then put the glass down. "I'll be upstairs. Knock if there's a problem."

Vinny was already in bed, but wide awake. "What's happening?"

"I'll start packing. But you rest, you're tired."

"We're going?"

"Bleeker is telling them now. We'll head for Liverpool before noon."

I pulled the steamer trunk out from under the bed and started packing. Before I had finished with my socks and underwear, Bleeker was at the door.

I stepped into the hall. "Trouble? They want to stay?"

"They want to go—except the Commodore. He wants to carry on as a one-man show."

"This is a joke?"

"As real as rain."

"Good. Give him cash for a ticket home—he'll need it sooner than he thinks."

"Really? We should do that?"

"Why not."

Bleeker shrugged and I watched as he shuffled off toward the stairs. "Good enough," he said.

And in that moment, in the tangled shrubbery of my brain, I saw again the face of the man I killed, and could still not believe I had done that.

Had I? Done it? Willed it? Or was it, in the fierceness of the moment, something that simply happened? You are there instead of somewhere else. The man sneers. He will abduct you and maybe kill you. He sees the gun in your hand, but scoffs. He comes at you. You pull the trigger. All of that—it simply, horribly happens, and here you are, in this house in a foreign country, watching the back of Bleeker's head as he disappears down the stairs.

∾ CHAPTER 30 ∾

LINN'S WATERLOO HOTEL

The next morning, Bleeker, out early, returned with a telegram confirming passage for us aboard a ship sailing the next day.

Moments later, as we assembled for breakfast, the Commodore,
with perfect aplomb, announced that he'd changed his mind and would
be returning to New York with us. Bleeker was beside himself. He had
to scamper off again to the telegraph station, posthaste, to secure an
additional berth on the ship.

The Commodore didn't say what his future plans might be, nor did
he explain what it was that had changed his mind—though I suspected
Harry Nobbs may have shoved him out an upper-story window and
dangled him by the ankles until he came to his senses.

Moments after the Commodore made known his decision,
Minnie did an interesting thing. She walked right up to him and,
for a tense moment, looked him in the eye. "Eat rain," she said,

then slapped him in the face, hard, and went off to her room to be alone.

After we'd gathered our things and the luggage was loaded, and after Bleeker had finished his business with the landlord and with the theater manager, we were off to the depot and boarded a train for Liverpool. It was a long, slow trip, with many stops and delays.

We slept that night at Linn's Waterloo Hotel, where I'd stayed on my first trip to England, when I was six. Everything was much as it had been, same furniture, same rugs, same pictures in the same frames, and so many memories flooding in on me. The drawers of the bureaus, when opened, gave off the very smell that I remembered, the smell of wood aging and curing in gusts of salty sea air blowing in off the Irish Sea.

That first trip, when my feet were on English soil for the first time, a boozy fellow at the hotel, a German in a gray suit, had his eye on my mother. He was ogling, leaning toward her in an obvious way, his hand touching hers. There came a moment when my father took him gently by the arm and in a friendly manner led him out the door, into the courtyard—and, while I watched from the doorway, he kicked the fellow in his bum and sent him sprawling in the mud.

How proud of him I was when he did that! But there was a sadness too, because even then I understood that, as a dwarf, I would never be able to do anything like that, kick a full-grown man into the mud. In those early years, I liked being a tiny person, I enjoyed the attention and the excitement—but there were things normal people could do that I never could, and the limitations weighed on me. They still do.

Nevertheless, there I was, in Liverpool, and less than twenty-four hours earlier, in a park in London, I had shot a man. Still couldn't kick anyone into the mud—but, with a kind of terror, I'd discovered I could snuff out a human life.

I had seen the morning paper—UNIDENTIFIED MAN KILLED IN PARK. A brief report mentioning the bullet in the head, and the absence of any clue as to who the killer might be. The man's money had not been taken, nor had his gold watch or the diamond in his lapel. He carried a pistol in a shoulder holster, and it was suspected he may have been involved in some underworld intrigue. A short person, perhaps a neighborhood youth, had been seen in the vicinity.

The face of that dead kidnapper was every minute alive for me. I was the one. Twenty-seven years of age and thirty-seven inches tall. I had fired that gun. And after that, how, I wondered, how will it feel to dash out onstage singing "Dandy Jim" and "Yankee Doodle"?

The next morning, I went down for breakfast early. The ship didn't sail till noon, and Vinny welcomed the opportunity to sleep late. Harry Nobbs and Ned Blossom were at a table with Julia. I was on my way to join them, but came up short when I spotted a familiar face at a corner table. Nickerson himself, King of Envelopes—envelopes that flew from hand to hand, with secret words, secret memories, secret suspicions, secret secrets.

He was already on his feet and coming toward me, one hand extended, the other in his pocket.

"You're sailing at noon," he said. "On the *City of Washington*."

"You, too?"

"Just arrived, pulled into port late yesterday."

"To see the Queen?"

He angled his head, left and right. "The Queen, no. But others. Right now, top of the list, I'm here to see you."

It sounded ominous. He wants me to spy on the Chinese? Or the Russians?

"Didn't learn till I reached port that you had quit Bennett Street and were on your way home."

He put a hand on my shoulder and steered me toward the back door, and out we went, to the lawn chairs on the patio. The same door, same bushes, same muddy grass that I remembered from years ago, when my father kicked a fellow for making passes at my mom.

And only now, as we slid into our chairs, did I notice. Nickerson's right hand—it wasn't there.

"You take the good with the bad," he said with a shrug.

"What if it's all bad?"

"Lick your wounds and start over."

Zatagatooz, I thought, wondering how, how did he lose that hand? In a shoot-out? An accident? Attacked by a nasty flock of crows?

He leaned forward. "You recall your trip through Kentucky?"

"Vaguely," I answered. But can that really be what I said? *Vaguely?* Kentucky where crazy Ike Hokus with his fast-shooting double-barrel LeMat came close to killing me and a whole bunch of us. Where Morgan's Raiders robbed a general store in broad daylight and left three kids dead on the street. Did Nickerson know about any of that?

"You made a stop at Bowling Green. A woman from Greenville gave you an envelope, the widow of a Union soldier."

I remembered her. Hazel eyes, she had.

"She told us a lot. Morgan had a friend with a house in Greenville— he often went there to rest up. That's all we needed. We posted a squad in the area. When Morgan turns up, the widow sees him, notifies the squad, and she's with them when they surround the house. She spots him hiding in the bushes. She points. Guns are aimed, but he doesn't surrender and tries to slip away. *Bang*, he's dead. September 4, 1864. Two children that woman has. The husband had been ambushed by a Confederate soldier, and this was her payback. Did you know we nailed

Morgan? You must have been dog-weary and dizzy after the long tour and the shit you went through at Chambersburg."

I hadn't known about Morgan. How did it slip by? Morgan dead. Tearing up railroad tracks when we were in Kentucky.

"Dead indeed," Nickerson said, "and if not for the envelope you passed along, it never would have happened. Just one of more than a dozen important outcomes from the envelopes you handled. I thought you would like to know."

"That's why you came?"

"That, and to ask where you're headed next."

There it was, slicing home like a knife. War or no war, Greenwood wasn't shutting down. It was ongoing and everywhere, wherever there was an enemy, and even among friends. Wherever there were secrets to be uncovered and delved into.

"Heading home," I said. "Going to build a house near Vinny's mother, in Middleboro."

"Then?"

"We'll see if Barnum has any cash left to keep me afloat."

"I spoke to Sam Hurd before I left. He mentioned Japan and China."

I shook my head, with a vague smile. "That's an old idea Barnum had toyed with. Four dwarfs with our huge entourage—to China? Japan? Are you serious?" Then, before he could go any further down that road, I tilted my head and switched the subject. "Did Confederate agents torch Barnum's Museum?

"If they did, we'll find them. We're still working on that."

Then a pause, a suspended moment, Nickerson's gaze stabbing right through me. "By the way," he said, leaning forward. "Nice piece of work, last evening."

I floated a blank stare.

"In the park," he said. "Well done."

"You know?"

"My men have been trailing that fellow for months. Him and his gang, plotting all sorts of post-war revenge. Before the surrender, they used Canada as a safe haven. But when we caught a bunch at the border, this unit came here, imagining it might be safer."

As he said that, I knew, suddenly, why I didn't like him. It was the nose—long, straight, and thin. Razor-sharp it was, and how can you feel good about a guy whose nose can cut open a sealed envelope?

He leaned forward with an intense, stabbing stare. "You're sure about Japan?"

"Dead sure," I said.

And he, still with that firm gaze, dropping the words as if they were heavy stones. "Never say dead. Never."

He hovered a moment, then was swiftly up from his chair, through the door, and back into the inn. I wondered if I would ever see him again.

The next morning we boarded the *City of Washington*, the same packet ship we'd come over on. A handsome three-master with square-rigged sails, and a smokestack belching smoke from an engine that drove the propeller at the stern. There was a diagram of the ship in the dining room—the deck forty feet wide and more than three hundred long. While we stood at the rail, waving farewell to strangers on the pier, the ship slipped away from its mooring, and we were off on our long journey.

As we moved down the Irish Sea, great flocks of birds appeared, some crossing overhead, others flying alongside of us, looping around and staying with us for a while. Jerry Richardson knew them all. "Plovers," he shouted, pointing. And, in another direction, "Petrels. And kittiwakes. And over there—gannets." This surprised me. Jerry, a denizen of New York, married to a piano, obsessed with sharps and flats, allegros and andantes—him? He knows about these birds that live by the Irish Sea? Even as he pointed, I could not, through the distance, make out the differences, except that the gannets seemed larger than the others.

"Where are the frigate birds?" Harry Nobbs called.

"They'll come. They'll come. But not yet. When we're closer to the Azores."

Puffy clouds hung on the horizon. The sun was a torch in the sky, but a cool wind blew across the deck. The ship rose and fell in a lazy rhythm as it moved toward the St. George's Channel, which opened onto the North Atlantic.

I didn't know what a frigate bird was.

"You will know it when you see it," Richardson said. "The big one, the man-o'-war bird—it's super-big. Huge black wings, each wing about forty inches long. They can glide forever. Totally black—but, under the neck, the males have a red pouch that they inflate to attract the girls. The girls have a white underbelly."

If they were as big as he said, did I really want to meet one?

We ate oranges, drank tea, played cards, and studied the horizon. Minnie was having a good trip, no hint of the mal de mer that had afflicted her on the way over. There were moments when she actually enjoyed the up-and-down movement, the leaning and the swaying. In the lounge, at a gaming table, she rolled dice with Harry Nobbs and Ken Keeler. They taught her how to play blackjack and poker. And still she smoked her cigarillos, and still the Commodore looked right past her.

The cabin Vinny and I occupied was small, but more than ample for our dwarf bodies, even commodious. There were two single berths, upper and lower, but we were small enough to snuggle comfortably in the lower. On the opposite wall, above a narrow table, there was a framed painting that depicted a whale. Vinny removed it and hung, in its place, her Celtic fertility cross.

She still had confidence in that cross. But now it was a confidence that was more like a fuzzy hope, the kind of dream that a gambler holds on to after losing more times than anyone could remember. Something, obviously, was wrong, in me or in her, or in both of us, and there were moments when I did wonder.

We talked about the new house that she wanted, in Middleboro. If there was to be no baby, we would at least have the house. We could build it, watch it go up, make it happen, and whenever we were out on tour, we would always have that house to go home to.

One afternoon, in the lounge, while Minnie played poker with Harry Nobbs and Ken Keeler, Vinny and I sat several tables away, with pencils, a ruler, and a few pieces of foolscap. We were designing the house—the rooms, first floor and second, with windows low enough for us to see through, and stairs with low risers, easy to climb. The kitchen with a low sink and stove, all as she wanted. But ceilings high enough for our guests.

And a room for the baby, which Vinny insisted on, a room with a crib. Because she still had a thread of hope. If Sarah, in the Bible, the wife of Abraham, could deliver a firstborn when she was ninety years old, then why couldn't it happen for us, while we were still young? The end of the war did that, it created hope, a sense of release and optimism. It made all things seem possible.

"We'll plant a garden," she said. "Benjamin will help. I want hollyhocks and roses. Tiger lilies."

We were dreaming. But it was good to dream. All those years when the big guns were hurling their shells, who could think about planting a garden?

"You will need a pond," Minnie said, joining us after beating Nobbs and Keeler at poker, a fistful of greenbacks in her hand. Those two guys, I knew them—they made her win. They were pumping her up, lifting her spirits.

"What's a new house without a lily pond?" she said. "And a crowd of frogs jumping in and out and making baby frogs. Tiny pollywogs."

Make a pond? Just like that?

"Yes, yes," Vinny chimed in, "Ben is home now and we'll do that, we'll pay him to dig a pond for us. He'll love it. He'll fill it with lily pads. And all sorts of wonderful things growing at the edge."

"And if you want," Minnie started to say, "if you want, you can—"

I put up both hands and cut her off. "Enough—the pond's enough!" Just then, before I could say more, the ship tossed wildly. Minnie went sprawling on the floor, and the greenbacks flew out of her hand and fluttered across the room.

As the ship settled down, Minnie looked up at me from the floor. "For God's sake, Charlie, you didn't have to make the damn boat jump like that. All I was going to say was that you could stock the pond with fish, and whenever you're hungry, you could go fishing. But forget it. I am *not* going to say what I just said. And never will. *Ever.*"

She scrambled about, retrieving her greenbacks. Two boys who'd been playing dominoes helped her. The dominoes, too, were all over the floor.

Then the ship leaned far on its side, and again it tossed about—and in a moment, sooner than we knew, we were all on the floor. My right arm struck the floor hard and my head bounced. Stunned, I was brought back to that moment in the park when I pulled the trigger and a bone-wrenching jolt ran up my arm and through my body. For a moment, I didn't know who I was.

THE MAN-O'-WAR BIRD

... born to match the gale ... thou art all wings ...
To cope with heaven and earth and sea and hurricane ...
—*Walt Whitman, "To the Man-of-War-Bird"*

With the boat rocking and swaying as it did, it was never easy to walk around on deck. Often it was plain treacherous, especially when high waves came crashing over the bow. But I did find a spot where I was out of danger and could gaze at the sky and the ocean with relative ease, without fearing for my life.

Each of the three masts had a rope ladder descending from the top and anchored to the deck about ten feet from the bottom of the mast. I found I could make myself safe and almost comfortable by going up about five or ten rope-rungs—then, turning, I sat on one of the rungs and secured myself by looping my arms around the side ropes of the ladder. Some days I sat like that for more than an hour.

On a day when the ocean seemed calmer than usual, I spotted a pod of whales, massive black bodies appearing and disappearing as they pushed their way through the water. It would be hell if the ship were to meet them head-on, and they seemed to think so, too. Very shrewd of them to stay out of the way.

Far off, I saw clouds hanging close to the water, like snow-covered mountains. It seemed another whole continent out there, sitting on the rim of the ocean.

Day after day, the ship carved its way through the water, plowing along from mood to mood—a mood that was memory, and a mood that was the future, with all of tomorrow's hope and uncertainty. Bright days and dark days. One afternoon, sunlight filtered through the clouds—seabirds appeared and disappeared, then appeared again, diving through the mist and splashing in the water.

My thoughts drifted, as the clouds drifted. In two months, Vinny would be twenty-four. And I, already twenty-seven. Fast, fast. Dwarf time, it races, bouncing and bumping through the white-water rapids of the universe. But there, on that ship, on the rope ladder that I clung to, I felt, strangely, that time had slowed, and I seemed, somehow, not quite myself.

I thought of my two sisters with their swept-up hair high on their heads, laughing and smiling, singing those Zatagatooz songs they used to sing—

Zootagataz, Zatagatooz—
Some days you win, some days you lose.
Hold on to your money—drink milk and honey—
And never forget to put on your shoes!

Frances Jane was now thirty-one. She'd been widowed many years ago and had remarried. Libbie was thirty-six. She too lost her husband to an illness, and it was recent, not long after the Lincoln assassination. We were wondering if, like Frances, she would marry again. But too soon, much too soon for her to know. She was still recovering from the loss.

My mother, who still baked blueberry pies and chocolate layer cakes, was dragging along through her fifties. She had continued to mention, in her letters, that she wanted to move to West Haven, to be near her relatives, but she was reluctant about the packing and the moving. And she was, for sure, still enjoying her rocker by the front window, watching the wagons as they rumbled by.

A far cloud dipped down and touched the ocean, then lifted away. I searched for more whales but didn't see any. I looked for dolphins and did see a few, leaping gracefully out of the water, knifing along toward some far-off dream that drew them on.

I thought of Barnum, aging but forever young, plunging along like the dolphins. Fifty-five and starting over, a new life after the fire. Getting old wasn't part of his plan. His mind forever busy, designing and redesigning, sprouting new ideas like wild grass on the side of a mountain.

And Anna—Anna Swan—gigantic, statuesque Anna. Sixteen when I first met her, and now soon to turn twenty, with no prospects in sight, no giants that had caught her fancy. She had come to America at a bad time. How do you fall in love with a country when it is shooting at itself with muskets and mortars and cannon shells? And you barely escape with your life when the Museum burns down. One of these days, I suspected, she would visit her family in Nova Scotia and never return.

I saw three large birds passing overhead. One was Anna, and one was Mary Darling. And the other, doing fancy loops and turns, was my father—ten years in his grave, but alive and flying.

Then a smaller bird, closer, with brightly colored feathers. That one was my mother.

The ship rocked—it leaned, it swayed. The beams creaked and groaned. We had a day of rain, then a day of fog, the sun a dim, murky disk in a gray-black sky. The ship sounding its foghorn, with answering calls from an invisible ship far off.

On a sunny day, the sea calm, Vinny and I were on deck with Minnie, and Vinny spoke to her. "Don't worry," she said, "there will be a man for you. It will happen. Everything good, in due time."

But Minnie didn't believe that. I saw it in her eyes. She was trying to believe, doing her best, but something inside her was saying no. As the ship slipped along, riding in calm waters, she leaned against Vinny—holding, hanging on.

It would have been a good moment for dolphins, to see them leaping the way they do, sleek and graceful. Minnie would have liked that.

Life is a road, my father used to say. Up a hill, down a hill, hope for good weather. And now the road was the ocean, it was taking us home, to that new house Vinny was dreaming of. To the daffodils, roses, fireflies on summer nights. And the crib for the baby, if that should ever happen. And whatever else that might be waiting for us.

We were seven days out of Liverpool and far into the Atlantic, roughly halfway through our journey. Iceland and Greenland somewhere to the north, beyond our ken. And to the south, nearer but not visible, sat the Azores, with their grapes and pineapples, their volcanoes, and their birds.

Again I was perched on the rope ladder that descended from the top of the mainmast. I was a little higher than usual, some fifteen rungs up the ladder.

The sail at the rear of the ship blocked my view in that direction, but I had a clear view to my left and right, and above. Far to my left, a white cloud sat low, it seemed an island on the water.

Then I saw it, far up there, gliding. Jerry Richardson said I would know it when I saw it. There it was, so big in the sky, riding the air, lifting, then descending, then rising again, gliding. A man-o'-war bird, alone up there, enjoying his solitude, his sky-wide freedom.

Then down, down, in narrowing circles, toward the ship, closer and closer, until he was level with the deck, still gliding, using the barest amount of wing motion—and with a sudden twist, he pulled up short and gripped the railing with his webbed feet, and perched there, barely twenty feet away, looking at me. My eyes on his eyes, and his on mine. This huge black fellow, the shoulder feathers iridescent, black but shimmering with a purple-green glow—and the red pouch at the throat, his pride of manhood, and the long yellow beak with a downward turn at the tip. On each foot, four toes connected by a web—clawed toes for grabbing fish. I knew what he was thinking. He could snap me up for lunch, eat me in midair and drop the shoes and the bones in the ocean. Thinking about it, considering. Or was he contemplating something else?

He spread his wings, showing them off, then closed them. And still we studied each other. Did he want my autograph? My address in Connecticut? Was he not a bird but some little-known ancient god, so old he'd forgotten his own name?

Again he spread his wings, and this time, releasing his grip on the rail, he flapped hard and was aloft, swiftly toward me. In an instant he brushed past, feathers grazing my face. His claws were tucked harmlessly away, but he did touch me with his feathers, as if to let me know who he was, as if to say he could do what he wanted with me but was saving me for another day. Off he went, rising in the distance, wings outstretched, lifting on the wind.

When I returned to the cabin, Vinny was peacefully asleep. Later, she told me she'd been dreaming of that garden she wanted, full of roses and tiger lilies.

I asked her what kinds of birds she wanted. She said the birds would figure it out on their own—which would come and which would keep their distance. The birds mattered, but she wanted them to be free, making their own decisions.

"We're going home," she said. "Maybe we can do some good—cheer people up, make them happy. Right, Charlie? After this awful war. A few new songs, some new routines. Why do they enjoy little people so much? Why do they feel so good when they see us?" If we were to go on the road again, she thought we should visit the South, where there was so much ruin and destruction.

It did grieve her that she'd missed that frigate bird. Maybe he would return for another visit. Possibly, yes. Another day. He might take it in mind to fly off with both of us, and that, she thought, would be an adventure. I thought so, too. Better than dancing my Highland fling, which gave me the pains in my legs. Better than yet another ten-minute impersonation of Napoléon, which I'd presented, already, maybe five thousand times.

We had sunlight, then we had rain. One day, on those high waters, late afternoon, it snowed. The next morning, when we awoke, a thin sheet of ice covered the deck, but as the sun muscled its way into the sky, the ice melted.

That man-o'-war bird, I never saw him again, though I do remember him, I sure do. Because a bird like that, and a moment like that, how can you ever forget?

ACKNOWLEDGMENTS

Special thanks to Eleanor Jackson for her commitment to this book. And to John Glynn and Whitney Frick, for their insights, their close readings of the text, and their tireless fascination with the world of Tom Thumb.

My thanks, also, to the DiMenna-Nyselius Library at Fairfield University, the Barnum Museum in Bridgeport, and the Bridgeport Public Library, where I gathered information relating to the Civil War, the Barnum era, and Tom Thumb. The books and documents I consulted are too many to name here, but it would be inappropriate not to mention the importance of Barnum's several autobiographies, written at various points in his career, and Lavinia Warren's autobiography, parts of which appeared in newspapers during her lifetime. The full manuscript was eventually found by A. H. Saxon—he edited the text, provided a valuable introduction and informative endnotes, and *The Autobiography of*

Mrs. Tom Thumb finally appeared in book form in 1969, some sixty years after Lavinia's death.

While the historical facts were important to me, I hasten to emphasize that *The Remarkable Courtship of General Tom Thumb* is a work of fiction, and on several occasions, following the demands of fiction, I've placed the characters at locations where they never were, and in situations that they never experienced in real life. It's fiction's way of building dramatic tension while probing the ironies and the problems life offers, as well as the blessings.

With that said, readers may be surprised to learn that some of the most unlikely events were indeed factual. There was a time, shortly before the war, when a slave owner in New Orleans did try to give a slave girl to Lavinia, as a gift. And a time, at the height of the war, when Lincoln hosted a wedding reception for Tom and Lavinia at the White House, days after their marriage in New York. In such moments, the writer sits back, and life itself writes the script.